Forbidden Footsteps

Forbidden Series ~ Three

Cynthia B. Ainsworthe

Other Works by Author

Remember?
2015 Words and Passion Publishing
Amazon and Barnes & Noble

Front Row Center's Passion in the Kitchen,
2015, 2014 Words and Passion Publishing
Amazon

Front Row Center,
2015, 2014 Words and Passion Publishing
Amazon

When Midnight Comes and *Characters*
Two short stories in the horror anthology *The Speed of Dark,*
2013 Chase Publishing Enterprises
Amazon

ISBN: 0-9802459-8-2 Paperback
ISBN: 13: 978-0-9802459-8-1 Paperback
ASIN: B01G7QOHHM Kindle ebook

IN DEDICATION ...

To Cindy, my loving daughter, who inspires me to tell a story from my heart. No mother could want for a nicer, more giving, and devoted daughter. Her love is the life-force for my writing.

To Terri Garber whose generosity of spirit and her kindness shown to me are one of my blessings. Her love for life has inspired me to create more than one feisty and strong female character in my novels. Thank you, Terri, for your friendship, support, and encouragement.

To all those affected by the terrorist attacks in Paris, (and elsewhere in the world), all the innocent people who lost their lives or whose lives were changed forever, and to those at Charlie Hebdo, who did nothing more than exercise their right to freedom of speech.

To all my fan readers who enjoy my writings and have remained loyal and encouraging. If it was for your support, my words would only be read by very few.

WHAT OTHERS ARE SAYING …

5 Stars! "Cynthia Ainsworthe's writing is fun, sexy and exciting. She uses her creativity and femaleness and turns it into pure sex. They are well-written reads. Once you start to read one, you won't want to put it down because you know you're in for a juicy ride." ~~ Terri Garber, renowned actor of screen and television. Quote by Terri Garber used with her permission.

Ms. Garber portrayed feisty *Ashton Main* opposite *Patrick Swayze* in the television miniseries adapted from John Jakes' novels *North and South, Book 1, 2, and 3,* as well her role as *Leslie Carrington* in *Dynasty;* roles in *As the Word Turns; Sporting Chance; Law and Order; Cold Case,* and innumerable other credits.

5 Stars! "I have read thousands of works from amateurs to Bestsellers that are looking to be adapted to film. Cynthia's writing is a perfect example of the quality that I look for in such a novel. The elegance of dialog and titillating description fits in nicely with those of the Bestsellers and transitions beautifully to the screen." ~~ Scott C. Brown, renowned Hollywood Screenwriter & Producer of screen and television.

Mr. Scott C. Brown is known for Andre Norton: The Grand Dame of Science Fiction & Fantasy (2016), Temecula Uncorked and Superman vs Doomsday (2017).

5 Stars! "Original and Riveting … Front Row Center is a superbly crafted, riveting and original … face-paced narrative … confidently recommended for readings who prefer their romance literature to be sophisticated, complex, thoughtful, thought-provoking, and thoroughly entertaining …" ~~ Midwest Book Review on novel *Front Row Center,* review at Amazon.com.

5 Stars! "This romance has it all … lust, love, suspense, danger … Great job!" ~~ Huffington Reviews on novel *Remember?,* review at Barnes & Noble.com.

IN ACKNOWLEDGMENT ...

My heartfelt thanks to those who assisted me in the creation of *Forbidden Footsteps*. Sincere advice is a treasured gift.

To Trish Jackson, my wonderful editor who is never too busy to answer one more question. She supports my writing with excitement and encouragement. Thank you for being there and for your boundless expertise.

My gratitude to Florentina Musset of Chez Mamie Lise for well wishes and permission to feature her charming restaurant in a scene situated in Annecy, France. The ambiance of her restaurant contributed greatly to create a lovely moment for my characters and assisted in bringing my story to life.

"Fragile heart ...
scattered pieces ..."
~~ CB Ainsworthe

Forbidden Footsteps

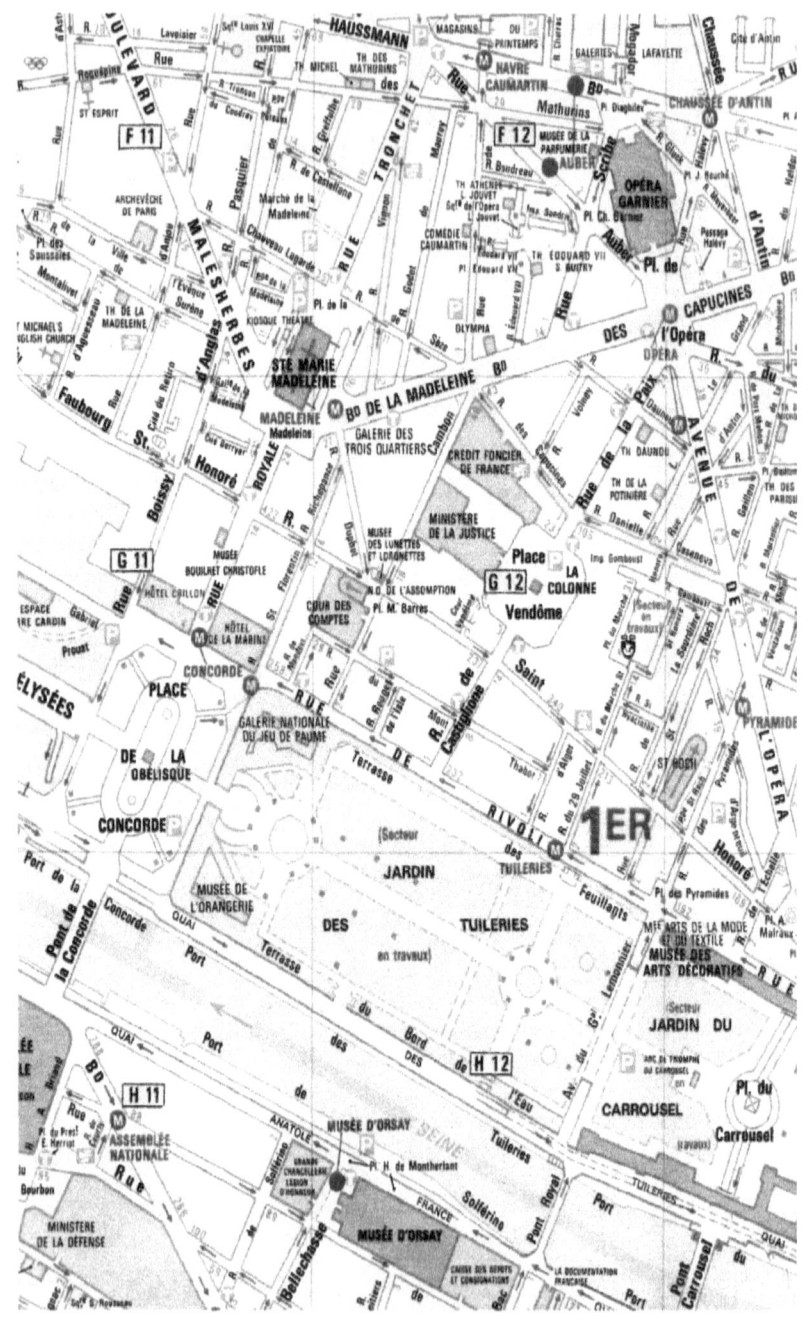

Paris, 1st Arrondissement

One

"VA AU DIABLE! Go to hell! I'm sick of you poking your nose into my business." Jean-Claude LeGrand's eyes blazed.

"Don't you dare cause a scene in this house," his father said in a quiet tone through gritted teeth. "Everyone is staring at you and you had better apologize to them at once. If you don't, I will expose everything, and your career will be in the Seine." He took a hefty sip of his dirty martini.

Jean-Claude turned his attention to the guests who were still gawking at him, and smiled, showing perfect teeth. "I apologize sincerely. Blame it on my French blood." He tilted his head to his father, took his handkerchief to his nose, and spoke in French. "How much do you know about Davis?"

Charles LeGrand raised an eyebrow. "I see your allergy is acting up …. It is rude to speak in French when our hosts speak English. I didn't bring you up to be rude."

"You didn't answer my question, Papa," Jean-Claude countered in English.

Expose me? What does he know?

"I know he's more famous than me." Charles took a sip of his drink. "Why the interest? You want Davis to back your career? Haven't I done enough for you?"

"His stepdaughter is of more interest to me." He glanced in Cindy's direction.

"Ah, that could be a problem." Charles discreetly gestured to her with his hand. "Did you not notice her wedding band?"

"Since when did that stop me, Papa?" A smug grin came to Jean-Claude's lips. "She seems to be a delicious challenge."

An American woman is just what my appetite needs. I've been savoring French pastry for far too long.

"Some challenges are best unmet." Charles narrowed his eyes at his son.

"You play it too safe. Always have." Jean-Claude studied Cindy as she chatted with other guests. "Taking a risk in uncharted waters is where the fun is, and can be the most satisfying."

"Don't be foolish, Jean. Have you forgotten about Monique in Paris?"

His father's concerned tone irritated him. "I'm bored with her.

She's so Parisian and entirely predictable." He adjusted his tie.

Jean-Claude caught Cindy's eye. She responded with a coy smile. "Besides, I don't feel I have to marry my mistresses." He kept his eyes on her as he talked. "You're paying alimony to what—four or is it, five wives now? I don't pay alimony to a single one. It's time I venture for new experiences."

Charles chuckled "Your new experiences always result in the same old ending."

Jean-Claude smirked. "Papa, I'm too old for you to be giving me advice about my personal life."

"At thirty-two, you still act and react as a child." His father continued, "Like it or not, I worry about you. Besides, I don't want you to make trouble that would cost me this relationship with Monsieur Davis. He could be important to my career."

"Go back to your martini." Jean-Claude spoke while looking at Cindy, "There's an interesting woman I need to know better."

~~***~~

"Who's that good-looking man?" Cindy Hastings asked. Her gaze focused on the gorgeous guy talking to Larry's manager, Brent. "Seems to be a French Don Draper out of Mad Men—acts as if he knows the world and owns it."

What were they arguing about? He sounded really angry. Doesn't a hot temper translate to being passionate in bed? She frowned. *He couldn't be like Vic, could he?*

"Aren't you rushing things, dear daughter?" Taylor Davis placed her hands on her hips. "You haven't decided if you want to stay married to Vic yet. Give yourself time."

They stood at the periphery of the living room at the kitchen entry of her mom and stepfather's Bel-Air home.

There goes Mom—always giving advice. If she knew anything about how Vic really is she would want me to leave him. He's made my life a living hell. I need a man who would appreciate and respect me. Europeans have a kind of chivalry, don't they? Something Vic wouldn't even begin to understand.

Cindy smoothed out the wrinkles in her black dress. "I was never one to put things on hold." She kissed Taylor's cheek. "Mom, I know you mean well. My marriage with Vic was over when he refused to get help for his gambling, and put me in debt. I'm just glad I never added his name on the deed to the Tampa home you gave me."

"Want to talk about it?" She felt her mother's scrutinizing gaze. "We can have a nice long chat after the party."

"Not yet." Cindy studied Jean-Claude. *His navy blazer looks expensive. I bet he does know how to treat a woman.* "I have other things on my mind." She fingered her hair and wet her lips slowly with her tongue, as a cat might do when eyeing a tasty bird. "Care to introduce us?"

"No." Taylor raised an eyebrow of motherly concern. "That's Charles LeGrand's son, Jean-Claude, and yes, he's drop dead gorgeous. He's like a fantastic pair of shoes—you want them, but they're not in your size."

"I wouldn't mind walking a few blocks in them though." Cindy edged closer to her quest.

"That's rich, coming from you. You always rebelled against anything French." Taylor grabbed a handful of nuts from the counter as she critically surveyed the man her daughter fancied.

"I've changed." Cindy took a step closer toward him. "People change all the time."

"Maybe ... and maybe not." Taylor touched Cindy's elbow to get her attention. "Look, it's clear you're on the rebound. Take it slow. This is no time to be looking for a replacement."

Cindy spun sharply around and her eyes narrowed. "I don't think you're in any position to talk after what happened to Dad."

"That was a deep cut." Tears rimmed Taylor's eyes. "There isn't a day I don't think about what happened." A sigh escaped. "I thought you and I had moved beyond that—we had found some peace between us."

"I'm sorry, Mom." She hugged Taylor and kissed her cheek. "I shouldn't have said that. I never meant to hurt you." She bent to pat the white and black toy poodles, where they sat at Taylor's heels, as if seeking safety from the strangers' feet. "Good girl Gigi and you're good too Jacques," she said quietly.

"I know, Honey." Taylor kissed her daughter's hairline at the temple.

"Excuse me, Mom." Cindy broke away as her voice trailed off, "Introductions need to be made."

~~***~~

"Why are you tidying up?" Larry came up behind her. "Our houseman should be doing this."

"Tim and both catering staff members are busy serving guests and collecting abandoned glasses." Taylor tossed used napkins and paper plates into the trashcan. "I can watch the party goings-on from the doorway. Charles LeGrand's son is handsome. That could be a problem for Cindy."

Larry picked up a sponge and wiped the kitchen counter down to help her.

"Our party seems to be a success." He noticed Taylor eyeing her daughter.

"More of a success for Cindy, if she has anything to say about it." She refilled the chip bowl.

"Really?" Larry grabbed a jar of nuts from the cabinet. "Anyone we know?"

"Jean-Claude LeGrand, of all people." She faced her husband. "You know his reputation."

"Yeah," Larry studied her face, "the old 'love 'em and leave 'em' routine."

"Exactly!" Taylor opened a package of fresh cocktail napkins. "And Cindy's on the rebound. She's vulnerable—prime for the pickings of a roué."

"Roué?" He arched his eyebrows.

"It's French for playboy." She stopped refreshing the party food. "And I bet he's been one for years. He's had plenty of lessons from his father."

"Careful, Tay." Larry lowered his voice. "Charles and I have a business deal in the works to put out a duet album. Keep a lid on your feelings. You could blow it for me."

I hope Tay doesn't worry too much about Cindy. They lost their closeness since Paul, and I don't think Cindy's ever forgiven her mom.

"Mum's the word." She kissed his cheek. "I'll be the perfect supportive wife with a wary eye on his son."

Joe Winton entered the kitchen. "Great party, Lar. Your business deal with LeGrand could open the French market for y'." He brushed his short white hair back with his hand.

"That's the idea." Larry chuckled, then looked at his much older adopted brother. "Who knows? I might actually learn more than two words of French."

Taylor smiled with approval. "You learning French isn't on my mind at this moment. Cindy's rebound reaction is what troubles me. Vic treats her like a possession to be tapped for money whenever he needs it. I don't think she realizes how low her self-esteem has gotten. People in her situation are vulnerable."

"C'mon," Larry suggested, "let's get out there and give Tim and the other servers a break."

I wish she wouldn't worry so much.

He glanced across the room at Cindy and shook his head.

Maybe Tay was right The way that girl was staring at Jean-Claude could only lead to trouble. Is Cindy strong enough to resist his advances? I hope she doesn't get hurt.

Two

CINDY STOOD BEHIND Jean-Claude. Her eyes widened with a devilish glint and her hand quickly smoothed her hair before she casually bumped into him.

He turned to see the object of his disturbance. His smile slowly emerged, showcasing his white teeth. He was tall and dark, and studied her with intense black eyes.

"Pardon, mademoiselle." He inclined his head with an approving look. "Have we met? I don't recall the pleasure of meeting such a beautiful woman."

I love his accent. Cindy extended her hand.

Jean-Claude lifted it to his lips and gently placed an enticing kiss on it. His eyes slanted up at her with a silent message.

"I'm, I'm," she stammered, "Cynthia Hastings, though my friends call me Cindy." *God! He's gorgeous!* "You speak perfect English." *Why did I say that? That's so lame.*

"Merci, Cindy." He still held her hand and rubbed his thumb slowly across the ridge of her middle finger. "Like my father, I sell more records in America if I speak the language. I understand from your stepfather that you are half French?"

"Yes. My mom is the French one in the family." Her eyes evaded his penetrating gaze before continuing. "I avoided everything French most of my life—a rebellious phase—avoided the culture and language, until now."

"Ah, until now? And what has changed your mind?" He took a fleeting look about the room. "My father's music? I understand your mother is a fan of his, n'est-ce pas?"

Cindy felt color come to her cheeks. "I thought that would be obvious."

"Maybe you listened to a few of my songs?" He shrugged in a typical French fashion. "I know I'm not as famous as my father, but I have time to prove myself. My music is more contemporary than the legendary Charles LeGrand."

"Music isn't the only thing of a French nature that might interest me."

He's so smooth. Is he interested or being polite?

"I should be mingling." Jean-Claude took a step back. "Guests will think you are my new love." He discreetly pointed to the wedding band on her left hand. "I see you are married. He has a treasure to adore every night." Clearing his throat, Jean-Claude's eyes narrowed as he scanned the room again. "Is he here? I would like to meet that special man who could whisk you away."

"Vic's in Tampa. I'd rather not talk about it. I've left him." Cindy sipped her drink. "When I make my mind up, there's no going back for me." *Is he turned off by my marriage?*

"Fini?" He gave an approving smile. "I like a woman who knows her mind. Are you certain there can be no second chances for your Vic?"

"Very certain." Her jaw set in determination. "No one takes advantage of me and gets forgiveness."

Is he still interested? He's so handsome and famous. Am I good enough for him?

"Bien sûr, Mademoiselle Cindy." He made a small bow. "I now know your rules. Merci for that illustrious example." A light chortle escaped. "I have rules, too."

"Want to share?" She looked directly in his eyes. "Rules are meant to be broken—when it's fun."

"You are a true coquette, and delightfully beautiful." He finished his brandy in one gulp. "And with that, I must greet the hosts or they will believe we French are truly rude."

"No issues from Mom on that point. She raises the French flag at every opportunity." Cindy looked at him from beneath her long lashes.

I think I blew it. Was it my marriage? He's absolutely a gorgeous hunk. More than I ever dreamed of for a new start.

His light laugh drifted away as he headed in the direction of his father.

Disappointed, she couldn't help glancing at him at every opportunity although she tried to avoid direct eye contact. *What's he doing?* Her heart leaped. *Is he coming back?*

Her frequent deep breaths must have communicated an opposite message to her outward indifference.

~~***~~

Jean-Claude grinned as he stalked his prey. *This one is going to be easy.* "So we meet again," he said.

Cindy smiled briefly, then an awkward silence evolved between them. She shifted her weight from one foot and then to the other.

"Do I make you feel nervous?" Jean-Claude's confidence caused him to smile slowly and then wet his lips. *She's clearly interested.*

"No." She smiled and tilted her head. "Why do you ask?"

He held out his hand, palm upturned. "Well, when a woman shifts her weight like that when a man is standing in front of her, that's a prime indication that she's feeling tense."

Color came to her face. "Ridiculous! I'm comfortable around all sorts of men. Nothing upsets me."

He inched closer. "Did I hit a beautiful nerve?" His hand touched her elbow. "I have a French talent for calming fascinating women, such as yourself." *She's beautiful.*

Cindy brushed the hair from her neck and tried to appear unflappable. "I'm certain all your talents have a French flair, n'est-ce pas?"

"So you *do* speak French." His eyes searched hers. "All this time, I thought it was English only."

"I barely speak a few common words." She briefly glanced at Taylor. "Mom is the one who's fluent in your mother tongue. 'Non, oui, pardon, and s'il vous plaît' is the limit of my French vocabulary."

The hum of the guests suddenly seemed to close in on him and encroach on his privacy. "Cindy, let's talk on the patio. It's quieter there. All this noise is distracting." He extended his arm in the direction of the doublewide sliding glass doors.

"Fine by me." A coy smile hinted at her feelings.

Jean-Claude led the way to the patio. Cindy sank into a blue and white striped cushion on a wrought iron chair. She placed her glass of rosé wine carefully on the umbrella-topped table. He chose the chair opposite to her. A refreshing April breeze blew her blond bangs briefly as he took a moment to bask in her beauty.

With her elbow on the table, Cindy rested her chin on her hand. "Well, what was so important that you needed to bring me out here and away from the others?"

"Beauty such as yours, should not have to compete with the voices of mindless persons. I want to hear every word you speak and appreciate you to the fullest." He reached for her hand across the table.

"Isn't that a bit offensive?" She withdrew her hand from his and nodded in the direction of the party within. "Those 'mindless persons' as you call them, are my parents and their friends. You live up to the old saying." Cindy sat straighter and tapped her foot in an irritated fashion.

"What is the 'old saying' you speak of?" *She has a temper. I love that!*

"The French are rude and snobbish!" Cindy's narrowed eyes punctuated her point.

"Ooh, là là, mademoiselle. Pardon-moi. It's my English. I didn't mean to offend." Jean-Claude leaned closer with his elbow on the table. *This one is fiery. I'd love to taste her heat.*

"Well, you did." She remained indifferent. "I noticed you said 'Pardon-moi' instead of the more formal 'Pardonnez-moi'. Why is that?"

"Mais oui. I thought you said you didn't understand French." *She's intriguing.* "You know more than you're letting on, mademoiselle."

"I've learned some from my mom." She took a sip of wine. "I always resisted that part of my family's culture."

"And, why is that? Are you ashamed of your French heritage?" *I can teach you to love your French nature.*

"No. I'm not ashamed. It was part of my rebellious phase as I was growing up and it just stuck."

He tilted his head to soften her defenses. Cindy's suggestive smile gave him hope. She leaned closer across the table. His hand stroked the top of hers.

His eyes searched hers intently. "Would it be too forward of me to ask for your number?"

"You're not the first wanting my number." Her tongue suggestively wet her bottom lip. "And I don't provide that information on a chance meeting."

"Even when you know you want to?" *She's not making this easy for me.* "Chance meetings are the best—there are so many forbidden facts to be discovered."

"That's true, providing both parties want to risk discovery." Her voice had an edge to it.

"Where there is no risk, there is no life." His eyes traveled to her décolletage.

"That is just your ploy to know me better." She glanced back at the party. Taylor stood watching them through the doors, and clearly observing their private conversation. "We better rejoin the others. I think Mom is missing us."

"Bien sûr, Cindy." Jean-Claude got to his feet and assisted by pulling out her chair. He reached in his jacket pocket, retrieved his card, and pressed it into Cindy's palm.

She gave him a curious look, then slipped the card in her pocket.

I must have her.

Will she call me? I can wait. If not, Papa can always call Larry for me. I'll have to watch out for her mother. She seems to know the score.

Three

CINDY STUMBLED OUT with a cup of cold latté to the patio where her mom and Larry sat enjoying their morning coffee. She patted the poodles as they sat together in another chair at the table.

He reviewed something that looked like his notes for the planned English and French duet album with Charles LeGrand, while her mom leafed through a fashion magazine.

"I didn't think you'd be up before noon." Taylor patted the seat, inviting her to sit.

"Why?" Cindy made a face as she dropped into the chair beside her. "I didn't drink that much at the party last night."

"I thought you might like the luxury of sleeping in." Taylor laid the magazine on the table. "Marital stress can make one tired."

"That's my mom, just come out with it, no matter who's around." Cindy took a sip of her iced coffee and stared at the pool.

Why can't she just leave me and my marriage alone. She doesn't know a thing about it, and I'll never tell her. She would only worry more.

"Don't be like that." Taylor shifted in her seat. "You know I care."

Larry finished his drink in one gulp. "Excuse, me ladies. I have arrangements to attend to. I'll be in the studio."

He got up and left the two of them alone.

"What was that all about?" Cindy looked out to the pool and set her jaw. "I wasn't rude to him."

"No. But you were a bit terse with me." Taylor sipped her coffee. "He doesn't like to see discord in our home."

"His home, you mean." She crossed her leg away from her mother.

"No. It's *our* home. I can tell from your body language that you're upset with me." She leaned toward her daughter. "All I've ever done, was want the best for you."

"Look, Mom. We will never be as close as you want us to be." Cindy looked directly at Taylor. "There's been too much water under that bridge. You can't make things better because they will never be better between us."

Why do I always push her away when I really want to be closer?

"Cindy, what's bothering you?" Taylor touched her daughter's hand lovingly. "You're lashing out at me because you're in pain. Talking things out can make big problems into small ones."

"Mom, I'm miserable—married to a man I can't trust. You know I never dated much before Vic. I need to spread my wings and live life." She looked up at the clouds. "I'm not getting any younger and I want to have wonderful experiences and make fantastic memories before I'm thirty."

It feels so odd opening up to Mom like this. I'm not confident like her— Vic ripped that from me along with killing my baby.

"Cindy, I'm fearful as to what choices you might make." Concern lined her mother's brow. "Hasty decisions can lead to lasting heartache."

"You're an expert on that one. Aren't you, Mom?" Cindy clenched her teeth. "You didn't think twice when you took up with Larry."

Why do I always say things like that to her? It's like years of pent-up hurt have eroded any kindness I might have toward Mom. Maybe I'd feel a lot different if Dad was still here to help me.

"That's not fair, Cindy." Tears rimmed Taylor's eyes. "There isn't a moment that I don't regret the pain I caused you and everyone else. I've accepted the fact that your dad is out of your life because of me. If I could fix that, I would—but that's not reality."

"Mom, I'm sorry." She hung her head. "I'm just so confused and I want a happy life with someone who isn't seeing me as a nuisance until the next poker game."

"I wish you had come to me before this had gotten so far." Taylor stroked her daughter's hair. "Moms are always there to lend an ear."

"I wish I had too." Cindy grabbed a tissue from her pocket and wiped her eyes.

I've made such a mess of my life. Why can't I be like Mom? Everything turns out good for her. What more can go wrong for me?

Four

TAYLOR'S PHONE RANG, jarring her thoughts from a travel magazine. She grabbed her cell phone from the coffee table. It was Vic. She wondered if she should let voicemail answer the call.

She grimaced and swiped the screen.

"Yes, Vic. What do you want?" Cool anger colored her words.

"Is Cindy there?" He sounded tense. "I've tried calling her, but she won't take my calls."

"I don't blame her one bit." Taylor hugged an overstuffed sofa pillow. "After what you did and then to deny the issue ... that goes beyond nerve."

He paused for a moment. "Look, I know you mean well. But this is between Cindy and me." Desperation tinged his voice. "If she's there please let me talk to her. Tell her it's important."

"I don't know if she's up yet." Taylor left the living room to see if her daughter was awake while holding the phone, and purposely didn't cover up the mouthpiece.

She tapped on the door. "Cindy, are you sleeping?"

"No, Mom." She cracked the door open. Cindy hid a yawn with her hand.

"Vic is on the phone." Taylor screwed up her face. "Do you want to speak with him? You're not obligated."

"Let me get my robe on first." Cindy reached for the garment from the back of the chair. "Tell him I'll be there in a minute."

"Did you hear that, Vic?" Taylor walked down the hall that led to the living room as she talked. "She'll be with you in a minute. Don't expect Larry and I to be sending any more money for your gambling debts. Seventy thousand was quite enough to pay off my daughter's ATM withdrawals and credit cards that you ran up!"

"I didn't call asking for money." His voice sounded humble. "Her boss wants to know when she'll be back, and so do I. As to the money you sent, it was Larry's money and not yours."

"Don't get snide with me, Mr. Ne'er-do-well. The fact still remains that we sent that money for our daughter and not for you!" Taylor started pacing.

Cindy entered the room. She reached for the phone from her mom, clicked on the speaker function, and held the phone away for Taylor to hear. "Don't ask for money—you're getting none."

"I'm not calling for money." He took a deep breath. "Landry wants to know when you're returning to work, and so do I. I miss you."

"You miss having a maid and someone bringing home the bacon. All your money goes for poker games, dog racing, and God knows what else." Cindy's lips thinned. "I don't know when I'll be back, or *if* I'll be back. Besides, Mr. Landry knows I'll be gone for at least six weeks because I already discussed that with him." She tapped her foot rapidly. "So your ruse of my boss wanting to know when I'll be back failed."

"How can you say that?" Vic spoke with hurt tones. "It's only been less than a week. You're not giving us a chance."

"Yeah. Like you were giving us a chance when you withdrew money on my credit card at the ATM?" Cindy walked to the open media room. Taylor followed to listen to the conversation. Cindy kept the speaker on for Taylor. She put her finger to her lips to warn her mom not to speak. "And what's worse, you keep refusing to admit you have a gambling addiction. You have to help yourself in this—I won't!"

"I don't have an addiction." His tone hardened. "It's only a little fun with the guys. I've had a bad run. My luck will change. One of these days I'll hit the big one, and then what'll you say? Look, I got a lot of people wanting their money. They don't play nice, and I'm not about to give up my life for you! You're sitting pretty in Bel-Air—sitting on all those golden eggs. You could at least share. We are still married. Besides, these guys know where you live. They'll get their money one way or another."

"Is that some kind of threat?" Cindy turned her back to Taylor. "No one will control me—least of all you. Your empty threats have no effect on me."

Vic's words had a strident quality. "You'll be sorry when you find out they aren't empty. Don't come crying to me when that happens."

"Vic. I'm hanging up. This conversation is over." She went back to the living room. Taylor sat down on the sofa and patted the cushion inviting Cindy to sit.

"What about Landry?" he asked. "You can ignore me but you can't just ignore your boss."

"Can't you remember what I just told you? Mr. Landry knows I took six weeks' vacation. After that I don't know." Her steely tone cut the air.

Vic suddenly sounded meek. "What about the bills? Who's going to pay the rent, gas, electric—all that stuff?"

Taylor rolled her eyes.

"You figure it out. You have a job." Cindy sat next to her mother. "Give up gambling and you can pay the bills. By the way, don't think you can shack up at Mom's Tampa home. I had the locks changed. That's *my* house and not yours! I canceled all my credit cards and our checking account, too." Tears welled up in her eyes. Taylor offered her a tissue. "Now you're forced to grow up and fend for yourself. I'm not your mommy!"

Cindy ended their call with a look of determination. She blew out air and stared at the phone for a few seconds.

"Honey," Taylor sidled closer to her and grabbed her hand, "I wish I could fix this for you. Don't make rash decisions. You have a career to think about. These things take time. You've worked so hard to achieve all your promotions—don't toss it away."

"More important than my career, I have my *life* to think about." She turned to face her mom. "I might have a dozen jobs in my life—but I only have *one* life. These have to be my decisions— good or bad—I have to make these tough calls. I'm not a little girl anymore. And there are some things I can't tell you about Vic."

Taylor gave her a warm hug. "Wrong. You'll always be my little girl. You can tell me anything." For a moment, she felt she was hugging her five-year-old daughter.

I wish she had never met that bastard. What did I miss all those years ago when she first met Vic. What has he done that she refuses to tell me? Were there signs I didn't pay attention to? I always had a gut feeling. I should have spoken up then. If I did, would things be different for her now? What will Cindy's future hold if she quits her job? Hollywood isn't a good place for her to start over—fast lifestyles, wrong men, and drugs. She's too unhinged to make wise decisions. Are Vic's threats empty?

Five

CINDY THANKED LARRY'S driver, Drew, when he dropped her off.

"You're very welcome, Cindy. You have my number, so all you need to do is call when you're ready to be picked up."

After her phone call with Vic, she looked forward to this pleasant, if not costly expedition. Hopefully it would help her forget for a while. Armed with Taylor's Platinum Amex card, she decided to shop to her heart's content, and Rodeo Drive in Los Angeles was just the place for it. The warm sun and cooler temperatures made for a pleasant walk.

A striking navy and white striped jacket caught her eye in a store window.

That would look nice over a pair of white pants and a yellow scarf to set it off. Hmm, white shoes and bag to match. Yes, and Hollywood sunglasses to complete the look. I need an entire image change. The plain sensible Cindy is yesterday's news. Watch out, world. I'm here and I want all the fruits.

With a determined look, Cindy entered a fashionable and prestigious boutique. Enjoying the feel of the fine fabrics, her hands grazed over the various items offered on racks.

I see why Mom has always liked expensive clothes. Well, I'm not going to deny myself anymore. The brass ring is mine and I'm holding fast to it.

A salesgirl came up to her. "Is there anything you would like, Miss?" Cindy read the name badge.

"Yes please, Judy. I'd like to see that striped jacket in the window." The girl went to the clothing stand where the garment hung.

Cindy called after her, "I think a pair of white pants, size ten, and a yellow scarf, too—if you have it."

The girl collected the desired items and showed her to the dressing rooms. After hanging the clothing on a hook, she said, "Miss, if you need any assistance, I'll be outside the door."

Minutes later, Cindy exited the cubicle and twirled in front of a large mirror.

Judy smiled. "That outfit flatters your figure perfectly."

"Thanks." She beamed and admired her image. "If you carry any white shoes and bags, that would be perfect."

"Of course." The girl gave a broad smile, clearly happy with a hefty commission. "As soon as you change, I'll have an assortment for you to choose from. I'm certain I can find that scarf you wanted, too."

Judy quickly left on her search, humming an unrecognizable tune.

Cindy made her selection of shoes, bags, and scarves. She spotted the perfect sunglasses to set off her Hollywood look.

Vic wouldn't even recognize me now. Why am I thinking of him? Jean-Claude is far more interesting and intriguing. I wonder what he looks like in a towel? Lots of guys look good in a suit and then they're a big disappointment when the shirts come off.

She did a double take when seeing the charge of eight hundred seventy-three dollars and ninety-six cents. She swallowed hard.

Will Mom scream at me? I overdid it. I can't do this again. Larry's already paid off Vic's debt on my credit cards.

She held the stylus up for a moment, and then shrugged and signed her mother's name.

"You were very lucky." The sales clerk handed her the three designer shopping bags. "All your purchases today are forty percent off during our pre-season sale."

Cindy took the packages with a smile masking her worry about the cost.

Holy crap! If these weren't on sale, what would the price be? I don't even want to calculate that one.

Outside the store, when she fished her cell phone from her bag to call Drew, she found Jean-Claude's card. His cell phone number was listed in the lower left corner. She noticed the country code of thirty-three.

Should I call him? Would he think I was being too forward?

Cindy dialed the plus sign on her key pad and then the number. It rang once, twice, three times. She looked down at her hands. They were shaking. She aborted the call.

I'm being foolish—acting on the rebound—still, he's drop dead gorgeous. I need to get my head on straight and take a deep breath. Yet, I wonder how long he'll be in the States? Should I let this chance pass me by? Does a chance even exist?

~~***~~

Larry left the home studio and entered the living room. He stood at the sliding glass doorway and watched Taylor on the patio. It looked like she was reviewing the grocery list Tim had prepared.

I'm so lucky to have her in my life. After that fiasco with Clive—I'll never take her for granted.

"What?" She looked up at him. "Come over here and sit by me."

"That's a lovely thought, and a lovelier picture." He strode over to her and pulled up a chair.

"Were you working on a new song?" Taylor shielded her eyes from the sun with her hand.

"I've been reviewing LeGrand's material." He picked off a grape from the cluster in a bowl on the table. "Charles'—not Jean-Claude's. It looks like this will be a 'go' for us. I like his songs. With a few key changes, it might work."

"Will you have to learn French? If so, I'm a very good teacher." He loved that coy, teasing expression on her face.

"And, I would be an apt pupil." He leaned closer and kissed her lips. "How would you like to spend some time in Paris?"

"I'd love to, but what about Cindy?" She pushed the grocery list aside. "My darling daughter, as you know, has always resisted everything French. Not to mention, I also now associate bad memories with that city—memories involving Clive."

"You don't have to come if you don't want to. Besides, I think Cindy is warming up to the French culture, since meeting Jean-Claude." Larry studied her reaction. "It's been nearly a year since the Clive episode. Please try to let go of it."

A skeptical look came to her eyes. "Would Charles be going, or Charles and his son?"

"Both. Charles invited us along when they fly home. We'll be recording in Paris. He's been kind to give me top billing on the album and offered first-class roundtrip airfare." He grabbed another grape and popped it into his mouth, chewed, and swallowed.

"That's only because you're a world-renowned celebrity and he's known mostly in Europe.... We don't need the airfare—not with our private jet." Taylor let out a heavy sigh. "I think if Cindy gets wind of this trip involving Jean-Claude, she'll be packing before the reservations are made. I fear she'll move too fast. She's still dealing with a bad marriage. She's so naïve—and vulnerable now."

"Look, Tay." Larry stared into her eyes. "You can't protect her. She has to make her own mistakes and learn from them."

"Yes. I know." She reached for his hand across the table. "It's too bad she didn't learn from mine."

Six

CINDY SQUINTED IN the bright sun, and a gentle breeze blew her hair as she joined her mother and stepfather out on the pool patio.

"Welcome back." Taylor reached out to her and patted a seat cushion.

Larry looked at his watch. "I was wondering if you got lost."

She took a seat at the circular table. *How am I ever gonna tell Mom how expensive my outfit was?* "Shopping always takes longer than planned." Cindy looked out at the far trees. "All the trying on until you find the right style."

"How well I know that." She felt her mother's gaze. "When I worked at Gérard's, some women took half a day before making a purchase."

Cindy pulled her chair closer to her mom and lowered her voice, "Mom, can I talk to you privately?"

"Certainly." Taylor stood up and started toward the sliding glass doors.

In the living room, out of Larry's earshot, she cleared her throat. "Mom … I-I-charged a lot for this outfit, even bought shoes, bag, and a scarf."

God, I hope she won't be upset.

"How much damage are we talking about?" Taylor's posture stiffened.

Cindy's voice was almost childlike, "Nearly nine hundred dollars." She shifted her weight. "But it was forty percent off."

"Nine hundred!" Her mother's eyes nearly popped. "This Amex account doesn't allow monthly payments. I have to pay that bill off next month."

"Do you want me to take them back?" She knew her eyes pleaded otherwise. "They were on sale."

With hands on hips, Taylor glanced at Larry and then back to her. "No. But let's not make this a habit. Larry will be okay as long as you don't have a repeat performance."

Cindy's cell phone rang. She didn't recognize the number and walked away from her mom to answer the call.

This better not be Vic calling from an unknown number. I wouldn't put it past him with his sneaky ways.

"Yes." She moved to the wall farthest from the patio, and turned to see her mother had rejoined Larry outside.

"I love that greeting, but I haven't asked a question yet."

Her heart missed a beat and she gasped out loud. "How did you get my number? I didn't give it to you."

"Not directly, mademoiselle." Jean-Claude sounded suave and mysterious. "Your number was listed in my 'missed calls'."

"How did you know it was me who dialed your number? It could've been someone else,"

He's a bit forward, and yet so smooth.

"I didn't. I took a chance." His voice was deliciously seductive, "Ooh, là là. Taking chances can make for some very satisfying conclusions."

"Exactly why are you calling?" She glanced at her wedding band.

"I would like to invite you to share a dinner with me, this Friday. I can pick you up at seven. Wear something casual and chic." She heard his confidence.

"A bit certain of yourself, aren't you?" Cindy rolled her eyes. "I haven't even said 'yes'."

The nerve of this guy. He must be a spoiled brat.

"I'm so sorry if you find me a bit forward." His voice softened to a near purr. "You are such a beautiful woman. I'm compelled to know you better."

"May I call you back with my answer?" She started tapping her foot.

"I'm hoping that you would answer me now." He sounded urgent. "Please don't break my heart."

"I'll be ready. This Friday evening at seven."

"My heart is already singing your name." Jean-Claude's tone lightened. "I'll choose a special place for us."

"Great. See you then."

Is he for real or playing me? His English needs updating. It sounds like he got those lines from a 1930's script.

She wrung her hands.

I've been away from dating for so long—this feels awkward. I just hope …

~~***~~

Jean-Claude sat on the sofa across from his father, leafing through an entertainment newspaper while Charles, seated in a modern pale blue upholstered chair, reviewed the song list he had compiled in his Beverly Hills Hotel suite. A tray of partially consumed cheese and fruit rested on the coffee table. Two glasses of Merlot sat near the opened bottle. Torn French bread completed the repast.

Jean-Claude tossed the paper on the end table and tapped his fingers on his knee.

Charles looked up from his papers. "Feeling edgy?"

"Not at all, Papa."

What irritating subject will he bring up, now?

"I think that American mademoiselle is occupying your thoughts." Charles put his list down and leaned forward, elbows on knees.

"Not at all." *He's always prying.* "She's just another. Like all the rest."

"I don't believe you." His father smiled. "Remember. I'm your father. I know when you're excited about something."

Jean-Claude stood up and looked down at Charles. "I don't have time to chat. I have to get ready."

His father looked at the time display on his phone, then raised an eyebrow. "It's two o'clock. You have plenty of time. Cindy must be a special woman in your estimation."

Jean-Claude headed to the bedroom as his words trailed off, "I need to shower." The plush carpet softened his irritated footsteps.

~~***~~

In his Tampa home studio, Mark Barnes jotted down the notes on a score sheet as the new melody developed in his mind, then played the phrase for confirmation that he liked what he heard. The doorbell chimed, breaking his train of thought.

"Just when I'm on a roll," he mumbled, "who in hell is that?"

Mark hurried to the door. He looked through the peephole and saw Vic.

He's got a lot of nerve after what he did to Cindy.

Opening the door, he greeted him with an irritated expression. "Hi Vic. What's up?"

"Can I come in to talk?" Vic removed his sunglasses. "I really need to speak with you." His eyes appeared tired and bloodshot.

"Look man, this isn't a good time. I've got a deadline on this song I'm composing." *He needs to get a life.* "We can talk here. Make it short."

"Cindy won't listen to me. I want her back and she's shut down." He sunk his hands deep into his pockets. "Well, I-I need a loan. The bills are coming due. All I need is a couple of grand."

"Not my problem, Vic." Mark made a face. "You need to help yourself by going to a Gamblers Anonymous meeting. Admit to yourself and others that you have a problem. I'm not about to enable you by giving you money."

"It was just a harmless game of cards." He raised his brow as if he really believed he was innocent.

"Well, that *harmless game* has caused Cindy to leave you and go to Bel-Air." *I'm not believing the nerve of this guy.* "In all likelihood, it has cost you your marriage."

"I think Cindy just needs time to cool off." Vic dug his toe into the welcome mat.

"Keep telling yourself that." Mark chuckled. "I doubt it, though." He adjusted his weight and grabbed the doorknob, ready to close the door. "Vic, if it was in your and Cindy's best interest, I'd give you a loan. But it's not, so I won't. Get a second job and stop the gambling." He started closing the door.

"You think you have all the answers about me. There's plenty you don't know. Cindy isn't all she appears. She's spoiled and selfish—even changed the locks on the Tampa house."

"I gotta go. Bye." Mark hurried back to his studio.

Should I call Tay and tell her about Vic's visit? Nah, better leave it alone. Cindy and Taylor have enough to deal with.

~~***~~

Friday seemed to have come quickly. Cindy wore a path from the living room to the entry. Her palms grew moist. She stopped momentarily to check her hair and makeup in the foyer mirror. She knew she looked good, and smiled at the confidence the new outfit had given her. Confidence was a feeling she hadn't experienced since marrying Vic.

Music wafted from the open door of Larry's studio. Taylor sat in a chair reading the latest romance novel.

"Do you want us to buy a new carpet?" Taylor didn't look up.

"What?" She stopped pacing. "What are you talking about?"

"You keep walking back and forth like Marie Antoinette wondering when the blade will fall." Her mom turned a page.

"No I'm not." Cindy retouched her lipstick in the hall mirror. "I just hope I'm not underdressed."

"You look perfect. This is California—not Manhattan." Taylor placed a piece of paper in the book before closing it. "You weren't this nervous dating Vic."

"It's not the same, Mom." She kept an eye on the entry as she talked. "Jean-Claude is very sophisticated and he's *French*. What if I come off as stupid or not worldly?"

I can't believe I'm actually going out on this date. Is it too late for me to cancel?

"No worry on those points." Taylor turned to look straight at her daughter. "You are worldly—well-traveled, and can easily fit into any situation."

"You're not the one going on this date." Cindy went back to the foyer. "What if I have to grope for words."

"Knowing the French male psyche, I don't think groping for words will be your issue." Taylor laughed lightly. "You'll have to deal with *his* groping issues and not yours."

"I can handle him." *How dangerous of a wolf is he?* "He's not the first flirt I've dealt with."

"Remember, you're still married." Her mom's eyes narrowed. "You don't want to give Vic any unnecessary ammunition for a divorce. Don't walk in forbidden footsteps."

Cindy spun on her heels. "You were married to dad when you were flirting with Larry. I see no difference. Everything turned out okay for you—even better than okay."

An uncomfortable moment grew thick and heavy.

Why did I say that? I really don't want to hurt Mom, but she doesn't know anything about Vic except the mask he puts on when he's trying to impress people. If she knew how vicious and dangerous he really is, maybe she would understand. I can never tell her anything about that, or about his friends. What if his threats mean something? He wouldn't dare send one of his goons here, to Mom's house, would he?

She shuddered.

Some of the people he mixed with were truly frightening.

"All I'm asking is that you learn from my mistakes." Taylor's voice was kind. "Please take this very slow. Enjoy his company and get to know him before you do anything reckless."

Cindy's eyes bored into her mother's. "I'm not about to go to bed with him." She took a deep breath. "And if I do, it's none of your business."

"Well, I guess I've been told." Her mother picked up her book and opened it to the marked page.

The poodles started barking and ran to the front door. Cindy looked out the window. A black limousine pulled into the circular drive and came to a stop. Not waiting for the chauffeur, the passenger door opened; a tall, distinguished, and elegantly dressed Jean-Claude got out. He stood there briefly adjusting his cuffs, then ran his palm over his hair. He wore a finely tailored beige sports coat over a pale yellow shirt opened at the neck. He walked with a cool and confident stride to the stoop, barely breaking the crease in his brown linen slacks. He rang the bell.

Tim promptly went to the entrance.

Cindy stood behind the houseman beside Gigi and Jacques, their tails wagging, and waited to the count of ten. She nodded to Tim to open the door.

Jean-Claude's manner exemplified subdued cockiness. "I am here to pick up the lovely Mademoiselle Cindy."

Cindy grabbed her pocketbook from the foyer table and moved in front of Tim. "I'm all ready. I hope I'm dressed all right."

Her smile caused him to do the same. He kissed her in a typical French greeting, first one cheek and then the other.

God, he's so handsome. They know how to grow hunky men in France. So gallant. Totally opposite to Vic.

"I would ask to visit your family, but we have reservations and I don't want us to be late." He smiled with seductive charm.

"That's fine." Cindy took his hand willingly. "I'm a grown woman. I come and go as I please. No problems here."

Hmm, how will the evening end. At his place?

Seven

CHARMING WHITE PICKET fencing bordered the front of The Ivy restaurant on North Robertson Boulevard in West Hollywood. Slatted green shutters framed the windows against worn brick walls. Cindy stood a moment, capturing this picture in her mind.

The pure country à la français décor lent an idealistic feel. As they waited to be seated, the French hostess mentioned it wasn't unusual to see more than one famous face sitting at a toile-clothed table. Flowered chintz chairs with similar curtains completed the look. A fireplace in the sitting area imparted a romantic ambiance that was difficult to resist. Jean-Claude smiled with approval as he eyed the surroundings.

Of course he'd pick a restaurant like this. Must make him feel at home. Is this part of his planned seduction? I'm not had so easily.

The maître d' greeted them. Jean-Claude gave his name. The host responded back in French to his guests.

Oh brother! That maître d' is trying to impress. Mom would love this place.

They followed him to their reserved table.

"Do you approve? I want to give you a new dining experience for a start." Jean-Claude scanned her face with his dark eyes.

"'For a start'?" Cindy arched her eyebrow. "A start of what? For what we might do after dinner?"

"That remains up to you." He smiled with cool confidence, demonstrating he had traveled this path many times before.

"I told you—I have rules." She took the napkin and stiffly placed it in her lap.

"And, I answered you that I have rules, too." He reached for her hand as she felt his foot touching hers under the table.

He's so damn charming. First his hand, and now his foot is flirting with mine. What will be his next move? Taking me to his place? He has a lot to learn about me. I'm not one of his bimbo's.

"Yes. I recall that." Cindy cleared her throat to control her nerves. "Let's look at the menu. You'll notice that I'm not listed."

"We haven't looked at the dessert listing yet." His thumb stroked the top of her hand.

"You won't find me on that one either." She took a deep breath and straightened her posture. She hoped he didn't feel her hand trembling. "I'll have lime chicken, snap peas, and a baked potato."

"Good. I like a woman who is decisive. And to drink?" Those dark eyes searched her face again, obviously looking for a reaction to his allure.

"You're the Frenchman at this table. You decide." She bit her bottom lip.

He released her hand to examine the beverage menu, then took his handkerchief to his nose with a light dab.

He's done that before—must be an allergy.

The waiter promptly served water and took their orders. Jean-Claude chose French champagne sangria cocktails for them both. Waiting for the drink order, a thorny silence evolved as Cindy sipped her sparkling water.

"So, Jean-Claude, what type of music do you sing?"

He's certainly easy on the eyes. His charm seems automatic. So why am I feeling so unsure of myself?

He gave a boyish look and a warm smile before replying. "Pop-rock. Certainly not the weepy and torchy ballads my father sings."

"I don't think I've heard your music." Cindy reached for a roll at the same time as he. Their fingers briefly touched. She jerked away and tried to keep her voice even. "Any of your music released in America?"

"Not yet." He cleared his throat. "With assistance from your stepfather, I hope that will change."

"If you sing solely in French, I don't think you'd find the sales skyrocketing." Her tone spoke of someone well versed in marketing. "We Americans like English songs—lyrics we can understand."

"Aah, but French is the language of," he reached for her hand and placed a gentle kiss on her palm, "... the language of love."

Give me a break! Is he for real? How corny—what a cliché. He's got to do better than this.

She pulled her hand away. "I'll excuse that on the basis of 'lost in translation'." It was all she could do to restrain her laughter. "I'm certain it sounds better in French."

"You told me you prefer I speak in English." He arched a brow. "Have you changed your mind?"

"No. I haven't changed my mind, nor my rules." She ran her tongue along her lower lip.

"We'll see." He took a swallow of his drink. "The evening is young and holds many possibilities."

"Possibilities are always present." The server placed the entrées in front of them. "I have the freedom to choose which possibility to explore—that's the way we do things in America—women call the shots."

Jean-Claude lifted his fork to his mouth. "That's where the mystery lies." He ate a piece of swordfish, then raised his drink to make a toast. "Here's to exciting perplexities and the beautiful woman named—Cindy. May she one day reveal one of her fascinating and intriguing mysteries."

"You're rather sure of yourself." She took a sip of her drink while looking directly into his eyes.

If he thinks he's going to take me to bed, he's got another think coming. I've given up on Vic, but I'm not some sex-crazed teenager.

"I never take myself, nor those in my life for granted." He tore off a piece of his French dinner roll.

"What about those in the periphery?" She scrutinized his expression. "Do you take them for granted?"

"You are speaking of yourself?" He chewed on his bread. "You think you are in my 'periphery' as you call it?"

Cindy pushed her vegetables around on the plate. "I think you don't know me well enough to be in your life—periphery or otherwise."

Jean-Claude leaned forward on his arms and looked suggestively at her. "Time and proximity can change that. It's your decision. Wouldn't that be a nice thought?"

She bit her bottom lip and replied smugly, "We'll see …. The night has barely begun."

Damn, he's hard to resist. It's been so long since I dated. I can't help feeling a bit unsure, but I'll never let him see it. What would Mom do?

Eight

MARK TENDED TO the broccoli, avoiding the steam from the pot hitting his face while Adrienne finished setting the table for their evening meal. She came up beside him to check on the salmon in the oven.

"Is the lemon sauce ready?" She lifted the lid and gave the contents a quick stir.

"Should be." He drained the green vegetable, placed it in a bowl which he carried to the table. "Vic came over to see me a few days back."

"What did he want?" Adrienne finished pouring water into their goblets. "Or don't I need to ask?"

Mark set their salmon filled dinner plates on the table.

"Seems he misses Cindy." He pulled his seat out. "But I'm not sure I buy that one. Some of the things he said were almost like a threat."

"He asked you for money?" She sat down and put a napkin in her lap. "He misses Cindy's salary more than he misses her. How did he threaten you?"

"Vic didn't threaten me—merely eluded to unknown stuff about Cindy. You're right about him missing Cindy's money—wanted two grand." He took a bite of his fish. "I didn't give him a dime. He needs to get help. He has to admit to himself he has a problem."

"Mark," Adrienne pointed her fork for emphasis, "I don't feel sorry for him. He took his wife for all she's worth and has no remorse. He doesn't want help because of the rush he feels when he's gambling." She took a swallow of water. "Until he thinks of someone else besides himself, he deserves what he gets. He gets no pity from me."

He took a forkful of broccoli. "Cindy must be in a lot of pain. I hope she doesn't act rashly on the rebound."

"That is troublesome for Taylor. Mothers worry no matter what the age of their children." Adrienne spooned lemon sauce on her salmon. "In a way, I wouldn't blame Cindy if she did take up with someone before being totally free of Vic."

Mark nodded as he chewed. "But," he swallowed his mouthful, "she could be jumping from the fat into the fire. The next guy could be worse than Vic."

"I can't fathom anyone worse than a guy addicted to gambling…" She stabbed a broccoli floret. "… unless the next guy is mixed up in drugs. And Cindy's too levelheaded to associate with that sort of man."

"I agree." Mark helped himself to the lemon sauce. "At times, I think Cindy's more sensible than her mother." He took a swallow of water. "She was shaken to the bone with worry over Taylor and that Clive mess. Maybe she's less cautious now—feeling life is too short to waste."

"Mark, after that Clive debacle, I should think she would be even more careful." She pointed with her fork again. "She needs to learn from her mother's mistakes."

~~***~~

Jean-Claude took Cindy's hand and helped her out of the limo. She noticed the street sign said "Wilcox Avenue".

"Are you familiar with The Sayers Club?" he asked, as he led her toward an imposing entrance.

"I've heard of it, but I haven't been here before," she said. "I've read about this place. The article said it was the most exclusive and swanky nightspot in Los Angeles for famous guests in music, television, and major motion picture industries."

This is definitely the place to see and be seen. Guests have to be on "the list" for admission.

Jean-Claude didn't wait at the end of the line. With Cindy in hand, he went to the head of the queue and whispered in the ear of the doorman controlling entry.

The man raised his eyebrows and flashed a broad smile. "Yes of course, Mr. LeGrand. The gentleman just inside this door will show you to the back room and your table."

He nodded and escorted Cindy through the doorway. Her ears adjusted to the hum of conversation as she spotted more than one famous face at the bar. After being seated at a table in the room's periphery, Jean-Claude extended his arm on the back of the brown leather sofa and his hand lightly caressed her shoulder. She noticed the exotic rug under her feet, then saw the movers and shakers, some laughing loudly.

"Did we get here too late?" She pointed discreetly at the DJ moving his equipment to one side near the stage edge.

"I don't think so. I was told it's jazz night. In France, it's called Le Jazz Hot." His eyes searched the room for a waiter. "Do you like jazz?"

"Not particularly." She slipped her hand into her purse, relieved that she hadn't forgotten her phone. "I never listened to it much."

"I'm glad I can bring a new experience to you." He drew her closer. His breath warmed her ear.

Aren't you the smooth one. Not so fast, Mr. LeGrand.

"What type of jazz do you think will be played?" Her blue eyes stared up at him.

"I hope it's smooth." His lips came close to hers. "I love smooth things ... silky things."

Cindy coughed. "Maybe we should have something to drink before ... before the entertainment starts."

Moments later a young waiter handed them the drink menus with professional aplomb. Jean-Claude ordered an expensive bottle of champagne. Cindy's eyes popped when she spotted the prices.

One bottle of expensive champagne is what I make in two weeks! Is he flashing his money around to impress me, or does he really live large?

She placed her menu on the table. "I'll have the French Seventy-Five instead of champagne."

The waiter noted their orders, then left.

Jean-Claude's lips formed a sly smile. "Ooh, là là. You honor me. You ordered a drink named after my heritage."

"Not at all. I prefer cocktails to most wines." Cindy grabbed a few nuts from the bowl on the table. "My Mom is the wine-drinker in the family. Champagne flows through her veins."

"That's because she's French." His fingers lingered on her neck. "That means you're French, too."

"As I told you before, I'm only half French." She chewed on a cashew. "The English in me cancels out the French."

"I think not," he said with a smug expression as his hand stroked her hair. "You merely need to release the French passion that dwells deep inside you."

"You don't even know if I have any passion." She tilted her head with a skeptical expression. "I'm not a carbon copy of other women."

"I never meant to suggest you are." He took a deep breath. "Cindy, I want to get to know you and you're not making that easy."

"I'm sorry." *I didn't mean to offend him. I just don't know how to read his thoughts.* "Look, I was coming from the typical idea of a Frenchman's stereotype. I wasn't being fair to you."

"No harm done." His suave confidence was difficult for her to resist. "I understand."

The waiter brought their drinks, placed a few cocktail napkins on the table, then put the opened champagne bottle in a chilled wine bucket.

Jean-Claude's eyes undressed her soul. "We'll enjoy the music with no expectations. Agreed?"

Cindy lifted her glass as in making a toast. "Agreed." She took a sip and studied his reaction.

He's so good looking. It won't be easy to resist his advances—if he makes any.

Oddly for Cindy, she recognized the jazz band from Larry's association. She recalled he said they were extremely famous with multiple gold and platinum albums to their credit. Jean-Claude focused on their performance and appeared to enjoy their brand of music. Cindy had to admit to herself that the melodic saxophone was smooth and not what she expected. Between songs, he glanced at her and punctuated the moment with a charming smile.

After the musical set finished, and the band left the stage, Jean-Claude motioned for the waiter.

"Yes, sir." He beamed politely. "How may I assist you?"

"L'addition s'il vous plaît." He blushed and smiled apologetically. "Pardon, monsieur. I meant to say, 'The check, please.'"

"No bother, Mr. LeGrand. We frequently have European customers. I understood you perfectly." The waiter produced the bill from his leather folder and provided a pen. He held a penlight over the check for the signature.

Jean-Claude took a Mont Blanc pen from his inside jacket pocket and signed his name with a flourish, then turned his attention to Cindy.

"Where would you like to go now?" His dark-eyed gaze penetrated hers. "A quiet drink at my hotel?"

"I—I really don't think I could on our first date." *He's certainly not subtle.*

"That's encouraging." His fingers traced along her chin.

"Encouraging? How so?" *I wish I could figure him out.*

"Well, you said, 'first date'. That means there's hope for a second." His finger lifted her chin as if he would kiss her.

Is he going to kiss me? I don't know how that would make me feel. Can I cross that line yet?

"That remains to be decided." *He's the pure definition of tall dark and handsome all wrapped in a package labeled trouble.* "We might go out again. Or, you could be busy with your dad and Larry in the recording studio."

"I'm only here on vacation." His fingers played with the softness of her neck and caressed the perimeter of her ear. She started to melt from his touch and glanced at his hand on the table.

God, his hands are so sexy, strong, slender fingers, and so well-defined. I bet he would know how to caress a woman all over. What in hell am I thinking! I'm still married. Does being separated give me more leeway?

She grabbed her pocketbook from the tabletop in an effort to leave. "We better go. It's getting late."

"Bien sûr, Mademoiselle Cindy." He quickly slid out and offered his hand to her. "I'll call my driver. He will be here un moment."

Jean-Claude dialed his cell phone and spoke in French. Cindy only understood a few words. She eyed him with approval.

He definitely knows how to treat a lady. Is what they say about French men true—they are the best lovers? He has a hot, passionate temper. Dare I find out?

Nine

BRIGHT LIGHTS FROM affluent Manhattan Beach's pier and neighboring businesses reflected in the Pacific Ocean, which lent a carnival-night feel to this famous landmark. Shimmering waves soothed the darkened sandy beach as couples walked in the moonlight with shoes in hand.

Cindy and Jean-Claude strolled along the pier toward the expansive water. The breeze cooled her comfortably.

"Did you enjoy the jazz at The Sayer Club?" He tilted his head and looked boyish.

"Surprisingly, I did."

He definitely wants to take me to bed. I've thought so all evening and now I can feel his vibes.

"Thank you for expanding my musical knowledge."

"Are there any other areas where I could expand your knowledge?" His smug smile suggested more.

"I'm married, Jean-Claude." *He's not very subtle.* "I don't think I'm lacking in that department."

"Pardon-moi. You misunderstand. Maybe it's my English. I didn't know if you wanted to improve your French." He pulled out an e-cigarette from his shirt pocket. "I never meant to suggest we have a nuit d'amour."

"Night of love?" She raised her eyebrow. "I'm sorry. I assumed that was your intention. Your body language says otherwise."

"Mon Dieu! Jamais!" He explained, "I would never be so bold as to assume we would be lovers after one date." Jean-Claude took a puff. "I hope you don't mind this, the cigarette, I mean. I've been trying to quit. I've had no tobacco for six months."

"That's admirable of you." *He's shifting the subject. Why?* "May you have self-control in other habits you wish to stop. Addiction can be a dangerous beast and one some can never deal with."

"You aren't referring to yourself, I hope." He slipped his arm around her waist and left a gentle kiss on the side of her hair.

"Definitely not me … but someone I know very well." *I shouldn't be thinking of Vic. How I wish he hadn't used me like that.* "Before you ask, it's not my mom or step-dad."

"Could this be the man you left?" He stopped walking and turned to face her, placing his hands on her shoulders. "Great pain should never be borne alone. Talking to others can soften the sharpness."

"I don't know you well enough for that."

Is he nervy or what! I'm not about to share anything so private with him. We hardly know each other.

He leaned closer to her, gazed into her eyes and placed his hand at the back of her neck. "You are very special, Cindy. You have a mystique I find intoxicating and one I crave." His lips gently pressed hers. She kissed him back with tenderness and genuine emotion.

"I hope you won't think ill of me." His boyish smile expressed an apology. "I wanted to kiss you since the first time I saw you at the party."

"I'm very flattered." *I can't believe I let him kiss me. I did enjoy it. Will he kiss me again?* "I'm glad we met."

"Moi aussi." Jean-Claude kissed her gently again communicating an unexpected loving and caring attitude.

"I think we better get back to the limo." She took his hand.

I'm glad it's night. He can't see me blush. Jean-Claude must be accustomed to women who are far more sophisticated than me. He's way out of my league.

"As you desire, mademoiselle." He took his cell phone from his pocket, dialed a number and spoke in French.

Walking back to the coastal city, Cindy expounded on the trivia she had gleaned from her mom and Larry.

"Manhattan Beach is a very old city, and extremely expensive." She looked up at the black sky. "Do you know the history if it?"

Jean-Claude shook his head. "Why don't you tell me."

"A lot of high profile individuals live here. Actors, too," she said. "During the 1920's the sand from here was transported to Waikiki Beach. Can you believe that? I heard it took over ten years."

"Really?" His gaze studied her face. "You are so fascinating. I never knew those facts."

He seems interested in my mind. Is this for real or a con?

"There were a lot of films shot on this beach, as well as TV series."

"You are a wealth of information." A light chuckle escaped as he brushed away a strand of hair from his forehead.

"There's a lot I don't know." *He's really a nice guy.* "I can't speak French."

He paused in their stroll and faced her. "Maybe it's time you learn new things?"

She looked up at him, took a deep breath. "Yes. It might be the time for me to learn …."

His gentle kiss ended her sentence, making her feel slightly lightheaded and breathless.

He's not the first man to kiss me. Why do I feel like this?

Couples strolling the pier took no notice of them.

"I—I 'd like to call you by a nickname." Her tongue moistened her bottom lip as his eyes studied her. "Would you mind if I called you 'JC'?"

His endearing smile confirmed her request. "Oui. I would like that." He lifted her chin with his fingers. "This will be our symbol, as a remembrance of our moment … when you felt close enough to give me a special name."

She raised her face to receive another kiss. His lips brushed her cheek as he whispered, "Cindy, you are very dear to me."

~~***~~

Taylor sat at the kitchen counter enjoying her morning coffee, Gigi and Jacques at her feet. Wanting to keep abreast of what events happened in Larry's world, she read the latest copy of the Entertainment Trade News. Shuffling footsteps grew louder from the hall to the doorway.

Without looking up, she asked, "You got home fairly early. Did you have a nice time with Jean-Claude?"

Cindy opened the refrigerator door and poured a glass of orange juice, then sat down on a stool opposite her mother. "It was very nice. He's extremely interesting."

"Want to share?" Taylor sized up her daughter's body language. "I'm just curious."

"Nosy is more like it. I'm not a teenager anymore." She took a deep breath. "He was a complete gentleman. And, if I want to have a relationship with him in the future—that will be my decision."

"Calm down." She put her paper aside. "I was merely making conversation. I didn't ask for details."

What do I have to do so we can bridge this gap? Can it be bridged? If only she would accept my love, but she's so secretive. She thinks I'm prying into her affairs, and I know there's something she's kept from me for a long time. If only she would open up.

"Look, I'm sorry, Mom." Cindy took a large swallow of juice. "I just assumed …"

"On a happier note, Larry, myself, Charles, and Jean-Claude are going to Paris soon." *Will she want to go with us or return to Vic?* "Lar and Charles will be recording their duet album over there."

Cindy seemed to jerk and sit more upright. She was staring with wide eyes. "I don't suppose there would be room for me." Cindy added more juice to her glass. "It's been a long time since I tasted a genuine croissant."

"Of course you can join us." Taylor leaned closer with her elbows on the counter. "What about your work? Can you get away?"

"I told you before, I took six weeks off as a leave of absence." She flicked the hair off her shoulder indifferently. "My boss is good with it."

"Still. Be careful about what your boss might think. You don't want him to be interviewing a replacement while you're away." *I hope she knows what she's doing.*

"Mr. Landry knows about Vic's gambling because I told him." Her tone held a matter-of-fact quality. "He was fine with it, and told me to take all of my vacation time if I wanted—so that's what I did and I'm not sorry. If I can go to Paris with you I'll be able to get farther away from Vic and he won't be able to bother me."

"We'll be leaving next Monday. You have your passport?" Taylor's brow furrowed.

Cindy's lips thinned with a hint of defiance. "Yup. That was one of the first things I packed."

She looks smug. What is Cindy up to? Looks like she's fleeing from more than the pain Vic caused.

"Good. If needed, we can supplement your wardrobe in Paris. The new line will be hitting their stores soon."

"Sounds like a plan, Mom." Cindy's text function beeped on her cell phone. She pulled it from her pocket. "I gotta take this message." A broad smile emerged. "It's from JC."

"JC?" Taylor raised her brows.

"That's a nickname I gave Jean-Claude." Cindy slipped off the stool and headed to the living room.

"Oh, I see."

Seems Cindy is smitten with him. I hope he's not too sophisticated for her. She's so inexperienced. Vic was only the third guy she dated before marriage. Is that the big attraction for her? To make up for the time she lost before

marrying Vic? I hope he doesn't break her heart.
~~***~~

Cindy paced on the patio and spoke softly on the phone. She didn't want to be overheard by her mother who would generate another round of questions. The mid-morning sun shone brightly. She squinted before putting on her sunglasses.

"I'm so glad you texted me. I wanted to thank you again for a lovely evening." Cindy sat on the oversized chaise. The cushion hugged her petite form. "You're very interesting to talk with."

"Likewise. I find you fascinating. Your free spirit is a breath of fresh air for my soul." His soothing voice charmed and softened her reserve.

"I can tell you write music." She twirled a strand of hair behind her ear. "You have a very lyrical way with words."

"You flatter me. My father is the true star in the family. I merely shine from his shadow now and then." She heard him take a puff from his e-cigarette. "That is the story of my life—always chasing my father's fame and never quite living up to expectations."

"I have no expectations about you." Cindy adjusted her seat. "I accept you for who you are. No pretense. No promises. It keeps things simpler that way."

I feel sorry for him. To be judged by his dad's success must be hell.

"Everyone has expectations. It's part of life." She waited for him to continue. "On a happier note, Larry has offered to fly my dad and me back to Paris on his private jet. Will you be joining us?"

"Yes. I will." Joy rushed through her. "Mom and I already discussed that. Like I said, I have six weeks off and I need a change of scenery."

"There's no better place than Paris for a fresh start." The sound of sniffing came to her ears.

"Exactly. A fresh start is what I need." She let out a small giggle. "You can show me the sites."

Why did I say that? Now I sound forward. It's such a relief to know I'll be so far away from Vic. If he means what he said about his friends being able to find me here, they'll be surprised.

"Showing you the sites will be my pleasure." He hesitated. "I, I hope you don't tire of me. I don't live a glamorous lifestyle, not as your stepfather."

"Don't believe what you read in the rags." She sighed. "Larry and Mom live a pretty humdrum existence. They only go to mandatory parties for one award or another."

"It will be a long flight, n'est-ce pas?" She heard him blow his nose.

"Yes. About twelve hours." She yawned. "I think the jet will gas up at JFK or Boston before landing at Charles De Gaulle."

"You yawned. Did I keep you up too late last night?"

Cindy felt herself blush as if he could see her. "No. You got me home soon enough. I had a hard time falling asleep."

"Moi aussi." He confessed, "I kept thinking of a beautiful blond who captivated my heart."

"Don't start off too fast." She twirled her hair absentmindedly. "We hardly know each other. Don't let this fire burn so hot that it goes out quickly."

"Jamais, never, Cindy. I know when my heart speaks the truth." *Is he for real?* "No one in my past is like you."

Ah, he has a past. Well, so do I. Is his past dark?

"I don't know if I can believe your words." Cindy sat straight up and swung her legs over the side of the chaise. "I haven't dated much since meeting Vic. I'm out of practice."

"Practice can be quite enjoyable." She envisioned his smug smile. "I can show you."

"I don't doubt that one." She giggled with nonchalance. "I don't know if I'm ready to learn."

"Your heart will let you know when the time is right." His voice lowered. "Listen to your heart and learn to live."

"You might be right, JC." *He seems so kind and loving.* "I'll call you later when I get a chance."

Ten

THE FLIGHT TO Paris passed without incident. Taylor noticed Cindy and Jean-Claude held hands while dozing on a sofa, as Charles, Larry, and Joe appeared to have enjoyed the comfort of the leather-upholstered seats. Gigi and Jacques, seasoned travelers, spent most of the time curled in a blanket on a comfy chair. On final approach to Charles de Gaulle airport, Taylor placed them in their carriers.

"Larry," Charles rubbed the sleep from his eyes, "you can use my limousine for your ride to the hotel. It's the least I can do for the fine hospitality you've shown to me and my son—flying us to Paris on your jet."

Taylor felt ill at ease with his offer. "Won't that be out of your way?"

I don't want to impose. The French detest pushy Americans.

"Not at all." Jean-Claude stretched his long legs. "My father lives on Île Saint Louis, and I don't live far from him."

She visualized the streets near the hotel. "Sounds like you're near the Regina."

What damn luck! He'll be sniffing around Cindy and I can't help worrying that she's too vulnerable right now.

"Mais oui." Jean-Claude smiled with a hint of smugness. "My apartment is well within walking distance."

The steward came by and made certain all were fastened in for landing, then sat in his jump seat and secured his belt.

~~***~~

Charles LeGrand's entourage of driver and security personnel surrounded him and the Davis group at the arrival terminal where the limousine waited. On the periphery, paparazzi photographers captured this candid moment of the French singers' arrival—both that of Charles and Jean-Claude.

Charles climbed in the backseat first, followed by Jean-Claude, and the Davis group took the seats opposite them. Charles noticed how attentive Taylor was with the poodles as she removed them from their carriers. *Madame Davis certainly loves Gigi and Jacques.*

I wonder if she notices how attached my son is to their daughter. They're as close as Gruyère and ham on a baguette. I hope he doesn't break her heart. There's so many crushed loves he has left in his wake.

"Madame," Charles smiled when Gigi raised her head from

Taylor's lap, "would you be wanting to take a nap? Or my driver can take you somewhere you might want to visit after he takes me to my residence?"

"Merci bien." She hid a yawn with her hand. "I think Larry and I would like to relax before we meet for dinner tonight."

"Bien sûr." He eyed his son and Cindy. "Et vous, Cindy? Do you want to relax before our dinner?"

"I think not. I'm too full of energy." A suggestive smile escaped toward Jean-Claude. "I'll decide what I want to do by the time we arrive at the Regina."

"Certainement, I mean certainly." Charles eyed his son and Cindy with concern.

Mon Dieu! She can be a problem for him. Taylor's not saying much, but I see her glare at her daughter. Jean-Claude had better behave himself. I'm tired of bailing him out of his scrapes and near scandals. At thirty-two, he should have more common sense and not act as a schoolboy. I've spoiled him too much. If his mother was still alive, maybe he would have turned out differently.

~~***~~

Jean-Claude realized the limousine had already pulled up in front of Hôtel Regina. Larry got out first, then Taylor with the poodles, and lastly Cindy.

The doorman immediately approached the famous American couple. "Bonjour Monsieur and Madame Davis. It is so nice to meet you again. Your luggage will be taken care of immediately."

"Merci." Taylor smiled, then turned back to Cindy, who hung back, and stood by the open car door.

He wondered what she was up to. *Did she and her mother have an argument?*

"Cindy," Taylor sounded reserved, "we need to check in. Come along."

"No." Her daughter's lips thinned with a set jaw.

Jean-Claude rubbed his forehead. *She's going to get me in trouble with her parents.*

"What do you mean, 'no'?" Her mother's eyes widened. "This is where we're staying—you included."

Cindy glanced at him in the backseat. "I'm staying at JC's place." Her devilish smile escaped.

Jean-Claude punched numbers on his cell phone and waited for someone to answer.

Taylor spoke softly through clenched teeth, "Have you lost your mind? Don't be a pushy American."

Larry came up behind her. Cindy returned to the backseat and snuggled close to Jean-Claude.

"What's going on?" he spoke quietly in Taylor's ear, but Jean-Claude still could hear him.

"Said she's staying with Charles' son." Taylor focused on her daughter. "I have no idea what's happening to her."

Monique answered Jean-Claude's call and he gave his orders rapidly in French. "Get out. Fifteen minutes. I'll explain later."

When he ended the call, Cindy's defiance was set on her face. "Mom, I can think for myself. JC doesn't mind. He can show me the sights."

Mon Dieu. Did I just see her remove her wedding band and place it in her purse?

"Pardon, madam." He coughed politely and stepped out of the limo. "This is as much of a surprise to me as it is to you. Quel surpris! But not a surprise that I find to be objectionable. It will be my pleasure to entertain Cindy. I find her très intéressante— extremely interesting."

I hope to God Monique can be out before we arrive. Perhaps we can spend some time at Papa's first.

~~***~~

Taylor wrung her hands as she walked into the living room of their suite. She wished she had a cigarette. Larry offered her a rum and coke from the mini bar. Worry and anger lined her brow as she clenched her jaw.

"I don't know Cindy anymore." She took a large swallow of her drink. "What was she thinking? No! That's the problem. She wasn't thinking—reacting to her mess of a marriage."

Larry gripped her shoulders. "You're doing yourself no good going on like this. Your daughter is sowing her oats, so to speak."

"Sowing her oats!" Darts shot from her eyes. "Selling her ass is more like it. She's not even officially separated from Vic and is ready to sleep with Charles' son. And for what! To prove how grown up she is?"

"Maybe she feels so desperate that she's acting out." Frustration creased his face. "True, acting out in the wrong way, but she's floundering—might see Jean-Claude as the proverbial 'life raft'."

"She should be turning to us and not Jean-Claude." Taylor looked out of the double windows at the traffic below. "We won't do anything to hurt her. My God! She doesn't even speak French."

She turned to face him. "What if she needs a doctor—she wouldn't know how to communicate."

"Tay, you're overreacting." He upturned his palms and tilted his head boyishly. "Cindy is sensible. She'll be back at the Regina tonight or tomorrow at the latest. Besides, we don't know that Jean-Claude will step over the line and go to bed with her. He might have a girlfriend and not even be interested in Cindy." He crossed the room and wrapped an arm around her shoulder.

"I overheard him talking to someone on his phone—probably a girlfriend—something to the effect of getting out in fifteen minutes." Taylor took another swallow of her drink. "Get real, Lar." Her worry didn't soften. "He's a man, a *French* man. I don't know of any who would turn down an opportunity for a night of amour—especially from a distraught, naïve American woman. The invitation is lying there on the mat for him."

"Your worry won't solve anything at this point. Why don't you call her?" She found him rubbing her shoulders comforting. "Ask if she wants to eat dinner with us."

"I'd like to do that, but my gut tells me otherwise." Taylor rested her head on his chest. "I pray to God no harm comes to her."

"It won't." Larry stroked her hair. "I don't have a bad feeling about that guy. Cindy's not a kid anymore. She'll be okay."

Eleven

A BLACK LIMOUSINE pulled to the curb of *rue Saint Roch*, off from *rue de Rivoli*. The driver opened the back door. She got out first. Jean-Claude's long legs emphasized his height as he bent forward to avoid hitting his head on the roof. He peered up and down the street, then spoke in French to the driver.

Cindy craned her ears to listen to his conversation.

Damn! I wish I had followed Mom's advice and learned French.

The driver retrieved the luggage and placed them on the sidewalk.

Jean-Claude punched a keypad to the right of the massive, ornate blue door. She noticed the finely sculpted brass handle, worn shiny from decades of use. He opened the door to reveal a charming courtyard containing flowerpots bursting with geraniums and daisies in bloom. He motioned for her to enter.

Two staircases on opposite sides led to what must be the higher dwellings.

"Please wait here a moment." He reached in his pocket and wiped his nose with a handkerchief. "I need to see if the maid has finished cleaning."

"I don't mind things strewn around."

Is he a fussbudget? Might be. His slacks barely break a crease when he walks.

"Non, non." He dashed to the outside stairs. "I won't be a minute."

He stopped briefly to pet a dog sitting by a potted plant.

Awe, JC likes animals. He's a good person.

A strong breeze kicked up. Cindy turned up the collar of her turquoise trench coat and hugged her shoulders, then rubbed her arms.

It's cool for April. Feels more like a Florida winter instead of Spring.

Ten minutes later, Jean-Claude came briskly down the steps. He sported a broad welcoming smile as he extended his hand out to her.

"Come. I'll show you the way. We're very lucky. The elevator is working." He grabbed their two small bags.

"A working elevator is special?" *What type of place is this? I hope there's running water.* "I pretty much take elevators for granted."

"This is a very old building. The parts that needed repair had to

be specially made. I had to climb the stairs for almost two years."
He chuckled. "That's why we French embrace everything that is
new—new things work as they should with no worry of failure.
My place is on the quatrième étage—the fifth floor in American
terms."

"Five floors to climb? I'm glad I don't have to endure that
one." Cindy entered the tiny elevator.

The old accordion-styled grating growled and squeaked as he
closed the door. Jean-Claude pressed number four. The ascent
was slow.

*I hope this relic doesn't stop mid-floor. Maybe the stairs would've been
safer.*

She eyed him and licked her lips.

*But I wouldn't mind being stuck with him for a while. A faulty elevator
could prove interesting.*

The glass and metal enclosed cage came to an abrupt stop with
an upward and downward jolt before finally resting to a
welcoming silence. He pushed the grate door open, took their
luggage, and stepped onto the firm beige carpeting. She followed
and took in the surroundings. Off-white damask wallpaper and
worn wood chairs in the hallway gave the feeling of antiquity.
Quaint sconces lit the way.

*I hope his décor isn't like Mom's—full of French antiques and crystal
drops.*

Jean-Claude strode swiftly down the hall to the end, then turned
a corner to his apartment. Cindy brought up the rear as he fished
in his pocket for his keys. He opened the door.

"Please. Welcome to my home," he offered.

She slipped over the threshold as he flipped a light switch and
closed the door. The sound of multiple lock tumblers broke the
silence.

"As I said before, thank you for not refusing me at the hotel. I
know I was abrupt and quite out of line." She wrung her hands.
"But after all I've been through, I couldn't bear the thought of
spending this time dealing with my mom's idea of right and
wrong." She started to say more.

He put his finger to her lips. "Hush. There is no one here to
judge you. I accept you for who you are. Your past is but a
painful memory. Your present is here with me, and I hope the
same for your future."

He took her by the hand to the expansive parquet-tiled living room. A small black baby grand stood at the far end—a true luxury in the first arrondissement in Paris if she remembered correctly what her mother had told her. His thoroughly modern décor of white and black with red, mirror, and chrome accents pleased her. The art on the walls was by Dali. Only one poster by Toulouse-Lautrec gave any indication of French influence.

He assisted Cindy with removing her coat, and placed it on a hanger from the coat closet near the entry. She felt his eyes boring into her. "You have a lovely home."

I wonder if his bedroom is just as seductive.

"It keeps me dry when it rains." Jean-Claude strolled to the bar adjacent to the piano. He lifted a bottle of red wine. "A drink, a nap, or both?"

"Both, I think." She sat on the white leather sofa, kicked off her heels, and rested her feet on the mirrored coffee table. "I didn't sleep well on the jet, even though your shoulder was quite comfy."

"Comfy?" He titled his head and raised a brow, then poured the wine into two glasses.

"Sorry. I shouldn't use slang for you." She hid a yawn with her hand. "It means comfortable. The same type of verbal shorthand that French people use for 'How are you?' as in 'Ça va?'"

"Merci for that lesson." He handed her a glass, then sat down beside her and began massaging her neck. "I might have a lesson to teach you." His lips grazed her ear, his breath hot.

"Hmm, that feels so good." Cindy closed her eyes and let her worries be replaced with longings for her new love interest. "You have strong hands—must come from hours at the keyboard." She took a sip of wine.

"Yes, my profession does have side benefits." His massaging touch grew more sensuous. "Enough about me. I want to know about you. You are so fascinating—like no other woman I've known—you speak your mind and don't play games like French women."

"Well, I'm not as frank as Mom. But I come close."

When will he make his move? Do I have the strength not to go to bed with him? Did Mom ask herself this question when she met Larry?

"Be proud of who you are and never look back. Remember," his lips came close to hers as he spoke, "the past pushes you forward with a hand."

"And pulls you back with the other." Her palm went to his knee.

His lips teased her neck in a trail of kisses before resting on her mouth. Cindy kissed him back with unrestrained passion—passion that had been controlled and stifled by a troublesome marriage. This moment was hers and she relished the feel and exhilaration.

Jean-Claude ended their kiss by standing up and taking her hand. "Come. We both need a nap, not to mention other things."

Talk about being direct! Isn't he rushing things a bit?

"I like the idea of … 'other things'," she cooed. "By the way, I'm on birth control."

He shrugged. "I use condoms."

He led her down a long hall, passing the entry, to his lavishly appointed bedroom styled in the same fashion as his living room, extremely modern.

"It's nice that you want to protect me." Cindy noticed his overt confidence and found it appealing.

"I use condoms to protect myself." He immediately turned down the bed linen and then started to undress.

She took her time disrobing down to her bra and panties. Turning around, she observed he was already in the bed.

Jean-Claude patted her side of the bed. "Viens ici."

"Come here?" With hands on hips, she made a face. "No one commands me."

"It was a request." He flashed an inviting smile. "I must savor your beauty."

"A lot seems to get lost in translation between us." She climbed into bed, removed her under things, then snuggled to his chest.

There's no turning back for me now.

"Intimate moments need no translation." His lips mouthed her earlobe. "Let me show you."

Jean-Claude leaned over her as his lips brushed against her cheek. Cindy turned to him, her mouth partially opened. Their tongues mingled as the heat of passion built. His hand caressed her breast and lingered on her taut nipple, giving a gentle squeeze and making her gasp.

Her fingers traveled down his muscular abdomen, over his soft dark hair, then teasingly toyed with his manhood as she heard his breath quicken. Jean-Claude's kisses trailed down her neck to her breasts. Taking her nipple in his mouth, his tongue teased her deliciously. She moaned and arched her back when his fingers found her deep recesses. His exploring drove her desire higher as her thighs parted wider, inviting him to join her in sweet craving. His kisses traveled down her body, ever more arousing, and continued to her most sensitive area.

"JC, don't tease me," she cried. He kneeled between her legs and gently entered her, pausing inch by inch, making her beg for all of him, his movement slow and lingering. She pushed her hips up to meet his every thrust as the heat of passion drove her higher. She controlled his rhythm, and she liked that power. He gave himself to her, on her terms. Filled with uncontrollable desire, she frantically grabbed his buttocks and gave into the supreme feeling of ecstasy that swept over them.

Panting breaths, moist hairlines, and heavy limbs remained intertwined in the afterglow.

Jean-Claude rolled off from her. "Formidable!" He looked at her tenderly as his finger traced her lips. "You are special to me, Cindy. Please, don't go back home. Stay with me."

She started to speak. He stopped her with a kiss. "Don't answer me now. Just think about what I ask. I need you in my life."

Twelve

CINDY STRETCHED AS she climbed out of Jean-Claude's bed, and made her way to the bathroom. The clanking of pans and the kitchen faucet running filled her ears. She smiled at the sound.

He's so considerate. Making breakfast for us. She made a face. Vic never did that. He wouldn't walk across the room for a bowl of chips—I always had to serve him.

After taking care of nature's needs, she took his terrycloth robe hanging from a hook on the back of the door and paid no real notice of a minute amount of fine white powder on the sink counter. The robe had the scent of men's cologne and made her smile. Tying the belt, she strolled down the hall, into the living room, and then into the kitchen. Cindy came up behind him, rose on tiptoes and kissed his ear playfully. Jean-Claude wiped his hands on a towel, then turned to face her and smiled.

"Did you sleep well?" His arms encircled her waist.

"Very well." She snuggled into his chest. "You are the perfect sleeping pill."

"Sleeping pill?" He looked mildly confused. "I'm sorry. I don't understand all American slang."

"It's medicine for sleep—it makes you sleepy." Cindy looked up at him.

"Ah, un somnifère." He looked at his watch then patted her derrière. "You had better dress if you want to have breakfast with your parents."

"I'm not certain I want to." She pouted.

Why should he want me to see my parents?

His fingers lifted her chin. "You need to face them and tell them of your decision—to stay here with me."

"I didn't say I would." *Does he really care?* "Would you be upset if I returned to America with them?"

"Mais oui! I meant those words I said to you." He held her firmly in his arms. "I don't invite a woman to live with me every day. You are special to me."

"I want to believe you." She fidgeted, shifting her weight.

"Then believe me." He kissed the tip of her nose. "Now dress yourself. I will walk with you to their hotel. It's only a block from here. You should apologize to them for missing their dinner at the hotel."

Cindy made a face and then broke from his embrace, humming one of his tunes she had recently learned.

~~***~~

Half an hour later, Cindy and Jean-Claude stood at the hotel's dining room doorway. The hum of tourists filled the room. She spotted them at a circular table in the corner, close to the garden dining area. Joe looked like he was enjoying his usual coffee, while Taylor and Larry ate croissants. Larry rose and extended his hand to Jean-Claude when they had reached the table. Taylor gave a long, hard look at her daughter.

"I thought you would like to know I'm fine." Jean-Claude assisted Cindy with her chair as she continued, "Nothing bad happened to me." She glanced at him admiringly as he sat down next to her.

"It's nice that you're okay." Taylor's voice held an edge. "We're your parents and worry about you. More importantly, I'm your mother and your welfare is my main concern."

"Stop worrying." She took a croissant and a petite bottle of jam from the waiting basket on the table. "I'm a grown woman and I know what is best for me. Mom, cut the damn umbilical cord."

Why did I say that? I don't want to hurt her. Damn! I'm not wrong, though. She treats me like a teenager and it makes me so mad at times.

Larry cut in, "Let's have an enjoyable and quiet breakfast. I have to meet with Charles in a few hours. I don't want tension to spill over into my singing. Hopefully, we'll record a couple of songs this afternoon."

"Certainement, Monsieur Davis." Jean-Claude looked at Cindy. "This day is made more beautiful by your lovely daughter, n'est-ce pas?"

Taylor leaned forward in her seat. "Jean-Claude, don't you find it difficult communicating with Cindy? She speaks little to no French."

Joe raised an eyebrow at Larry, but kept his mouth shut.

"Jamais! Never!" He gave Cindy's hand a reassuring squeeze. "We communicate quite well for the important things." He paused poignantly. "Sometimes, no words are needed for the most intimate of communication."

Joe coughed loudly into his napkin.

"I see." Taylor's expression morphed into one of steely politeness. She directed her attention to her daughter. "Do you feel the same? Have you come to a decision that could alter your entire life in a detrimental way?"

Cindy took a deep breath for courage. "Mom, I don't want us to argue, even with courteous words in public. Vic and Tampa are my past ... Jean-Claude is my future." She looked at him with love in her eyes. Another deep breath. "I will not be returning to Bel-Air with you. I'm staying in Paris .... I'm going to live with JC."

I can't believe I'm actually saying this. I hope JC doesn't mind—and doesn't hurt me or let me down.

"JC?" Her mother quipped, "I see you're still calling him by a nickname." She sighed. "I guess that's the norm since it's obvious you two have already slept together."

Larry leaned to Taylor and whispered, "Don't go there. There's no point."

Joe, who had been silent up to now, tried to defuse the situation. "Look. We all have things to do today. Let's put the squabblin' down and get on with it. Paris is awaitin'."

"Sure, Joe." Larry turned to Taylor. "Let's get our things from the room and be on our way. You have to help me find how to get to the studio to meet up with Charles."

The three rose leaving Cindy and Jean-Claude to contemplate that morning's discussion.

~~***~~

Jean-Claude sipped his café au laît as he digested the recent encounter with Taylor and Larry.

Well, it could have been worse, but was not as good as I had wanted.

He watched Cindy take a bite of her jam-laden croissant.

He touched her hand. "That wasn't so bad."

"It wasn't good." She took the steaming cup of cocoa to her lips. "Mom isn't going to change, and I refuse to remain her little girl. She has to let me go at some point."

"You hurt her feelings." He stroked the top of her hand. "She's your mother and deserves respect."

"JC, don't give me that crap. I've heard the way you've talked to your father on the phone." Cindy wiped her lips with her napkin. "Don't be a hypocrite. Besides, Mom and I have a history and it's not pleasant, and not one I want to discuss."

"Je comprends, ma chérie. I understand. But my father and I have an understanding. He knows my harsh words don't color the love I feel for him, or the love he feels for me. I still respect him."

He looked earnestly at her.

Is Cindy's heart really this hard?

Her eyes pleaded with him. "I love Mom, I truly *do*. Please try to understand. She pushes my buttons and I hers."

"Push buttons?" A question colored his expression. "There is so much in your language I don't understand."

"It means she irritates me, gets under my skin, makes me angry." Cindy sighed and reached for her purse. "Enough of this talk. You promised to show me Paris."

"Did I?" Jean-Claude chuckled. "Promise is not in my vocabulary in any language." He pulled out her chair as she rose. "No promises, but many offers."

He took a handkerchief from his pocket and wiped his nose.

"Your allergy acting up?" Cindy eyed his slightly red nostrils.

"Yes. It's the end of April and the flowers are in bloom."

This isn't the first time she's mentioned my allergies. Maybe I should be more discreet.

Can I mold her to my tastes?

Thirteen

"WHY HAVEN'T YOU taken me to see the sites?" Cindy stood behind Jean-Claude as he sat at the piano playing one of his songs. She left a gentle kiss on his ear.

I love the smell of his cologne.

"I have to work some time. Sightseeing is a luxury my fame can't afford." He took her hand from his shoulder and left a kiss. "I don't have a security team like the famous Larry Davis."

"Joe is the only one here with him, and he really isn't a security guy." She sat down on the bench beside him. "I thought you would enjoy sharing Paris with me. Showing me the city you love from your eyes, and not from a manufactured brochure I can pick up anywhere."

"D'accord. If you want to see the Paris I enjoy, then we'll start tonight." He played another musical phrase. "Wear a skirt, heels, and no pants."

"You're not serious, are you?" Her eyes popped. "I would never go out without panties. What are you thinking?"

"Sorry. It must be the language. Much lost in the translation." He turned and kissed her cheek. His hands cupped her face. "If you would meet me halfway and try to learn French, then we might understand each other better."

"I've never been one to want to learn a foreign language." She studied the intensity in his eyes. "Don't push me on this one. We communicate perfectly well enough."

"Yes, we do." His lips met hers with constrained passion. Her mouth opened to receive him. He ended their kiss slowly. "But I'd love to hear you speak to me in my mother tongue."

"Since you put it that way—bringing tongues into the conversation—I'll think about it." She leaned into his arms.

Jean-Claude's kisses trailed down her neck and to her throat. She ran her fingers through his hair as his hands fondled her breasts giving a firm squeeze. Cindy's heavy pant caught on a gasp.

"Let's go to the bedroom," she said nearly breathless. "The piano bench is far from comfortable."

He broke his caress and looked in her eyes. "I make the choice of where and when."

She sat straighter. *What's with him? He was so tender.* "I'm not one to obey commands. I have rules—I told you that from the beginning."

"Mais oui. And I told you the same." He chuckled as he returned to the keyboard. "American women are so indisciplinée—uncontrolled."

"You got that one right!" She got up from the piano. "When are we leaving for wherever you have planned?"

"À vingt-deux heurs—ten this evening." His focus remained on the keys.

"And what do we do before then?"

"We can stroll the back streets, away from those who might recognize me." His suave smile tugged at her heart.

"Or we can spend our time here. Your bed or sofa offers a comfortable diversion."

I don't want to walk the streets. I want to feel his love.

"Later. Waiting sharpens the senses." His hands brought her face close to his. He teasingly brushed her lips with his and then pulled back. "I want your senses sharp as nails tonight."

"No need." She licked her lips. "My sensations are always finely tuned."

Cindy took his hand and led him to the bedroom.

~~***~~

Joe sat at an outside table at Café Carrousel, across from Hôtel Regina, talking with his French friend Frédéric Millet. Both enjoyed the Parisian afternoon with a bottle of beer.

"What do you know about Jean-Claude LeGrand?" Joe brought his glass to his lips.

"Not much." Frédéric leaned back in his chair. "Just what the press puts out. He's a famous French singer. Likes the ladies, and changes them almost as often as he changes the sheets. Never been in trouble with the flics."

"Flics?" Joe's brows rose.

"Police, gendarmes. No record of crime." His voice lowered, "Though in the clubs, some of his associations seem questionable and not of the best sort."

"Interestin'." Joe motioned to a waiter. "I'm hungry. Will y' order for us?"

Likes the ladies? Maybe Taylor's right. Cindy could be hurt.

"Bien sûr, I mean, of course." Frédéric pulled out a cigarette and quickly lit it.

The waiter promptly produced two menus and a basket of French bread. Joe pointed to his selection and his friend placed the order.

"Why are you interested in this French singer?" Frédéric took a long puff and then crushed the cigarette in the ashtray. He tore off a piece of bread from the basket on the table and placed it on a napkin. "Is there something he's involved in with Larry?"

"He's datin' Cindy." Joe took a sip of beer. "Why didn't you finish your cigarette? Tryin' to quit?"

"Yes. I try to quit constantly." He chewed quickly. "Back to Cindy, I thought she was married to Vic. Did they divorce?"

"She left him. Somethin' 'bout gamblin'." Joe watched a pigeon and a few sparrows peck at the crumbs on the sidewalk. "Now she's takin' up with this Jean-Claude guy. Taylor's worried 'bout her."

"Je sais. I know. Taylor loves her daughter very much." He took a swallow of his beer. "Would you like me to contact my investigator friend and see if Cindy is in any harm?"

"You're readin' my mind." The waiter brought their order—a ham and cheese sandwich for Joe and an order of escargot for Frédéric. "I don't think there's really anythin' goin' on, but I want to be on the safe side."

Frédéric's eyes narrowed with skepticism. "I doubt there is anything to discover. Jean-Claude LeGrand has always been living a clean life. But, if it makes you feel better, I'll get my friend to snoop around."

For Cindy's sake, I hope nothin' turns up on this guy. Still ... he's too damn slick not to have dirty laundry buried somewhere.

Fourteen

LARRY STUDIED THE French lyrics as his Parisian singing partner looked on with a bemused smile. Beads of perspiration dotted his forehead. The stifling heat in the recording booth caused him to repeatedly wipe his moist hands on his black jeans.

"Do you need more time? Are there any words you're not certain of?" Charles leaned closer.

Larry pointed to a phrase on the sheet music. "How do you pronounce this?"

He looked at the words in question. "Ah, 'toute la journée'. That means all the day. Pronounced toot-la-jour-nay."

"Got it." Larry sipped water from a bottle. "D'accord." He smiled, pleased that he could speak a few simple words in his friend's language.

The orchestra behind them in a separate glassed area began the song. Charles led the first few strains. Larry would come in during the chorus and take over the second stanza. Taylor appeared nervous as she looked on.

The recording session lasted the entire afternoon for two songs. Charles had no difficulty with one of Larry's songs and demonstrated his fluency in English. By the end, the American singer felt more secure in this foreign language.

This won't be as bad as I thought. Glad Taylor coached me with most of the words and their meaning.

Charles patted Larry's back. "Très bien, mon ami. You sang my song very well. We'll record more tomorrow. I hope I gave your song the same amount of justice."

"I have no issues on your part." He ran his hand through his hair. "What time should I be at the studio for our next session?"

"I'll be here at nine in the morning." Charles went on to explain, "Have a lunch, and then continue in the afternoon until five. If we don't need to record each song more than twice the album could be completed in two or three more days."

Larry's eyes popped. "That short a time? You have a lot of faith in my ability to pronounce every French lyric properly."

"Don't worry. My fans don't expect perfection. They expect expression and soul." He chuckled. "American singers are very popular with the French."

"Likewise." Larry felt mildly relieved. "American women drool over a man with a French accent."

Charles smiled. "Well, dear friend, it appears we are a winning combination on both sides of the Atlantic Ocean."

~~~***~~

Frédéric and Claude Beaufort enjoyed lunch at an outside table of the famous Les Deux Margots café on *6 Place-Germain-des-Près* in the sixth arrondissement. The sidewalk bustled with tourists holding cameras and locals headed for different destinations. None took much notice of the armed national police—now commonplace since the terrorist shootings. A gentle breeze fluttered their napkins as they waited for their waiter to refill their breadbasket.

"Frédéric, how deep do you want me to dig?" He took a mouthful of salmon. "It could take some time if you want me to go beyond the usual tabloid stuff that's already been out there."

"Deep. She's Taylor's daughter and is on the rebound. If Jean-Claude has a past, I need to know." He sipped his wine and then took a forkful of omelet before continuing. "I can't see him taking any woman seriously."

"He does have a reputation. Parties, women, and drink—that's his rulebook." Claude retrieved a small notebook from his inside jacket pocket. "Give me the details about Cindy. It might help."

"Blond, pretty, naïve, at odds with her parents. Separated from her husband, Vic." Frédéric took a swallow of wine. "Not much more to tell. Left Vic because of gambling."

"I'll start after lunch." The waiter brought a fresh basket of cut baguette. "This will be an interesting assignment. Far better than the boring adultery cases."

"Don't spill any tasty beans to the press." Frédéric watched his friend take notes. "Taylor and Larry are my friends and I don't want their daughter pulled into anything messy."

"Frédéric! When have I ever given up a confidence?" His eyes grew wide. "You insult my friendship."

"I merely wanted to remind you." He took the napkin to his lips, then called out to the waiter, "L'addition, s'il vous plaît."

"I've always been up front with you." Claude leaned closer. "I have never revealed your identity to any of my connections."

"Yes. I know." Frédéric reached into his wallet to pay the bill. He tossed fifty euros on the table. "I still remember your involvement with the paparazzi when Princess Diana was at the Ritz." His eyes narrowed. "Do you still deny you were one of those who tipped them off?"

"Jamais! Mon ami, I respected her and her courage. She fought the system." He sighed. "Such a shame. Her glorious causes resulted in her death."

~~***~~

"Undress. Remove all your clothes."

Cindy watched Jean-Claude cross the bedroom floor and draw the drapes, leaving only the dim light from the lamp on the night table.

Cindy's brow furrowed. "Why? What do you have in mind, besides the obvious?"

"I'm in control, mademoiselle." He stood commanding with hands on hips. "You will like it. I promise."

"I'm not certain about this." She began to unbutton her blouse. "Pain does not turn me on."

"There will be no pain." He stepped closer, then sat in the chair next to the bed. "But, sometimes pain can lead to the most exquisite pleasure."

"Look." She stood squarely in front of him, bare breasted. "If you have any kinky ideas, forget about me. If you hurt me in any way, I will scream."

Surely he can't be another Vic. He doesn't appear to be the violent type, yet he did sound kind of scary when he was arguing with his father at Mom's party. If he tries to force me to do anything I don't like, I'll leave and I won't come back.

"Scream with pleasure will fit the situation." He appeared smug. "I always leave the ladies satisfied—eventually." He opened the nightstand drawer and pulled out a sleep mask.

"What's that for?" Concern rutted her brow. "I told you. I don't want to get into anything weird." She removed the remainder of her clothes.

"Don't worry, ma chérie." He handed the blindfold to her. "Put it on. When you deprive the sense of sight, feeling becomes more intense."

Hesitantly, Cindy pulled down the bed covers, lay down on the bed, and slid the sleep mask over her face. She noticed the faint scent of lavender. Moments passed. His breathing pierced the silence. She reached out to him. She felt nothing but the void of the air.

"Where are you? If you don't answer me, I'll get up and leave."

I didn't feel him sit on the bed.

"Shh." His voice was low and soothing. "Anticipation heightens the senses. Breathe deeply and be aware of what you feel."

A sensation of light stroking at her neck, as that of a kitten's whiskers, teased her curiosity. What could be causing such a delicious feeling? Her hand went for her sleep mask. Jean-Claude grabbed her wrist mid reach.

"No. Not yet, ma chérie." He coaxed, "Relax and enjoy."

The sensual tickling sensation traveled downward to her breasts, first circling one nipple and then the other. A small moan escaped her lips as the teasing trailed farther, slowly, to her seat of utmost pleasure. She raised her hips as craving took control of her senses. Cindy's hand went to touch herself.

Jean-Claude stopped her. "No. Wait. It will be worth it."

"I want you." Her breathing came in short pants. "Please. What game are you playing? Why is this taking so long?"

His palm pressed against her mons, light at first then firmer. She rose up to seek more of her pleasure. His fingers explored her inner being, teasing her with each caress.

Why is he still dressed? I feel his pants against my thigh.

She was a slave to his expert ministrations. She spread her legs further apart, sending a silent invitation for him to be one with her. A moist and warm glow grew within her as his kisses replaced his fingers.

Oh God, when will he enter me?

"I need you now!" She reached for the back of his neck. Again his grip stopped her.

His slow kisses grew faster and firmer. She moaned loudly. "JC! I need you. I can't hold back much longer."

Abruptly, his teasing caresses stopped.

She tore off the mask and looked at him kneeling before her with a satisfied smile.

"What have you got to smile about?" Her eyes darted at his with frustration. "Get undressed and give me what I want."

"What you want? Ah, but it's not what *I* want."

"You don't play fair! You make me want you and then hold back?"

JC is twisted.

Cindy grabbed her clothes and proceeded to dress.

She noticed the long feather on the night table. "I don't like your game. I have a mind to pack up my things and return to my parents while I still can."

Jean-Claude pulled her into him. His breath caressed her ear and left a teasing kiss.

She jerked back. "Oh, no. None of that!" Cindy slipped on her shoes. "I don't like your little game and I've had enough of being brought so far and then no further."

"I never said you wouldn't feel satisfaction." His hand massaged her neck. "Just not now. The next time we make love, the intensity will be as you've never felt before." He kissed her lightly and teasingly bit her bottom lip.

He's so deliciously dark and dangerous, but … why do I have this sinking feeling that he has secrets. I know I should run back to a safe life, but there's something irresistible about him … he's captured my heart. I don't think he'll abuse me the way Vic did. But … Could I be wrong?

Fifteen

CINDY STROLLED DOWN *rue de Rivoli*, looking in the various shop windows. She skirted two uniformed national guardsmen who stood talking while keeping an alert watch up and down the street. Tourists clamored at the ubiquitous stalls selling the typical souvenirs, while Parisians stopped at the clothing and boutique stores. Morning waned and her stomach told her it was time for a midday meal. She was glad that Jean-Claude had business elsewhere, especially since hours earlier he was the cause of such physical frustration.

Two blocks from *place de la Concorde*, near *rue Cambon*, she stopped and peered at the display of books in the window. A youngish man with cropped blond hair placed a new English novel toward the front. He looked up and smiled. She smiled back and brushed her long hair away from her shoulder. He looked interesting.

A gentle chime announced her entry as she crossed the threshold and stepped onto the noise-deafening tweed carpet. A longhaired gray tiger-striped cat purred and sauntered in front of her.

The man from the window greeted her with an English accent. "Hello. Welcome to Prose and Poetry." He extended his hand. "I'm Stuart Dumont." He pointed casually to the cat. "Please excuse Hugo—he likes ladies."

"Nice to meet you and Hugo." She shook Stuart's hand. He held onto hers a little longer than was necessary and stared into her eyes. Something caused her heart to miss a beat.

She bent down, petted the cat, then stood and surveyed the various offerings of both English and French books stacked in small piles on the front tables. The novels in the bookshelves were neatly arranged by subject.

"I love animals," she said. Hugo's tail tickled her legs.

She sorted through the pile of books on the front table. Her hand lingered on an English poetry book.

Dad was so proud when my poem won first prize. I was only in fifth grade. He reacted as if I had won a Nobel Prize in literature. We were so close.

The warmth of her smile matched the single tear on her cheek and reflected the love in her heart.

We celebrated by going to an ice cream parlor. Those were good times. He even encouraged my artistic efforts. I miss him so much. I hope JC will give me more good and not pain. She bit her bottom lip to dry her eyes. *Vic made fun of my paintings. I gave up the dream to follow in Dad's footsteps. Maybe I'm not supposed to have joy—after causing Vic to hit me and lose the baby.*

Cindy turned away from the man, took a tissue from her pocketbook and dabbed her eyes. She couldn't let him see she was crying.

"Are you looking for something special, or just browsing?" He tilted his head boyishly. "We have a vast array of subjects—both English and French."

"I'm looking for a book to learn French." She bit her bottom lip. "I have a French friend and I think I would understand him better if I learned his language."

"He must be very special if you want to take on such an arduous task." Stuart started walking. "The foreign language area is this way, in the reference section. You might find it easier to enroll in Berlitz near *place l'Opéra*. I think their approach is total immersion."

"No. I want to take it slow, to see if learning French is my thing." She picked up a level 1 French language book and leafed through the pages. In the back were CDs to supplement the lessons. "This looks like it'll do the trick. It has English translation—immersion seems too difficult for a quick lesson."

"That's a good choice." He took the book from her and proceeded to the checkout area at the back of the store. "Anything else? French-English dictionary, or a phrase book?"

"Yes. Add both the phrase book and dictionary." Cindy reached for her wallet from her purse. "How much?"

"Fifty euros." Stuart took her money and placed the book in a bag. He glanced at the clock on the wall. "I don't mean this to sound forward, but I see it's lunchtime. I usually go to Café Carrousel, right across from the gold statue of Jeanne d'Arc. It's a lovely site and the food is quite good. If you haven't already eaten, maybe you'd like to join me?"

She took her purchase. "Well, I-I shouldn't and wouldn't if you didn't seem all right …. Yes. That would be nice. The only people I know in Paris who speak English so well, are my parents." Cindy chuckled. "Let's face it—parents are not always the most interesting to chat with." She felt the cat rub her ankles. "I guess

Hugo's the store mascot?"

"Yes, and my family member. He lives with me. When I'm away, I have a very good friend look after him. I named him after the famous French author—Victor Hugo and after the famed Hugo Award for literature. He's more of a dog than a cat—comes when he's called and begs for treats." He watched Hugo, purring loudly, rub up against her ankles. "I hope he's not making a pest of himself."

"Not in the least." She reached down and petted the feline again. His purr grew louder.

In less than ten minutes, they sat at an outside table facing the famous statue and the entrance of Hôtel Regina. Le Louvre was opposite the hotel on the corner of *rue de Rivoli* and *Avenue de Général Lemonnier* which made a commanding view. A waiter quickly came with two menus and a setup of salt, pepper, olive oil, and red wine vinegar.

Cindy read her menu as she talked. "How did an Englishman end up in a bookstore in Paris?"

Stuart responded in kind without looking at her. "My parents told me to follow my heart. I did that by traveling to Paris from Switzerland."

"Switzerland?" The waiter came to the table to take their orders. "But you sound English, not at all French or German."

"My parents had me schooled by an English nanny. Because of that, English is really my first language."

They each gave their orders, and he gathered the menus and handed them to the server, who placed a basket of French bread on the table and set their places with napkins, placemats, cutlery, and a carafe of water.

"That is so interesting." Cindy poured water into her glass not giving the waiter a chance to serve her. "Why did your parents want you to learn English? Were they English?"

"No. They're both French, but relocated to Geneva." He pulled a slice of bread from the loaf in the basket. "Before we get too far into this conversation, shouldn't proper introductions be made?" He again extended his hand. "As you already know, I'm Stuart, Stuart Dumont. And you?"

She felt color come to her cheeks. "So sorry. I should've told you my name before. I'm Cindy Hastings. Soon to be divorced, and with that my last name will be Allen."

"Too bad about your marriage." His gaze searched her eyes. "Do you feel bad about it?"

"On the contrary, it can't come soon enough." She took a swallow of water. "Though, no papers have been filed."

"Oh, I see." The waiter returned and placed a tossed green salad in front of her and sandwich mixte for Stuart. "How does your husband feel about this?"

"I don't really care." She lifted her fork and eyed him with a knitted brow. "Why all these questions? You writing a book or something?"

"You caught me." He took the cola to his lips and swallowed. "Yes, I hope to write the next great novel. I was lucky to be able to buy the bookstore. It gives me time to write and I live in an apartment above the shop." He paused a moment. "I didn't mean to pry. It was nice to meet an American who wasn't in a hurry to get on a bus for the next tour taking off from the City Rama office over there." He pointed his fork. "Speaking French when on dates gets so old. It's refreshing to communicate in English."

"I know exactly what you mean. My French friend speaks very good English—seems to be fluent—yet I feel I have to speak very correctly in simpler sentences for him to understand." She pushed her greens around in the bowl. "Tell me more about yourself. You look very young to own a bookstore."

"I look far younger than I am." He sighed. "Not much more to tell. I'm adopted because my mother was too sick to care for me. My parents gave me an English first name in honor of my birth mum. I never met her so I don't have any feelings for her one way or the other."

"Fascinating." Cindy's napkin fell off her lap. They both reached to retrieve it, knocking heads in the process. "Oh crap! I'm so sorry." She rubbed her sore area. "I'm okay. No harm done."

His eyes, which were a deep blue, lingered on her face a moment too long. "I hope I'm not keeping you from your boyfriend." He gently rested his fingers on her hand.

"You aren't." *He's so nice. I wonder if he has a girlfriend.* "JC is out and about somewhere—in a recording studio or meeting up with his manager."

"JC? A singer?" He removed his hand. "I don't recall a singer named JC."

"Jean-Claude LeGrand." She brushed her bangs away from her brows. "The son of Charles LeGrand."

"Oh yes, the French playboy." He studied her face, clearly looking for a reaction.

"He doesn't seem like a playboy to me." She sat straighter. "He's treated me very well."

He's a bit nervy for having just met me. What gives? Does he have a beef with JC? Did he lose one of his girlfriends to JC?

"No, no, no," he stammered. "I meant no offense. I said no more than what is in the papers."

"I give no credence to tabloids." She wiped her lips. "It's clear I've taken way too much of your time. I'm sure that you want to get back to your store or write down what I've told you for another chapter in your book." She stood to leave.

"I'm sorry. I meant you no harm. Look," he took his business card from his pocket and placed it in her hand, "if you want to call me, I'm always ready to listen."

She handed back his card. "Keep your card for someone who cares." Cindy placed her package from the bookstore on the table as she went for her purse. "I can pay for my own lunch."

"No bother." He took crisp euros from his front pants pocket. "It's my treat and was a pleasure talking with you. Please accept my apology?"

"Yeah. Okay. Whatever."

Too bad. I thought he could be a nice friend. Now he blew it. He's not bad looking either. What do I care—I've got JC.

Cindy grabbed her things and started walking around the corner down *rue de Rivoli* toward *rue Saint Roch.* She turned down the side street to Jean-Claude's apartment, then glanced back and saw Stuart on the corner looking at her. He turned his head away.

What's he doing? Following me? Why? He doesn't seem like a bad person. Damn! Now he knows where I live. If he follows me again, I'll tell JC.

~~***~~

Jean-Claude vaped on an e-cigarette in his living room. He chatted on the phone to his friend from the nightclub—a nightclub that had become his second home.

"Don't worry about it, Maurice." He leaned forward on his knees. "She'll be ready."

"Be careful. You nearly got caught last time." He warned, "Your father had to call in a lot of favors to get you out of that scrape."

"I wasn't as cautious as I should have been." He sighed. "After tonight, she'll do anything—anything I tell her. A few kisses in the right places and there will be no problems. Tout est parfaît."

Maurice's voice faded. "If you're sure, I'll clue in Henri. He'll make certain there are no interruptions."

"See you at the club—ten thirty tonight." He heard the key in the front door. "Have to go. She's back."

Does she need more prepping? No. I better not overdo it.

Sixteen

CINDY ENTERED WITH Jean-Claude. He had a firm grasp of her hand as they wedged through the throng to the leather bar. Dark and noisy, Club Noir blared music from unseen speakers. Patrons had to yell over the din. Some communicated with hand signals. Stainless steel, mirrors on the walls, and avant-garde paintings accented the ultra modern décor of black, white, and gray. Some gyrated on the dance floor brightly lit from underneath. Others sat or stood at the bar located at the back of the room. Heavily made-up women and slick-dressed men greeted him as they passed. Cindy had a good idea this was typical as an afterhours meeting place for the rich and famous on Paris' left bank. She guessed that, like The Sayers Club in L.A., only those "on The List" achieved entry to this exclusive nightspot.

JC seems to know everyone here. He must be as famous as Larry. I wish I knew what they're saying to him. Doesn't anyone here speak any English?

He gestured to the bartender and said something in his ear. Soon, a bottle of Dom Pérignon in an ice bucket with two crystal flutes appeared on the bar.

Impressive! What other surprises does he have in store for me?

He noticed Cindy staring at the dance floor and smiled. "What do you think? You are looking at the décor? It was once considered out of date, but now it is regarded as vintage-trending." Jean-Claude lifted the bottle. "Champagne? It will be a nice beginning to our evening."

"Sure." Cindy moistened her lips. "I feel I'm the only one here who speaks English."

"They understand English—just won't speak it." He filled a glass and handed it to her. "There's no reason for them not to speak French—this is a French club."

"Obviously." She sipped the bubbling liquid. "I bought a book today to learn French."

He raised his brows. "Really? I thought you recoiled from most things French."

"I've had a change of heart—mainly because of a certain famous French singer I know." Her eyes locked onto his.

"My father, perhaps?" His famous onstage smile charmed her.

"Nooo. The singer I'm looking at now." She reached up and fondled the hair at his nape, then slipped a foot out of her stilettos for a moment.

"Do you want to sit? Are your feet hurting you?" Jean-Claude's genuine concern embraced her as his arm went around her shoulder.

Cindy glanced about the room. "Where? There doesn't seem to be any tables free."

"Pas problème," he scoffed, then turned to the bartender and communicated something.

Two waiters appeared. One carried a small round marble-topped table, and another held two chairs. They proceeded to place them on the periphery of the dance floor.

"Merci, mon amant." She felt proud to make an effort in her lover's language.

"I'm your lover?" He assisted her to sit down, then took his seat beside her. "I thought our situation was a bit more casual."

"Quoi? What?" *What game is he playing? He's been screwing me since our arrival in Paris. Does "mon amant" have a different meaning to Parisians?* "I think of you as my lover. We've been sleeping together."

"Bien sûr." He leaned closer for her to hear. "As long as you realize I never said 'Je t'aime' to you. I don't want any misunderstandings."

"Aren't you the cool one!" She pulled back in surprise. "You operate from a different definition of our relationship than I."

"I don't understand." He looked boyish and innocent. "You need to speak more plainly—better yet, you need to study that language book you bought."

His hand ran up and down her shoulder as his lips kissed her ear. Cindy blushed while strangers' eyes observed his less than subtle advances.

Why is he acting like this in public? Another part of his game?

She squirmed. "Not here, JC. People are watching. They could take photos from their phones."

"You're in Paris. No one knows you here. Relax." He kissed her neck as his hand squeezed her thigh.

"Yes. But they know *you*." She tried to pull away. His encircling arm wouldn't let her go. "I don't need to be in the French press."

"There's a private area in the back." His lips brushed against hers. "We can have complete privacy. Love shouldn't be confined to the bedroom." He stood up and seized her hand while Cindy took her purse. "Come. I'll take you where your inhibitions will be erased."

Jean-Claude nodded to the bartender as they headed to a back door on one side of the bar. He swiped a card through the key slot. The door opened, revealing a nearly black room. As Cindy's eyes adjusted to the darkness, She could make out a few couples in various stages of lovemaking. A knot filled her throat and her stomach tightened.

What in hell is this? An orgy meeting place? Just what type of man is JC?
He led her to a doublewide lounge chair, upholstered in leather.

"Viens. Come, sit down. The waiter will bring our champagne." He guided her to sit beside him.

"I'm not totally comfortable with this." Her body tensed. "I don't make love in front of others."

"Is that what we're doing?" His hot breath caressed her ears. "You still have your dress on. Can't make love with fabric covering your luscious body ... though that would be an interesting challenge to pursue."

Damn! What's wrong with me? This dark side of him is so intriguing. I should run away and never come back, but I can't. Will I ever learn? I want to change, but I ...

"If it's all the same to you, I'll keep my clothes on."

"As you wish." His lips found hers.

Jean-Claude opened his mouth and sought her recesses. Cindy's tongue mingled with his in heated passion. Her hand traveled up his thigh slowly to his groin. Her fingers lingered on his rising manhood. He sighed as his hand caressed her breast while his lips ran kisses down her neck. She continued to tease him with her touch. He fired her desire further when his fingers explored up her skirt sending delicious sensations of urgency through her. Her soft moan escaped in a tortuous breath.

I can't do this—not in public, but I'm such a slave to my sexual needs.

"I need to go to the ladies' room." She pushed his lingering fingers from between her legs.

"Fine." His eyes pierced her soul. "I'll lead the way."

Jean-Claude stood up, took her hand, and walked into the near total darkness. A string of rope lights at a threshold indicated the restroom entrance at the far side of the room behind a partition of tall green faux plants.

Opening the door, she noticed that the painted symbol was that of a man. Her eyes adjusted to the bright light. A long counter of sinks with mirrors, urinals, and stalls came into view. She stopped in her tracks.

"JC, this is the men's room." Cindy started to leave. "Where is the ladies' room?"

"Out of order." His smile had a sardonic quality, and yet somehow it appealed to her.

In one swift movement, he lifted her up and placed her hips on the counter between two sinks. He produced a small knife from his pocket.

Her eyes grew wide. "What are you going to do? Don't hurt me. I'll scream!"

"Shh, relax. I would never hurt you." His strong hands grabbed her knees and forced her legs apart. "You will enjoy this all the more. Remember our lovemaking earlier."

"You mean when you left me hanging?" Her breathing deepened.

"This time, satisfaction will be for both of us."

Cindy felt his knife tear at the crotch of her pantyhose. She pulled back as fear started to grip her mind. His kisses smothered her mouth. Sounds of an opening zipper creased the air as he pulled her hips closer to the edge of the counter.

"Enjoy this." He assured, "No one will see us. Inhibitions serve no purpose."

Jean-Claude's fingers tore farther at her hose and then explored what he sought, driving her desire higher. He smiled as he discovered that her heat matched his. Cindy moaned and shut her eyes. Grasping her hips tighter with one hand he pushed her skirt up to her waist, and manipulated her thong panties to the side.

I want him now. I feel so liberated. This is so crazy and exciting.

She felt him ease into her in one slow and teasing stroke. Her legs went to encircle his waist, pulling him in further. Jean-Claude moved slowly in a teasing rhythm. She threw her head back as pleasure filled her being.

"Faster." She panted between words. "Don't hold back."

"Teasing will make it better." He stopped his movement. "I want this to be good for you."

"I need you *now! Fuck me now!*" Cindy shut her eyes and held back a scream.

He picked up his pace as she savored every delicious stroke of pleasure. Her breathing grew faster. She laid her head on his shoulder. Their frantic momentum brought her hands in a viselike grip on his buttocks. Spasmodic movements signaled the ultimate ecstasy that took over her entire body. Her fingers went to the wet hair at the back of his neck.

"I never felt so alive before." She breathed in his ear. "This was intoxicating. I'm glad no one came in to find us."

"Ah, but that's what made it better—the danger." He slowly pulled away from her and started to zip his pants.

A man entered and smiled at Jean-Claude. "Très bien, Jean-Claude."

Cindy turned colors, quickly slid off the counter, and adjusted her clothing. She hurried out the door as her lover followed.

~~***~~

Frédéric sat across from Claude at an outdoor café on *rue d'Arcole* on Île de la Cité. A light breeze flirted with the placemats, while the sun hung low in the sky. Tourists crowded the street, eager to explore the oldest section of Paris, and made eavesdropping difficult for a curious ear.

"What did you find out?" Frédéric studied the menu. "Anything to worry about?

"Besides the obvious?" He chuckled. "Jean-Claude has been relatively clean."

"Relatively?" His jaw tightened. "What do you mean exactly?"

"Other than having a former lover found in the Seine a few years back—no arrests, no scrapes." Claude took a pack of cigarettes from his pocket and offered one to Frédéric. His friend motioned refusal with his hand. "He does have some questionable friends. Possible drug users and such. But nothing directly connected to him."

"Obviously, if he does, he hides it well." Frédéric felt mild alarm.

Claude cupped his hands to light his cigarette. "One thing—that young woman who had been in his bed whose body was found in the Seine—she had bruises about her face, and red marks encircling her wrists and ankles."

"So unlikely to be suicide? Maybe, an accident, or murder?" He leaned closer.

"The flics called it an accident." Claude shrugged. "Pretty cut and dry. She liked coke—hung around with the S&M crowd. Her cocaine level was high on autopsy and the ligature marks looked old from multiple times of being forcibly restrained. The bruises were explained as a result of the fall and hitting the rocks."

"Just the same," a waiter approached, "there could be a connection. I need to tell Joe of your findings."

"I have no problem with that." Claude pointed to an item on the menu for the waiter. "What I told you is in court records—no hidden secrets."

Frédéric gave his order and watched the waiter leave.

If Jean-Claude has dangerous connections, she could be in peril and not know it. I hope Cindy's common sense will save her. Taylor thinks she's vulnerable. She might be more vulnerable than anyone imagines.

Seventeen

"WHY ARE YOU calling me?" Cindy sat in Jean-Claude's living room. "Vic, I told you before! We are finished! Take yourself to a lawyer and let me get on with my life."

"Then there's no hope?" She heard him take a deep breath. "No way to get you back?"

"None." Her lips thinned while her heart raced with anger. "After everything you did to me and the baby …. Why would I want to stay with you?"

"Can you spot me a couple of thousand?" He sounded urgent. "I know Larry would give you the money."

"What nerve!" She stood up and went to the window holding her cell phone to her ear. "You didn't call for a reconciliation. You called to beg money. Vic, get help for your addiction!"

Cindy ended her call, took her purse and a light jacket from the coat rack. Her hands were shaking and she wasn't sure if it was from anger or nerves.

A walk is just what I need. I have to get him out of my life. I can't go back to that. I can't let myself be in that situation ever again.

~~***~~

Taylor started preliminary packing in their suite. Nearly every item she placed in the suitcase was punctuated with a sigh. Larry sat in a chair by the window as he watched her.

"We still have three days before we leave." His voice had a hint of lightness. "What's the hurry?"

"I don't like to wait till the last minute." She sighed again. "Packing helps me think."

"Of what? Cindy?" He went to her.

"Yes. She's constantly on my mind." Tears rimmed her eyes. "We'll never be close. That's where her power is—withholding her love to punish me. Even my dying breath won't bring her closer." Larry hugged her tightly as an item of clothing fell from her hand to the foot of the bed. "She doesn't mean to hurt you. Cindy's in so much pain, that she can't see the pain she's causing you."

"What are you saying?" Taylor pulled her head away and looked up at him, her eyes darting about his face. "She's pain-blind?"

"You could say that." He chuckled. "You coined an excellent name for it. Give her time. She loves you. Like a mother's love, a daughter's love runs just as deep."

"We've never been close, even during her childhood." She shook her head in dismissal. "She was always daddy's little girl. Rarely would she ever turn to me for comfort."

"That's not unusual." Larry stroked her hair as she snuggled into his chest. "Daughters often see their moms as a source of competition—even subconsciously."

"Whatever the reason," her voice muffled by his shirt as her tears wet the fabric, "the pain is still the same."

He lifted her chin to look at him. "Let her grow, make mistakes, and learn from them. Hopefully her mistakes won't be life-altering." His warm smile spoke of comfort to her. "She just might discover that it's a blessing to have a mom."

"Lar, I hope you're right." Taylor wiped her tears away with her fingers. "I fear she sees me as a curse at the moment. She hasn't returned any of my calls. I left her a ton of voicemails and texts."

"Let her come to you. You reaching out might seem as desperation to her." Larry took a handkerchief from his pocket and wiped her streaming tears.

"What you're asking of me is so difficult." Her sob escaped.

"Difficult for you, but the best for her and any future relationship with Cindy." He held her tighter as her chest heaved with sorrowful sobs.

~~***~~

Cindy felt proud to have navigated herself to Galleries Lafayette on *boulevard Haussmann*, behind l'Opéra. Expansive windows displayed the trending fashion for women, men, children and home, creating an urgency to enter and discover more.

This was a pleasant diversion. Armed with her French phrase book, she charged headlong through the brass and glass doors. Security men waited just inside, close to the vertical scanners.

She gazed up in awe at the immense stained glass dome in shades of blue and green with red accents, and at a height that would rival some churches.

I could get lost in here and never want to leave. I have no idea where to start.

Cindy saw an information display by the elevator, picked up the English flyer and studied the various offerings at each level. She glanced at her watch and took the up escalator.

At the top floor was the cafeteria. The outside dining area granted a majestic view of the city. Taking a tray from the stack with cutlery wrapped in a napkin, Cindy looked at the vast array of entrées, salads, cheese, fruit, and splits of wine. She opted for what might be considered a hamburger, a slice of Swiss cheese, and a hard dinner roll. Just before reaching the cashier, she added a bottle of water. *I hope I have enough cash on me.* The check-out line moved swiftly.

"Vingt euros s'il vous plaît, madame," the cashier announced in a perfunctory tone.

"What … I mean, quoi?" Cindy's brow furrowed a moment.

The cashier pointed to the lighted display. "Twenty euros," she clarified in abrupt English.

Cindy fished the money from her purse.

Twenty euros for this meager meal! What would it be at a café? Fifty euros? If I stay here, I might have to get a job. I don't want JC giving me spending money. If I do find employment, I better learn French—and learn it quick.

She chose a vacant table in the less crowded outside dining area, enjoying the refreshing breeze even though it was necessary to anchor the napkins with the eating implements. She sliced the roll in half and placed the meat patty with the Swiss on one half.

Damn! I forgot to get the catsup.

Cindy studied the crowd around the condiment display.

It's not worth the effort to get it now.

Taking the quasi burger in her hands, she opened wide to take a bite. The hard crust forced her to chew in exaggerated fashion, as if chewing on a tough Kaiser roll.

A shadow fell across her table. She looked up.

"May I sit with you? Or, are you saving the seat for someone else?" Stuart's eyes twinkled.

"Please, by all means." Cindy watched him pull out the chair opposite her. "It'll be nice to speak with someone who understands what I'm saying."

"You said that before." She found his smugness mildly amusing.

"Yes. I did, didn't I." She opened a bottle of water and poured it into her glass with a half smile.

Stuart spread his bread with a cheese mixture. "Why are you smiling? Did I make a joke?"

"No. I find it funny that you seem to pop up when I need my spirits lifted." She took a sip of water. "You're not following me, are you?"

I know he tracked me to the corner of rue Saint Roch.

"Not at all." He looked deep in her eyes. "Mere coincidence."

"Then why are you eating here? I would think that a neighborhood café would be more convenient—especially where your store is located."

Is he speaking the truth?

"Gallerie is far cheaper than a bistro or café, the food is good, and you can't beat the view." He looked out toward the Paris rooftops and the Eiffel Tower beyond. "I eat here quite often. I enjoy the walk, and it's not that far." He took a bite of bread, followed by a sip of tea. "How's the French lessons coming along?" Stuart pointed to her phrase book on the table.

"Not well." Cindy took a deep breath. "I must have a mental block of some kind. The conjugations are driving me mad, not to mention the construction of sentences. The grammar is all backward."

"All the English speaking world feel as you." He swallowed some tea before adding, "Truth be known, English grammar is opposite to most other languages."

"That may be true, but it'll never feel normal for me to think 'I you like' sounds correct for 'I like you'."

"Do you like me, then?" He chuckled.

"Yes, I do … as a friend." With a mouthful of burger, Cindy spoke between chews, "I was giving that as an example of how this language frustrates me. True, I learned some phrases from Mom, but I never really thought about the construction of what I was saying."

Stuart reached for her hand across the table. "Think of me as your oasis from all things French."

"I thought you are French and learned English from your nanny." She reminded him of their earlier conversation.

"Yes. But my parents told me that they knew both my parents were English." He poured additional hot water into his cup and dunked the used teabag up and down. "So you see, not one drop of French blood runs in my veins. I'm fluent in French because of my parents and environment—truly bilingual. I guess some would consider my mother tongue is French because I'm a French citizen."

Her eyes cast down to the table. "If I decide to stay in Paris, I think I'll have to find a job. That's another reason why I need to learn this damnable language."

"Yes. You have a point there. Plus, I doubt you'd find anything that pays a decent wage without being a French citizen, not to mention as an American you would have to get a valid work permit. As far as I am aware, you can only do that from outside of France. You would have to go to the French Embassy in the United States to apply, and who knows how long it would take if they approved you." Stuart retrieved the teabag from his cup and gave it a squeeze with his spoon. "Of course, I wouldn't mind having a pretty American employee in my shop. I'm not able to pay more than enough for spending money, but I could give you cash off the books, and therefore you wouldn't need a work visa. During good months, maybe a bit more."

"Are you certain?" Her eyes narrowed. "You're totally serious?"

"I don't make offers lightly, Cindy." He reached out and stroked her hand. She pulled it away.

"I want to be upfront with you." She coughed lightly in her napkin. "I'm seeing JC. He and I have an understanding."

"Engagement? Marriage?" He took the cup to his lips, never taking his eyes off hers.

"That hasn't come up yet." She bit her bottom lip. "But ..."

"But ... you expect it to," he completed her comment. "Never mind. The offer stands no matter what your relationship is with Jean-Claude. I'll be glad for the help. The American tourists would like to speak with one of their own."

"I'll give it some thought." Her eyes brightened. "Your offer might be just what I need to make a favorable decision."

"Whatever you decide—do what is best for you, and not for others." He finished his tea in one swallow. "I'm only working a half-day. How about we take in a museum? The Métro will have us there in no time."

"That sounds like fun. Two friends absorbing some French culture." She smiled and stood up, eager to be on a new adventure.

She hung onto his arm as they headed down *rue Auber*.

Cindy's cell phone rang as they approached l'Opéra Métro entrance. She motioned to Stuart. He stopped and turned to her. Her caller ID identified "Sonny Fugatzzi, salon".

"Hi, Sonny. What's up?" She put her free hand to her ear to muffle the city noise.

"I thought you should know that Vic showed up to the shop asking for money." His voice seemed tenuous.

"You didn't give him any, did you?" She knew Stuart could see her concern.

"No. But I didn't know if he needed the money for you." He paused. "I thought something might be up with him because if you were short of cash Larry would help you out."

"Right." She stared at Stuart as she talked. "Look. I can't really talk much now. I'm in Paris with Mom and Larry. I've left Vic— gambling debt. Larry helped me out. I might stay here for good. I don't know yet. Gotta go. Love to you and Robert." She slipped her phone into her purse.

Stuart moved closer to her. "Anything I can do?"

"Nah. All is good." She forced a smile even though her mood had turned to anger. "Now, let's check out that museum."

"Hold onto your purse. Pickpockets love the Métro." He guided her by the elbow. "We'll take the underground train in the direction of *pont de Levallois-Bécon*, get off at *Villiers* to make a connection onto Line 2 and get off at *Monceau*—near the park."

"Glad you're navigating." She took his hand in hers, and with the other held her purse firmly as they descended the steps to the dim and noisy tunnel with a prominent scent of exhaust fumes. "I'd get lost in this maze."

He laughed lightly. "I doubt that. You'd have it mastered in no time. You're too clever not to pick up on things quickly."

She thought about her new friend as she stood on the platform beside him.

Stuart is extremely nice. He's considerate and not controlling like JC. JC has that dangerous edge—the bad boy image, and something about his controlling nature is appealing to me. I couldn't want for a better lover. He takes risks—that's so exciting.

More passengers-in-waiting came up behind them. Wary, she looked over her shoulder, before turning her attention to Stuart. She studied his face.

He seems dependable. The kind of man I should be with. Can I depend on JC? Hmm, he has that player reputation. What if Mom is right? Should I swallow my pride and return with them to Bel-Air? What if I did? Would Vic send his goons to scare me?

Eighteen

PARC MONCEAU PROVIDED beautiful and serene respite from the city's hustle and bustle. Spectacular roses in varying degrees of bloom decorated the English style garden plantings. Small sparrows willingly accepted treats from people sitting on benches. Stuart took Cindy's hand as he gave a brief history of the park. He glanced at her frequently.

Cindy is so beautiful, and fun to be with. Why is it I'm always the guy missing the bus? She thinks Jean-Claude is the one. Such a shame.

She slid him a sideways glance and smiled.

"I think you're the only friend I have here in Paris." She looked straight ahead.

"That's a start." He beamed. "I'll take friendship. Sometimes friendship can evolve into more."

Am I moving too fast? Why did I say that? Dumb!

"Maybe..." She inclined her head. "If both parties are free."

"I guess you're not—free I mean."

I love the way she looks at me—tilting her head in that beguiling way.

"So far, I'm not." She looked straight ahead as if to avoid his eyes.

They followed the path to *avenue Velasquez*, walked two blocks to 63 *rue de Monceau*, the entrance of Musée Nissim-de-Camondo.

"Stu, life changes things all the time—sometimes moment-to-moment."

"You're teasing me now." Crossing the gravel courtyard, he guided her to the entrance. "Friendship is fine for me."

"Me, too." She gave his hand a squeeze.

Stuart paid the entry fee, then handed the ticket coupon to Cindy. She raised her head up looking at the immense spiral stairway with highly decorative wrought iron banisters and a tapestry woven with a family coat of arms. The black and white tiled marble foyer lent a classic feel, while the ivory carved statue to the right provided elegance and old-world glamour to the décor. Voices of the few tourists echoed from the rooms yet to be discovered.

Cindy studied the pamphlet that provided a self-guided tour. "Such beautiful furniture and paintings."

Stuart entered the main salon on their left. "Elegance was very much in vogue when this home was constructed." He strolled with his hands in his pockets. "The family who lived here had a very sad history."

She lifted her questioning eyebrows. "Care to share. I'd love to hear it. Might make the visit more significant to me."

"Okay. Stop me if you get bored." He took a deep breath. "This was a private residence of Moïse de Camondo, a Parisian banker, originally from Istanbul. He was a passionate collector of French furniture and art objects from the eighteenth century. Sometime in 1911, he hired the famed architect René Sergent to build this house. He meant to give this home to his son. That didn't happen because Nissim, a French aviator, died in World War I. I've read that the design was modeled after Petit Trianon in Versailles. He insisted on all the modern conveniences of that time."

"Go on. I'm enjoying this." She chuckled. "You're my own private tour guide."

They entered the next room decorated in shades of blue. He continued, "Well, since his son died, he bequeathed his home to Arts Décoratifs, and it hence became the museum we are now touring."

"Wasn't there any other family that Moïse could have left this home to?" She turned the pamphlet over as if looking for an answer.

"That's the sad part." He bit his lip. "Tragically, Moïse's only daughter, Béatrice, her husband, and their children, all perished in Nazi death camps, ending the family's distinguished history."

She talked while looking at a portrait of Béatrice. "Why did they go to the Nazi camps?"

"They were Jewish." He reached for her hand. "Unfortunately, hate and destruction leaves a lasting mark on history."

They strolled from room to room. Stuart glanced at her frequently as an object or a painting would catch her eye and cause her to pause.

How firm is Jean-Claude's grip on her heart? He's a playboy. Knowing his reputation, I'm willing to bet he's probably just using her. Dare I think I have a chance?

Nineteen

CINDY ENTERED THE apartment and tossed her pocketbook along with the museum pamphlet and French phrase book on the side table. She removed her light jacket and hung it on the coat rack. A deep voice came from the living room.

"Où étiez-vous?" Jean-Claude rose from the easy chair near the piano. "Where were you?"

"I had a lovely walk in a park and then visited a museum—soaked in a bit of French culture." She stopped. "Why are you talking to me in French?"

"I thought it was time you learned. If you're not interested, then why did you buy that language book." He pointed to the lesson book she had just tossed on the table. "It doesn't look as if you even opened it."

"I wasn't in the mood." She got a bottle of water out of the small refrigerator. "We communicate fine. No need to rush."

What feather has gotten up his ass?

He hovered behind her. She turned around and nearly bumped into his chest. "And before you get on my case about me not learning your language, what about that perfectly good pair of pantyhose you ripped? That was rude."

"I heard of no complaints from you afterwards." He turned on his heels and returned to his seat. "Besides, I told you not to wear any pants. If I had told you of my plans, the experience wouldn't have been nearly as exciting for either of us. You're lucky I didn't shred your panties."

Cindy unscrewed the bottle and took a gulp of the cold liquid. "I don't want to argue. You and your culture are still new to me." She sat on his lap and slung her arms around his neck. "I'm still getting used to you. Lord knows our lovemaking is divine. Other than that, I don't really know you."

"What else is there to know?" His warm smile enticed her.

"Where do you go during the day?" Her eyes searched his face. "It's as if you come and go like a ghost, hiding in the shadows."

I wish I could tell if he's concealing something.

"I'm a singer. I sing. I have a manager, an agent, songs to review that I might want to record." He turned his head as if to avert her gaze. "I meet with people who do things for me, people I connect with."

"You sound more mysterious now than ever." Her fingers toyed with his hair. "Can I come with you to some of these meetings? I'd like to meet your friends."

"You wouldn't understand them." He scoffed, "They all speak French and are not about to speak English just for you—a silly American girl."

"Is that how you see me?" She removed her loving embrace from his neck. "A silly American girl? Someone not to be taken seriously?"

"I don't express myself correctly." She slid off his lap and stood before him with arms folded across her chest. "Because of you not understanding French—my friends would feel uncomfortable around you."

"JC, I put a lot on the line here to be with you." She sat on the sofa opposite him. "I told my mother to leave me alone and that wasn't the easiest thing to do."

"I never asked you to be with me. And when you invited yourself into my life," she went to speak—Jean-Claude raised his finger for her not to interrupt, "… to live with me, I accepted you and welcomed you into my home."

"And your bed!" She tapped her foot.

Why is he being like this? Did I make a mistake? Is he using me?

"Mais oui. But that was a mutual choice." His voice lowered in a loving tone. "Cindy, please be patient with me as you request the same from me. I have never had a liaison with a woman who was not French." He sat next to her. His finger traced her ear. "When are your parents leaving? My father said they have completed their recordings."

"In a couple of days. At least that's what Mom told me in a message." She closed her eyes and started to purr as his hand caressed her neck.

"Don't you think you should say goodbye to them?" His finger went from her ear to her throat in a light stroke. "You might not see them for a long, long time."

"No." Her mood shifted to serious. "It's better this way. I might call her tomorrow. Calls are better than face-to-face encounters."

"Remember, you only have one mama." He kissed her long and passionately. "Go freshen up for me. I'll meet you in the bedroom."

"Giving orders, JC?" She didn't like being told what to do. That very thing had so enraged Vic on more than one occasion. He couldn't handle it, and her obstinate nature had led to him attacking her.

"Not an order. Strongly suggesting." She felt his eyes on her as she left.

In the bathroom, Cindy noticed a sprinkling of fine white powder on the gray sink counter.

Hmm, what is that? Talcum powder? I didn't notice JC using anything like that. Could it be drugs? Nah. JC doesn't even smoke marijuana.

She brushed the thought from her mind while dialing her mother. Her mom answered on the first ring.

Taylor's rapid words pierced her ears. "I'm so glad you called. I've been worried sick. Are you okay. You can come back with us. We're flying out tomorrow."

"Slow down, Mom." *She's so anxious. I hope we don't argue.* "No. I won't be returning with you and Larry."

"Are you certain?" Taylor's disappointed sigh saddened her. "You don't speak the language, you have no friends here, or any form of support. What about money?"

"JC is happy for me to stay with him."

Now she'll give me a list of roadblocks!

"If things don't work out for you and him, then what?" Taylor's voice became frantic. "You can't get employment because you're not a French citizen. You have no friends in Paris."

"I do so have a friend ... well an acquaintance ... Stuart Dumont. He speaks perfect English, and owns a bookstore on Rivoli."

"An acquaintance is hardly a friend." Taylor reasoned, "It's not likely he would take you in if Jean-Claude tires of you."

"Mom, listen for a moment and let me speak." She took a deep breath. "You know I love you. I always will. But this, I have to do for myself. It'll make it easier for me to get away from Vic if I stay here for a while. If it turns out not good, then I'll call you and return home."

"You make it sound so simple." *It is simple, Mom. Let it go.* "What if Jean-Claude has dangerous connections? That's not uncommon in the music industry. Plus, there's the issue of possible terrorist attacks."

"You're really fetching on that one." *That club he took me to felt a bit dangerous, but I don't think it can be compared to Vic and what he did to me, not to mention his threats.* "He's given me no reason to suspect such things. With the French National Police patrolling nearly every corner, I feel quite safe."

"Can we meet tomorrow before Larry and I leave? I'd love to give you a hug and a kiss goodbye."

That would be too hard on us both.

"Mom, let's just say goodbye now." *It's so difficult to say these words.* "No tears. Just happy thoughts."

"Since you want it that way, then will you at least accept a parting gift?" Taylor's pleading tone nearly softened her. "I'll leave an envelope with the Regina's concierge. It will have your name on it. Ask for Jean-Luc at the front desk. He'll be wearing a name tag."

"Mom," she sighed, "what are you up to?"

"I'll leave you some euros. Save the money for an emergency." Taylor's voice nearly cracked, "I feel you might need it for your safety."

"Whatever you say, Mom." A tear fell to her cheek. "I really need to go. Give my love to Larry and Joe. Safe flight. Wish me the best with my French."

I can't blame her for being so worried after what happened to her in France. I know she only wants to help.

Cindy ended the call then splashed water on her face. Opening the door, she saw her lover on the bed, naked to the waist, waiting for her. She never tired of gazing on his muscular chest covered in a blanket of dark hair.

Jean-Claude took a tissue from his night table and wiped his reddened nose. "So sorry. Allergies again." He patted the mattress. "Viens! Come. You need to warm up your side of the bed."

"Just the bed?" She walked to him with a seductive gait and removed her clothing item by item. "I think more than the bed needs warming."

Twenty

CINDY STOOD BY a private guest phone in Hôtel Regina's lobby as she opened the envelope her mother had left for her. *Ten thousand euros! What was she thinking? Why so much? Is Paris really that expensive? I never paid much attention to the prices.* She slid the note out from the money and read her Mom's parting message.

Cindy,

Please be safe and take care. Call us for anything ... to talk, with a question, or when you want to come home. Remember to check in with the US Embassy officials on 2 Avenue Gabriel at the northwest corner of Place de la Concorde. They are your friends and can help with most any situation.

I love you and always will.

Hugs and kisses,

Mom xxoo

Cindy folded the message and put it in her wallet.

There was something else in the envelope. A business card. The printed name read "Frédéric Millet" and gave his phone number and address.

Why did Mom think I needed his info?

She placed Frédéric's card behind her driver's license. The secret lining of her purse secured the envelope of euros. Crossing the hotel's lobby, she eyed the concierge's nametag and smiled back at Jean-Luc. The doorman tipped his cap as he assisted her with the revolving door.

A warm breeze kicked up from the direction of the Seine. Her bangs fluttered against her forehead and she pushed them away from her eyes. Waiting to cross the street, she stood on the corner of *rue des Pyramides* and *rue de Rivoli*, facing Café Carrousel. Children's voices and squeals from Jardin des Tuileries could be heard over the city's traffic sounds of honking horns and chattering tourists of various nationalities.

Charming. I see why Mom wanted to return here year after year.

She crossed quickly with the light, then her steps took on a more leisurely pace as she scanned the shop windows. She came to *rue Saint Roch*, paused a moment, then continued down Rivoli.

At Dumont's bookstore, she opened the door. Welcoming chimes rang and Hugo ran to greet her. She patted the cat's head. Stuart looked up from a display of English language crime novels near the counter at the back of the store.

"Just can't stay away, eh?" His smile gave her a warm friendly feeling as he approached. It almost felt as if she had known him forever.

"Your store is a magnet for me." She pointed to the latest American release. "I don't need a dictionary to understand what I'm reading for these books." A halting pause ensued. "Truthfully, I wanted to thank you again for the excursion to the museum and park."

"I enjoyed it too. I've been there many times before, but never enjoyed it as much as through your eyes." He stepped closer. "We can go to another museum sometime, or even today, if … if you're free."

"Free?" Her light laugh filled the air. "I'm without a job—I'm constantly free. One can only shop the windows so much to fill time. I don't dare spend too much. I hate the idea of begging Mom for money."

If it wasn't for JC, I could really be attracted to him. He's so incredibly nice—always thinking of others. He's good-looking too—in a different way than JC. He's basically everything Vic isn't.

"Then we have a … a date?" he stammered and looked at the clock on the wall. "I'm the owner, and I don't expect any deliveries—we can leave now."

"Now?" She looked mildly surprised. "What do you have in mind for only a few hours?"

Stuart winked. "I'll keep that as a surprise." He took his jacket from a hook on the wall, and paused a moment while he spoke to an employee in low tones, clearly giving instructions.

Coming back to Cindy, Stuart grabbed her hand. "Come, fair maiden Cindy. Let's be on our new adventure." He opened the door.

~~***~~

While Stuart obtained tickets at Musée Rodin of Hôtel de Biron on *77 rue de Varenne* in the seventh arrondissement, he noticed Cindy admiring the replica statue of "The Thinker". He hoped that this museum might, in some obscure way, further his cause and bring her heart to his.

Jean-Claude is so wrong for her. He's slick, overly confident, and blatantly conceited. He uses women and then discards them soon after. She needs a man who can step out of himself and appreciate all she has to offer.

"I have the tickets. Let's go in, unless you want to study Le Pense some more."

"Le Pense?" She made a face.

"That's the original French name for 'The Thinker'." He handed her a pamphlet that accompanied the entry fee. "I know a bit about this place. Want me to share? I don't want to bore you with a lot of facts. We could just enjoy the art without the details."

"No. Detail away. It will enrich the experience for me." She started to the front steps. "Whatever you don't mention, I'm certain I'll find in this flyer."

He placed his hand lightly at her waist. *Hmm, she didn't pull away. Maybe she didn't feel my touch.* His heartbeats quickened.

"Well, he sculpted 'The Thinker' in 1906 and said it represented himself." *She seems genuinely interested to learn more.* "Since you like hearing me talk, here goes …." He breathed deeply. "Auguste Rodin was the preeminent French sculptor of his time and very beloved in this country—considered as one of the fathers of modern sculpture. His work is highly realistic and mostly based on mythology, not to mention highly sensuous."

Past the threshold, they walked toward the enormous hand exhibit, titled "The Cathedral". As he talked, Cindy slowly circled the pair of white hands carved in marble. She then glanced at the intricate marble design on the floor.

"Rodin also sketched and painted, and that probably played an important role in his growth as a sculptor. You might have seen his famous work, titled 'The Kiss'. It's been exhibited the world over."

Cindy nodded. "Yes, I remember that well."

They continued roaming the rooms. "He lived here as his private residence since 1895. I think he owned this place and upon his death, it was left to the Paris government."

Cindy stopped at another striking sculpture of two lovers embracing in torrential passion. Stuart studied her reaction.

Does her desire run as ardently as that couple in stone?

He cleared his throat. "That piece is 'The Eternal Idol'. It is admired by many and thought to be one of his finest works. It seems to have captivated you."

"It certainly stirs the imagination." She blushed. "Prompts thoughts that one shouldn't have—at least with a friend." She looked up at him.

That word again—friend! What can I do to make her see me as more? I wish she would allow herself to see Jean-Claude for what he really is—an egotistical idiot!

Stuart followed Cindy as she meandered from room to room, taking in the various sensuality each new sculpture offered.

She certainly seems to be enjoying the art. How I'd love to be the one who captured that gleam in her eye. I'm tired of always missing the boat. I'm not going to let it happen this time.

"Since you appreciate Rodin's talent, you must see this one." He took her hand and led the way to another room. She paused before the marble art. "What do you feel about this one? It's another celebrated piece. 'Eternal Springtime' was received with wild acclaim."

"It's magnificent." Cindy turned to face him. "All this art is so beautiful. He was a man of great depth and feeling. It's clear he admired women and lovers. I can almost feel their heat."

"That's the point." Stuart placed his hand on the back of her waist and drew her closer. Her delicate perfume wafted into his nostrils. "Passion is the moment, the present—it's what is real."

His lips grazed her hairline at her forehead. *She's not pulling away.* He hoped she couldn't hear how his breathing had quickened. He couldn't help it. She was intoxicating. "The past is a memory. The future is a vague mist. But the present—that's now, that's tangible."

"You have such a beautiful way with words." She touched his cheek. "You're sensitive and feeling. There is no reason why you wouldn't be a famous author."

"I only speak from my heart." He fought with himself not to kiss her as his lips brushed the tip of her ear. "I have so many feelings that I want to express, I almost scare myself. Men are supposed to be strong and not feel. I could never quite fit into that mold."

"I'm glad you didn't." Cindy smiled briefly. "If you weren't as you are, I might have never been drawn to you."

"Drawn?" He tilted his head boyishly. "That's encouraging."

"I'll be truthful." She sighed. "Yes. I feel something. I can't explain it, not even to myself. I don't want to be torn. JC is in my life, and now I have this strong attraction to you. We started as friends, and in a span of a few days—it seems to becoming more."

"I can understand how that would be a little complicated. I won't rush you." *I think I have a chance. Or could she merely be working through her confusion. She still has a husband on the scene. Damn! This can get messy and I could lose out.* "Let's sit in the museum's garden and enjoy the fragrant roses. They're in full bloom."

Stuart led Cindy to the back exit of the museum that opened out onto a luxurious small parklike area with multiple benches. Rodin's replica statues highlighted the walkway. They sat on a bench in a cozy area secluded by ornate plantings and manicured low hedges.

He took her hand in his and stroked the top lightly while looking deep into her eyes. "Do you want to share your feelings? Sometimes what is seen as insurmountable mountains turn into small ruts when once said."

"Stuart, you're so like me in some ways. I was never one to drag things out. But here goes." Cindy took a couple of deep breaths. "I left my husband, I tell people it was because of his gambling, and that was a major part of it. He destroyed all sense of trust by lying and throwing us into debt. That's over.

"Then I met JC. His tall, dark and handsome ways captivated me, plus his French accent didn't hurt. I know I was vulnerable. I knew that at the time, but I thought I was in control of my emotions. The truth is, when you've been married to someone and you take the initiative to leave him, it's a big step. It's like you're crossing a line and it caused a lot of conflicting feelings." She took a labored breath. "Even though he gambled away all our money and did other things that I don't like to talk about, I had made that vow. At the time, I was deadly serious about it. I tried to make my marriage work." Her fists clenched as tears filled her eyes. "But, there are some things that you can never recover from, and that's what helped me to make the decision.

"So when JC showed an interest in me, I thought I loved him—now I'm not so sure." Cindy looked in his eyes. "You're so easy to talk to, and he's not like that."

Stuart's eyes remained fixed on hers.

She sighed. "He's never once said he loves me. I'm old-fashioned in a way. Deep down I need to feel that I'm loved, and instead, I'm starting to feel used—the new flavor of the month."

He looked in her eyes. "It's difficult to be with someone who doesn't share the same values, and you're so perfect. You should be treated with respect."

"It makes me wonder if all French men are like him—a misogynist without a true care for women's feelings." Her finger drew an imaginary design on her knee.

Stuart slid his arm around her shoulder.

Cindy looked out to the garden as she spoke. "My mom's been trying to talk sense into me, and I guess maybe she was right. Maybe he is all wrong for me. Yet, I don't know that for certain, and I don't feel I'm at the place where I want to leave him."

"What would make you feel the time is right … to leave him?"

I wish she could see his true colors. With his reputation, he must be some kind of bastard!

She opened her mouth to speak. Stuart leaned into her and gently kissed her lips. It was a kiss of love and a yearning to embrace her heart. If only he could still his racing pulse.

"Will that help you come to a decision?" *Did I move too fast? She didn't pull away.* "I probably shouldn't have done that. I don't want you to feel as if I'm like all the other French men you've come to loathe." He didn't release her.

"I-I enjoyed your kiss." Cindy's fingers traced the line of his jaw.

Did she sound a little breathless?

"Funny," her eyes gazed into his, from one to the other and back again, "I don't feel any guilt. I don't care about Vic, but I'm kind of in a relationship, and that kiss would normally have had me reeling with bad feelings."

"Maybe it's a sign that your relationship is already over. Or it never really started."

This is going too smoothly. Something bad is bound to happen. I'm never this lucky.

"Or it's me voicing my confusion—my thought of the moment until I feel JC's arms around me and I succumb to his charms. He's very handsome and very charming." She cast her eyes downward. "Stuart, I think too much of you as a friend to jeopardize that." A devilish smile curled her lips. "But, I did enjoy our kiss very much. Your lips are talented."

"Now you're encouraging me." He chuckled. "Don't do to me as I'm convinced JC is doing to you."

Why in hell did I say that! That only pushes her into his arms.

"No, Stu—if I may call you that?" She looked sincere.

"I like that nickname." He rubbed her cheek in tender strokes. "Every time I hear that name, I'll think of you."

"I've talked about me all afternoon. What about you? I don't think you have a girlfriend. Right?"

Stuart nodded. "You're right. I don't have anyone special in my life at the moment—except for you."

Cindy smiled. "You haven't shared much about yourself with me except that you were adopted. I can't imagine what that would be like. Have you ever made contact with your birth mother?"

Stuart shook his head. "The adoption records were sealed. I've searched for her on the Internet, but I only know her first name, and where I was born. I think everyone wants to know where they come from, and when you're adopted, you can't help wondering why your mother couldn't keep you."

"I hope you find her one day." Cindy looked at her watch. "We better be going. You have the store to close and I need to get back to the apartment."

"Back to Jean-Claude?"

How can I compete against a rival like that—looks, money, fame—he has it all—including Cindy.

"Yes." She bit her bottom lip. "Stu, let's just take whatever we've started slow—whether it's friendship or grows to something more. Good things are worth waiting for. I might stop in to see Frédéric— his shop is a few blocks up from yours."

"Frédéric?" *Is this another guy interested in her?*

"Frédéric Millet is an old friend of my parents. He owns a little shop that sells miniature Parisian stores and buildings for tourists. He does quite well. Every vacationer wants to take back a little bit of Paris with them. He's very nice and Mom has known him for a very long time. He even flew over to attend my wedding, though I don't really remember him."

How old is he? Hmm, she said very long time—he could be rather too old for Cindy.

"I'll have to check out his shop." Stuart's throat tightened. "We got off the subject of possibilities." He squeezed her hand. "Can we build on our friendship?"

"Friendship always makes for a good beginning." She kissed his cheek. "Let's just wait. My feelings are such a scramble of clouded thoughts. I made one rash decision to stay in Paris, I don't want to make another without careful thought."

She's worth waiting for. But once again when she warms his bed, will I forever be frozen in her category as a friend. Unless…

Twenty - One

STUART'S LONG-BURIED curiosity about his birth mother had been re-ignited by Cindy's questions. He sat in his store researching her name on the computer. Again. His fingers frantically typed and clicked any link that might lead to additional information. As he had told Cindy, all he had was her first name, the name of the adoption agency in Geneva, Switzerland, and the hospital of his birth.

It would be nice to know the circumstance of my adoption. What illness was so serious that she couldn't care for me? What if it's hereditary? That could affect my health and I not even know it. I wish my parents could be of more help. They don't know any more than I do.

He went from website to website always coming to a dead end. He thought to search hospitals in Geneva, but the display showed multiple pages of listings.

This search could take the better part of a month, or even a year to sift though all this data.

An English customer stood in front of him casting a shadow across his desk. "Sir, I was hoping you could help me."

Stuart looked up. "Yes. What type of book are you seeking? Or is it a phrase book or language dictionary?"

The elderly man shifted his weight and adjusted the black rimmed glasses on his nose. "I'm looking for an old classic by Dickens. 'A Tale of Two Cities'." He chuckled. "I thought I had packed it and when I arrived at the hotel, I discovered I must have left it on my library shelf."

"I have a copy in the back of the store." Stuart started to rise. "Let me show you properly." He led the customer to the English classics section of used books. "I'm surprised you don't want to read something more current. Didn't you read that book when in school?"

"Yes. Many times." The man reached for the title. "But a good book is like a good friend—always worthy of a revisit." He adjusted his glasses again. "I think I recognize your accent. Is that London or Oxford? In what part of England did you grow up?"

"I'm a French oddity. I had an English nanny. I don't know where she was schooled. She taught me English from when I was a wee tot. I'm a French citizen with an English accent."

"Blimey! That is curious. Do you speak French, too?" He stroked his chin.

"I went to French-speaking schools." His brows raised. "I guess I'm fortunate that I don't sound foreign in either language when I speak."

Stuart left the man to browse the shelves and returned to the computer at his desk. He went back to his search. His eyes strained and he scrunched up his nose as he tried to access a list of past patients. Stuart typed in his birth date in hopes that would aid his quest. Still, nothing. The section leading to patient records flashed "Interdit" in bold letters. *Forbidden!*

Damn confidentiality protocol! It always comes back to that.

He signed off from the search engine and returned the screen to his own website.

I need a walk and a coffee. Maybe something will come to me later.

~~***~~

Frédéric dusted off the miniature figurines on the glass shelves. Customers milled about looking at the various scenes on display. Some were of Montmartre, others of the Latin Quarter, and still more of the famous broad boulevards similar to the *boulevard Champs Élysées*. He held his breath whenever a patron would pick up a fragile tiny building to check on the bottom for the price written on a sticker.

A middle-aged woman gathered pieces and placed them on the glass-topped counter. She moved to another display, collected some items, and repeated the process.

Mon Dieu! Is she going to buy all of those? There must be twenty pieces there, if not more.

He noticed the impressive jewelry she wore of diamonds, emeralds, and gold. Her gold Rolex watch ticked away the time.

Is she famous? I don't recognize her face. She seems American by her gestures. I hope she doesn't fling her arms about and break something.

He went behind the counter and then motioned to his young employee, Émilie, to stand nearby.

"Madame, I see that you like the little houses that I sell." He smiled broadly. "Are you planning a special arrangement in your home for these? A way of taking a taste of Paris home with you?"

"That's exactly what I'm planning." She didn't look at him as she spoke, but kept surveying his unique merchandise. "I would like to have a display table, specially made, all glass enclosed— maybe a coffee table or a multilevel wall hanging."

"I have little people, cars, buses, trees, and pavement you can add." *I hope I didn't push too hard. Americans don't like forward sales people.* "Madame, that was just a suggestion. I didn't mean that you should—"

"No problem. Yes, I would like all that you mentioned. I don't know when I'll be back and I might as well get the complete set." She opened her pocketbook.

Frédéric spoke in French to the young girl, "Get the best specimens of all we have, at least ten trees, and such, and don't forget the pavement needed for a large display."

While Émilie went about her work, he proceeded to add up the customer's purchases. He swallowed hard and hoped that she wouldn't change her mind when seeing the total cost.

"Madame, the total amount due is one thousand two hundred seventy-six euros even. That includes the VTA."

"VTA?" She looked mildly confused.

"Pardon, Madame. That is VAT. In France we call it VTA." He took her black Amex credit card and swiped it.

The stylish customer signed the slip, grabbed her purchases and opened the door to leave. A young man held the door open for her before entering. Frédéric looked up in anticipation of another sale.

"Bonjour, Monsieur. How might I help you?" He extended his hand.

The man gave a firm shake. "I'm Stuart Dumont," he said in French. "I own the English bookstore down this street not far from *place de la Concorde*. I think we have a mutual friend. Cindy Hastings? Taylor Davis' daughter?"

"Mais oui! I know her, though I know her mother a bit better."
What does this guy want? Is Cindy in harm?

"I probably shouldn't be speaking with you, but she, Cindy I mean, is my friend, too. I believe you know she's been seeing Jean-Claude LeGrand, and I … feel uneasy about that association." He ran his hand through his hair. "There is something not quite right about him—too smooth and perfect. Cindy is still somewhat of an innocent. She doesn't know the city, nor the language."

"Say no more." Frédéric let out a sigh of agreement. "You're speaking my exact thoughts. I have a friend who is a private investigator, and have given a thought about having Jean-Claude researched. Cindy's mother is worried about her daughter's involvement with him." *I don't know this Stuart. I better not tell him too much. Certainly not admit my friend has already checked out this singer.* "Do you feel she is in danger?"

"No, not at the moment." Stuart shifted from one foot to another. "Can we go to a café for a talk?" He glanced around at the other customers. "I really don't want to discuss this here."

Can I trust this guy? He seems okay, still … I should hear what he has to say. "Café Carrousel okay with you?"

"Fine. I know the place. Great view of Jeanne d'Arc." Stuart headed for the door.

Frédéric turned to Émilie. "I shouldn't be long. Don't close up until I return."

~~***~~

"What has Cindy told you about Jean-Claude?" Frédéric sipped his red wine.

"Nothing to set off alarms." Stuart took a taste of his espresso. "Just a feeling I get. You could say I don't like the competition, but I also sense a certain vulnerability in her and it worries me."

I hope Frédéric doesn't want her, too.

"Competition?" He looked surprised. "Are you hoping, or has she said something to you more concrete?"

"Don't I wish!" He shook his head in disappointment. "I have a slim chance against that famous singer. Any guy would pale next to him."

"That's true." Frédéric looked out at the golden statue. "How do you expect me to help, other than having my friend Claude do a small investigation?"

"I'd like you to keep an eye out for her." He hesitated a moment and scratched his chin. "There's something else. If I may?"

Frédéric nodded. "Go on."

"I was adopted. I'm actually British by origin, although you wouldn't be able to tell from the way I speak French."

Frédéric's eyes widened, and he waved Stuart on.

"I-I would like to find out what happened to my mother, and her identity of course. I have done searches on the Net and came up dry. What I did find out I've written on this paper." He reached into his pocket and passed the folded note across the table to Frédéric. "Cindy mentioned briefly that you were a friend of the family and helped her mother out when she needed some digging into a person's past."

"How much did she tell you?" Frédéric's brow furrowed as he took the paper, opened it up and scanned the information.

"No details. Only that you have an investigator friend who could find things out." Stuart motioned to the waiter for a refill. "Are you still in contact with him?"

"Yes. I don't see him often." The waiter placed another glass of wine and cup of espresso on the table. "He likes to blend into the shadows. It's better for his business that way."

"Do you think he'll take this one on?" He leaned in to Frédéric. "I can pay."

"I don't even know if he's free. If you're not in a hurry, he might be able to help." He took a cigarette from his pocket and lit it. "He's in high demand, but I'll talk to him."

"Thank you so much, mon ami." Stuart beamed. "I pray that he will take the case, and hope that what he discovers doesn't indicate I could come down with a serious illness."

"What?" He drew on his cigarette as smoke rose above his head. "Was your mother seriously ill?"

"My adopted mother said she was too ill to care for me." He reached for his wine. "If she was that sick—that could be an illness that I'm carrying. Health history of one's parents is very important—diabetes, cancer, heart disease, a slew of conditions could affect me." Stuart took a swallow and savored the taste. "By the way, you look very young to be the owner of a shop and a friend of Cindy's mother for a number of years."

"I'm older than I look. Good genes." Frédéric chuckled. "My mother always appeared ten to fifteen years younger than her age."

Thank goodness. He probably isn't interested in Cindy then. My gut tells me JC has a past—a very dark past. I must protect her from that. But how?

Twenty - Two

"I THOUGHT YOU said she was ready." The harsh male voice sounded over Jean-Claude's phone. "You didn't give me anything to film the other night."

"I had no way of knowing she was so hot." He wiped his nose with a tissue then took his e-cigarette from the coffee table in his apartment. "Maurice, I tried to hold her back. She came too soon."

"Well, the couple of shots on my cell phone won't bring home any big money from Davis." His voice held the firmness of granite. "I can only buy you so much time with the hope of big bucks."

"Can't you put him off a few weeks?" He vaped on his cigarette. "I need more time. This could be a big payoff. If all goes well, I could be set for the next five years. Davis is worth millions."

"Why don't you ask for the money before the film is made?" Maurice Junot reasoned, "The threat of something can be just as lucrative."

"I'm not certain that's wise." He went to the window, and looked over the rooftops to Jardin des Tuileries. "Davis is too smart to bite on a bluff."

"Seems like good poker to me. Your name nor that of your father's would never come into play." Maurice's cockiness rang in his ears.

"When I think back on it, you should have been waiting in the stall for us instead of coming in at the end." Jean-Claude turned and went to the kitchen for a small bottle of water. "If you had done your job, I wouldn't have to set up another clandestine shoot."

He sounded frustrated. "The room was so dark, I didn't see you leave."

"It wasn't that dark in the club's back room. I could see clearly enough to get to the men's room." He took a large swallow of water. "You didn't get my face in the photos, did you?"

"Of course not! That would defeat the plan. I didn't get much of her face either—not enough to bring in any money." He chuckled. "If I had gotten your face—it would be great for the tabloids but would ruin your career."

"Don't send me the photos. I don't want any trace to you." Jean-Claude went back to the sofa.

"How much longer do you think you can put off the bill collector?" He heard city traffic over the phone as Maurice talked. "You better watch out. They play rough. Remember what happened a few years back to that girl? This time you could be sharing an address with Jim Morrison at Cimetière du Père Lachaise."

"Yeah." His eyes narrowed. "I'll watch my ass. If Cindy has to pay the price—what of it. I'm growing tired of her American ways. She has lost the fascination. Once the film is made and the money is mine, she can take a hike, drop off the earth, or go to hell for all I care."

"Be careful," Maurice cautioned. "Davis has to be handled with kid gloves, and you don't want your father on your back."

"Don't worry." Forming a tight fist, he crushed the empty water bottle. "I can take care of Papa."

~~***~~

Cindy watched Jean-Claude's haphazard movements as he tossed a few items in a carry-on bag.

"So, how long will you be gone?" She pulled off an orange segment from the fruit in her hand, a remnant of her breakfast. "Why can't I come along?"

"I told you before—it's business." He looked exasperated. "I don't bring women to my recording sessions."

Is he hiding something? Another woman?

"My mom goes to Larry's recording sessions." She popped the orange piece into her mouth and chewed. Juice dribbled from the corner of her mouth. Her tongue peeked out to capture the drops.

"I'm not Larry Davis and you're not Taylor." He placed the few remaining items in the suitcase. "I'll only be gone less than a week." He kissed the tip of her nose, then called out as he headed to the front entry, "Go to a museum or do some shopping. I left a few hundred euros on the side table next to the door. Don't forget to lock up every night."

Cindy heard the front door open and then close. She plodded to the living room and picked up the carelessly tossed money.

Hmm, seven hundred euros. JC is certainly generous. If I'm careful and count pennies, I could live on that for two weeks. What is the true purpose of his trip away? She flopped down on the sofa. *Nope. I'm not going to that dark place—suspicion and jealousy.*

She went to the bedroom and changed from her nightshirt to a pair of trim-fitting jeans, loose shirt, and slipped on a pair of comfortable loafers. She had made up her mind. She was on a mission.

Cindy walked the short distance to *rue de Rivoli*. The birds chirped and the sun cast delightful shadows of Paris waking up to a new day. The traffic was already heavy with delivery trucks speeding on their way to various destinations to amuse or feed Parisians and tourists. As she passed the shops, owners opened pull-down shutters and rolled out awnings. Some called out, "Bonjour, mademoiselle". She smiled and kept walking.

I hope Stu has opened his store. If I'm too early, I'll get a coffee or a cola somewhere.

Cindy peered through the window. Lights shone from the back of the bookstore. She saw the movement of someone but couldn't make out the identity. *Is that Stu? What time does the store open?* The sign in the window read "Ouvrir 8 heurs à 18 heurs. Fermer les dimanches et les fériés".

I think that means the store is open from eight in the morning until six at night. Hmm ... I guess it's closed on Sundays and holidays.

She looked at her watch. It was seven fifty-five. She tried the doorknob. It was locked.

Should I wait?

She tapped lightly on the window of the door. Muffled footsteps grew louder. A young girl unlatched the locks and pushed a button to what seemed to be a burglar alarm system. The shop employee opened the door and smiled.

"Madame, le magasin n'ouvert pas à ce moment." The girl must have seen Cindy's confusion. "Pardonnez-moi. The store isn't open yet. We'll open in a few minutes." She started to close the door. Cindy's foot prevented that occurrence.

"Is Monsieur Dumont here yet?" Cindy fingered the strap on her pocketbook.

"Oui. He's here. Please wait. I will tell him that you are here." The girl let Cindy wait on the sidewalk and closed the entry.

Moments later, Stuart approached and opened the door.

"What brings you to my doorstep so early in the morning?" He beamed and led her to his desk at the back of the store.

"It's not that early." She hugged her purse in front of her chest.

"I thought two friends could share breakfast together—that is if you can spare the time?" She noticed his half-eaten croissant and cup of coffee by the computer.

"Certainly." Stuart took a stack of invoices from his desk, piled them up and pushed them to one side. "I don't have any pressing business and I have a full staff to man the decks."

"Are you sure?" She bit her lip and looked at the partially consumed food. "It looks like I've interrupted your morning meal."

He glanced at the pastry. "That's not an issue. I haven't had a leisurely breakfast in months. I mostly eat on the run." He took his draped jacket from the back of the chair and ushered her toward the door.

Hugo followed. Stuart raised his finger in a no-no sign. The cat backed up and watched his "daddy" close the door.

On the sidewalk, she looked in the direction of the famous royal gardens. "You're so good—the way you talk about French history. I'd love to know more."

"You're serious?" He paused on the sidewalk. "We can have a bite in the Tuileries gardens and I can tell you a few tidbits."

"I was hoping you'd say that." Cindy took his hand as they crossed the street.

Located near the center of the park was an outdoor food pavilion that sold snacks, sandwiches, and drinks. After making his purchase, Stuart put the change in his pocket and returned to Cindy sitting at a small circular table under an awning of tree limbs. He handed her a coffee and a pain au chocolat pastry. He took the orange juice with his croissant.

"So," she took a bite of the decadent treat, "where's my history lesson."

"Hmm, I'll tell you about this place." He reached for her hand. "Stop me if—"

Cindy finished his sentence, "If I bore you." She smiled broadly. "You never bore me."

"I don't know that much—other than the main facts." He looked out into the distance. "In 1539 these gardens were started as part of the Catherine de Médici's palace grounds and were opened to the public in 1667. Part of the Louvre was made of wood and bordered this park on each side. It was burned in 1871 by the Paris community as an act of revolt against the government." He took a swallow of his juice. "Many tourists dislike the gravel paths—complaining of dusty shoes and feet. I don't know much more than that about this park."

"I used to run for the hills when history or anything dealing with the French would come into a conversation." She blew on her coffee before taking a sip. "But, you make history come alive. You're fascinating. You should be a teacher."

"It's nothing special." He bit into his croissant, chewed, and swallowed. "I'm a parrot, spitting out all the dull facts I learned in school."

He stared into her eyes as if trying to read her mind, and rubbed her hand. "Is something bothering you? Jean-Claude? You look sad."

"You could say that." She sighed and watched a cluster of sparrows pecking on the ground, eager to eat the food droppings left by others. "JC's gone for a few days—nearly a week for some recording session. Said he didn't want me around—that it was no place for me."

"I'd never leave you alone in Paris or any place else." His thumb rubbed the ridge on the top of her hand. "You have any plans?"

"No. I guess I'll roam the streets, eat at the cafés—try to fill my time." She knew he could tell by her look she was hoping he would react favorably.

He made a face, took out his phone, swiped his finger on the face, and checked his calendar. "I can take a few days off—if you want to spend some time with me."

"I don't want to intrude on your work."

Will JC be jealous? He didn't like it when I told him Stu had accompanied me to the museums. If I spend this time with Stu and JC gets wind of this, all hell will probably break loose.

"Not a problem." He paused as if thinking. "Have you ever been to Annecy—near the French and Switzerland border?"

"No. Paris is the only place in Europe I've visited." *Sounds exciting, but would I be back in Paris before JC returns?* "Is it a long trip? I want to be back in Paris in less than a week."

"I'll have you back in less than four days." He finished his juice in one gulp, then took the croissant. "Eat up. I'll walk you to your place where you can pack. I'll go back to the store and make reservations." He looked at his watch. "I'll meet you at the bookstore in ninety minutes."

"I don't know what to say."

Stu certainly moves fast. Am I doing the right thing? I want to go with him.

"'Yes' in any language will do." His smile encouraged her.

"Yes! I'll go." She squeezed his hand. "Let's take Annecy by storm. I'll walk to JC's apartment alone. No sense in creating gossip for the neighbors."

"The TGV train will have us there in a matter of hours." He stood and gave her a large warm hug. "This will be a fun adventure—for both of us. If we're in luck, we'll be there today and won't have to take a night train."

"Night train?" She made a face. "Maybe you should make reservations for tomorrow."

"I don't want to wait. I read where the TGV expanded their schedule to accommodate the tourists. We're bound to find something." He stood and took her hand. "Let's hurry. We have memories to create."

Twenty - Three

THE PARIS SKYLINE flew by at lightning speed. Cindy looked out as the landscape rapidly transformed into suburbs and then rural views with grazing cows and fields of beautiful wild flowers.

This new adventure and diversion was an emotional tonic to smother the negative, deep-rooted ominous instincts that gnawed at her gut.

Is something wrong with me or is it JC? I get the feeling that I've displeased him in some way. But how? He has that dangerous dark side that is intoxicating—it's the part of him I can't resist, but will that side cause me harm? Is it my insecurities causing these doubts? Memories of Vic?

She smiled at Stuart dozing beside her.

Stu is stable, kind, and loving. I feel I can depend on him. Yet, I can't get involved with him while I'm still with JC. I'm not that kind of person—I won't become my mother. Never!

She turned back to the view out the window. Far off mountains came into view as they approached the Alps.

Stu wants a relationship with me. He's made that clear. But JC has captured my heart. Every time I'm in his arms my heart and body melts. Is Stu some kind of test? To see how much I care about JC?

JC has never said he loves me, but our relationship is still new. Now that I think about it, he's never spoken about how he feels about me at all. Why can't he talk about it? Doesn't he have any feelings for me? I think I'm falling in love with him. Maybe I already love him. If I didn't, how could I share his bed? I'm so messed up. I don't know any of the answers.

Paris is known as the city of love, and I can see why. If I were home in the US, I would probably be single right now, and stay single.

The train slowed, and then came to a stop to pick up additional passengers. Cindy watched what appeared to be a French family with two small children clumsily walk down the aisle trudging with luggage and a stroller, as they searched for vacant seats. Another woman holding her Yorkie, followed and found a window seat next to an older sleeping man. Once settled, she gave kisses on the small pup's head and spoke lovingly in French to her fur baby. Cindy smiled.

She acts with her Yorkie like Mom does with her poodles.

The train started and rapidly picked up speed. Cindy looked at her watch, and checked the timetable. She nudged Stuart from his dozing.

"Stu, wake up." He slowly opened his eyes and rubbed them with the heels of his hands. "We're going to arrive soon."

"What?" He squinted as if trying to focus on the landscape. "What town did we pass?"

"I'm not sure." She looked at the timetable again. "I think it was Eloise."

He straightened up in his seat. "I'll get the luggage."

Stuart flashed a broad smile, then retrieved the carry-on cases from the overhead storage area. She watched him.

Stu has such an attractive body. Damn! If I wasn't committed to JC, I wouldn't mind being in his life …. At least he's a friend. Friends are a blessing, too.

~~***~~

"It's seven in the morning. You must've had an early creative spark to be dressed and at the keyboard this early," Taylor spoke to Larry sitting at his piano in the media area of their Bel-Air home.

"I did." Larry looked up at her. "I have this melody tumbling around in my head. It won't go away until I get it down on paper."

"I haven't heard from Cindy. Not a text, phone call, nothing." Taylor held the previous day's mail. "I want to contact her, but I'm afraid it'll be counterproductive."

"She'll come around." He struck a chord on the keys. "She always has. When she needs something is when we'll hear from her."

"I wish she would just let me know she's okay." She rifled through the envelopes. One item stuck out. "Cindy's received a notice of some kind from the Hillsboro Courthouse in Tampa. Do you think I should open it? It could be important. I should've gone through the mail yesterday."

"Maybe it's an old parking fine that she's forgotten about." Larry jotted notes on the musical score sheet held up by the music stand. "You better text her."

Taylor checked her watch. "I will. It's not too late there." She promptly sent her daughter a brief message, RECEIVED MAIL FOR YOU FROM HILLSBORO COURT HOUSE. SHOULD I OPEN IT?

Moments later, her cell phone chimed that a message was waiting.

I hope it's Cindy. Wish she would call instead of texting.

Cindy's reply came on the screen, MOM, GO AHEAD. OPEN

ENVELOPE. CALL IF IMPORTANT.

"She told me to open the letter and call her if it's important."

"Good news and bad," Larry mentioned with nonchalance. "Good for you if the news is bad—you get to speak with her, and bad for Cindy in that she has something serious to deal with."

"Shush." She silenced him with a hand motion. "Let me read this." Her eyes grew large. "I'm not believing this!"

"Believing what?" Larry stopped playing his newest creation.

"Vic has gotten a no-fault divorce from Cindy. Cut and dry. It became official last week, he even requested she give up his last name … ah, she has to formally request that herself."

"I thought for certain he'd want to hang on and finagle his way to the Davis money pit." Larry made a face. "He must've found another pot of gold to tap." He rubbed his hand on his knee. "Glad he won't be sniffing around her in the future."

"Exactly!" Taylor dialed her daughter's number. It rang once, twice, three times.

"Hi Mom," Cindy greeted. "Tell me what the Tampa courts want."

"You're free! Vic obtained a no-fault divorce, official two weeks ago. He requested that you revert back to your maiden name, but what I can tell from this document—you have to do that yourself. It's noted here on the paper that Vic will be packing up your things and shipping them out to Bel-Air." Taylor heard Cindy's deep breaths. "You okay? This is what you wanted, right?"

"Of course, Mom. I'm okay and deeply relieved …. Now I can get on with my life."

She heard voices in the background. "Are you alone? I hear voices."

"I'm in a public area." Cindy hesitated. "Mom, I really have to go. It's after four in the afternoon here and I'm on a trip."

"A trip? Where? With Jean-Claude?" She looked at Larry with wide eyes and mouthed "a trip!"

"That is exactly why I don't call you—too many questions …. I'll be fine—here in Annecy with Stuart Dumont—the bookstore owner. He's only a friend. Don't worry. Bye."

The line went dead. "Well if that doesn't beat all." Taylor sat beside Larry on the piano bench. "My baby daughter has taken up with someone else, though she said he was a friend—Stuart Dumont." She stared into space. "Why has Jean-Claude lost his allure? At least LeGrand's son was a known evil—this new man might be worse."

"Don't go borrowing trouble." He gave her a warm hug. "He could be perfectly normal, maybe even dull, and truly a friend."

"If Cindy is interested in him, I doubt he's dull—a friend? That's possible. But how long will he remain as a friend? That's the question."

"Put your protective mama bear claws away." Larry chuckled. "If she's anything like her mother, he'll be in the friend status for as long as she wants, and not a minute longer."

She turned to him. "This isn't funny." Her jaw set. "This is Cindy we're talking about. Dealing with a separation is one thing, a divorce is worse and more difficult to cope with. She's even more vulnerable than before."

"Well, I won't tell you not to worry." He placed his fingers on the keyboard. "Worry is in your blood. You'll even worry about what will happen in the future that might cause you worry."

"Oh stop it!" Taylor pouted. "You can't understand. You're not a mother. The worry gene develops during pregnancy."

Twenty - Four

CINDY AND STUART wandered the streets of Annecy. The old picturesque buildings and canals that opened onto Lac d'Annecy made a spectacular view. Distant snow-tipped Alpine peaks created a romantic storybook backdrop to the landscape. Armed with a local map from the tourist office at the station, and wheeling the carry-on, Stuart tried to locate Hôtel du Palais l'Isle on *rue Perrière*. Cindy brought up the rear, treading on the old cobblestone street while admiring all the quaint offerings.

I feel like I'm in a Swiss chalet village—very colorful. Is Stu trying to impress me?

Stuart turned back to her. "I've found it. This is home for a while."

Cindy picked up her gait. "Good." She sighed and paused to look at a terraced café tucked into a narrow alleyway. "I'm glad we didn't have to walk any farther. Too bad this is a pedestrian only area. A taxi could've dropped us off at the door."

Those pedestrian bridges certainly drip with history.

"The main thing is we're here." He retrieved the travel documents from his shirt pocket. "This hotel has thirty-four unique guestrooms. It's supposed to be quite nice. Very modern baths and a view of the canal and lake."

"What did they do? Hire you as a PR man?" She saw his hurt feelings. "Stu, I was only joking. This is a very lovely hotel from what I can tell from the outside. It has a Swiss feel to it."

They entered the lobby. Stuart went directly to the reception desk and spoke in French to the concierge. She went up to him and handed over her passport.

"I can pay for my own room." Cindy tugged on his sleeve to get his attention. "Stu, I said I can pay. I have money."

The gentleman returned the passport to her. Stuart took the keycard. He spoke instructions in French. Cindy nodded, not understanding every word spoken.

She pulled him aside and lowered her voice as he headed to the stairs. "You only have one key. Where's the other one? Don't we have two rooms?"

"There's only one key because we only have one room." They started up the main stairwell. "We were lucky to get that. They had one last minute cancellation and I booked it."

"Don't you think it would've been nice to consult me?" *What nerve! He's not going to make me pay for my room with sex.* "Where will you sleep? I'm taking the bed."

"We'll both have the bed." He reached the landing. "The beds are queen or double in size and that should be big enough."

They climbed another flight to the middle floor. "I don't think I can climb any more steps with my carry-on." Her breath came in weighty pants.

"You don't have to." He breathed heavily and checked the room number on the key. "Our room is on this floor." He opened the door and entered the hallway. "They serve a nice buffet breakfast and there's a bar to have a relaxing drink."

Passing a few guest room doors, Stuart located their home for the next few nights. "Here it is. Room Prestige 203." He swiped the keycard and opened the door.

Stuart stared through the glass slider that opened onto a small balcony decorated with flower boxes. "This is a great view of the canal, lake, and the old Isle du Palais." He flopped backwards on the bed, pulled the tourist brochure from his pocket, and proceeded to read.

"We're south of Geneva, and only ninety minutes from Italy." He flipped through the pages. "Says this area is one of the best examples of French medieval history."

Cindy turned on the air-conditioning, set her small overnight suitcase on the bed, and started unpacking.

"This is a nice place. Very beautiful. Though the room could be larger. I can hardly walk around the bed." She grabbed her toothbrush and paste and headed for the bathroom. Her voice echoed off the walls. "How long are we here for?"

"I booked it for two nights. Sorry about the room being small. I had no idea."

Cindy came back into the room.

"Is that too long—two nights, I mean?" He looked hopeful for a positive reply.

She flicked the hair away from her shoulder. "I don't think so. With the TGV, it was only a two or three hour train ride. I see there are no national police or guards hanging around. Is that just a Paris thing?"

I hope JC doesn't arrive back in Paris before me. If he does, what will I tell him?

"Other cities have additional police security, too. Since Charlie Hebdo, the terrorist shootings, and bombings, more police and guards are on the streets. Personally, it makes me feel safer." Stuart returned to reading the tourist information. "This place is called the 'Venice of the Alps'. We're a short walk from the medieval castle Château d'Annecy, the cathedral, and the lake. There's even a museum here, Musée d'Histoire d'Annecy. That river is Rive Thiou and it flows backwards—drains the lake. That's unique—most rivers drain into a lake."

"Though museums aren't my mainstay for fun, it might be interesting to check it out." Cindy took a brush from her case and placed it on the dresser. "And if I ever need a bit of trivia for conversation, I'll remember that tidbit about the river."

"If you didn't like museums," he propped up on his elbows, "why didn't you speak up? I wouldn't have bothered with the two we visited. We could've done something else."

"I didn't say anything because I was enjoying your company and you made the tour interesting." *Damn! I don't want to hurt his feelings.* "I enjoyed seeing all that art because of you, Stu. Your enthusiasm made me want to know more." She put her hands on her hips. "Hmm, that bed doesn't look very wide to me."

"I can call up for extra pillows and we can put them between us." His expression pleaded that she would say no to the idea of a barrier.

"That might be a good idea. There's no shower curtain. Unless we want to spray water all over the bathroom, you'd better ask for one." *He's pouting. Stu's hoping for more.* "Remember, we're friends. I don't want to have deep thoughts—just fun."

"We could always shower together, save water, and only make one wet mess of the bathroom." His smile looked amusing and hopeful.

"Just call the concierge, Stu. Stop the joking. We have Annecy to explore."

He reached for the room phone, dialed, and then requested the additional pillows.

"What do we do now?" she asked. "Take a nap? Check out the bar? Take a walk?"

He looked at his watch. "It's a bit late to take in any museums. Why don't we walk and get to know the place?"

"Sounds good to me." She finished unpacking. "Why did you

pick this hotel? Have you been here before?"

"Annecy is as new to me as to you." He sat up, scooted forward, and dangled his legs off the end of the bed. "I've heard people mention how lovely it was and wanted to visit this resort." He stood up and placed his hands on her shoulders. "And … you make this city more lovely because you're in it."

"You have a way with words." *He never stops trying.* "I can see the novelist in you. Maybe Annecy will inspire you."

"I don't need Annecy to inspire me—you do that." He lightly kissed her lips.

Hmm, I do like his kisses … so very gentle and loving. Almost makes me want more.

Twenty - Five

GUY CLOUTIER, YOUNG and tall, walked into the seedy Montmartre bar. Even though the warm weather forced Parisians to forego heavy jackets for light cover-ups, he wore his zipper-accented black leather jacket as a merit badge earned in a Boy Scout troop. It concealed his .38 pistol. A silver colored chain went from his belt loop to his pocket that secured his wallet. Multiple tattoos covered his exposed hands and wrists. Another design, one of a skull with a spider decorated the left side of his neck.

Others at the bar softened their conversation as he passed, and their gaze held subdued alarm. Rumors surrounded him and he enjoyed the fact that those same rumors created respect and fear from spectators. The bartender quickly poured his favorite drink and passed it to him. An older man gave up his stool. He took such a courtesy as an unspoken expectation and sat down without a word. He ignored the "No Smoking" sign over the bar, and pulled out a cigarette from his pocket. The bartender leaned across the counter and lit it for him. Guy inhaled deeply and exhaled the smoke directly at the bartender's face. The man went back to his duties, wiping the bar down with an old damp rag.

Guy's cell phone rang. "Yeah. Got a job for me?" He turned his back to the bar.

"It's not your boss. It's Maurice, Maurice Junot," he spoke rapidly.

He left the stool and moved to the back of the bar. Guy kicked the door open with his heavy, black motorcycle boot and stood in the litter-strewn alley. The odor of rotting garbage, old beer from half empty bottles, and cat urine permeated his nostrils.

"What's up?" He dragged on his cigarette. "Got a bee stinging your ass you want me to nail? I always strike hard and true. No witnesses."

"Not so fast, Guy." He took a breath. "This is about Jean-Claude's bill. He needs more time. He has a plan that could set him up for the next five years."

"I don't call the shots—Maçon does." He noticed a prostitute adjusting her skirt as she tottered unsteadily in her heels to her favorite corner.

"Is that his real name?" Maurice sounded edgy.

"Can't say—won't say …. So what is this plan? A heist?" He started up the alley, scuffing up dirt with each step.

"No details yet." He breathed deeply. "Please ask Maçon, or whatever his name is, to hold off. Give Jean-Claude more time. If he whacks him, then he'll be losing a good customer." Maurice's voiced tensed. "Remind him of all the converts he brought to the cause. He wouldn't have those new customers if it wasn't for Jean-Claude's loyalty."

"Let me straighten you out on a few details." He took another long drag from the cigarette. "Jean-Claude brought those new customers in to pay off his old debt. Where's the profit? He uses tac-tac and doesn't pay. His highs and red runny nose come to him for free? He hasn't brought in any new talent lately—he has no credit with the source."

Maurice's voice sounded desperate. "I'm begging you man. Speak to your boss."

"If you won't give me details on this wondrous plan, give me a name—something to whet my tongue. It sounds like bullshit to me."

Could Jean-Claude be onto something? I don't believe it.

"Davis. Larry Davis." Maurice paused as if to let the name sink into Guy's brain. "The multi-millionaire—world-famous singer."

"What's the connection?" *Maurice and Jean-Claude are both full of shit!* "That straight bastard is as clean as hell. He doesn't use."

"I told you before," he sighed, "I can't go into details. Just trust me on this."

"See what I can do."

He better not be selling me a bunch of fucking shit.

"Thanks, Guy. I appreciate that." He heard Maurice's relief.

"As payment for this favor, send me some new traffic …. Three OD'd last week. Damn shame. They were good customers." He ended the call.

Guy strode back into the bar. He said nothing, and scanned the room for a familiar face who owed him money. Finding none, he finished his whisky in one swift gulp and left.

~~***~~

Joe sat on Larry's patio, Gigi and Jacques curled at his feet, while Tim prepared lunch. He had felt ill at ease about Cindy's relationship with Jean-Claude from the first moment. Taylor was special. Ever since she had come into Larry's life, Joe had regarded Cindy as part of the family, and now she was his niece.

He stared out at the pool as the light played on the water, dancing in light ripples from the breeze.

He picked up the phone from the glass-topped circular table and dialed the long distance number with his chubby fingers. Tim handed him a chilled beer and a pilsner glass.

Hmm, Taylor insists beer is served in a fancy-assed glass. I prefer to drink from the bottle. He listened to the ringing on the other end.

Damn, Sal! Pick up the phone.

"Hey, Joe." Sal coughed. "How goes it?" He was glad that Sal Mourtos, his old street buddy from his teen years, still maintained a close friendship.

"It's okay." He poured his beer into the glass. "The same ol' shit, just a different tune."

"So, why you callin'?" He heard a puffing noise over the phone. *Sal must be smokin'.*

"Cindy's over in Paris. She and her ol' man split for good. Taken up with this slick French singer—too damn slick not to have a few skeletons lurkin' around in the closet." He took a swallow of beer.

"Paris is a bit rough for me to tail him from New York City." Squealing tires came over the receiver.

"Don't expect that. I want y' to see if the big drug boys know of him." Joe adjusted his seat as his brow rutted. "Maybe they supply him through one of your guys."

"Man that's a long shot." Sal sighed. "His supplier might get directly from Columbia and not deal with the guys in New York."

"I know." He watched the foam flatten in his drink. "It's worth a try. Cindy's important to me. Taylor and Larry would be heartsick if she got into any bad stuff, or worse, became a user."

"It's an outside chance. I could come up empty." He paused a moment. "Give me what info you have. Shoot."

"Don't have much. Name is Jean-Claude LeGrand, son of Charles LeGrand, famous French singer, lives in Paris, flashy, likes the ladies, and enjoys spendin' money."

"Any tabloid stuff?" Honking horns clouded his voice.

"None that hit over here." Joe took another swallow of beer. "How you gonna translate the French press stuff?"

"Gotta a friend from Haiti. Not a problem." Sal breathed deeply. "Look ol' buddy. I gotta make a delivery. Can't make the boss unhappy—don't wanna end up in the East River."

"Later." Joe hung up the phone.

Twenty - Six

CINDY AND STUART walked the old well-worn streets along the canals. Every block or turn brought a new enchanting view that was picture-worthy. Romance was the underlying tone with a lively crowd of twenty-somethings'. The setting sun turned the vivid blue lake into hues of azure and navy.

"It's a bit too soon for dinner, but there was a lovely café near the hotel. Want to go there?" His head tilted and a charming smile lit his face.

"Good idea." She checked her watch. "We have an hour before these restaurants start to serve dinner. What spot were you thinking of?"

"Café des Ducs." His eyes pleaded a "yes" response from her. "Looks quaint. If you don't like it, we can leave."

"If *we* don't like it—the both of us not liking the place—not just my liking." She clarified with a smile.

He is so darn adorable with boyish ways.

They walked nearly back to where they started. The small tables under the faded yellow awning created a charismatic backdrop. Colorful red geraniums in pots enhanced the old-world ambiance. He pulled out the chair for her as she sat down. A waitress appeared promptly clutching a small menu. The server took a pad and pen from her pocket, ready to take their orders. Stuart ordered a cooling Pastis, which Cindy had seen before, but she preferred to try Lillet Blanc.

"Tell me," she casually placed her hand on the table. Their fingertips barely touched. "Have you any idea where we might dine?" Her finger moved closer to his. He didn't pull away. "I don't mean we have to hurry with our drinks and then eat. I was just curious."

He turned his head to study the restaurants that faced the canal.

"Chez Mamie Lise seems interesting. Though we can't really see it from here." He shrugged. "I don't know if the fare is good or not, but it would be a fun adventure to find out. The brochure recommended the food."

"Fine by me—as long as they offer something else besides fish."

Glad the waitress is coming with our drinks. I'm more than ready.

"Well," he raised his eyebrows, "we are staying on a lake. I'm certain wherever we eat, chicken will be offered for non-fish eaters."

Cindy blushed. *What a stupid thing for me to say—not liking fish. Duh! Of course fish will be the mainstay.*

He placed his hand next to hers, and his fingers slowly crept on top of her hand. She didn't pull away.

"How's your Pastis? I can smell it from here." *I'm not good at small talk.*

"It's nice. Want a taste?" He raised his glass to her. She took a sip and felt his eyes watching her every move.

"It certainly tastes of licorice." She made a face. "Not one of my favorites."

"No licorice and no fish. I like learning your likes and dislikes." His fingers stroked up to her wrist.

I like the feel of his hand on mine. "I have yet to learn yours." She smiled as the last word escaped her lips.

He's so charming. If JC and I had broken up before this trip, I wouldn't be going through this hell, but he's expecting me to be there for him.

"How's the Lillet?" His boyish charm was hard for her to ignore.

His hand has now traveled up my arm. Next, will be my shoulder? "Very good. This is Mom's favorite. So I thought I couldn't go wrong with what she likes." Cindy laughed. "I misspoke. She loves escargot. I hate them."

"I enjoy those black creatures, too." He leaned closer. "Have you ever tried them?"

"No. And I don't intend to." She stifled a smile. "I don't like them on principle."

"What principle? Most things French?" Stuart inched closer and draped his arm on the back of her chair. "I'm French. Don't you like me?"

"Of course I like you. I wouldn't be here if I didn't." *His thumb is making delicious lazy patterns on my back. Should I pull away? I don't want to.* "You're not like other Frenchmen I know." Cindy sipped her wine. "You don't sound French .... Your accent is English."

"Ah, but I'm French in all the ways it counts." She watched his tongue moisten his lower lip.

"What ways are those?"

Why am I playing this game with him? Why can't I stop? I'm playing with fire.

"If you give me a chance, I'll show you." Stuart lifted her hand to his lips and left a lingering kiss as his eyes gazed up at her.

She pulled her hand from him.

He's nearly irresistible. I have to be careful here.

"Let's finish our drinks and have a lovely walk to Chez Mamie Lise."

~~***~~

Stuart and Cindy followed the street along the river Le Thiou to a pedestrian bridge to the first island, and then to a second bridge. He glanced at her frequently, and took her hand when they reached the *quai de l'Isle*.

Everything about her is so charming, and almost naïve. I wish she could see that Jean-Claude is all wrong for her.

Continuing on to *place Saint-François de Sales* and then to *rue Saint-Maurice*, they turned left onto *rue Grenette*. He checked the numbers on the buildings against the map he held. There it was, Chez Mamie Lise.

He opened the door for her.

I hope we don't need reservations. This place is perfect to champion my cause.

They entered. A pleasant woman greeted them in French. He requested a secluded table for two. The hostess went to her pedestal and studied the seating chart, and then escorted them to the main "La Cosena" room. Their table was at the window where they could view the passersby strolling with souvenir purchases or dangling cameras.

A waiter appeared, and handed them the menus and filled the water glasses. Stuart noticed the lack of English translation for the food listings. He handed his menu back to the server saying, "Un menu en Anglais pour la mademoiselle, s'il vous plaît."

"Certainement. Un moment, monsieur." He left and nearly instantly returned with an English menu for Cindy.

She reached over the table and gave his hand a gentle squeeze. "You're always thinking of me—what I might like or want to do."

"I do what I can." He looked around. "I hope you like it here. It looked interesting from the outside."

"It's charming. I love the rustic wood tables, and the way they've decorated the walls with pots, old dishes, and wine racks—even that old coffee grinder."

"I wasn't certain as you seem more urban. You appear to love the life and excitement of a city."

Is she just being polite or does she really like this place?

"That's true." Under the table, her foot touched his. "I love the hustle and bustle with all the lights and noises of a city. But, it's nice to take a break to somewhere that's more calm—makes it easier to think." She looked in his eyes. "It was extremely considerate of you to request an English menu for me. JC would've insisted I struggle with a French one."

"Maybe he wants you to learn his culture?"

I hate defending him to her. But if I talk against him too much, that could push her away.

"He should be more thoughtful regarding what I want, and what will make me happy." She laid the napkin in her lap, then looked up at the rough-hewn wooden beams across the ceiling.

Stuart bit his tongue before speaking. "I could say something about him—but that wouldn't help you—merely serve my own ego."

"I understand." He felt her foot move back and forth against his. "You're probably right." She paused and looked at a far wall. "I feel as if I've been transported to Switzerland in this restaurant. They have food canisters and cute figurines. A bit of rustic refinement."

"You expressed that perfectly."

Her foot is rubbing mine. Is she sending me a message or merely being playful?

Did he have any chance at all to win her over? His heart beat a little faster at the thought.

"Have you decided what you would like? How about we start with a Kir and go from there?"

"That's wine, right?" She scrunched her nose. "I don't like any dry-tasting wine."

I love that thing she does with her nose, so adorable. "It's a fruit liqueur with white wine. It's not dry. Anything else before the main course? Salad or appetizer?"

"I think the onion soup. It will remind me of Mom. She makes the best French food." Cindy remained focused on the menu.

"I thought you didn't care much for French food?"

I love getting to know her. There is so much yet to learn.

"What child doesn't like their mother's cooking?" She took a sip of water. "It gives me a warm feeling when I eat something that reminds me of her. Some of her dishes are a bit too rich, though."

She inclined her head and twirled a strand of hair at her neck. "What are you ordering? Probably something I wouldn't like."

"You'll find out when it's served." He hoped his wily smile would intrigue her.

"Well, aren't you the sly one?" She languidly moistened her bottom lip with her tongue. "I'll have steak and fries with the shallot sauce. The chicken is filled with mushrooms—so that's out of the running. No dessert. I'll be too stuffed."

"Ah, you don't like mushrooms, escargot and—"

She cut him off, "And people who want to know too much too fast."

Ouch! Cindy cut me down and hard on that one. "I was going to say 'and fish'."

"I'm sorry." She reached for his hand and gave a gentle squeeze. "I didn't mean it the way it sounded."

"No harm done."

Was that cutting remark meant for me or words she wished she could say to Jean-Claude. That has to be wishful thinking on my part. What has he done to capture her heart so quickly? I'm a man like him. We all have the same equipment. Women! Such an eternal mystery!

The waiter stood at the table and placed a basket of freshly baked bread nestled in a red napkin. Stuart ordered in French out of respect to the employee. Collecting the menus, the server left with a polite "Merci."

Moments later the waiter served the Kir. Stuart raised his glass in toasting fashion.

"To a most lovely and intriguing lady who enhances everywhere she goes by her beauty and sparkling personality." He smiled as they clinked their glasses together.

"Thank you. Those are ego-boosting words, Stu." She took a sip. "This is delicious. I can't place the flavor."

"I think it's blackcurrant." He took another taste. "I'm glad you like it."

"I do. What shall we do after dinner? Roam around a bit?" She tore off a piece of bread.

"That would be nice. A way to let our dinner settle."

Did she remove her shoe? I feel her foot against my ankle.

"This place doesn't look very big on nightlife around here—not like L.A. or New York." Again, she reached out and touched his hand for a moment.

"There might be a few spots in Annecy. I'll ask the concierge when we get back to the hotel. They would know what to recommend." *She wants to go to a nightclub? Is that to avoid or prolong when we have to go to bed?* "Were you thinking of going someplace else after dinner?"

"No. Not really." She turned and stared out the window. "The days are so long here. The sun never seems to set."

"We're more north of the equator. The further north the location—the longer the days and the shorter the nights."

Her toes are playing on my ankle. What gives with the mixed messages again? Making small talk and flirting with her feet?

After the appetizer, the server brought the main course.

Stuart saw the look Cindy gave. "What's wrong? Isn't that what you ordered? Steak and fries?"

"It's not my order it's yours!" She swallowed hard. "You're eating frog's legs. They're right up there with snails."

He chuckled. "They're delicious." He offered a bite from his fork. "Tastes just like chicken."

Cindy shook her head. "That's what they say about snake, and I wouldn't eat that either." She removed her foot from his ankle.

A person eating frog's legs upsets her? "What I'm eating sounds elegant in French. It's 'La fricassée de cuisse de grenouilles poôlées'. Really quite good and a treat for me."

"Enjoy away!" She cut into her medium-rare beef. Red juices flowed to her fries. "I'm a simple girl and enjoy simple things."

"So ... nothing exotic entices you?"

Cindy eats in a most sensuous way. I wonder if she knows she's teasing me with the smallest gesture, or is it natural? If it's in her nature, I could be entirely wrong. She might not be sending any signals at all.

"No. Nothing." She took a bite of fries. "Like I said, I'm a plain girl, with simple tastes. Nothing more complicated than that." Cindy raised her glass before taking a gulp. "I hate drama, too. Arguments and shouting will send me packing every time. That's why I'm so glad to be done with Vic. He ridiculed my attempt at painting. I aborted that effort. Dad always encouraged me and thought I had talent."

"We're similar on that point." He swallowed his food. "Life is too short for hurt feelings and negative actions."

That's another thing we have in common—plus the love for spontaneity. Sounds like she argued with her husband. She told me he gambled. Now, I find out he made fun of her—what a bastard.

Stuart put his fork down. "We're nearly finished with our meal. Is there anything else you would like? Dessert? Coffee? A liqueur?"

I know what I would like to end the meal and begin my night. I can't go there. She's not receptive.

"Just a walk. Create some lovely memories." She looked at her watch. "The sunset will be soon and I can take some beautiful photos from my phone."

"Fine." He gestured to the waiter for the check.

Twenty - Seven

CHARLES LEGRAND STOOD gazing out of his apartment window on the prestigious Île Saint Louis. He saw his faint reflection in the pane. Tension deepened the lines from his nose to mouth, and at his eyes.

"Where are you? You missed your recording session." He spoke into his phone as he approached the Louis XV chair near the antique desk. "Jean-Claude, you can't be taking off like this without a word. You have a career to work at."

"Papa. You're making too much of this. I had things to do." He laughed. "Not unlike you—living in the most exclusive area of Paris."

Female voices sounded over the phone. "Who's that with you? Monique or someone else?"

"That's not important." He blew his nose.

"Not important to you, but very important to me if it's Davis' stepdaughter, Cindy." His tone strengthened. "I told you, don't ruin this deal with me and Davis. It's good business for me."

"Give it up, old man." Jean-Claude jeered, "You're dried up, and next week they'll be holding a funeral for your career."

"Where is your respect?" Charles felt his forehead pound. His fingers rubbed against the budging vein. "I'm your father. You should show me honor. Going from woman to woman is disrespectful to the family and your name."

"It's the LeGrand name you're concerned about." He let out a ragged breath. "I was always the little boy you had to put up with as you went from one affair to another. You put Mama in her grave. She died of a broken heart."

"Your mother died from a heart attack." He took a pen from the antique desk and started clicking it repeatedly. "Besides, she took a lover, too."

"Not until you were on your third," Jean-Claude sounded incensed. "If it wasn't for you, she would have been faithful. She sought love you never gave her. The same love I seek from you and never receive."

"That's not true." He leaned forward with elbows on knees. "I worked hard and long hours to provide for you and your mother. I loved you and still do."

"What's the point, Papa? If I don't feel it, it doesn't make a difference."

Charles heard his son hang up. The sound of the dead phone reflected the fear and anguish he felt for his son.

~~***~~

Frédéric and Claude lunched at the ultra famous Le Brasserie Café de la Paix on *5 place de l'Opéra*. Frédéric didn't splurge often, and regarded this old-world restaurant as a treat. The lavish surroundings exuded Second Empire elegance and proudly displayed its listed frescoes and sumptuous gilding. He ate his smoked salmon while Claude savored ham and cheese crêpe covered in a delicate cream sauce. They shared a bottle of rosé wine. Attentive, yet unobtrusive waiters stood at hand to fulfill the slightest need without being asked.

"Claude, I haven't heard from you for a while." Frédéric lifted the fork to his mouth, chewed, and swallowed. "Have you learned anything about LeGrand?"

"Nothing that would rock anyone's world." Claude took a swallow of water. "He goes to sex shops in Montmartre—Pigalle to be exact."

"C'est vrai? Really?" *Does this mean trouble for Cindy?* "He goes alone?"

"Oui. Toujours ne personne. Always alone." Claude brought a forkful of crêpe to his mouth. "He doesn't bother with the cheap peep shows."

Intrigued, Frédéric probed further, "Anything else? Anything that might harm Cindy?"

"He likes sex toys." His friend spoke with a nonchalance as if it was common practice for most. "He was seen in one of those live sex shows—the type that draws in droves of tourists."

His eyes widened. "You said he was seen *in* a live sex show. Was he a participant? Or in the audience?"

"In the audience. I have it on good information that he pays for private performances." Claude took a mouthful of wine. "He might have cultivated them as friends and have free-wheeling orgies at his apartment."

"I doubt that, with Cindy living with him." Frédéric took out a pen and a pad of paper from his pocket and started taking notes. "Anything considered bizarre or freakish?"

"Maybe he's grooming her for some little 'Ooh là là' experiences." Claude finished his crêpe. "She's relatively young and inexperienced—prime for his tastes. He can mold her the way he wants. Encourage her to develop exotic tastes."

"Taylor would be heartsick to learn of this." Frédéric dabbed his mouth with a napkin. "Is there anything else?"

"He frequents this exclusive club for the mega rich. Sex runs rampant in the back room. It is rumored they might have cameras for the exhibitionists." Claude leaned in closer. "Beyond the sex thing, he does have a very shady friend, Maurice Junot who has a connection to Guy Cloutier."

"Tell me more about Junot." Frédéric franticly scribbled. "What does Cloutier deal in?"

"Junot is an errand boy for LeGrand. He arranges meetings with women that Jean-Claude fancies. Cloutier—known as the 'nail', is an enforcer, a bill collector, and deals cocaine on the side. You don't pay your bill—gambling or drugs—he collects one way or the other—even his last name means nail in a way, from the word 'clou'."

"Is there a direct connection between LeGrand and Cloutier?" Beads of perspiration formed on his forehead.

"None that I can find." He leaned closer to Frédéric and lowered his voice to a near whisper. "Cloutier deals drugs for Maçon." A waiter came by and refilled their water glasses. Claude paused his conversation with his friend. When the server left he continued, "Maçon is just a cover. No one knows his real name. He gets his shipment out of New York." He glanced around checking if eavesdroppers heard his words. "Maçon plays rough. Murder is not beyond his reach. Anyone having dealings with him is fair game for an untimely death." He pointed a warning finger to his friend. "Don't do any research on your own. Keep your nose clean, and sell those little houses to the tourists."

"Mon Dieu! Cindy could be in real danger if LeGrand knows Maçon." *Will she believe any of this if I tell her?* "Be careful, dear friend. I don't want to lose you."

"I'm good at what I do." He took a deep breath. "I'm a survivor .... By the way, I haven't investigated Dumont's parents—been too busy chasing LeGrand, Junot, and Cloutier. LeGrand has gone underground for the present."

Is Cindy with him, getting hooked on drugs?

"Do you know if he's alone? Is Cindy with Jean-Claude?"

"He left alone. The woman who manages the apartment complex where he lives, said an American woman stayed behind and then left on her own."

"That doesn't mean she's not with him—only means she left later. She could be in a lot of trouble."

This is very bad. How can I protect Cindy? Taylor is counting on me.

"Calm down." He chuckled. "I did more research. Seems Dumont left his bookstore for a few days—went to Annecy. Told his store manager that Cindy was traveling with him to that city." He smiled broadly. "I don't have an excellent PI reputation for nothing—I'm thorough."

A look of surprise crossed Frédéric's face. He motioned for the bill. "This meal is on me. Thank you. I appreciate all you've done."

"Don't worry." He smiled as he rose. "I'll keep on it …. Oh, when you see Dumont again, tell him that I'll need a sample of his DNA and that of the suspected mother. I'll drop the swab off to you when I've finished with the LeGrand case. Mention that the DNA test will cost a thousand euros. I can't foot the bill for that. I'll get better results if DNA of the alleged father could also be obtained." He paused before leaving. "Thanks for lunch. Nice place."

Twenty - Eight

AFTER DINNER, CINDY and Stuart strolled hand in hand along the canals. This was a safe haven for her troubled mind. She didn't want to clutter her thoughts of what could be and only wanted to live in the moment of now. The moonlight danced on the rippling water. Music blared from the few nightspots that added diversity to Annecy's old town. Everywhere displayed a testimony of French medieval history with a strong Swiss influence. Like Paris, Annecy was a lover's retreat.

"Are you still enjoying yourself?" He inclined his head. "Or do you find walking somewhat of a bore?"

"Not in the least." In their clasped hands, her thumb stroked his hand. "The company makes all the difference."

"Do you want to go back to the hotel?" He hesitated a moment. "We've had a busy day and should probably rest up for tomorrow."

What's going to happen when we get to the room? Is he using a new tactic to get me into bed for more than sleep?

"What's planned for tomorrow? More of the same—wandering the streets, maybe do some souvenir shopping?"

"What we'll do, is going to be a surprise." Stuart looked smug as they crossed the bridge. "I've been doing my research."

"Aren't you a mystery man …." She sidled closer to him, bumping her hip sideways into his. "How do you know I will like what you've planned?"

"I don't." He smiled and squeezed her hand. "I can only hope."

"Hope?" She sent him a flirtatious grin.

"Yes … I hope for a lot of things." They approached the entrance to their hotel. "You can fulfill some of those."

"Some of what?"

I know exactly what he's hoping for. I can't fulfill it. Yet, this game is fun.

"My hopes and wishes." Stuart entered the hotel's lobby, then lowered his voice as they stood at the elevator. "You know precisely what I'm talking about." He smiled charmingly. "I love every teasing side of you."

"Too bad you didn't notice the elevator when we first arrived." She chuckled. "It would have saved us from climbing all those stairs."

"I never noticed. I was too excited that you were on this trip with me." A wistful look came from his eyes.

In their room, Cindy noticed the four extra pillows on the bed, and a new shower curtain hanging in the bathroom with fresh creases from having been unfolded from a package. Stuart went to the window and drew the curtain, and closed the drape along the balcony door.

"Looking for privacy?" *Is he trying to set the stage?* "I hope it's only for modesty's sake and not something else?"

"You have the answer to that one." He removed his belt and started unbuttoning his shirt.

"Are you going to undress in front of me?"

Does he think his body will turn me on? Yet, I did like his kiss—and he has a nice ass.

"Yes." He removed his shoes and then socks. "Don't hold back on account of me. You can start disrobing, too. I don't mind."

Why does his smile have to be so damn appealing?

Cindy pulled out her nightshirt. "I'll get ready in the bathroom. I'm taking a shower before bed."

"Good plan." He started to follow her with unzipped pants. "I'll take one, too."

"Not with me, you won't." Her eyes flared and then softened.

"Who will wash your back?" He upturned his palms, and then stepped closer, as she entered the bathroom.

"I'll manage."

He's certainly direct. His accent might be English, but his approach is all French—maybe even American.

"Will you please, leave?"

Will I have to fight him off? What in hell did I get myself into? With JC I know the score, but Stu has a way of surprising me.

"Okay." Stuart started back toward the bedroom. "Call me if you need anything." He snatched a towel and closed the door.

"Yeah, right," she mumbled under her breath with a hint of disgust.

The warm stream and soapsuds relaxed her. Images of Stuart filled her brain—of them sharing forbidden kisses, and clandestine embraces, while his hands caressed her body, touching her breasts, squeezing her buttocks, his mouth buried in her neck. *This isn't right. I should be thinking of JC—not Stuart.* She smiled thinking of this daydream.

"Hey! What's happening?" She jumped back from the water and

let out a yelp. The water had turned nearly ice cold.

Stuart burst through the door. "What's wrong?" He stood on the other side of the curtain. "Are you okay? Did you fall? Can I help?"

"I'm fine." She laughed. "The hot water cut off and it was a shock."

"Must be a water hog guest taking a shower at the same time." He went to the warming rack, took a towel. "I have something that might help."

"I'm finished anyway." She turned off the shower, peeked around the curtain, and took the towel from his hands. "Thanks. I can dry off in the tub if you're going to remain in the bathroom."

"I'm leaving." She heard the door close.

Wet drops from her hair cascaded to her shoulders as Cindy entered the bedroom. Her nightshirt came to her mid-thigh, and she felt Stuart's eyes on her legs, and then his gaze followed her as she went about the room from combing her wet hair to laying out her clothes for the next day. The extra pillows were stacked in the chair by the dresser. Stuart was under the sheets on the side closer to the balcony door.

She perched on the edge of the bed and glanced at his bare chest. His neatly folded clothes were in a stack on his suitcase.

Is he naked under the bed covers?

She bit her lip. He lifted his hand and traced a random pattern on her back with his fingers, causing delightful shivers through the silky fabric.

"Ooh, Stu." She sighed. "You shouldn't do that."

"What?" His innocent tone vaguely veiled his intent. "I'm only helping you to relax after a long day of traveling and walking."

"The best way for me to relax is to go to sleep."

Can I resist him? Do I even want to?

He sat up and leaned close to her back. She felt his bare rippling chest though her nightshirt. He kissed her ear lobe. "How about a good night kiss? A kiss couldn't hurt."

She faced him. "One kiss will lead to another, and then another, and then—"

Stuart ended her words with a kiss as she fell back on the pillow. Cindy returned his kiss as her lips opened to receive his passion. Their tongues mingled with fire pent up from long periods of yearning. His hand went to her breast. She relished his feel.

Reality abruptly shook her. She grabbed his wandering hand at the wrist and broke away from his mouth.

"Stop it! I can't. I won't." She gasped. "I'm not like this. This isn't me. When I'm with a man—it's only that man and no one else. If I do what we both want now—I'll hate you and myself in the morning."

"Are you certain Jean-Claude is meant for you?" He kissed her fingertips. "He might be merely a stop along the way to the one you're meant to be with."

"I can't answer that." She gazed deeply in his eyes and touched his cheek with her fingers. "You and I could be more than friends—but not now—not like this."

She got out of bed, hauled the pillows over, creating a soft barrier.

Will I say no to him next time?

Twenty - Nine

CINDY SLOWLY WALKED in the breakfast buffet line viewing an array of tempting offerings. Stuart stood next to her. She chose a selection of ham and cheeses and two pieces of pain au chocolat pastries. They took their selections to a table by the window in the cheery brunch room.

He pulled out her chair. "Did you sleep well?"

Cindy cut off a piece of meat and cheese and piled it on her fork. "Very well, and you? Any nightmares after our amour disaster?"

"It could have had a different noun to describe the result." Stuart poured sugar into his coffee.

She sipped her orange juice. "Umm, yummy, this is really good."

"You're avoiding the subject." He buttered his croissant. "Why do you say one thing and your actions communicate the exact opposite?"

"Do I?" She raised her eyebrows with little girl innocence. "I had no idea."

"Encore! Mon Dieu!" He reached for her hand and looked directly in her eyes. "My feelings run deeper for you than friendship. I thought you understood my heart."

"Stu," she rubbed his hand, "let's keep this as a friendship. Yes, I like to play, but I'm in no position to give you what I can't."

"You mean, your body … or your heart?" Sadness rested on his face.

Cindy avoided his eyes. "Both." She withdrew her hand and took the pastry, smearing butter on a torn-off piece. "Let's enjoy our last day with no talk of feelings. I need to laugh and enjoy. Complications are messy."

His lips thinned with clear disappointment. "D'accord, okay. If a day of fun is in order, then that is what you shall have."

"Thanks for understanding." She squeezed his hand. "You're a good friend."

"Yes, a good friend who nearly became more." He sipped his coffee.

"Stop. Don't go into those woods." She moistened her lips. "They're loaded with barbs and thorns."

I hate hurting his feelings.

"Just let me know when to put on my suit of armor and I'll trudge onward. No thorn or barb will strike me." He dropped strawberry jam onto his croissant.

"If there is a right time, I'll let you know." She stared out the window. "The weather seems perfect to enjoy the lake. Why don't we do that?"

"Fine. You ready now?" He wiped his lips on the napkin.

"Okay." Cindy started to rise. "We can have a nice walk and see what water activities are out there."

In the absence of a breeze, the calm water reflected a mirror finish. Cindy and Stuart strolled along the metal-railed pathway that outlined Lac d'Annecy, enjoying the fresh lake air. In the distance were small terraced villages and estates. The clouds caressed the mountain peaks. A romantic couple passed them, arm in arm, and punctuated their moment with a kiss.

I know Stu wishes that couple was us. I thought this trip would be good for me. Now I'm not so sure. Why can't he be satisfied with just friendship?

She looked up at him and smiled. Her hand squeezed his waist.

He's such a good person. I hope Stu finds someone who will truly make him happy. I don't think that person is me.

Stuart picked up his gait, and it seemed that something had caught his attention. "Come on. I think this will be fun."

"A boat?" *I don't think I'm going to like this.* "I'm not at my best around water."

"Ridiculous!" He hurriedly walked to the vendor renting pedal boats, then extended his hand for her to follow. "Don't be afraid. You can pedal?"

"Of course I can pedal! Any idiot can pedal." Stuart paid the fee, and put his cash in his front pocket while the gentleman secured a boat for them.

"Wait a minute." Cindy pulled out a large plastic zippered bag. "Put your money, cell phone, and wallet in here. If we fall in—the important stuff will be dry."

"You think of everything, don't you?" He flashed her a broad smile and handed her his items.

"Not really. I always keep a plastic bag with me—remnants of what Mom taught me." She placed the bag between them on the cushion. "Every now and then I do something right. I didn't feel like carrying a purse today and put my essential stuff in this bag."

She grabbed his hand to steady herself as she took her seat on the canopied boat.

They sat side-by-side on the cushion and placed their feet on the pedals. He looked at her. "I find very little wrong with you."

"That's the problem."

He's not seeing me objectively.

The vendor gave Stuart last minute instructions in French.

After a moment or two of coordinating their pedaling efforts, they had propelled themselves a third of the way from the bank. The wind disturbed the lake's serene surface, and created small ripples lapping at the narrow shore. Cindy looked up at the sky. The red canopy above them started flapping although there were no storm clouds.

"Is the weather very changeable here?" Her eyes remained upward.

"It can be." He noticed her looking at the fast moving cloud. "We're at the foot of the Alps. I don't feel a change in the air. If it changes, it's rather quick."

"Do you think we should return?" She looked at her watch through the clear plastic bag. "It's been almost an hour."

He looked back at the location from where they started. "We've pedaled quite a distance. Going back would be a good idea." A line of waiting tourists stood at the vendor's platform. "People are waiting for their turn."

"How do we turn this thing around?" *I hope we're not stuck out here.* "I didn't understand his instructions to you."

Stuart laughed. "Never fear. I'll steer. Stop pedaling until we're turned around. I'll pedal and we will end up in the right direction."

She followed his instructions and soon they were only minutes away from their drop-off point. The vendor steadied the boat as they disembarked. Cindy brushed her bangs aside and put her hand to her forehead to shut out the glare from the water.

He sought her hand and they started walking away. "Where to now? Parasailing? Canoeing? Something else?"

"Parasailing? Not on your life!" She stuffed the plastic bag in her jacket pocket. "Let's stick with water sports. Besides, that was fun."

"Do you want to go back to the pedal boats?" He stopped.

"No. How about renting a canoe?" She shaded her eyes with her hand again. "I think I saw canoes lined up during one of our walks—not far from our hotel."

"You're on. Canoeing it is!" He chuckled. "You lead the way."

"Me?" *He's joking, right?* "I have no idea how to get back to the hotel. I never paid any attention to the maps. How could I possibly find the canoe rental?"

"I'm only joking." He laughed quietly. "I know where they are. Follow me."

They strolled down the shaded tree-lined pathway along the river, and then turned to the right where a canal came into view. In the near distance, a line of canoes of various bright colors peeked between the obscuring foliage. Stuart picked up his pace.

He called back at her, "Here it is. Hurry up before a line forms."

What's the rush? So what if we have to wait.

"Calm down. There's no fire." She came up behind him.

"You have my money with the other items in your plastic bag." Mild frustration widened his eyes and he upturned his palms.

Cindy handed the bag to Stuart. He reached in for the cash, paid the man, and gave the sack back to her. She returned it to her pocket. The man held the canoe as they stepped in and took their seats. Stuart sat at the back and took a paddle in hand.

"Don't move around too much." He pushed off with force against the bank. "Canoes tip over very easily."

"I'm not a dolt." She made a face. "I know that."

He paddled down the channel, passing picturesque buildings and footbridges. Cindy started to stand up. The boat swayed dangerously from side to side.

"Cindy, sit down!" Fear etched his face. "We'll tip over!"

"No we won't." She started towards him. "I want to try paddling for a change."

The boat rocked more violently. From the corner of her eye, Cindy saw a couple of bystanders stop and take pictures of them. What was their problem? She wasn't about to tip the boat over if that's what they thought.

She grinned at Stuart, stood upright, and caught her toe on a wooden rib. For a brief moment, she thought she had managed to save herself, but she couldn't stay up, and fell headlong onto him. The last thing she heard was laughter from the onlookers as in one swift movement, she, Stuart, and the canoe flipped over.

Cindy flapped her arms and legs as she came to the surface and saw his face in front of her. He held onto the overturned canoe.

I look like a damn fool. Why in hell didn't I listen to Stu?

He did not look happy. He spat out water. His clothing clung to his body.

She felt something soft rub past her leg. "My God!" she screamed. "Something touched me! What's in the water?"

Stuart laughed. "Well, considering that this water comes from the lake, and the lake has fish, what do you think it was?"

"Very funny." Her annoyance surfaced. "I didn't need a comment like that. Fish *do* bite."

"There are no piranhas in the lake." He edged to the bank. "Help me get this thing over to the edge where we can secure it." He scratched his head. "Do you have the bag?"

"What?"

I didn't do any souvenir shopping.

His voice held urgency. "The bag! The bag!" More laughter sounded from the onlookers. "The plastic bag with our money, phones, watches!"

"I didn't think to look." She searched her pocket. "Yes." A large sigh escaped as she pulled out the plastic bag. "It didn't fall out of my pocket!"

"All is well then." Stuart grabbed the canoe and yanked firmly. "It would be nice if you could help me. It's not as light as it looks."

Cindy wiped her dripping bangs away from her eyes. "I was fixing my hair." She pushed on the back end of the boat.

"You need more than your fingers to make your hair right." He started to laugh.

"It's not a laughing matter, Mr. Dumont." She gave a final push on the canoe that nearly caused him to fall over onto the bank.

"The lady has muscles." He teased with a smug smile.

"And don't you forget it." Determination flashed in her eyes.

"And a temper." He stood with hands on hips. "You are a sight! Give me the bag so I can take a photo."

"Not on your life, buster!" Cindy walked up to him. "Instead of pointing out all my faults, how about going back to the man who rented us this canoe? We can't walk this boat back by ourselves. I'm not getting back into it. If you want to paddle it back—fine. But I won't!"

"Where are the paddles?" He looked out at the canal. "I don't see them."

"Even though I'm such an idiot for tipping us over, I had enough brains to grab the oars before they floated away—they're under the canoe."

He thinks he has all the answers.

"That was smart thinking. By the way, they are called paddles and not oars." He looked around. "I don't see any steps to the sidewalk."

"They're directly behind you." Cindy smirked. "Now who's the one with all the brains? I might have tipped the boat, but I found the stairs."

"Touché, Mademoiselle Cindy." He started up the steps, then turned back to her. "Stay here. I'll be back with the man."

"I already figured that one out." *I shouldn't have talked to him like that.* Her voice softened. "For what it's worth, I'm sorry for tipping the canoe."

He thinks he's so smart and I'm a stupid female. He's got another thought coming.

She climbed a few steps and watched him leave, his wet shorts clinging to his form.

Damn he's got a nice ass. Almost as nice as JC's.

Thirty

CINDY RUBBED HER hair with a towel as she exited the bathroom wearing a bright, printed dress. Stuart smiled and stood up from the bed, wrapping the towel tighter around his waist.

"The bath is all yours." She walked over to the mirror. "This is our last night. Let's make it special." *I shouldn't have said that.* "You've spent so much already. Tonight will be my treat."

"How 'special' do you want to make it?" He took a tourist flyer from the surface of the bed. "Romantic-special or lively fun-special?" Stuart flipped a few pages. "No. You will not pay. This trip was my idea and my gift to you as a friend."

"I think fun-special is a good idea." *He might be running short of funds.* "Maybe I want to give you a gift, too. You should allow me to pay for something."

"It's not part of my French nature." He stood up and handed her the brochure. "Look it over while I shower."

Cindy leafed through the printed offerings.

~~*****~~

They dined in Le Petit Chalet on *rue Jean-Jacques Rousseau*, off from *quai de l'Évêché* in Annecy's old town. The décor transported Cindy to quintessential Switzerland. The rough plank walls, crossbeam ceiling, low ambient lighting, and understated refined table settings created a cozy and romantic feeling in a relatively large room, with a welcoming fire. On one side, a comfortable low-armed sofa served as seating for a long plank table with wooden chairs opposite. End tables with a living room styled lamp gave a warm glow.

Cindy stood in restrained awe with Stuart at her side as they waited to be seated.

This place looks expensive. I hope I brought enough cash with me. I can't allow Stu to pay for my dinner. Did I bring enough to pay for his meal, too?

"Stu," she tugged on his jacket sleeve, "it's beautiful here. It looks full. Do you think we'll have to wait for a table? Should we go elsewhere?"

"Don't worry." He ran his finger along his turtleneck opening, as if he felt an itch. "We have reservations."

"You think of everything."

Is he trying to woo me or just being considerate? Probably a little of both.

"Remember, I'm paying the bill." She shifted her weight and fingered her purse. "I won't have you paying for this entire trip."

"Don't worry about it." He looked directly at her. "It's better that you save your money. Emergencies can occur when you least expect them."

"Since we're not on the slopes, I can't imagine what."

Why is he so insistent?

The hostess showed them to their table by the windows, and handed them the menus. A server filled the water glasses. While Cindy reviewed the restaurant's offerings, the waiter placed a bottle of rosé wine on the table, then poured a small amount into each glass. Stuart tasted and said, "Très bien," indicating his approval.

"What would you like to order?" he asked as he read the items listed. "How about a nice cheese fondue with a tossed salad? Or something more substantial—Chateaubriand steak with Béarnaise sauce?"

She noticed the price of the beef item and compared it to the regional dish. "I think the fondue would be fine for me. I'm not in the mood for fancy dining."

Cindy discreetly peeked at the money in her purse.

If he takes me up on paying for this dinner, that could just about wipe me out of cash. I wish I didn't leave the money Mom gave me in my cosmetic bag at the hotel.

"What are you looking for?" He took a swallow of water.

"Just checking my makeup."

Dang! I don't want him to know I'm worried about paying the bill.

"I think I found a good place to end the evening." He sipped his rosé. "The wine is very good. You should taste it. Not dry at all."

"How did you know I don't like dry wine?"

What else does he think he knows about me? I'm not biting on his "end the evening" comment.

"You mentioned that to me before." He sported a smug smile. "Remember, I'm a writer of sorts and love to observe people."

"I hope I'm not going to end up in your novel. It looks like you're constantly formulating plots or characters in your mind."

He knows nothing about me—not what really counts.

"Maybe." He sat straighter in his chair as if to create distance. "I don't know if I'll write about the French Revolution or the court of Henry VIII. Both subjects fascinate me."

"Since I wasn't alive during those historical periods, I find it difficult to see where I would fit into that manuscript." She took a taste of the rosé. "Hmm, quite nice."

"It's not a textbook I'm considering." He leaned forward and interlaced his fingers on the table. "I picture fictional characters living in those historical times, dealing with the challenges of survival, having goals as present day people."

The waiter brought their steaming fondue, tossed green salad, and a huge basket of French bread cubes for dipping into the pale creamy mixture. Two long-stemmed forks rested on separate cloth napkins.

"Interesting." Cindy took a whiff of the fondue, inhaling the faint scent of wine. "Your idea of using history as a backdrop to your characters is intriguing. A much better read than that of dates, names, locations, and who did what." She stabbed a cube of crusty bread with her fork and swirled it into the melted cheese. "History never held any appeal for me." She pulled out the treat and blew on it before continuing. "I wouldn't mind reading something like what you described."

"That's the idea." Stuart took the cheese-laden morsel to his mouth and chewed. "I have a ton of research to do, though. All the facts have to be correct."

"Some American authors have done the same—Herman Wouk and John Jakes are a couple I remember." Cindy pierced another piece of bread.

"Do you read their work?" He appeared fascinated about what she had to say.

"No. But I did see the TV miniseries based on their books." She took a swallow of wine. "Herman Wouk's novels Winds of War and the sequel War and Remembrance were a twenty-part tome. John Jakes' North and South, Love and War, and Heaven and Hell were put to the small screen, too. I saw the reruns on some channel that I don't recall. Those three books were a trilogy."

Why did I say that? He knows what a trilogy is—duh! He's a writer.

"I don't know if I have a massive length of work inside me." He chuckled. "Time will tell."

"Have you written other things?" she asked. "Articles? Short stories?"

"Yes. A few have been published." He swallowed some wine. "I was the starving artist of a sort and that's why I own a bookstore.

It's a lot easier now. I worked for a while as a waiter at cafés to keep life and limb together, saved my money to open my business and buy my apartment. When not busy, I can write." His smile charmed her. "You could say I have the best of both worlds."

"No special girlfriend in your life?"

He seems to have let his guard down.

"None." He reached for her hand. "Would I have asked you on this trip if I had?"

"Well, I don't know." *He seems to be speaking from his heart.* "You *are* French, and Frenchmen have a reputation for dating more than one girl at a time."

"Cindy," he cleared his throat, "that is not me. I'm a simple man with straight-forward values. I don't believe that subterfuge has any place in any relationship—romantic or otherwise."

"But, what about all those innuendos that are so common in the beginning of a romance?" She took a bite of salad. "Isn't that being less than honest?"

"That is," he touched the tip of her nose, "the fine art of playful wooing—creating the mystique of anticipation, the hinting of what could be, and then pulling back."

Her eyes fixed on his. "That's what we've been doing during this trip, isn't it? Reaching out and pulling back. A game devised to never cross the line."

"That was, and is your game." He reached for her hand and stroked it lightly. "I played along because I sensed you hide a deep confusion, somewhere in your heart. If you want to share any troubles—I'm here. I'm your friend. Yes, I would like to be more—but, that's up to you. Either way, friendship—your friendship will be enough."

Cindy felt tears rim her eyes. She looked upward to restrain her emotions.

Why does he know me so well after such a short time? Even Vic never truly knew me or seemed interested—never wanted to know how I felt. What do I feel? JC will be back in Paris in a few days. How will I feel then?

~~***~~

"Come on," Stuart said. "Time to move on."

He held Cindy's hand as they made their way to their next destination after the restaurant.

"Are you going to tell me where we're going?" Cindy asked.

Stuart hesitated a few moments, then shrugged and said, "Sure. Of course. Le Garage. It's the most explosive nightspot on *rue*

Sommeiller."

Stuart hoped it would meet with Cindy's expectations. The brochure had said it featured an ultra-stylish, modern club, a chic bar, with an abundance of chrome, leather furnishings, and the aura of joie de vivre for the young and young at heart.

The throbbing beat hit them as they entered through an imposing doorway. Stuart spotted a free table at the far end of the room. He took Cindy's hand and led the way walking along the periphery, weaving through the gyrating bodies on the dance floor, which was alive with laser lighting, and great acoustics for the DJs, who apparently provided a variety of music of pop, rock, and R&B.

He hoped this choice of entertainment would please her.

On the way to their table, Cindy suddenly screeched. "Take your hands off of me!"

"What's wrong?" Stuart checked behind her. "What happened?"

"That guy in the tan jacket and black turtleneck just grabbed my ass! He slid his hand under my skirt."

That son of a bitch! He needs a lesson.

"I'll take care of him."

Cindy's voice hinted fear. "Stu, don't make a scene. Let's go to our table ... better yet, let's leave."

He ignored her words. Stuart tapped the man on the shoulder. "Hey, you grabbed my lady's ass."

The man turned around and boasted a blatant arrogance. "So what of it?" he slurred in French. "She's got a nice ass—firm, too." He was obviously drunk.

Stuart drew a tight fist and made direct contact with the man's jaw with a thundering blow.

Blood flew from his lips and spattered onto his tan jacket as the drunk dropped to the floor, cursing loudly.

Stuart rubbed his knuckles and waited for the man to get up. Two brawny security men closed in and separated them. He turned to Cindy and saw her astonished expression with a slack jaw and bulging eyes.

He ran his fingers through his hair. "Let's get our table and enjoy the evening."

"Are you all right?" She rubbed his hand. "You're hurt. Your knuckles are bleeding. I can't believe what just happened. I don't know what to say." She took a tissue from her purse and pressed it to the cuts on his hand.

"No one should treat a woman like that—as if she's a piece of meat. I hope his jaw hurts." His hands shook and he was still angry.

I don't want this incident to spoil her outing.

Still breathing hard, he gazed at her tenderly. "Come on, let's get on with our evening and forget about it."

As they reached their table Stuart turned and looked back. The rowdy man had been escorted out. Patrons focused on them and spoke softly, clearly discussing Stuart's actions.

Will he be waiting for me when we leave? If he is, I'll deal with it then.

He pulled the chair out for her, and she brushed the hair from her shoulders as she sat down.

"This place is perfect." Cindy had to yell to be heard. "I'm so sorry I was the cause of that." She pointed to his wounds.

He cupped his hand to his ear to hear and simultaneously focused on her mouth to read her words. "Glad you like it. Don't worry about my cuts. He deserved it."

"Do you want to dance?" She glanced at the dance floor and then back at him.

His voice strained to be heard, "Let's order a drink first. They serve any American cocktail."

"I guessed that by the selection of American music." She tapped her foot in rhythm. "I'll have a Pina Colada," she shouted.

Stuart caught the eye of a waitress and talked close to her ear. She scribbled down their request on her pad and left. He dabbed at the cuts on his knuckles with the tissue. They seemed to have stopped bleeding.

Cindy glanced around the room as if capturing new memories in her mind's eye. A few minutes later the girl returned with their order, placing the drinks and a few napkins on the small circular table.

Cindy asked in a raised voice. "What are you drinking?"

"Scotch rocks."

I wish I knew what she's running from. Vic or JC? Am I reading too much into her reactions?

"That's an American drink." She took a large swallow of the creamy, icy drink.

"Actually, it's from Scotland. Quite popular in the UK as well as America."

Is Cindy making small talk or does she really care about what I like?

"Yes. I remember Mom saying something like that." The music stopped. She adjusted her voice to a lower tone. "I like good tasting cocktails. Never did like the taste of straight liquor."

"Scotch is usually an acquired taste." *I wish she would open up to me. Her joviality seems forced somehow.* He pointed to her drink. "I enjoy tropical cocktails, too." He looked at the vacant dance floor. "Do you want to dance when the music restarts? I'm not too bad at dancing."

"Maybe not. I'm a bit tired after that unplanned swim in the canal this afternoon." She took another sip, then bit her bottom lip. "What else are you not too bad at? Care to share?"

She's teasing again. Why? What does she want from me?

"I'm good, even excellent at a lot of things …. Things that you say you're not interested in—at least you have said in the past. Has that changed?"

"I have no idea what you mean." She winked.

She's toying with me, like a cat with a mouse before the end.

"Mon Dieu! You know every bit of what you're doing. If I didn't know better, I'd think you were born and bred one hundred percent French."

"I am French," she conceded. "At least fifty percent. Mom's all French."

"I knew it!" *That explains some of her coquette nature.* "You seem very proud of your non-French heritage."

"I am." She clipped her words. "The other half is English."

"What a combination!" Stuart chuckled. "The English and French haven't always been friends. Maybe that accounts for the war that wages inside of you—the push and pull against yourself trying to find out who you truly are."

"There's no such war." She folded her arms across her chest and pouted. "You think you know me—know everything about me—and you don't."

"Cindy, I make no assumptions." *She's unfolding her arms. Is she softening?* "You are far too complex for any man to know you in a few days' time. Your mystique would require a lifetime of love and understanding, and then I doubt that all would be known to such an honored man."

Stuart saw the glistening of tears fill her eyes. A tear fell. He wiped it with his handkerchief.

I didn't want to upset her. What is it that is causing her so much pain? Will I ever have a chance to be in her life and make a difference? She needs a man of substance. Cindy needs me and not Jean-Claude.

"Stu," she reached for his hand across the table, "let's leave and have a nice walk back to the hotel." Cindy took a deep breath. "We have a long train ride in the morning and I want to get to bed early …. I need to feel loved and comforted." He went to speak. She put her finger to his lips. "Don't say a word. I want to feel your arms around me."

Is this another game? What does she mean by "comforted"? The comfort of a friend? Or a lover?

Thirty - One

JOE SAT IN his favorite Italian restaurant in the Bel-Air area of Los Angeles. A bowl of spaghetti and meatballs sat before him. A small pitcher of beer rested on a paper napkin. He drank his ice-cold brew in large swallows from a frosty mug. His mind played on his worry involving Cindy and Jean-Claude.

What if this guy is playin' her, which I'm sure he is, and she gets hooked on drugs? A new stress for Taylor. Taylor has a bum heart. Lar could end up a widower.

His cell phone rang jarring his thoughts. He looked at the caller ID.

"How goes it, Sal?" Joe twirled a forkful of spaghetti.

"Same old shit, just a different source." The sound of a puff from a cigarette came over the receiver. "Got some info on LeGrand's son, Jean-Claude."

"Shoot. Don't tease me like those hookers on Hollywood Boulevard." He chewed the spaghetti and spoke with his mouth half full. "Any bad crap?"

"Not sure." New York City's honking horns and street noise filled Joe's ears.

"What the hell do you mean 'not sure'? Work with me here, Sal." He took a large swallow of beer.

"I had to call in a lot of favors to get any dope on this jerk." Joe heard his friend's deep breath. "It wasn't all that easy to get what I learned."

"Out with it. I'm gettin' fuckin' frustrated. Is Cindy in trouble or not?" He tapped his fingers rapidly on the table.

"Looks like there's a connection between Jean-Claude and this guy called Maurice. Seems Maurice is a runner of sorts—like what I do—only doin' it for LeGrand. Now Maurice is in tight with Guy Cloutier." Joe listened intently and dropped his fork in his food. "This Guy person works for a head man known as Maçon. Everyone knows that's not his legit name. Guy is a button man and made his bones years ago—enjoys doin' hits—a real mechanic."

Joe's jaw dropped as his eyes grew large. *Oh my God! I never envisioned this!*

"Has Guy had any contact with LeGrand?" Joe pushed his plate farther away and grabbed his beer.

"None. The only contact is with Maurice." Sal sounded excited. "Maurice and Guy are both dealers—crack cocaine is their candy—called tac-tac in Paris. LeGrand might be in the same action—if not dealin', then is certainly a customer. I mean, if he ain't usin' then why would Maurice be so buddy-buddy with him?"

"You got proof?" Joe took another swallow of beer.

"How in hell am I gonna get proof? I'm not in Paris and my contacts don't send no photos over the Net." He paused. "All I can say is I got reliable intel from a reliable source."

"Anythin' else?" Joe's brow deepened with ruts.

"He's a freak." Sal coughed loudly.

"How? S&M?" Joe added, "You need to lay off those damn cigarettes."

"Yeah. Been tryin' …. He likes to have his dames in submission—ties 'em up, likes to force the screwin' on 'em." Joe heard his friend drag on a cigarette. "No real harm to 'em—at least no charges filed. Guess he gets the willin' type that like that sorta thing."

"Has he gotten any of these women hooked on crack?" Joe pulled his plate of spaghetti closer to the table edge. "He might want to bring in more customers to help pay for his drug bills."

"Don't know nothin' 'bout that. It could happen." Sal sighed. "Don't y' think Cindy is too smart for that? She's not a kid in school lookin' for the next new high."

"I sure hope so." Joe rubbed his chin. "From what I saw of her, she seemed pretty levelheaded. She did act nutty over Jean-Claude—like a fifteen-year-old girl with a teen idol. That's why Taylor is so worried. Cindy just picked up and decided to live with him—don't know if he invited her or not to his place."

"That's a bag load of shit to dump on her mom." He paused. "They on the outs or somethin'?"

"Been bad blood since Paul." Joe chewed his spaghetti as he talked. "She never got over her father bein' out of her life."

Joe heard swearing drivers over the phone as Sal talked. "Y' want me to keep diggin'?"

"Yeah. Keep your nose to the ground." Joe looked outward with a vacant stare.

"Got it. Later."

What type of shit has she gotten herself into? Taylor will be crushed if anythin' happens to her. Should I tell Lar, or keep this to myself?

~~***~~

The walk back to Hôtel l'Isle de Palais provided a relaxing and pleasant respite from the energetic atmosphere of Le Garage. The full moon, supplemented by the old-world style lamplight lit the way. Stuart took Cindy's hand and hoped her less-than-positive earlier response had melted into one of welcoming his touch.

"We're having a nice stroll." He inclined his head to see her face. "A tranquil ending for a couple of friends."

"Or could be lovers ... someday." A flirting smile curled at her lips. "I've never had a man stand up for me the way you did in there. It feels good to know you care that much about me."

"Of course I wouldn't ignore anyone insulting you—by words or otherwise." He arched an eyebrow. "Your coquette nature must be ingrained, like the beautiful vein running through a piece of marble—always intriguing and yet steadfast." His thumb stroked her index finger as their hands remained clasped.

"I can't help it." She held her head down looking at the pavement. "Most of the time I don't think about what I'm saying—it just comes out."

"That's what's so charming." They rounded the corner and crossed the footbridge. "Your spontaneity is alluring. You don't work at being who you think you should be. There is no pretense."

"You hold me in high regard, dear friend." She let go of his hand as he opened the door to the hotel.

A little while later in their room, Cindy came from the bathroom in her nightshirt.

Stuart, wearing only his shorts, flashed her a smile as she walked to the edge of the bed. He stood there holding the four pillows in preparation to place between them and reinforce his restraint from touching her. She had made her intentions known during dinner and at Le Garage, and he didn't want to pressure her.

She turned down the sheets, and climbed into bed. As she reached over to turn off the bedside lamp, her shirt raised up and exposed the lower part of her buttocks.

Does she know I can see part of her derrière? If she does, she doesn't seem to care.

Only the filtered moonlight through the balcony sheers disturbed the darkness. He hoped she wouldn't be turned off by the condom on the night table.

Stuart cleared his throat. "Do we need these?" He still held the pillows.

"For what?" Her voice sounded as that of an innocent child.

"Temptation." He cleared his throat again. "I don't want us to do anything you don't want to do …. You mean too much to me. I don't want to risk losing your friendship."

"You are very unselfish, Stu." She patted his side of the bed. "Come to bed and let's not think of possible regrets."

"Are you saying … saying that you want me as more than a friend?" He swallowed the golf ball-sized lump in his throat, and tossed the pillows to the side.

"If we spend the night analyzing every word we say, the night will be lost." She reached her arms out to him.

Stuart slid into bed and wrapped his arms around her. She snuggled close to his chest. His hand caressed the softness of her shoulder as he kissed her hairline. His gentle kisses traveled to her neck and then to her lips. She opened her mouth eagerly, as if swept away by a longing. Their tongues joined in passion as the physical manifestation of his desire grew unyielding against her thigh.

Her fingers ran across the hair on his chest. She breathed deeply as his kisses went from her lips to her neck. Her soft moan encouraged his advances. He caressed her breast softly, and then more firmly. His mouth teased her nipples. She toyed with the hair at the back of his neck.

Stuart kissed her abdomen as his hand caressed her inner thigh, traveling slowly upward.

"Stop it!" Cindy rolled away from him. "I can't." She buried her face in a pillow, muffling her sobs.

"What did I do wrong?"

Poor Cindy. She must be in some kind of emotional hell.

"It's not you." She turned to him. "It's me. I should've never let us go so far."

"Is it Jean-Claude? You're feeling guilty?" Stuart handed her a tissue from the night table.

"No. Not guilt." She took the tissue, wiped her eyes and blew her nose. "It's a lot of things, but not guilt. You've never made me feel guilty—not once."

"Want to talk about it? You might feel better. Things seem better after they're out in the open."

I want to make her troubles go away. I feel so helpless.

"I haven't been fair with you, JC, my mom." Her chest heaved as if holding back a sob. "A few days ago I spoke with Mom. Oh God, this is hard for me."

"Go on, Cindy." He held her hand.

"Well, that bastard, Vic, he, he … filed for divorce." She cried into his chest. "He dumped me without a word."

"Didn't he contact you at all since your separation?"

What a cad!

"He only called for money—twice." She blew her nose again. He handed her another tissue. "I've been dumped."

"But, you were the one who left him." He stroked her hair. "You made the first move."

"That's not the same." She looked up at him. "He ended it officially. He's ready to move on."

"Isn't that what you did?" He caressed her cheek. "You decided to remain in Paris and live with Jean-Claude."

"But I didn't do it for the right reasons." Stuart offered her a glass of water from the night table. "I was acting out in a horrible way—like a spoiled child having a temper tantrum."

Her confusion goes deeper than I imagined.

"How do you feel now? Do you—are you in love with Jean-Claude?"

She took a sip of water. "I don't know how I feel. Confused, hurt, remorseful—yet I can't see how Vic and I could go on—not the way things were. And as to JC, I think I love him."

"You *think* you love him?" *She's in so much pain.*

"No." She bit her bottom lip as if strengthening her words would convince herself. "I *must* love him. I've invested too much of myself not to love him."

"Are you certain you shouldn't reach out to Vic?" *I hate saying these words.*

"He's got an addiction. Gambling." She looked up at him with a hopeless expression. "He won't seek help. He doesn't believe he's addicted. There are other things. He was … He abused me. When I was ten weeks pregnant we had a terrible argument, He wanted money—I wouldn't give him any more and …" She wiped her streaming tears. "He beat me and I lost the baby." A sob hung in her throat as her chest heaved. "He never cared that I lost the baby."

Her sobs choked her throat. "I never told Mom about my pregnancy and losing the baby."

That bastard! Drawn and quartering is too good for him.

"There's no excuse for what he's done to you. Yet I have no right to judge Vic." He drew her closer to his chest. "Denial is so very true for anyone suffering, struggling with a dependence—alcohol, drugs, gambling. Abuse often happens, too."

This explains so much about her teasing behavior. She's lost. Cindy plays the coquette as a way to reach out for help.

"I don't know myself. I don't know what I want." She rubbed her tear-drenched cheek against his hand. "I don't know what to do about JC. I've been unfair to him."

"In what way?"

I hate having to talk this honestly and supporting that sleazy singer.

"I moved in on him. He never invited me to live at his place." Cindy let out a ragged sigh. "I used him to hurt Mom and Larry—acted as a defiant teenager getting back at my parents."

"Don't be so hard on yourself." He kissed the top of her head. "You were in emotional shock, and are still in shock. The heart doesn't heal with one impetuous affair."

"When will this be over for me?" She looked up at him again.

"I don't know." His fingers glided along the side of her neck. "You will love again. And when you do, it will be the right man for you—a man who will be worthy of your gentle nature and loving heart. Don't rush it. Don't close your heart to happiness."

I can only hope one day she will see me as her right man—the one to live in her life.

Thirty - Two

MONIQUE FAVREAU WATCHED Jean-Claude refill his wine glass from the bottle of red sitting next to a selection of chèvre on her coffee table. Her humble apartment in Montmartre cloaked her extensive modeling income from one of the most famous couture houses in Paris on *avenue Montaigne*. She had been told her striking looks and blond hair created a cross between the youth of two timeless beauties of Catherine Deneuve and Grace Kelly.

"Does your new play toy know where you are?" She tapped her cigarette on the edge of the ashtray.

"No." He cut off a piece of cheese and spread it on a piece of crusty French bread. "I intend to keep it that way. She doesn't need to know I've been with you for the past two days or so."

"What if she asks questions?"

Can this American handle his bizarre tastes?

"That doesn't matter." Jean-Claude chewed and then swallowed the morsel. "I'll tell her I've been held up in a recording studio ... putting out the next hit album."

"She might not be satisfied with your secrecy." Monique took a sip of wine. "Americans want answers, especially women."

"I can handle her." He wiped his red nose with a handkerchief and then took his glass. "The thicker my accent, the more she succumbs to my wishes."

"Aren't you glad you can't manipulate me?" Her finger played with his ear. "I'm more of a challenge. That's why no matter how many part-time lovers you take, you always come back to me."

"I only come back because you won't let me put my mark on you." He winked and pointed to her blemish-free ankles and wrists. "I thrive on a challenge."

"I would've thought that my refusal would be no fight for you. You usually force your intentions—painful or not." Her fingers traveled to the hair behind his ear.

"C'est vrai, mon amour. You speak the truth. But," he took her hand and kissed her fingertips, "if I did that, where would your career be? A model with red marks at the ankles and wrists doesn't make for a pleasing impression to the client. You'd never see the catwalk again."

"That's one of the reasons I allow you to float in and out of my life—you respect what we have." She leaned closer and put her lips near his. "—a friendship that endures all your flirtations and affairs. You tire of them and return to me."

"As long as you keep your looks." His lips brushed against hers.

"Why do you tease me so?" *I love his games.* "Why don't you take me now?"

"You're not hungry enough." His sly smile intrigued her as she moaned when his hand crept up her skirt. "I want you to need me so badly that you use all your strength not to scream."

His fingers hit his desired mark. Monique moaned and spread her legs slightly. "Let's go to the bedroom."

She felt his hot breath on her neck as he manipulated her thong panties. "No. Here. I want you here." He panted.

Monique unzipped his pants and reached inside. Her fingers found his firm arousal. "Take me now."

His rough grasps tore her panties free. In one swift movement, they were one. Monique knew better than to deny him. That would be dangerous.

~~***~~

Cindy opened the door to Jean-Claude's apartment as quietly as she could. She heard no sounds as she tiptoed across the threshold and wheeled her carry-on behind her. She decided to go directly to the bedroom and hoped he wouldn't be there. The last thing she wanted was discovery, not when her emotions were in such turmoil.

I have no idea why I would think he would be upset if I went for a little trip. After all, he left first, and he hasn't been demanding or jealous.

She lifted the suitcase and placed it on the bed. As she unpacked her under things out of it, a brochure fell from her hands and landed by her feet. She picked it up and stared at the glossy photo of a lake in front of beautiful mountain peaks. Her fingers grazed over the image. A wistful look came to her.

I had such a wonderful time with Stu. I was as happy with him as when JC took me to The Ivy. Why should I make that comparison? JC is special. Stu is just a friend.

Cindy put her emergency money from her cosmetic bag back into the secret compartment of her purse.

I never thanked Mom properly for the cash. I wish things were easier between us. I don't know if I'll ever be able to cross that bridge—the gap just seems too wide.

Cindy gathered the few soiled items along with her toiletries and placed the clothes in the separate hamper Jean-Claude had set up for her in the bathroom. She opened the mirrored medicine cabinet to stow her toothbrush and paste. Closing the cabinet door, she caught sight of something. White powder.

Hmm, looks like baby powder, maybe foot powder. I've seen it in here before. Does JC have a rash? I never noticed. Yet I never paid attention to his every nook and crease. I better not ask him. That could be embarrassing.

She rubbed the back of her neck and studied her eyes in the mirror. They seemed puffy and irritated to her. Her throat was a bit scratchy and a dull ache had settled behind her eyes. Tea with honey might be in order. She hoped Jean-Claude wouldn't be out of nature's sweetener. She truly didn't feel up to walking all the way to Monoprix on the corner of *rue des Pyramides* and *avenue de l'Opéra*.

Cindy took the shortcut to the kitchen, bypassing the living room and searched the cupboards.

I bet I caught a cold from being drenched in that canal .... That was a nice memory, though. She smiled as she remembered the frustrated and yet boyish expression on Stuart's face. She took a cup from a hook under the cabinet, filled it with water and placed it in the microwave oven.

After preparing her honeyed tea, she mindlessly ambled into the living room, intending to lie down.

"Where have you been?" His voice was low, with a granite edge. He stood within striking distance of her.

Cindy nearly dropped the cup as her jaw slackened. "Wha, what do you mean?" She felt inner trembling and her stomach tightened. "When did you come in? I didn't hear the door open or close."

"I've been here all this time ... waiting for you." He clenched his fists at his sides.

"I-I went on a little trip for a day or so." She backed up a few steps. "You were gone and didn't tell me where you were."

"Don't get cute with me." His eyes widened with controlled anger. "You are living with me, sharing my bed, eating my food. I deserve—no, I demand respect."

"You never said I had to account to you for where I go and what I do." She stood straighter as her courage mounted.

"I told you back in Bel-Air that I have rules." He whipped his e-cigarette from his shirt pocket and took a long drag.

"And I told *you* that I have rules, too." She took a step closer to him, disguising her inner fears. "I can leave anytime you want."

I hope he doesn't take me up on that. Where would I go?

"Why do you want to torment me and threaten to leave?" His voice softened as he turned to sit on the sofa.

"I don't want to leave." *What game is he playing? Now he's acting hurt?* She walked over to him. "I said those words because I feared you were tired of me."

"Have I ever said I was tired of you, or I didn't want you around?" He looked crestfallen as his shoulders slumped forward.

Cindy sat in the chair opposite him. "But when you raise your voice or look angry at me, what else am I to think?" She sipped her tea. "Sometimes you nearly frighten me."

Jean-Claude blew his nose in a tissue. "I'm French. I get emotional. You wouldn't ask a leopard to remove its spots—you can't ask me to change my nature."

"I'm not asking you to change your nature ... merely add a little consideration into the equation." He looked confused as if not comprehending her words. "I mean to say, don't act angry with me, and question me as if I did something wrong." She took a deep breath. "JC, you hurt my feelings. When people care for each other they don't purposely go out of their way to cause pain by words or any other way."

I hope he's understanding me.

"Your feelings?" His back stiffened. "What about my feelings?"

"I care about your feelings." Her voice softened to a near whisper.

"You didn't leave me one note as to where you went." He sneered back at her. "How do you know I wasn't calling all the emergency centers in Paris? Wondering if you were in some terrible accident?" He rested his elbows on his knees as he leaned closer to her, as if trying to reach out to her. "You don't know the language, you don't know the city. Anything, and I mean *anything* could have happened to you."

"I had no idea." She got up, walked around the table and slid onto the sofa beside him. "I'm so sorry, JC." She snuggled to his shoulder. *He's so caring and I nearly cheated on him with Stu. And he does care. He really does.* "Please forgive me, JC. I didn't think you would care that much."

"You hurt me deeply." He took a firm hold of her wrists. "You were a very bad little girl."

She winced at his grip. "JC, let go. I don't like this."

"You don't?" He showed a Cheshire smile. "I recall you liking restraint before in the club's men's room."

"That was different." She squirmed and twisted her wrists, and noticed the red impressions he inflicted on her. "It was in public. I was lost in the danger."

"Danger doesn't always have to be in public." His mouth was close to her ear. "Danger can happen anywhere—even here."

Cindy writhed free of him. She glared "I'm serious, JC. Domination holds no thrill for me. It is humiliating and painful to both body and soul." She took a deep breath as she adjusted her shirt. "If you really loved me, you wouldn't want to control me."

"I never said I loved you." He stiffened with an air of authority. "I will remind you again. If you don't live with me, where will you go? Back to Mama and Larry?" His chuckle held a sarcastic quality. "That's not very adult—more like a teenage girl running from a boy who moved too fast."

"Don't try those mind games on me." Cindy stood up and backed away with a defiant shake of her head. "I'm a grown woman."

He doesn't love me. That's what he means, isn't it?

"Not grown enough, it appears." His eyes softened. "I'm sorry. I don't want to argue. I want to make love to you."

"I don't understand you."

He's acting odd. His mood is running hot and cold. What gives?

"There is nothing to understand." Jean-Claude patted the seat. "Come, sit here and let me show you how much I care."

"What if I don't?"

Will he try to tie me up? Besides sex, what else does JC want?

"Then I might leave, or I could see someone else." His smile lasted a moment too long.

He stood and took one stride toward her. Cindy inched back and gripped the chair to steady her balance.

What is he going to do now?

"If you are afraid of me, what's the point?" Reserved anger lined his face. "What's the point of any of it." He went to the hall closet and grabbed his jacket. "I'm going out."

"I noticed your English has improved. What's up with that?" She huffed. "Where are you going?"

Is he going to come back and kick me out?

His eyebrows rose in surprise. "Do you truly care? I don't play with little girls. I thought you were a woman."

"I am a woman!" She raised her voice as he left, slamming the door. "I don't play games. I play for keeps."

Cindy slumped on the sofa. Confusion consumed her and her symptoms of coming down with a cold reminded her she didn't feel much better.

What in hell just happened? He's angry one minute and then wants to make love the next. He's so moody, I don't know what to expect from him from one moment to the next. Maybe he does care and that's why he's angry. He said he didn't love me. Is he going to the arms of another? I don't want to go to Stu. I don't know how JC would react if he got wind of that.

Should I swallow my pride and call Mom?

I'll have to make a decision soon.

Thirty - Three

"BACK SO SOON?" Monique greeted Jean-Claude with a warm and assuming smile. "I expected you five minutes from now."

"You are so self-assured." He tossed his jacket on a vacant chair. Monique followed him into the kitchen. "Better to be self-assured than self-absorbed as some I know."

Did he and Cindy argue?

He opened the small refrigerator door, took out a bottle of water, unscrewed the top, and quenched his thirst with a couple large gulps.

Brushing beside her, he sat down on the sofa, resting the ankle of one leg onto the knee of the other. "Cindy and I had a disagreement. She doesn't interest me as much. Before you start, I don't want to talk about it." He sighed. "So, what's on your agenda? A bit of play?"

She shrugged. "I don't have a modeling gig for a few days. I'm free."

Jean-Claude glanced at the white powder laid out in neat thin lines on the small mirror on the coffee table. "Been doing a little tac-tac to suppress the appetite? Or suppress the loneliness?"

"You know me so well." She sat down beside him. "No. Not yet." She snuggled to him. "Now you're here, I might not need it."

"Don't make more of what we have than what it is." He pulled out the e-cigarette from his shirt pocket and took a couple of deep drags.

"What do we have?" She sniffed, and took a tissue to her nose.

"Friendship. A few side benefits add to our bond." He extended his arm around her shoulder and drew her closer.

"Don't you ever want to have a woman in your life to grow old with?" She took a drag from his faux cigarette, then shook her head. "I'll never get used to those things … back to what I said—do you see yourself with just one woman?"

"Why should I when I have you?" He laughed. "No one could measure up to the legendary Monique—queen of the runway—electric blue eyes and gossamer blond hair."

"You're making fun of me." Her finger traced a design on his knee. "I'm trying to be serious."

He stared at her. "I am serious. You're very special to me—I just don't know how much."

Monique took a swallow from his water bottle. "Why don't you ever tie me down when we make love—like you do to the other women?"

"I care about you. I already told you that answer—runway likes no marks." His expression was as if she should know the answer. "What we have works for us—works for me, anyway." He cleared his throat. "Don't get serious on me. I want no shackles."

"I've never done that to you." She reached for a cigarette from the table and took the lighter. "I've never made any demands. You go and see whoever, whenever, and wherever you want."

"And that's precisely why I always return to you." He stroked her cheek. "If I really think hard about us, I might find you mean more than I care to admit—and that could be the end of what we have."

"Don't think about it then." Monique started to get up. "I think we should express our feelings in a more physical way." She strolled down the short hallway toward the bedroom. "I'm always ready for your adoration."

Jean-Claude started unbuttoning his shirt as he followed her. By the time she reached the doorway, only her bra and panties clothed her.

~~***~~

In slim-fitting jeans and an oversized shirt, Cindy followed the sidewalk of *rue Saint Roch*. She looked left to Jardin des Tuileries. No. The park was too cheerful for her current disposition. She had just experienced Jean-Claude's anger, which left her emotions raw and ripe for further injury.

On the corner of *rue des Pyramides* and *rue d'Argenteuil*, a bright green-outlined flashing cross told her she had found the pharmacy. The bells on the door informed the sales clerks they had a new customer. Cindy rummaged through her pocketbook and hauled out the French phrase book. Flipping the pages, she found the section covering medical needs.

Her scratchy throat had turned into a full-fledged soreness that radiated to her ears when she swallowed and it hurt when she talked. She searched for the appropriate sentence in the book, and spoke slowly, trying to enunciate the words the best she knew. "J'ai mal à la gorge." She pointed to her throat. "I have a sore throat."

"Ah, oui." The pharmacist smiled and handed her a pamphlet

giving instructions on how not to spread a cold. "I speak English, mademoiselle. Do you have a French national health card?"

Cindy shook her head.

The woman paused a moment as if shifting her thoughts into English. "How long have you had this sore throat? Are you spitting up any blood? Have you had a fever? Any aches and pains in the joints?"

"My eyes ache and my throat is very painful—it hurts to swallow." Cindy looked behind the pharmacist at the neatly labeled drawers. She noticed that even common over-the-counter remedies were not displayed out in the open.

The French certainly regulate medicines. I can't even grab a bottle of cough syrup or aspirin without asking for it.

The medical professional opened a couple of drawers behind the counter, and placed a bottle of cough elixir, and an aerosol throat spray in front of Cindy.

"That is sixty-seven euros and eighty-eight cents." She placed the items in a small white paper bag while Cindy retrieved her wallet from her purse. *Over the counter medicine ain't cheap.* The pharmacist briefly ran down the do's and don'ts of taking the medication, and handed her an English information sheet that explained when it would be necessary to seek out a doctor's care.

Cindy managed a "Merci" as she handed over the exact amount. When she opened the door to leave, the woman called out, "Bonne chance."

She walked one block and turned left onto *avenue de l'Opéra*. The artistic window displays didn't interest her. Her less-than-happy mood, peppered with Jean-Claude's outbursts added to the uncertainty of her future.

What have I done wrong? Why can't JC say how much he cares? He must care deeply for me. If he didn't, then why his sudden anger? If he didn't love me, my little trip wouldn't have upset him. He's jealous. There must be a way to get him to open up.

Thirty - Four

MID-AFTERNOON IN the bookstore, Stuart placed the harness on the cat. Hugo purred loudly, seemingly eager for a walk. This was a habit he had started when Hugo had been a kitten. He had always believed socialization at an early age was key for a well-mannered pet. He attached the leash. Hugo rubbed up against his legs and reached up with a paw.

"Ready for a nice walk?"

The cat led the way, and glanced back at Stuart after a dozen steps, as if checking that his "daddy" was still there. They stepped onto *rue de Rivoli* and walked two blocks back to *rue Castiglione* before heading to place Vendôme. Tourists admiring the expensive watches, necklaces, rings, and the like crowded the famous square.

"This is your favorite spot," Stuart said. "Everyone stops to pet you."

Hugo looked up at him, meowed, and flicked his tail from side-to-side.

As they strolled along the square, Stuart smiled and paused to allow admiring strangers to pat and praise the feline. When they reached *rue de la Paix*, he picked the cat up and carried him to the corner that took them onto *place de l'Opéra*.

Feeling a treat was the order of the day, Stuart chose a seat in the outside dining area of expensive Café de la Paix. He had just settled, with Hugo curled up in his lap, when the image of a young woman caught the corner of his eye. He turned and saw it was Cindy. The waiter came to his table and he ordered café express double and a carafe of water.

Stuart took an abandoned Le Figaro newspaper from the seat next to him, and pretended to read an article.

Should I go over to her? She looks upset. Her eyes and nose are red. Has she been crying? Did Jean-Claude do this?

He noticed her coughing and taking a sip from a bottle she had pulled from a paper bag.

What is she taking? Something he gave her? What if it's a drug of some kind?

He felt Hugo gently "knead bread" on his lap with his claws completely concealed, and he automatically petted the cat.

The waiter brought his order and a bowl of water for Hugo.

Stuart smiled with the customary "merci" response. He glanced back in Cindy's direction. Her eyes appeared out of focus.

Should I go over to her? I don't think she saw me.

He poured water into a glass and then took a sip of his coffee.

Jean-Claude is not all what he seems. I can feel it. Still, she thinks she loves him, and there's the recent divorce she's dealing with. No. The decision has to come from her. I can't influence her feelings nor her choices.

He returned his attention to the newspaper and fought his desire to make contact.

Moments later, a pair of open-toed sandals and the hemline of a pair of jeans caught his attention. He glanced up at her face and noticed the signs of fatigue.

"Cindy," he pulled a chair out from his table, "please join me for a drink." He gestured to the waiter.

"I'm not feeling too well." She hesitated, then sat down. "I don't want to give you whatever I caught." She coughed into a tissue. Hugo crawled over to her lap.

"Not a problem." The waiter appeared. Stuart ordered tea and honey for her. "I rarely catch colds. It must be because of all the vitamin supplements I take."

"I think getting wet in that canal gave me this cold." She took a lozenge from her purse and popped it into her mouth.

"What you need is a good dose of steam." The waiter brought her tea. "My mama swears by that remedy."

"I don't think JC has anything that will produce steam, except for a pot of boiling water." She chuckled. "And I'm not about to stick my head over a pot on the stove."

"Drink your tea. I'll take you back to my place." Stuart estimated the bill, took out his billfold and placed euros on the table, secured under the water carafe. "It's not far from here. I have a steamer for colds."

The waiter appeared with the check. He took the money from the table and offered the change. Stuart waved his hand as a signal for the server to keep the coins as an additional tip.

Cindy touched his hand. "You keep a steam contraption in your bookstore?"

"At my apartment. I told you. I live above the store." He picked up Hugo and held him to his chest.

Cindy finished her tea in one large gulp, stood up and took his hand. "I feel so miserable, I'm ready to try anything at this point.

I wish there was a cure for a cold."

He chuckled. "You and millions of others wish the same."

~~***~~

Cindy blew her nose while Stuart pushed the buttons, releasing the door's lock to the apartment complex on *rue Cambon*. A very small courtyard with plantings of flowers flanked the entry to a communal stairway to an upper level. He led the way with Hugo in his arms.

Stuart unlocked two bolts on a door at the end of a long dark hallway, and waved Cindy in. She stepped to the side to let Stuart and Hugo enter after her.

His entry is so cramped. Is the rest of his home this tiny?

He escorted her to a small living area. Directly opposite was a table and chairs for two. She sat on the loveseat. There was only room for one other chair. To the left, a curtained opening showed an extremely small sink, a tiny under-the-counter refrigerator, and a clothes washer-dryer combination at the end of the counter.

"I don't want to be a bother," she called out while he busied himself in the kitchen.

"Ridiculous." Sounds of him opening cabinets filtered through the rooms. "That's what friends do for each other."

Cindy looked at the modern furnishings and décor. Floor to ceiling windows were flanked by expensive looking drapes that pooled on the floor. A pair of dumbbells rested in the corner on top of a stack of books.

I guess he works out. That's why his chest is so appealing.

She coughed into a tissue. "Where do you sleep?"

"I have a bedroom at the end of the hall with a bathroom. Quite luxurious for an apartment as small as this. Plus, there's a small toilet by the coat closet if you feel the need."

"What about guests?" She found the yellow and orange color scheme cheerful. "Or, don't you have any friends who sleep over?"

"That sofa you're sitting on opens out as a bed." He came from the kitchen with the steamer in hand. "For special guests of the female kind—they share my bed."

"Oh, I see." She watched him plug the steaming unit into a wall socket. "What about a female friend who is not so special—like me?"

Why did I ask that? I have no intention of leaving JC—not when it's so obvious he needs me.

He placed the steamer on the coffee table in front of her. "Those friends usually sleep on this sofa bed."

Gurgling water sounded as the unit heated up. "Sorry. I didn't mean to ask so many questions."

"Pas problème." He sat next to her. "Place your face over the steam and breathe in deeply." He draped the towel over her head to retain the steam.

Her words sounded muffled in her ears. "Stu, you're such a good friend. I'm lucky to have you in my life."

But I don't think JC would feel the same way.

Thirty - Five

AMELIA HOLLINGSWORTH, THE Duchess of Steffenfordshire, touched up her makeup in her lavish Mayfair townhouse. She checked her diamond-studded watch, anticipating a scheduled clandestine liaison with a young admirer, whom she paid handsomely.

Her cell phone rang. She made a face.

Reggie had better not be canceling on me. I'll replace him if he is.

She checked the caller ID.

"Hello, Fréd." She talked as she left her bedroom and made her way down the stairs to the foyer. "It's been a long time since I received a call from Frédéric Millet. Good to hear from you."

"Same here." Paris' street noise sang in her ear. "I need a favor. This friend of Taylor's daughter is looking for his birth parents. His name is Stuart Dumont. He was adopted at birth. Seems to be worried about his family's health history."

"Why call me?" She walked into the living room on the left. "How can I help with that?"

"I immediately thought of you when he said that his mother was in a hospital in Geneva. Said she was too sick to care for him."

"You think Clive had something to do with this?" Her brow wrinkled with worry.

What new hell has he delved into?

"I know this is probably not the case, but I thought it would be worth a try." She heard the pleading in his voice.

"My, my, wouldn't that just jar his lordship's preserves!" A mischievous smile came to her lips. "Clive Bradford, the Duke of Bryningmead, has a rightful heir to the title and estate. He hates to share anything."

"Yes, I know." Fear came from his tone. "Whatever you do, be careful. I need his DNA sample to give to my private investigator friend."

"I'll do what I can." She started for her personal book from her purse. "Is your address the same?"

"Yes. No changes." She heard Frédéric puff a cigarette.

"Fine. I have your information on my mobile phone." She tapped her foot. "It will take some planning, but I'll get it done."

Where is Clive? The club? Home? The laboratory?

"You were a tremendous help with Taylor." He paused. "You saved her life."

"I might be called a lot of names, like being the rogue in the family—but what's right is right." Her jaw set with determination. "No real harm should be done to innocent parties."

Amelia ended the call.

Sleuthing can be fun. I'd love to see Clive get what's due him. She looked at her watch again. *Where is that wicked Reggie? If he's late, I'll give him a good tongue-lashing. Better yet, I'll demand he give me one.*

~~***~~

Stuart and Frédéric enjoyed dinner at Café Marly, under the Richelieu wing of the Louvre's arcades. The trendy restaurant, with its view of the three glass Pyramides, had a reputation for superb quality and excellent menu choices. Chic white slip-covered chairs with maroon cording accents added to the rich feel and ambience. As Stuart perused the menu at their cloth-covered table on the outdoor balcony, he hoped he had taken enough cash from the ATM.

I hate running up debt on a credit card.

"Have you decided? A starter?" Frédéric picked up the wine menu.

Stuart cleared his throat. "I'm not that hungry. I'll have the lamb. You can choose the wine." *Even a cheeseburger is expensive.*

Frédéric continued reading the wine selection. "I'll have the sole. Do you mind drinking a white with the lamb?"

"Not at all." *I hope Fréd doesn't order the most expensive bottle.*

"Stuart, as you probably guessed, I wanted to talk to you about the project of finding your birth mother." He placed the napkin on his lap.

"Go on." *Could he have good news already?* "May I call you Fréd?"

Frédéric nodded. "Only if I may call you Stu?"

"Yes, of course you may."

The waiter came to the table edge. Frédéric gave the order for them both and returned the menus. The server filled their water glasses and left.

"You were saying something about my mother?" Stuart unfolded his napkin and laid it across his lap.

"I do have a private investigator friend who is willing to help you. A DNA test will be required from you—a mouth swab. He will provide the testing materials and give them to me." Frédéric lowered his voice. "It will cost you one thousand euros."

Stuart nearly choked on his mouthful of water. "A thousand, you say?"

"Accurate DNA testing is expensive, and with you having so little information for my friend to go on ... well, that requires more time and expense." Frédéric upturned his palm. "He is very good at what he does."

"Fréd, I'm certain he is." *Is this an expensive con?* "I would have to go to BNP Paribas for the funds. Would a cashier's check be okay?"

"He prefers cash." The waiter poured their wine and left a basket of hard dinner rolls. "But if you're insecure about this. You could give me the check and I would then pay him the cash."

"Still," Stuart leaned forward in his seat, "if he comes up with nothing, then I'm out of pocket for one thousand euros."

"Stu, I trust him completely." Frédéric broke apart a dinner roll. "I know he's honest and wouldn't cheat anyone. He's helped Cindy's mother out of a very dangerous situation."

Should I take this chance? "Fréd, how soon do you need the money?"

"Is a couple of days too soon?" The waiter brought their dishes. "I could call him tomorrow to drop off the swab at my shop and you could do the test there. It would save a lot of time."

"Yes. I could get the money by then." Worry came to Stuart's face. "It almost seems like there's some sort of rush? I've waited all these years wondering about my parents' identity."

"No rush at all." Frédéric shifted forward on his elbows. "From the information you already gave me, I have an instinct that you could have favorable results."

"Don't tease me, Fréd." He cut into his lamb chop. "You've whet my tongue. Tell me more."

"I can't." He squeezed the lemon slice over his sole. "If I'm wrong, I don't want to get your hopes up."

"Now you've aroused my curiosity." He reached for his wine. "You don't play fair, Monsieur Millet."

Frédéric chuckled and raised his glass. "Touché, mon ami. The main thing for you to remember is, that I am fair, especially with my friends—and you *are* my friend."

~~~***~~~

Galleries Lafayette had quickly become Cindy's favorite store. It seemed to her that when most Parisians wanted to sit and think about a trouble or difficult situation, they found a pleasant park bench or a cozy café. She took solace in perusing all the various items on sale, especially since Jean-Claude had stayed out all night after their argument, and she assumed he'd stayed at a friend's home. That upset her greatly.

Shoes were one of her weaknesses. She felt particularly lucky when a pair of Italian-made sandals had a forty-percent off sale tag. They felt like butter on her feet and she believed this treat did far more to improve her cold symptoms than any amount of cough syrup. She still had a cough that hung on, though, and she still felt ill. Her nose required frequent blowing, and her pocketbook nearly overflowed with tissues. The sun was warm on her back and walking always helped calm her nerves and gave her time to think. She decided to take the long way back to Jean-Claude's home.

At the corner of *rue des Pryamides* she walked one block and crossed to *rue Sainte Honoré*. While standing on the corner, waiting for the light to change, her heart jumped, and she gasped out loud.

Is that JC with that blond? It can't be.

She stared hard at them.

It is him. How dare he!

She quickly grabbed her phone and started taking photos of the kissing couple at the café. Then she switched to video function and used the zoom control.

What nerve! I've been faithful to him, turned down Stu, and for what? To be made to look like a fool? Gambling was Vic's mistress. Now JC has a blond! My god! His tongue is halfway to her toes.

Streaming tears left streaks of makeup down her cheeks—her badge of devastation. She couldn't help it. A few passersby watched her and shook their heads with pity.

I don't know what I'll do—but I have to do something. I can't take any more heartbreak.

Angry footsteps took her home, back to Jean-Claude's apartment. She punched the security numbers on the entry pad, ran up the five flights of stairs, down the hall and fumbled with the keys to the locks. Cindy slammed the door, pushing her back to it. A new flood of tears ran down her face. She weakened as her legs gave way and she slid down to the floor. Her strident voice cried out loud, "How could he do this? What's wrong with me? Is every man I care about meant to hurt and use me?" Cindy hugged her knees as she rocked back and forth. Her hair hung in her face.

After a while, she hauled herself to her feet, dried her eyes, and started packing her clothes into her carry-on. She didn't know how long she had been sitting there.

Cindy paused when she heard the door open.

I'm going to give him a piece of my mind. He understands English far better than he lets on.

Her determined footsteps took her to the living room, where Jean-Claude sat on the sofa reading a music magazine.

"Are you all calmed down after your little tantrum last night?" He looked smug and secure.

"My little tantrum?" She grabbed her phone. "My little tantrum? You haven't seen anything yet!"

"Why are you still upset? I spent the night with a friend." He went to kiss her.

Cindy pulled away. "Yeah, a female friend—blond with blue eyes." She tapped the face on the display. "I have video and photos, too. You can't deny this evidence. It's rock solid."

"You must have taken a picture of someone who looks like me." He laughed. "My face isn't that unique."

"Oh no, mister slick. You're not getting out of this one so easily." She scrolled through the photos to find the most incriminating one. "You're a French Don Draper. Most Frenchmen don't look like him."

"Qui? Who? I know of no such person." Jean-Claude looked confused and boyish.

"Don't play the innocent bit with me." She showed him the evidence. Her tears blurred her focus. "And stop being so damn charming. It's not fair."

"Oh, yes. That is Monique." He tilted his head as if he did nothing wrong. "She's a friend. It's a French custom to kiss a friend when meeting."

"You're kissing her on the lips!" *What bullshit is he trying to give me?* Cindy switched to the video function and shoved the phone in his face. "What about this, you bastard?"

Jean-Claude watched the video. His face became somber. "Monique was my lover. I broke up with her for you—you're the one I want. I was trying to let her down gently. I didn't want her to create a scene with you—coming over here and demanding that you move out because of her jealousy."

"From where I stand," Cindy crossed her arms in front of her chest, "that's a damn passionate and heated breakup."

"Cindy, please believe me." He stood and embraced her. "You are the woman for me. If you weren't, I wouldn't have let you stay one night with me."

I want to believe him. Is he telling me the truth, or telling me what I need to hear so he can get what he wants? I don't trust him anymore.

Thirty - Six

DRESSED IN HER newest spring Dior ensemble, complete with gloves, Amelia sashayed into the government laboratory in her usual devil-may-care manner. She was well aware that her exuberance for life and adventuring spirit kept those around her on their toes. Her second cousin, Clive, sat on a stool at the long table, peering into a microscope. Floor-to-ceiling bookcases occupied three of the four walls, with a bank of windows festooning the fourth. An array of papers and manuals rested on top of the counter. Clive didn't look up. His crisp white lab coat reflected his precise nature.

"What do you want, Amelia?" He jotted notes on a pad of paper. "Come to create a new hell in my life? Don't you have enough of your own?"

"I was looking for Alistair." Clive took a swallow from a water bottle near his work. In front of him a group of unopened water containers sat on the bench. "Aren't you afraid of spilling water on your precious notes?"

"I'm not a ruddy twit!" He flashed her a glance. "The ink doesn't bleed, and water won't contaminate anything on this table." He went back to study the slide under the scope. "Your husband's not here. Off in some research library. At least he's out of my hair."

"Well, let me give you a hug. It's been too long since we bonded." She flung her arms around his shoulders. His opened water spilled its contents over his work.

"Bloody hell!" Clive scrambled to clean up the wet mess by pulling off long hanks of paper toweling from the roll at the end of the table. "You have all the grace of an ape. We never hug— not since childhood. Have you gone daft?" He took his wet notes and wiped them down page by page. "Keep your hugging for your toy-boys and whatever other forms of affection you lavish on them."

She took the empty bottle, and discreetly placed it in a zippered plastic bag in her purse while he wiped up the mess.

"I'm so sorry, dear cousin. I meant no harm." She couldn't help her smug expression.

"Why are you looking so devious?" His eyes narrowed. "Amelia, what are you up to? Came here to ruin my day for a bit of fun?"

"You're so smart, Clive." She turned to leave.

"That's an understatement." He leaned on the table with clenched fists, skin white and tight over his knuckles. "The crown elevated me from an earl to a duke because of my genius."

If the crown only knew the truth.

"Of course. It's a pity that you have to lower and inconvenience yourself to deal with us who have less than your stellar intelligence."

"We all have crosses to bear." His words faded as she left the room and closed the door with the most noise she could muster.

Amelia scurried down the steps from the London research building to the sidewalk, crossed the street, and hurried to her car. Her breath caught in her throat, and her heart pounded. Before opening the door, she stood there a moment. She noticed her hands were trembling.

If Clive ever finds out what I'm about to do—it could be deadly for all concerned.

Sitting in the front seat, she took a pre-addressed, large, padded manila envelope from the glove compartment and inserted the plastic bag containing Clive's empty water bottle. She secured the seal.

This should arrive in a couple of days. I hope it leads to some answers.

~~***~~

Larry rested in a chair on the pool patio of his Bel-Air home. Tweeting birds complemented the serenity of the morning. Taylor flipped though a French cookbook seemingly not focusing on a single page. Her fingers tapped incessantly on the arm of the chair. The umbrella-topped table separated them.

"Okay, Tay." He put the morning paper aside. "Out with it. You've been stewing for over an hour. What is it?"

"Been stewing for longer than that." She turned her head toward the opened glass patio doors. "Tim, I'd like some coffee."

"Me, too." Larry returned his attention to her.

Tim's voice sounded from inside. "Sure thing."

Larry picked up his sunglasses from the table. "So, shoot. What's bugging you?"

"Cindy." Her lips thinned. "Isn't it always Cindy?"

"I know you constantly worry about her." He touched the top of her hand. "That worry isn't good for your health. I want you by my side for many years to come."

I hate to see the pain in her eyes.

She looked at him and smiled. "It's been over six weeks since we returned from Paris, and not a word from her—no calls, text, nothing except when I notified her of the divorce proceedings. When Cindy was in Tampa, she was only five hours away. Now being in Paris, she's a good twelve hours from us."

"Do you want me to call Charles LeGrand?" Tim brought their coffee on a tray and placed it on the table, then left. "I need to speak to him about the release of the debut album."

"Do you think he would know anything?" Taylor took her coffee and stirred rapidly. "Isn't he a bit estranged with Jean-Claude, like I am with Cindy?"

"I'm not certain there is that much distance between them." He took the cup to his lips. "It's worth a try. Who knows? Jean-Claude could end up being our son-in-law."

"Heaven forbid!" Taylor took a large swallow of the steaming brew. "He'd be as bad for her as Vic was. She'd be going from the pan into the fire."

"You don't know that for certain." *I should've kept my mouth shut. Now Tay's gonna worry about that.* "I was only joking. I didn't mean to give you more to stew about."

"I know." She grabbed his hand across the table and gave a squeeze. "Please call Charles. Not knowing anything is driving me mad."

He leaned sideways and stroked her cheek. "I'll call him, soon."

When he finished his coffee, Larry went to work in his home studio, which provided privacy, and thickly padded walls prevented others from overhearing his words. He looked at his watch and mentally calculated the time in Paris, then dialed the number. The European ringing tone sounded in his ears. *Charles, pick up, pick up!* He paced in the small ten by thirteen foot room.

"Allô," the male voice answered.

"Charles? Is that you?" Larry sat on a stool.

"Mais oui, mon ami." His voice held a smile. "It is so good to hear from you. Do you have a question about the album?"

"I was wondering about the release date." He adjusted his seat and then pulled on his shirt sleeve.

"Ah, the first week of September. My manager has set the date with your manager. I see no problems." He chuckled. "Has your French improved?"

"Not much. Not more than what was needed for our album." Larry stood and started his pacing habit. "I'm also calling about Cindy and Jean-Claude."

"Jean-Claude?" He sounded worried. "What trouble has he caused?"

Maybe Tay's instincts are on point.

"Is he usually in trouble? Anything serious?"

"Nothing serious." He took a deep breath. "Davis, what has he done to your daughter?"

"I don't know of anything yet. That's why I'm calling." *I have to be careful with him.* "We haven't heard from Cindy since we left Paris. I was wondering if you heard anything on your end."

"Je tu comprends. I understand you." He sighed. "Unfortunately for you and me, Jean-Claude only calls me when in need."

"In need? What kind of need?"

This could be bad. Now I'm starting to worry like Tay.

"Argent! Money, of course." Charles laughed. "Is it not the same the world over? Children always come to the parents for money?"

"Very true." *Does he tap Charles often? Could he be a gambler, like Vic?* "What about the women he dates? There were some photos of him in the press with a blond, and that person wasn't Cindy."

I'm glad Tay didn't see those photos in the rags.

"Oh, that woman must have been Monique." A light laugh escaped.

"Who's Monique?" *Cindy's too fragile to be hurt again.* "Cindy doesn't like to share."

"I don't think he's serious about Monique." A long silence ensued. "Don't worry. Your daughter is safe with Jean-Claude. If she wasn't, I would know."

"Know how?"

He's not reassuring me.

"When Jean-Claude becomes tired with une femme, he asks me to take them in for a few days at my home here on Île Saint Louis." He laughed heartedly. "He uses me to soften the blow."

"I don't mean to sound insulting, Charles—but that sounds rather crass to me and not very respectful to you."

"Respect? That's a quality he doesn't hold for me." His voice softened. "Things have never been good between us, and became even worse after his mother's death."

"I'm sorry to hear that". Larry started pacing again. "Do you think Jean-Claude is the type to settle down with one woman?"

"No. I don't. He takes after me on that trait." He chuckled. "Life is too short for one woman. Why settle with one, and then make all the others unhappy?"

"I like your sense of humor."

Tay was right. His son's a playboy and Cindy is another victim to feed his ego. Doesn't he get enough ego-boost from performing?

"Besides women, does your son have any difficulties?" *I hope I'm not crossing the line with him.*

"None that I know of." His voice grew serious. "Why are you asking these questions, dear friend?"

"Cindy is recently divorced. Her former husband, Vic, was a gambler and put her in a lot of debt." Larry paused his pacing and rubbed his brow. "She's in no shape to have her heart broken. I'm afraid if Jean-Claude breaks from her she might become seriously depressed."

"Oh, mon Dieu! I had no idea of what you are telling me." Charles breathed deeply. "Do you want me to talk to Jean-Claude and explain these facts to him?"

"I don't know if that's such a good idea." *I hope I didn't make things worse.* "He might assume that Cindy called us and your son might think she is talking behind his back—which she didn't."

"Handling Jean-Claude has to be done carefully." His voice lowered to a near whisper. "My son does have a temper, but I've never seen nor heard of him harming any female."

A temper!

"How bad is his temper?"

"He throws things. Might break a vase or a lamp." He hesitated a moment. "I truly don't think you need to worry about Cindy. As I told you earlier, if he was ready for a new woman, Cindy would be my houseguest before I put her on a plane to return home."

"I hope you're correct." Larry sighed deeply. "Please call me with any news. If you speak with Cindy, please tell her to contact her mother and me."

"Certainement, mon ami. I understand a parent's worry. I worry about my son, too."

What mess is Cindy in? Is Jean-Claude someone to be feared? Should I put Joe on this? He's got his PI friend, Sal, who might be able to snoop around. I can't share this with Tay. Should I fly to Paris and bring her back against her will?

Thirty - Seven

FRÉDÉRIC OPENED A box from yesterday's delivery. It was a shipment of new miniature Paris-styled buildings and a new line of miniature houses copied from the ones found in the south of France. He hoped this new selection would boost his sales. Catering to the tastes of tourists was a risky business. What was hot during one season could fall flat the next. The back door entry chimed. He didn't look up nor did he stop removing the bubble wrap and popcorn stuffing.

"Émilie, is that you?" He arranged the miniatures carefully on the floor.

"Oui, c'est moi." She hung her jacket up on the hook just in front of the storage doorway. "What have you got there?"

He glanced up at her. "A new shipment. I hope it will be popular with the tourists. One is never certain these days."

"Has the mail arrived?" She took the feather duster and started her daily duties.

"Not yet." He stood up from kneeling and picked off a piece of lint from his pants' leg. "I'm expecting a package any day now from London. If it arrives when I'm not here, call me right away."

"Mais oui." Émilie adjusted the figurines. "It is important, this package?"

"Extremely." He went to the counter and gathered up the previous sales slips. "I've got to get these sales records to my bookkeeper today. He hates it when I let them accumulate."

The mail carrier opened the door, setting off the chimes. Tall and lean, he stood with a package and a piece of paper in his hand.

"I have a delivery for Monsieur Frédéric Millet and I require a signature." The man stepped toward him.

"I'm he." Frédéric took the package and a pen from the man. He scribbled his autograph on the appropriate line. "Merci."

"Is that the package you told me about?" Émilie stopped her duties. "Is it special? A new product we'll be selling?"

The mail carrier smiled and promptly left.

"It is personal, I think." He tore open the flap and peeked inside. "Nothing to do with business." Frédéric glimpsed at her. "Can you manage till I get back?"

Émilie nodded.

"I've got a personal errand." He took his jacket from the same hook as she had used, then grabbed the newly delivered package. "I shouldn't be long."

Frédéric hurried out the front door and onto *rue de Rivoli*. He headed to his preferred café opposite the Louvre.

It was only nine, and the morning sun created long shadows. Already, the sidewalk was filled up with tourists and locals. The traffic seemed unreasonably congested. It took a long time to clear before allowing him to cross from one block to another. A tourist café was a perfect choice for the privacy he desired. The majority of café patrons at the height of tourist season rarely knew French, and thus lessened his fear of eavesdroppers.

Rounding the corner to Café Carrousel, Frédéric was relieved to see that his favorite table was available. He sat down and took the handset from his pocket, and dialed. He glanced around while he waited for the ring.

"Claude, I've got the sample." A waiter came to the table. Frédéric put his hand over the mouthpiece. "Un café noir et croissant, s'il vous plaît." He returned his attention to his friend, "Sorry about the delay, Claude."

"What type of sample is it? Hair?" His voice sounded far away.

"A water bottle." The waiter brought his order then left. "Will that be enough to go on?"

"It should be." Claude paused as if thinking. "Was there a note from the sender?"

"Wait. Let me check. I didn't think to look. Hold on a minute." Frédéric looked in the package and pulled out a note on expensive stationery. He read it quickly. "It says here that the person obtaining this sample witnessed the subject drinking out of the bottle."

"A hair sample would have been better, but this will work. Might take a little longer to process."

Frédéric lit a cigarette and took a deep drag.

Claude continued, "When will your friend be paying the fee? I can't move further without the cash."

"He said he has to go to the bank for the money." He took a sip of coffee. "When I get the funds from him, I'll have him use the swab you dropped off. I'll make certain I witness him obtaining the specimen in front of me, then I'll call you."

"Fine. I'm still digging on LeGrand. I'll be in touch when I have anything new."

Frédéric hung up. He buttered his croissant and smeared strawberry jam on the surface.

I better call Dumont. I assume the fresher the specimen the better.

He called Stuart and relayed what Claude had told him.

~~***~~

The chime on the bookstore door jangled. Stuart looked up from his desk near the back of the room and met Cindy's eyes. Hugo jumped down off his perch on one of the chairs, and rubbed up against her ankles. She stopped and picked him up, before continuing toward Stuart's desk.

He greeted her with a wide stride and a warm and welcoming smile.

"Well, what brings you this way?" He kissed her cheek as in a typical French greeting. "I see Hugo has made you welcome."

"Is he the only one who's glad to see me?" She kissed the top of Hugo's furry head.

"Of course not." Stuart went to kiss her again.

Cindy waved her hand. "You better not. I still have this cold that doesn't want to go away."

"Paris colds always last longer."

"I got wet in Annecy." She chuckled. "This is an Annecy cold."

"Ah, but your symptoms started in Paris." He took Hugo from her. "Seriously, I do hope you feel better. Are you taking all the remedies from the pharmacy?"

"Yes." She coughed into her sleeve. "I'm well armed."

"If you felt better, I'd invite you to dinner at my place." He looked for her reaction hoping she wouldn't be put off.

"I'm not too sick to enjoy a friend's company." She absently looked around the store. "I hear that most friends meet for dinner at a café or restaurant when in France. To be invited to someone's home is very special."

"You *are* special." *Is she sending a mixed message. Is she off JC? I hate to see her ill.* "I enjoy your company. Besides, that unspoken custom of eating at a café has practical roots. Most apartments are extremely small and would be difficult to do any form of entertaining. Also, the French value their privacy and will usually only invite family into their homes."

"Well then, I must be very special seeing that I've already been to your place." She pulled out a tissue from her bag and wiped her nose.

"How about tonight at eight?"

Cindy, please don't say no.

"Fine. I make no promises as to what shape I'll be in." She sneezed. "I won't be much fun."

~~***~~

Frédéric stood up immediately when Stuart entered, and motioned for him to come to the backroom, leaving Émilie at the front assisting a customer with a purchase.

Closing the curtains to the back entry, Frédéric took Stuart's cash and put it in a large white envelope. He slipped on vinyl gloves, then opened the sealed thick swab from the plastic screw-top container, handed it to Stuart and watched him stroke the inside of his mouth for nearly a minute.

"I hope my money won't go wasted." Stuart gave the specimen to Frédéric. "I thought obtaining cash would be quicker than waiting in line for a cashier's check."

"Stu, cash was a better decision." He secured the swab in the appropriate case it came in. "I don't know when the results will be available. We still have to obtain a specimen from a woman who may be your mother. That could take a lot of time. At least we know where you were born and that's a start."

Stuart nodded. "I trust you. Cindy said you helped her mother a great deal."

"Her mother and I are good friends for many years." They shook hands. "Don't worry. You'll have your answers."

Parting the curtains, he left quickly, presumably back to his bookstore.

~~***~~

Stuart hurried with his inventory check. He repeatedly looked at his watch.

I've got to get to the markets.

He pulled out his billfold from his pocket and checked if he had enough. Stuffing his money back in his front pocket, he called out to his assistant.

"Hélène, I'll be gone the rest of the day. Lock up." He grabbed his canvas market bag and went out through the back door.

The warm early afternoon air transported him back to his childhood, walking home from school on dirt paths lined by colorful wildflowers. He grinned recalling his mother on the porch watering her prized geraniums.

I don't know why I'm thinking about this. It's probably because of what Frédéric just said. There's a woman who could possibly be my birth mother.

His stomach clenched.

Could it really be possible? It seems so surreal after all this time trying to find her. No matter what, Mama is still my mother and I'll always love her and Papa.

Coming upon the market storefronts on *boulevard de la Madeleine*, he spotted a flower shop and on impulse picked up a mixed bouquet for that night's table setting. A few stores down, he chose the oldest and most plump chicken available in the poultry store. His next destination was the green-grocer and the patisserie. Humming in a low tone, with a smile, rushed strides took him back to the bookstore.

His assistant looked up briefly as he entered with his recent grocery purchases. Hugo meowed and followed him out through the back, and to his apartment complex entry. The feline purred loudly, clearly in anticipation of a treat. Stuart rushed through the courtyard, up the steps, and to his front door. Fumbling for his keys, he unlocked the door. Hugo went in first and ran to the kitchen.

"I'm coming," he said to the cat. "Daddy's been shopping. We have a very special guest coming for dinner."

Hugo purred loudly and weaved around his ankles, nearly tripping him while he opened a can of choice tuna, spooned it into a dish and set it on the floor next to a bowl of fresh water. Stuart unpacked the food items while Hugo feasted. He filled a large pot of water and set it on the small stove, turning on the flame to high. He inspected the chicken, and after he was satisfied, placed it in the water. Next he added the vegetables.

I hope this helps her with the cold. I want nothing but the best for her.

He looked down at Hugo. "Cindy is in love with the wrong man. She just doesn't know it yet …. I hope she realizes that before it's too late."

The cat meowed again.

"You're getting another treat after dinner. How about nice a chicken liver, heart, and gizzard? Hmm?"

Hugo tilted his head, meowed, as if he understood, and then reached up with his paw.

Stuart wiped his hands on a towel and placed the small dessert in the under-the-counter refrigerator. Taking a clear bubble-glass vase from an overhead shelf, he filled it halfway with water and placed the flowers in the container, doing his best to arrange them pleasingly. He set the table with the best-mismatched china he could assemble from his flea-market finds, and then stood back and eyed his handiwork.

Hugo pawed his leg as if begging to be picked up. He bent down, lifted the cat and stroked his back. "That's what I love about you … you're more of a pup than a cat." He kissed Hugo's head. "So what do you think, Hugo? Think the lady will like this?" He screwed his face. "I'll tell her the table was set with an eclectic style. No, I better not say anything—best not draw attention to my near poverty years. I hope tonight will turn her heart to me."

Thirty - Eight

STUART FILLED A tumbler with orange juice from a carafe on his coffee table and handed it to Cindy.

"I've never had a cold as bad as this one." She wiped her nose with a tissue while sitting on the loveseat. "Maybe I'm not adjusted to the Parisian weather."

Stuart dispensed wine into his glass.

Purring loudly, Hugo jumped up on Cindy's lap and proceeded to knead her thigh. She automatically stroked his soft fur.

"Have you seen a doctor yet?" He offered her some fresh fruit.

She took a slice of apple and bit into it. A drop of juice ran down her chin. She wiped it with the back of her hand. "If I don't feel better, the doctor will be my next stop. I bet it will be expensive ... I don't have a national health card to offset the costs."

"I'm willing to help you out with the bill."

I hate her being dependent on Jean-Claude.

"I couldn't impose on you like that." She sipped the juice and grimaced as if swallowing hurt her throat.

"It's no imposition. Friends take care of each other." *I don't have a lot of spare money—especially after giving Fréd all those euros. I could always tap my savings account if needed.* He stood up. "I better check on dinner." He watched her from the kitchen doorway.

Cindy got up from the loveseat. Hugo jumped down and looked up at her and raised his paw.

"You sure love to cuddle," she said to him.

"Stu, you set a lovely table." Awaiting dinner, she sat down on the cushioned chair.

The noise of pot covers meeting the counter muffled his voice. "Thanks."

Stuart returned, holding what he prayed would be a cure for her ills.

"Here it is." He placed the dish in front of her. "Piping hot, and I hope ... delicious."

"Awe, Stu," Cindy inhaled the fragrance of the steam rising from the bowl. "You made chicken soup. How did you know I would enjoy this?"

"A lucky guess." He beamed. "I thought the soup would help you to feel better." He inclined his head. "Chicken soup is pretty much the same the world over. Besides, it's also like having a taste of home." He served himself a bowl, then sat across from her at the table.

"You're so thoughtful." She took a spoonful, and blew on it before tasting. "Umm, scrumptious. You did very well my destined-to-be-famous French author."

"Merci, mademoiselle." He laughed. "I'm not an author yet. Lots of work ahead of me. However, I feel I have some talent. Friends seem to like my short stories. Though, friends can be extremely kind and not speak the truth."

"Have more faith in your talent." Cindy pulled off a hunk of bread from the baguette on the plate between them. "If writing is your passion, you should follow it." She took a tissue from her pocket and dabbed her nose. "If you don't mind, please speak in English. I'm not up to doing any mental gymnastics via translations beyond the word merci."

"Of course. English it is …. Back to what you said, following one's passion is very wise advice." *I could listen to her forever.* "Not so easy to follow."

"My stepdad has always lived by those words. He believes them wholeheartedly." She tore off a large piece of bread with her teeth. "His belief has served him very well."

"Yes." Stuart took a sip of his wine. "He's famous in the United States?"

"Extremely." She finished the soup and raised the bowl to him. "See. I ate every last drop."

"Would you like more?" *She likes my cooking!*

"I don't want to put you out and look greedy." She bit her lip. "But, it is delicious. I think I feel better already."

"Say no more." He took her bowl to the tiny kitchen area. *God bless that chicken who gave up her life to make Cindy feel better.* "I always have plenty of chicken soup when I'm feeling sick. My mama swears by its curative powers."

"Your mom seems like a nice person." Hugo jumped up and sat on her lap, resting his head on the table. She petted him affectionately.

Stuart returned. He spotted the cat. "Hugo! You're a bad boy. You know you're not supposed to be at the table."

Hugo meowed pitifully. "I don't mind. He's sweet." Cindy scratched behind his ears. He raised his head and appeared to smile. "See. He likes me petting him."

"He likes the aroma of the chicken is more likely." Stuart went to remove the feline.

"Please don't." She raised her hand. "It's comforting to have him purr and snuggle into me—comforting like your chicken soup."

"If you're certain you don't mind." *She's such an animal lover. Cindy's a good person. Jean-Claude doesn't care about her goodness.* "Let me show you some of his tricks."

"Tricks?" Her eyes widened. "I never heard of a cat doing tricks. They're so independent."

"Not Maine Coon cats." He took a small piece of chicken from his bowl. "Watch."

Stuart called Hugo to him and held the tidbit up in the air above the feline. Hugo sat up on his haunches, reached up with his front legs, and put his paws together as if in prayer. After a moment, Stuart rewarded him.

"He is adorable." Cindy looked amazed. "Does he do any other tricks?"

"Of course he does." *I'm glad Hugo is entertaining her. It eases my tension.*

He made a circular movement with his hands. Hugo lay down and rolled over as a dog would do. Stuart stood up and took a small ball from the cat's toy box. He gave it a slow roll on the floor. Hugo scampered to the toy, retrieved it, then brought it back.

"He's a puppy cat!" Her smile emphasized shining eyes. "I love it! Hugo is very special."

Stuart sat back down at the table. The cat leaped into his lap. "Yes, he's more than special. He's a true friend. No matter how I feel, Hugo seems to understand. Always happy to see me."

"Hugo and I have something in common." She reached for his hand across the table.

He tilted his head and raised an eyebrow. "What's that?"

"I'm always happy to see you. You make me feel good, even with this damn cold." She squeezed his hand.

"Those are pretty words from a pretty lady." He broke from her touch. "Why don't you go over to the sofa? We'll have dessert there."

Cindy dropped into the loveseat, while Hugo followed Stuart to the open kitchen area. Moments later he returned with two pieces of vanilla cake served on plates with forks, and placed them on the coffee table. He slid onto the loveseat beside Cindy and handed her the dessert. The feline curled up on her other side.

"I hope you like what I chose. I didn't want to serve you anything with a lot of milk because of your cold. Milk products might make your nose more stuffy."

What if she wants something more special?

"You did fine, Stu." She inched closer to his side, and took a taste of the cake. Cindy closed her eyes. "Umm, this is delicious. You chose the perfect finish to a great meal."

"You're spoiling him, you know." Stuart chewed. "Hugo. He's bonded to you already."

"Is that true of all coon cats—they love people?" The feline started purring again as if on cue. Cindy put her fork down and petted him.

"Yes." He swallowed. "But he warmed up to you from the first. He's a good judge of character, like his 'daddy'. I have to admit … I spoil him too much."

"Do you indulge in any other ways besides pets?" Her smile turned coy.

"Only people I care about …" His lips came close to hers. "… and love."

She put her fingers to his mouth. "Don't, Stu." Her eyes fixed on his. "I have a cold." Her pause hung in the air. "I haven't broken from JC. I don't know if I will leave him." She put her plate with the half-eaten cake on the table. "If you know nothing else about me, then remember this—I can't become involved with another when I'm in a relationship." She cleared her throat. "I'm a one-man woman."

"I meant no harm." *I hope I didn't push her emotionally away from me.* "Please try to understand. Your honesty compels me to want to be near you … to have you in my life."

"Truthfully," she blushed, "I see nothing special about myself. I'm a typical American woman who has lost her way and not certain how to find the path again."

He put his arm around her shoulder. "I wish we could find that path together."

"That's a journey I have to travel alone." She took a deep breath. "At least until I realize for certain what type of life I want."

"Share with me, Cindy." He kissed her cheek. "Let me help you."

"No." She touched his face gently. "I have to know that my decision is mine, and wasn't influenced by others. My decision has to come from my heart. I can't make life choices based on what others want from me."

"You are misunderstanding me." He gave her shoulder a squeeze. "I only want what is best for you. Yes. I admit, you would make me the happiest man in Paris, in all the world, if you left Jean-Claude and came to me." He laughed with a tinge of disgust. "What would be the point to influence you to my will? In the end you would only resent me, and later hate me, for taking you from the one you think you love." Stuart took a deep breath and swallowed hard. "If I can't have you in my life as a wife or lover, then having you as a friend is so much better than saying goodbye. Goodbyes are painful and can be very ugly."

Cindy closed her eyes for a moment, then sighed. "You have made me so relieved. I was feeling pressured from you." She raised her hand in affirmation. "I realize I've led you on with my flirting. As I said before, I was in pain …. I still am." Her eyes watered.

"Your Vic?" He lifted her chin with his fingertips.

A careless tear fell onto her cheek. "He's not mine anymore." She took a tissue and wiped her nose and dried her eyes. "He's not my only source of pain."

"Then what?" Stuart held her tighter.

She shook her head. "I can't tell you. It wouldn't be fair."

What is she hiding? Did JC do something?

"Cindy, I won't say anything to anyone. Share this with me."

"I won't." She looked directly at him. "If you knew, you would feel compelled to say or do something. I can't put you in that position."

Oh my God! This sounds really bad!

"Whatever it is, I can tell it's eating away at you. Don't shield someone who doesn't deserve your protection."

She looked up at him again. "I'm protecting you from doing something that might end up hurting you. If nothing else, I care for you, too, even as a friend."

She's using that word again—"friend". How I wish I was more to her.

Her words caught in her throat. "I might be making mountains out of molehills. I tend to do that sometimes."

"Going on a gut instinct isn't bad poker."

Why did I say that? Vic's a gambler. Now she'll be thinking of him.

"You sound like Mom." She chuckled. "She always told me to listen to my inner voice."

"What is that voice telling you now?"

This has to be about JC. He might be cheating on her and she suspects it. I remember seeing a photo of him with a blond in one of the tabloids recently. Grrr ... I'd like to ram my fist in his face!

Cindy let out a labored breath as her chest heaved. "I will wait and see if my suspicions are groundless—which they probably are—a lot of thinking bad thoughts, seeing bad situations that my troubled mind creates. That's not fair to the person I'm worried about." She lifted her head and looked to the ceiling as if to dry her welled-up tears. "I think it's time for me to help you with the dishes before it gets too late."

"Don't worry about those." He chuckled. "Bachelors never wash dishes until the sink is full."

"I doubt that about you." She took a momentary look around. "Your place is too neat and tidy for that." She glanced at her watch. "Seriously, I need to leave. I don't want JC to worry. He'll be returning from wherever he went."

Is she afraid of him? Has he threatened her?

"I'll walk you back. Hugo will enjoy the outing."

Hugo nudged her arm, then positioned himself on her lap.

"See, even Hugo wants you to stay. He's up for a tummy rub."

Cindy rubbed the feline's furry abdomen. The cat kneaded the air and purred loudly.

"Despite Hugo's desire for me to stay, I must be going." Hugo left her lap as she rose.

"Okay." Stuart took the cat's leash from the nearby shelf and attached it to the harness. "You're probably right."

Hugo came running to him and stood still for Stuart to fit the buckle fastener. Loud purrs filled the room.

The walk back to *rue Saint Roch* was all too swift for Stuart. Breathing the same air as Cindy gave him the illusion he was in her world, if only on the outskirts. They came to the entry of the apartment complex.

He held both her hands in his. "I guess this is where we say goodnight."

The streetlights twinkled in her eyes. "Yes. It was a lovely evening, Stu. You made me feel one hundred percent better." She smiled. "I'm afraid I was not so kind to you. I'm sorry for unloading all my troubles."

"You didn't—unload I mean. Maybe if you truly revealed whatever it is, you'd feel better. I'm always here for you."

I hate to release her back to him.

"That means a lot to me. You're my soft, warm, and silent strength." She kissed his cheek, then punched in the security pad code. The buzzer sounded and she was gone behind a forbidding door.

Cindy, your playful exterior hides a very troubled and complex woman. Can I ever have you? Should I drain my savings account and have Jean-Claude investigated? She's worth every penny.

Thirty - Nine

THE FOLLOWING MORNING, Cindy felt better than she had in ten days—since catching the cold that seemed to hang on forever. She had slept late. It was nine thirty. Stretching her arms high above her head, she sensed the only remnant of her cold was a slight nasal stuffiness. A note with a wad of one thousand euros rested on Jean-Claude's pillow. She took the scrap of paper and read it.

Ma Chérie, Cindy,

I'll be out most of the day. I hope you feel better. I have a surprise for you. Please leave by one o'clock this afternoon and don't return until seven this evening. Use the money with this note for shopping. Buy yourself something special. Enjoy your day.

Always thinking of you,

JC

Her remorse for her past insecurities turned to a twinge of guilt.

I should have never given Stu the impression that JC wasn't nice. Why did I hint to all those horrible things, when all this time JC has only been thinking of me. That was so stupid—always jumping to conclusions when I have no basis—no real evidence not to believe him. I bet he was truly breaking up with Monique. She was desperate and didn't want to let him go. Monique was trying to hang on to him with one last kiss.

She went to the bathroom, washed her face, and brushed her teeth. After a long look in the mirror, a pleased smile graced her face.

I'm starting to look like my old self. My eyes have cleared, my throat is no longer sore. JC loves me, though he hasn't said it yet. His actions speak of love. Some guys just can't say those words. Life is good.

Cindy combed her hair, piling it up on her head, then applied makeup. She hummed a current tune.

Walking back to the bedroom, she put on a different pair of jeans and a new, bright turquoise shirt she had splurged on when buying the sandals. The color intensified her blue eyes. She remembered her mother's timely advice, "Blue-eyed blonds look fantastic in bright colors, especially blue. Black looks good on everyone."

She snatched her purse, keys, secured the locks, and left the apartment. A new vibrancy colored her steps with a lighthearted quickness. Strangers' smiles amused her. The flowers seemed brighter and the birds sang sweeter. Jean-Claude had thought of her and planned a special gift—a surprise which intrigued her.

Cindy strolled down *rue de Rivoli* to her favorite haunt, Café du Carrousel, and sat at an outside table. The view of the Louvre continued to fascinate her.

I see why Mom loves it here. This is the most romantic city I've ever known.
She stared straight ahead at Hôtel Regina's entrance.

Mom's home away from home. Typical Mom—always picks the best.

Instead of the usual French breakfast offering, she opted for Le Petit Déjeuner Américain.

That's just what I need. Ham and eggs. A big cup of coffee and o.j., too. Normal food without sauces and everything cooked in wine—I felt I was back living with Mom. I love her, but all that French cooking—give me a hamburger any day.

Cindy spied a discarded American newspaper on the chair next to her. She flipped through it, seeking an interesting article that didn't have to do with stocks, finance, mergers, or world leaders. She found a small piece on fashion trends in New York City, and then a list of the bestselling novels.

Hmm, one day Stu will be on that list. He has a way of seeing the world as fresh and new.

The waiter brought the breakfast order. Cindy relished every bite and ate as if it had been some time since her last good meal. She didn't leave a crumb of croissant. After consuming the last of her coffee, she motioned for the check and managed to say, "L'addition, s'il vous plaît." The server tore the slip of paper from his pad and placed it on the table. She took out her euros and waved her hand indicating she didn't want the few coins of change, and mumbled "Pour vous. Merci." The waiter's face looked downcast as he clearly expected a larger tip from an American. Stuart had told her that most tourists didn't understand French law—all tips for meals were included in the bill's total. She had given him enough. She clutched her purse with the American paper and left, heading in the direction of *place de la Concorde.*

Weaving through the tourists, Cindy stopped and studied the goods displayed in a few of the fashionable shop windows. A particular bright-patterned scarf caught her attention.

That's pretty. She noticed the price tag and moved on. *Mom was right. Rue de Rivoli is very expensive. If JC ever kicks me out, I'll have to move back to Bel-Air. Ten thousand euros from Mom wouldn't last very long in this city. Oh, God, I hope that doesn't happen. I don't want to be mommy's little girl returning home because I can't fend for myself.*

Cindy cheerfully entered Stuart's bookstore. He met her halfway with a broad smile and shining eyes.

He gave her a warm hug. "I'm so glad to see you. Are you feeling better?"

"Marvelous. I haven't felt this good since before our trip to Annecy." She kissed his cheek. "I don't think I'm contagious anymore. Kisses are permitted."

"Wonderful. Are you hungry? Want some coffee?" He squeezed her upper arm.

"No, thanks." Hugo reached up to her leg asking to be petted. She picked him up and kissed the top of his head. "I had a wonderful American breakfast at Café Carrousel. No room for food or drink." She bit her lip. "Well, some water would be nice."

"You've got it." Stuart scurried to his desk, and pulled a bottle of water from the cooler by his chair.

She placed Hugo on the floor. "I have to thank you again for dinner." She opened the bottle and took a swig.

"It wasn't special—plain old chicken soup." He chuckled. "I'm not much of a chef. I cook basic meals—meat and vegetables."

"That's fine by me." She looked in his eyes a bit too long. "I like good food … and good people."

Stuart shifted his weight and appeared uncomfortable. "I see you have an English newspaper. We carry all the major English papers and magazines. I could hold back a copy or two for you. You wouldn't have to pay."

"Stu, that is so sweet." She kissed his cheek. "Fashion and mystery, or horror books are my thing."

"You got it, pretty lady." His eyes held laughter mixed with love.

It made Cindy feel guilty, but it wasn't as if she hadn't been honest with him. "I don't want to keep you. JC has a surprise for me." Cindy licked her lips to moisten them. "I have orders not to return to the apartment till seven tonight. He left a large amount of money for me to buy something extravagant. I might find a fashion treat along *rue Sainte Honoré*—most likely at Galleries Lafayette. I could shop all day in that store."

"I'm certain whatever is planned, it will be nice." He directed his gaze down at the floor. "He has very good taste."

"I'll fill you in on the details tomorrow." Cindy started to leave. At the door, she waved goodbye.

I wish he didn't look so sad.

Forty

CINDY'S JAW DROPPED when she entered Jean-Claude's apartment. Miniature American flags stood on nearly every tabletop in the living room. The coffee table held taco chips, a bowl of salsa, and popcorn. Potato chips, and a veggie dip rested on the end table. Red, white, and blue napkins complemented the accent pillows in the same colors.

Jean-Claude called out, as his voice became louder when he entered the room with a broad smile and hands on hips. "So how do you like it?"

"I'm totally amazed." She looked around the room again. "You did all this—by yourself?"

JC's so considerate. He's trying to say he's sorry for upsetting me.

"Yes, I did." He planted a brief kiss on her lips. "Have a seat. The surprise continues."

Eager to know more, she sat on the sofa while he went to the kitchen. Moments later, he brought a tray filled with food treats and placed them on the coffee table before her.

Her eyes widened. "JC, you have all my favorites! Hamburgers, hotdogs, chips, even root beer soda!"

"That's not all. Just look." He pointed to the small jars near the burgers with pride. "All American made—catsup, mustard, mayonnaise, both relishes—sweet and dill. Only the onions were grown in France. Even the buns are American." He sat down beside her.

"How did you find all these things?" Cindy took a burger and promptly started preparing it to her liking. "I've been craving genuine American food for sooo long." She took a bite. Condiment dressing oozed from the corners of her mouth. She swallowed and gave him a kiss leaving a drop of mustard on his lips. He wiped it off.

"I guessed that you were missing things from home. I wanted you to know that I care. My busy schedule has kept me away from you." He stood up. "Wait. I don't want you to have a coughing issue. I'll get your cough medicine."

"I don't need it. I feel fine." She took a chip and dunked it in the dip before savoring the taste. "I haven't been coughing all day."

"Symptoms can return." He walked down the hall to the bathroom. "I'll get the syrup."

He returned and handed the bottle to her. "Don't bother with a spoon. I don't want you coughing during your next adventure— that would spoil the effect. Take a big swallow."

"You're such a devil!"

JC's so adventurous and exciting. What has he planned? A trip?

She took the bottle from him and gulped a mouthful. "Okay. I was good and took my medicine." He sat next to her, kissing her neck as his hand stroked her thigh. "Not so fast, JC." *He's certainly hungry.* "I want to enjoy this feast you've prepared."

"Sorry. You are so enticing. I can't keep my hands off your luscious body." He watched her chew. "It's better you take your time and let the medicine work with the food you're eating."

"What?" *Did I hear him right? Medicine work with the food?* "Since when does cough medicine need food to work properly?"

"My English again." He laced his fingers together on his lap. "I mean that medicine works best with food in the stomach."

"Some medicines require an empty stomach."

He can be rather odd at times. Still, I trust him. Look at all this effort he's put in to make me happy. He wouldn't do this if he didn't care.

"That cough syrup isn't in that category." He chuckled. "I read the label. You probably didn't understand them because the instructions are written in French."

Cindy patted his hand. "You're always looking after me." She wiped her lips on a red napkin.

"Are you still hungry? Want a hotdog?" He pointed to the item. "I even obtained yellow mustard."

She kissed his cheek. "You're so thoughtful." Her fingers played with the hair at his temple. "So where's this new adventure you have planned?"

"In the bedroom." His smile held a Cheshire quality.

Cindy raised an eyebrow. "I know your—*our* bedroom. Nothing unusual there, except for a sleep mask."

"There's more." He stood up and clasped Cindy's hand, and led her down the hall. "New things can be fun."

I like the tone of this. He wants to change things up. A taste of safe danger?

Jean-Claude opened the bedroom door. Her eyes adjusted to the dim light provided by the two end table lamps. She recognized the black sleep mask and long feather on the pillow.

Hmm, I don't see any new toys he was hinting at. There is a towel on the bedspread. Gonna use oil?

He whispered in her ear with bad boy seduction, "Take all your clothes off slowly. I like to watch."

What's he up to? "You do the same." A moment of dizziness waved over her, and then subsided.

Maybe I still have a touch of a cold.

"Later ... after you're naked. Then lay down on the bed ... on top of the towel." He ran his tongue along the top edge of his teeth.

Cindy walked to the side of the bed and removed her clothing seductively, item by item. Jean-Claude's eyes brightened with desire. He lightly grazed the front of his slacks with his hand. She smiled knowing she turned him on, and wanted to tease him.

"Get on the bed—on the towel." He walked over to her as she reclined.

Her hand traveled up his pants' leg to his manhood. "Let that beast out." She licked her lips. "I want a taste."

"Not yet. Put on the mask." His hand started traveling up her leg. "Wait there while I undress and you can think of me."

Cindy put the blinder in place. She enjoyed the sensory deprivation. It heightened her sense of touch. The sound of unzipping, and the muffled rustling of clothing coming off made her yearn for him. She lifted the mask. His naked body made her want him all the more.

"No peeking." His voice was soft and low. "Naughty girls have to be treated in a very special way."

Cindy covered her eyes again. "I'll behave …. I love your cologne, it turns me on."

"Keep the mask on. Don't remove it until I tell you." She sensed him bending over her. His hot breath was on her neck. She inhaled his intoxicating fragrance. "I want this to be special for you."

"I promise."

What new delight does he plan? This is exciting. He must love me very much to put in all this effort for our love making.

She felt a light lingering and tickling touch start at her neck, then slowly travel down to her breasts. *That's the feather. I love that. Ooo. Don't stop.* The soft sensation circled her nipples, then went farther down to the inside of her thighs. He kissed her fully on the mouth. His lingering tongue teased her as she arched her back.

"No. Lie still," he murmured in her ear. "I want you to feel the most exquisite pleasure."

She felt a soft restraint, like velvet at her left wrist, and then at each ankle.

What is he doing? This is so kinky, and I love it. Why is my right hand still free? Maybe to caress him?

She felt him lie beside her. His firm manhood grazed her thigh. His mouth kissed her breasts and his tongue teased her nipples.

I want him so badly. How much longer will he make me wait?

"I smell a different cologne," she whispered.

His voice held soft firmness. "Shh, relax."

Jean-Claude's kisses traveled down farther to where they gave her the most intense pleasure.

I want to raise my hips to reach out to him, but I can't move.

Something wasn't right.

I feel the weight of him between my knees. Who's grabbing my right wrist? Such a tight grip.

Her mind whirled.

Someone's between my legs. I feel fabric on someone's leg. Didn't he remove his slacks? That scent isn't JC! I have to get free!

Cindy twisted and struggled to free her semi-restrained wrist, and tore the mask off.

"What in hell is going on?" A partially clothed man—a stranger—was kneeling between her legs, with his pants dropped to mid thigh.

Her mouth gaped. She stared wide-eyed at Jean-Claude.

Cindy tore free from the loose restraints, grabbed her clothes, and ran to the bathroom.

She slammed the door.

Uncontrollable sobs wracked her body and tears streamed down her face. As she dressed haphazardly, confusion clouded her mind. If only she could think clearly, but she couldn't. Her mind was fuzzy. She slumped onto the lid of the toilet seat, as tears flowed down her cheeks and moistened her shirt.

How could he do this to me? Wanting another man to make love to me? What type of animal is he? Why was I so blind?

A soft knock sounded on the door.

"Cindy?" Jean-Claude sounded kind and caring. "Are you all right? What did I do wrong?"

"Wrong?" She opened the door. A sob caught her breath. "You have the nerve to ask me that! You bring a strange man to our bed to have sex with me so you can watch! You're a perverted bastard!"

"There's no one here but us." He stepped back into the hall. "Come out of there and look for yourself."

"Don't lie to me." She went from room to room searching, all the while talking. "I know someone is here. I'm not going mad. He was naked to the waist with his pants halfway down. He smelled different than you. You were naked."

"Cindy, get a hold of yourself. Look at me."

She stopped her frantic movements and stared at him. "You're wearing slacks and no shirt."

"Yes." He walked slowly to her and placed his hands on her upper arms. "The stranger you saw is me."

Cindy shook her head vehemently. "But, your cologne?"

What's happening to me? I know what I saw and felt.

"I bought a new fragrance." He embraced her. "Snuggle up and see for yourself."

He pulled her into his chest as he kissed the top of her head. She pushed him away violently. "Don't touch me."

He's right about the scent, though. JC is wearing new cologne.

"Let's go and sit down." Jean-Claude tried to guide her to the sofa.

"No! Let go of me." She snatched her purse. "I have to go and think—by myself."

"Don't be ridiculous! Your cough medicine must have given you hallucinations." He started to the bathroom. "I'll get the bottle and you can read the warnings on the label."

"No! No!" She flung open the door. "I have to walk. I don't know when I'll be back or if I'll be back."

My God, my hands are shaking. I'm so very scared. I can't tell Stu—he'll murder JC. Where will I go?

Cindy nearly ran down *rue Sainte Honoré*. She dashed from one corner to another never paying attention to traffic lights. Screeching tires, honking horns, and French obscenities accosted her ears. Her eyes flooded with tears that blurred her vision. Her pace didn't slow until she rounded the corner which brought her to *avenue l'Opéra*, where the bright lights sharpened her senses. She took a vacant outside table at Café de la Paix.

Am I losing my mind?

She ordered a large American coffee from the waiter.

Why do I feel like my head's full of cotton wool?

Her eyes widened as she withheld a gasp.

Oh my God. What if JC put something in the cough syrup? Is that why he insisted that I take some? He thought I wouldn't know what was going on. And that white powder that I saw in the bathroom—more than once. Is he using cocaine? Did he give me cocaine? I'm getting paranoid. Why would he plan such a special evening just to drug me? This makes no sense. Did I imagine there was another man in the room? I thought JC was naked. I'm sure he was naked ... or was he?

The waiter served her. She immediately left euros on the table, not wanting to wait for the check.

This is too bizarre to be true. What would JC have to gain by having a stranger screw me? Perverted kinkiness? Nah, that's not him—he's too suave and refined.

She stirred her coffee and gazed out unseeingly at the square, full of people with loud voices.

What if he didn't break up with Monique and this was an elaborate plot to make me leave him? If that's true, then why go through all that effort. No. JC loves me. I have to believe that he loves me. This is just a horrible nightmare.

She glanced at the next table of women in their twenties. They laughed while pointing to a photo on the front page of a tabloid. Cindy craned her neck to observe the image.

What? Is that a picture of JC?

Her eyes thinned with suspicion and she leaned closer.

It is! With that blond, kissing—nearly the same pic as on my phone.

She turned her back to the other women, who were giving her strange looks.

I won't believe my fears. That's all it is—fears. I'm glad I don't understand French. I don't need to hear their obvious ugly comments.

Forty - One

CINDY STOOD IN front of the bookstore, staring down at the pavement before going in. Her confusion about Jean-Claude clouded her reason.

For the past three nights JC has been loving. He has accepted my not wanting sex. Why? Is he being considerate after my reaction and hallucination of him inviting another man to enjoy my body? What is being lost in translation? It's more than the language issue.

"Are you going to stand out there all day counting the cracks in the pavement?" Stuart's voice jarred her. He stood in the shop's doorway. "Or, are you going to come in and brighten my day?"

"I don't want to trouble you." *His eyes are so kind. Stu's very different from JC.* "I just want to walk for a bit."

A customer squeezed past Stuart and into the store. He moved onto the sidewalk to Cindy, shielding the sun from his eyes with his hand.

"Want company?" He placed his hand on her shoulder. "I have no pressing details to tend to."

"What if a customer has a question that your employee can't answer?" *He knows I'm upset. I can't share my mess with JC.*

"I trust Hélène. She speaks fluent English." He chuckled. "Even with an English accent."

Cindy took a few steps away. "You can tag along, if you want …. I don't feel very talkative."

"Ah, a contemplative mood." He walked back to the entry. "Wait here. I'll speak with Hélène."

Stu's so persuasive. He wants to protect me. I can't involve him. What I sense as a problem could be nothing more than my groundless fears.

Stuart came quickly from the bookshop and stood by her side. He lightly touched her elbow. She looked up at him.

"Where to? Up the Champs Élysées? Or somewhere else?"

"I was going to amble around—no place in particular." *I hope he doesn't pry.* "Walking calms me and helps me think."

He checked his watch. "It will be a nice outing before lunch."

Crossing the street, they hiked a block to *place de la Concorde*. Circular traffic, blaring horns, and the myriad of rumbling vehicles made one wonder why there was an absence of automobile accidents. Cindy remained silent. Stuart glanced at her frequently, but didn't press her. *Pont de la Concorde* took them to the left bank. She turned left onto *quai Anatole*. Stuart clasped her hand.

It's nice, walking with Stu. He seems to understand that I want his silent presence. How could he seem to know me so well in such a short time? There are times when JC is a million miles away.

Overhanging tree limbs shaded the sidewalk. Cindy hugged the stone wall to allow others to pass. Scattered along the way they passed stalls of vendors selling art, old books, stamps, postcards, and small antique-looking items of one sort or another.

Up ahead were four parked vans that appeared to belong to a production company showcasing a celebrity.

"What do you think this is?" She discreetly pointed at the crowd of professionals and onlookers.

"I have no idea." Stuart quickened his step to keep up with hers. "A movie star or singer? Maybe a famous American?"

"Let's see if we can recognize anyone." Cindy hurried to the horde of picture-takers holding their phones high in the air.

"By the time we catch up to them ..." he panted between words, "all the excitement will have passed."

"Spoil sport!" She kept her attention on the commotion up ahead.

Cindy reached the edge of the crowd. Stuart came up behind her. She stood on tiptoe and scanned the center of the activity. Professional photographers busied themselves with packing up equipment of lights, lenses, white reflective umbrellas, and battery packs. Others stowed away racks of clothing, a makeup table, and a row of wigs. She was about to turn away when her eye caught a glimpse of a familiar face. She stared.

It's Monique! If she broke up with JC, she doesn't look very upset.

Her envious curiosity rose as she took a longer look.

She's thinner than me. Must wear a size two. Her hair is blonder, too. Her makeup is perfect.

She bit her lip and focused on her own feet.

"What's wrong?" He took her hand. "What did you see?"

She looked up again and watched Monique entering a waiting van.

He took her hand and gave a gentle squeeze. "Come along. Let's get some lunch. The excitement's gone."

Cindy looked at his face and realized that Stuart had recognized Monique.

He probably knows JC has been involved with that blond.

Maneuvering through the traffic, they crossed the street, which brought them to the intersection of *pont Royal, rue de Bac,* and *quai Voltaire.* Stuart guided Cindy into the brasserie La Frégate, and indicated to the host that a table for two was in order.

They enjoyed the view of the Louvre from a window table. "This is a lovely restaurant. A tad upscale from Café Carrousel." Cindy admired the ornate décor and noted the bronze plaque with the numbers 1870. The waiter handed them menus and left a carafe of water with two glasses.

"I feel like having a grilled cheese sandwich if they can manage it."

Will Stu make small talk to take my mind off Monique and JC.

Stuart glanced around. "This place has a bit of history to it."

"All of France has history to it."

Too bad they don't serve hamburgers.

"Very true." He didn't take his eyes off the menu. "This precise location was that of the mansion of the real Marshal d'Artagnan who inspired the famous novel, The Three Musketeers by Alexander Dumas."

"Leave it to you to know all the history trivia." She chuckled. "You're my own walking encyclopedia." She cupped her chin in her hand. "You always make history so interesting."

"Thanks." His smile created fine lines at the corner of his eyes. "As I mentioned before, I only know facts on a few topics. Since Dumas was a famous French author, of course I'd want to know where his inspiration came from when creating his characters."

Stuart placed their orders.

"I wish my teachers had been as interesting as you. I might've learned more."

Where do I really stand with JC? Does he love me or not? Did I really imagine another man? JC wouldn't really do that to me, would he? He seems so nice and the way he talks to me makes me believe he does care deeply for me. Maybe I shouldn't have gone to Stu. His small talk isn't helping.

She glanced at his hand.

His knuckles haven't healed completely. He got that injury because of me.

"Don't sell yourself short." He poured water into their glasses. "You are very intelligent. Didn't you have, or still have a career in America."

Cindy took a swallow of water. "Yes. In Tampa. I was a manger of a benefits firm. I resigned just before leaving for Paris. I refuse to look back. What's done is done."

"There's truth in not being able to go back." He offered her bread from the basket. "Things are never the same as one remembers."

"In a way … that's sad." She broke off a small piece of bread. "I-I want to ask if your offer is still good."

"Which one? To have my heart or something else?" His eyes twinkled with amusement.

She felt color come to her face. "No. Not your heart." *What if Stu wasn't serious?* "I'm being too forward."

"How?" His endearing puppy-like expression charmed her. "You've proven yourself to be anything but forward."

"I've pretty much made up my mind that I won't be returning home—at least not for a while, and …" She fingered the stem of her glass. "I-I was wondering if I could work at the bookstore for a little while—just for some pocket money. Mom gave me a number of euros for emergency purposes. I don't want to spend that for food and such."

"Of course, you can." He beamed and reached for her hand across the table, giving it a squeeze. "I don't mean to step on your privacy—but, doesn't Jean-Claude give you spending money?"

"He does." The waiter served her Croque Monsieur and a dozen escargots to Stuart, then poured white wine into the glasses. "But, I don't like the feeling of obligation. It's as if I'm taking money from a parent. I'm too independent for that."

"How much do you need?" He leaned forward on his elbows. "I won't be able to pay you a full-time salary."

"I have no idea how much." She cut into her grilled ham and cheese sandwich. "I don't need a lot. Just enough so I can buy a piece of clothing, or stop at a café for a bite."

Holding a two-tined fork, Stuart stabbed an escargot from the shell. "Hmm, I could give you the money—a gift from a friend."

"Then, how is that any different than what I have with JC?" She chewed and then swallowed. "He gives me money just because I'm living with him. It's nothing that I *earned.*"

"I admire you for your convictions." He chewed on the black morsel. "You're a woman of integrity."

"I don't know about that. I impulsively pushed myself on JC." Cindy raised her glass and tasted the wine. She smiled. "Very good selection. Le vin, c'est si bon." A light chuckle escaped. "See, I do know a few French phrases here and there."

Did that come out of me? So corny.

"You don't have to speak French for my benefit. I'm not Jean-Claude." He forked another escargot. "Back to you working at the store … I see no problem." He chewed heartedly and swallowed. "I can pay you enough for your needs. I can't afford to give you a salary large enough for rent and utilities, mobile phone, and such."

"Oh no, Stu." She took another bite of food. "Mom has taken over the cell phone bill."

"You might want to get a mobile phone from here." He swallowed some wine. "Every time you use your American phone, the call bounces all the way to a tower in the States and back to here. You must be running up a huge bill."

"Oh my God, I never thought of that." *Poor Mom and Larry.* "Mom never said a word about the bill. Though, she hasn't called nor texted me in a long time."

Larry's paid out so much money already with the Vic issue.

"You'll need a day or so to get the feel of the store—the way we categorize the books and such. Nothing very technical." He flashed a broad smile. "I am absolutely delighted that you've come to this decision."

"How many days do you want me?"

Should I've had mention this to JC first? I hope I didn't walk into a hornet's nest.

"Three or four?" He looked hopeful. "The day after tomorrow?"

"How about one or two to start." *He's a bit pushy.* "I'm not certain when. I need to speak to JC first."

"For his permission?" Stuart cocked an eyebrow.

"No—not permission. It's only fair that I inform him." *How will JC react?* "After all, I *am* living under his roof."

"I understand." He wiped his lips with his napkin. "I shouldn't have pressed you on the issue."

"No matter. You have a new employee and I have a new employer."

He took her hand in his. "Remember, if the need ever arises, you can live with me with no strings whatsoever."

"I doubt that will ever happen—me staying at your place. JC and I are solid."

Are we solid? I won't tell Stu about my doubts. Will I regret this impulsive decision to work for Stu? Is this the first step to a ruined future?

Forty - Two

CINDY WAITED FOR Frédéric to finish assisting a customer purchasing a miniature Paris figurine. He nodded to Émilie to take over, and beckoned for Cindy to follow him to the backroom entry.

"What can I do for the most beautiful American girl in my shop?" He looked mildly concerned. "I don't think you want to buy a souvenir."

"I need to speak with a friend who has a bit of distance from my situation." She fingered her purse strap. "Stu is too close and I think he doesn't like JC, so his opinion wouldn't be objective. Please promise me that you won't share what I'm about to say with Stu. I know you and he are friendly, and … and if he gets wind of what I'm about to say he might confront JC—I don't want that. I care for Stu in a different way, but I still care."

"You have my complete secrecy." His face turned sullen as if anticipating grave news.

Frédéric guided her back to the small lounge area fitted with a table and two chairs. He poured her a cup of coffee from the maker on the small side table. Cindy added cream and sugar he retrieved from the mini-refrigerator. Stacks of corrugated cardboard shipping boxes and packing material for stuffing lined the walls from floor to ceiling. Rolls of strapping tape sat on one low stack of cartons.

"So what is this all about?" He prepared his coffee. "Did you and Jean-Claude have an argument?"

"Not exactly." She blew on the hot brew before taking a sip. "Things seem to have turned very odd, very quickly."

"How? Did he ask you to move out?" He sat next to her at the table.

How much should I admit to?

"Well, you remember I had a cold?"

"Yes. Are you feeling better now?" He drank his coffee while staring at her with inquisitive eyes.

"I feel fine. But, but while I had that cold, JC gave me some cough medicine. This sounds crazy," her voice trembled, "but I had a hallucination of some kind."

He inched forward in his seat. She saw the alarm on his face. "What type of hallucination? Out of body?"

"No. I was seeing things not there." *Does Fred know something?* "I saw a person who wasn't there."

"What was Jean-Claude's reaction? Did he take you to a hospital?" His concern intensified.

"No. The subject never came up." *This is so difficult to tell Mom's best friend.* "I grabbed my clothes, dressed and ran out of the apartment."

"Dressed? Weren't you already wearing clothes?" He took a sip without taking his eyes off her. "Were you making love and he did things you didn't like?"

"No. Nothing like that." *I'm making a mess of this.* "He did nothing wrong that way. I thought I saw another man with us—as if he wanted this man to have me while he watched."

"What makes you think the other person was not there." He looked at her as his brow furrowed.

"There was no evidence of anyone else—no clothes. Only a fragrance I didn't recognize—a man's cologne or aftershave."
I sound like some kind of nut.

"I don't understand." He took a swallow of coffee. "Did Jean-Claude leave the room when you were on the bed?"

"No. He was there naked. I saw him *naked*. JC had me wear a mask."
Fred is gonna think I'm a freak.

"That's not unheard of." He took a small bottle of water from the refrigerator and opened it. "Many couples use masks. Back to what you smelled. How was that different?"

"Well, since JC didn't leave the room to change his cologne, and then he smelled different—right before I felt a man's pants' leg against my thigh." *Should I mention the restraints?* "That's when I pulled the mask off and I saw a strange man with his slacks pulled halfway down his legs, ready to enter me. It had to have been a hallucination from some ingredient in the cough syrup. JC showed me the warnings on the label—though it was in French and I couldn't read the information for myself." She took a deep breath. "There was absolutely no evidence of another man. After this, when I went up to JC, he smelled like the new fragrance .... I guess my sense of smell was affected, too."

"Mon Dieu! Incroyable! Unbelievable!" Frdéric rubbed his brow while his eyes grew large with amazement. "I have never been told of any medicine for a cough—one that doesn't need a doctor's prescription, causing hallucinations." He took a large swallow of water directly from the bottle. "Is it possible that something was put in the cough syrup?"

What is he saying? JC drugged me? Never!

"JC would absolutely not do something like that. He even fixed me a totally American meal—all the items were American made. He went to a lot of trouble to arrange that surprise. If he didn't care, he wouldn't have gone through all that effort."

Frédéric spoke slowly as if choosing every word with caution. "Cindy, I want you to be very careful around him. I think it is time you returned home where you will be safe. You have your passport?"

"I carry it in a secret place in my purse with the money Mom gave me." She studied his face. "Why should I return home? JC has never threatened me. I know he loves me."

"Has he told you that he loves you in English or French?" Fred probed deeper. "Has he said 'Je t'aime'?"

"No. But his actions speak of love." She ran her finger around the top edge of her cup as she stared at the liquid.

"Aren't you seeing feelings in him that you wish were there?" He touched her hand. "You suffered the loss of your marriage. It's natural that you want to replace Vic with someone to love you."

"You're saying I'm on the rebound?" Her eyes filled.

"I'm saying that you are not seeing Jean-Claude as he is. You aren't seeing your relationship with clear eyes." He sighed. "Your vision is clouded with your love for him. That cloud has prevented you from seeing the truth in his feelings for you."

Cindy took a large swallow of coffee as she thought on Frédéric's advice.

Have I been inventing in my mind more than what is there? Am I nothing more than a casual fling to JC?

"Jean-Claude has dangerous associations—at least his friends have those dangerous connections. Like all cities in the world, there are very bad people living here." His voice softened, "Cindy, look beyond the romance of Paris. Criminals live here, too."

"JC's a criminal?" She felt her hand shake.

Have I been living with a monster?

"I didn't say he is." He leaned closer. "He has friends who are connected to criminals—very bad men. Your safety, maybe your life, is worth far more than any affair."

His words washed over her and seeped in, creating a cold fear. She tried to recall any suspicious persons near Jean-Claude.

The only odd thing was that club, and having sex in the men's room. Did JC know that man who entered? He didn't act as if he did.

"Cindy, please leave JC and go home to Taylor and Larry. Book your ticket today." He reinforced his words with a squeeze of her hand. "You need to be safe. This is not your time to be in Paris."

She nodded with a vacant stare.

I came to Fred for reassurance and all he gave me was more confusion and now, fear. I don't want to leave JC. Yet, should I? Is what Fred told me true?

~~***~~

Jean-Claude paced in his living room with the phone pressed tight against his ear. He puffed rapidly on his e-cigarette as he listened.

"I told you," Maurice's harsh voice jarred him, "Mâcon means business. He wants his money or someone will have to pay."

"If you hadn't botched our plan, I would have the money."

What in hell am I going to do now?

"I'm not the one who did anything wrong." Background street noise sounded from the receiver. "You didn't drug her enough."

"I had to be careful. If she was drugged too much, she wouldn't act like she enjoyed it. No porn is worth a sou without the woman acting sex-crazed." Jean-Claude took another puff. "Besides, because you wouldn't remove your pants, she caught on—I was naked and you weren't. Plus, you didn't wait for me to finish tying her wrist—that's where she made the connection. She knew I couldn't be kneeling between her legs and at the same time tying her wrist. Also, you didn't use my cologne! I told you not to wear your own—she picked up on that, too. I had to splash on a different scent to throw her off the track."

"I thought she was already tied down." Maurice sighed. "Besides, I don't want someone seeing my naked ass."

"But you don't mind your bare dick in a film?" He paused his pacing. "You make no sense."

"I'm proud of my cock." He chuckled. "Measure up better than yours ... I never thought she'd notice the cologne."

"Stop with the jokes. I get no complaints. The women always come back for more." He went to the bar at the end of the piano, and poured vodka into a glass. "Thank God she took long enough to change so you could get out of there with the camera.... So what do we do now? I have no film to blackmail Larry Davis."

"What do you mean 'we'? I don't owe Maçon a chunk of money." He laughed loudly. "My ass isn't the one on the line. I've been buying you time. Remember what happened to your girlfriend in the Seine? You want to see your American trinket end up the same?"

"You can't blame me for that." He sat on the piano bench. "I got her hooked, didn't I? She didn't pay for her tac-tac, and got wacked."

"Got a real short memory." Maurice's voice lowered with grave firmness. "She paid for her own tac-tac turning tricks in Montmartre. She never used more than what she could pay for. Never ran up a bill. She was payback for your outstanding bill."

"I never heard that!" He stood bolt upright and stared out the window.

"That's crap!" Maurice paused. "I called you many times and told you to pay up or someone would get hurt."

"I thought the threat was against my father." His jaw slacked. "When no one bothered Papa, I thought it was empty words."

"Maçon doesn't deal with empty anything—least of all threats." Screeching tires came over the phone into Jean-Claude's ears. "You had better pay up."

"How?" He started pacing back and forth. "That was the only plan I could come up with."

"Set up another situation with that American pépée of yours—your chick." He laughed. "Why not slip her some tac-tac, and make her a member of the club? Film her sucking a whole line of cocks, full face so everyone can see she's Davis' daughter. As an encore, have those same guys screw her one by one." He laughed louder. "You could title it 'Davis' Daughter Takes All of Paris'. He'd be paying you off for the rest of your life—and Maçon would have a new customer. It's a win-win all the way around. Hell, if she turns out to be a good customer, he might give you a packet for free every once in a while."

"I don't want to turn her." He took a long drag on his e-cigarette. "I don't want to make her a user."

"Then how in hell are you going to get her to agree to sucking off a roomful of dicks?" He breathed deeply. "American women are gullible, but not all are stupid."

"I don't love her, but I do care for her." His fist balled up as beads of sweat dotted his upper lip. "I might be able to arrange something. She did enjoy that episode in the club. Maybe a repeat is in order."

"That could take time—time is running out." He sighed again. "Look, I know Maçon. He's a man of his word. Either you pay up or someone will. Maybe your Papa."

"Maurice, you have to get me more time." *I've got to arrange for another film.* "I don't want anyone, and I mean *anyone* to get hurt."

"I'll do what I can." He dragged on a cigarette.

"Is my life in danger, too?"

Does Maçon have me followed? He must or else how would he know about who I see?

"Not yet. But I make no guarantees. Right now you're too good a customer." His tone stiffened. "If your bill goes unpaid, your life could be the ultimate payment—after others in your life have made their contribution. I have to go. I just spotted two of Maçon's boys on the corner."

The phone went silent.

I can't go to Papa—he'll throw me into one of those rehab hospitals. I'm not addicted. I can handle tac-tac. I can stop anytime I want. It helps me relax. I sing better after a hit or two. I must get Cindy filmed in the hottest porn ever made. Davis will pay anything to keep his nose clean. His wife would make him pay. This has to be done carefully. I have to make Cindy so hot that she'll screw anyone. Sex must become a drug to her.

Jean-Claude's brow knitted as he formulated his plan.

Forty - Three

HAPPINESS FILLED STUART'S heart when Cindy entered his store. She wore the same jeans, with a bright turquoise shirt. Slung over her shoulder was a hobo purse.

He felt Hélène's eyes on him.

She's a good employee, but can be so nosey.

"Did you come in to train already?" he asked.

"Not so fast. I need to use your bathroom." Her phone rang. She took it from her pocketbook and checked the caller ID. "Must be a wrong number. I don't recognize it." She scrolled the display. "Yup. A wrong number." Cindy placed her phone on the desk beside his computer keyboard.

"It's in the back, next to the lounge." He guided her down the narrow hall and to the restroom. "Just turn off the light after you're finished—trying to keep the electric costs down."

"Sure." She closed the door.

He returned to his work at the desk and saw a picture on her phone.

She must have touched her photo album key.

He looked closer at the image.

It's Jean-Claude and that famous model, Monique Favreau! They're kissing.

He looked over his shoulder listening for her footsteps.

I shouldn't break her confidence, still maybe I can help her in some way if I know what other photos she has of him.

He flipped through other romantic photos of Monique and Jean-Claude. Then he came to the video. Watching the brief film, his mouth opened.

Cindy's been carrying all this pain—keeping it to herself. He's such a bastard! She's still an innocent. How could he! Why is she still with him?

The faint sound of her footsteps grew louder. He placed the phone back in its former position on the desk.

"Want to get a coffee?" he offered when she returned.

She spotted a food stain on her shirt. "Damn! I didn't notice this before." She looked up at him. "I'll take you up on the coffee later. Have to change my shirt."

"Remember, I can get off work nearly anytime—at a moment's notice," he called out as her springy steps took her out the door.

Hélène made a face at him, clearly not appreciating his flexible schedule.

Later, Stuart stood stocking a shelf at the back of the store with the newest shipment when deliberate footsteps approached him from behind. A man's heavy tread. He turned to see Jean-Claude's angry glaring face less than a foot away. His breath quickened along with his pulse.

Jean-Claude jabbed his finger harshly onto Stuart's chest. "Keep the hell away from Cindy," he bellowed. "Maurice has told me all about your associations with her. She is my woman and I'm not about to share with the sap of a shop owner." Jean-Claude raised a threatening fist.

Stuart's eyes nearly popped with rage. Without a second thought, his fist connected with the singer's nose leaving a gush of blood as reward for his effort.

"You've had that coming all your life and I'm glad I could be the one to deliver that lesson." He grabbed Jean-Claude's shirt collar and dragged him out of the store, and threw him onto the sidewalk, breathing hard.

He waggled his finger at the pathetic figure bleeding and lying on the concrete. "Cindy is not a toy. She is a person to be respected—look up the definition in the dictionary!"

His hand stung, and he noticed the previous cuts on his knuckles had re-opened and started bleeding. He took a handkerchief from his pocket and wrapped it around the wounds.

Jean-Claude scrambled to his feet and wiped his bloody nose with the back of his hand. Stuart took a wide stance ready to deliver another blow. He smiled as the singer turned and walked deliberately down the street.

That bastard! He doesn't deserve to see another day! Too bad paparazzi wasn't around …. Should I tell Cindy? If I did, would she run into his arms?

~~***~~

Jean-Claude sat in the living room holding a glass of vodka in one hand and pressing an ice-pack to his nose with the other. He heard Cindy enter the apartment and go to the bedroom. He put the ice-pack down on the table.

Good, she's back. Time for a training session for her acting debut.

As he entered the bedroom, she unbuttoned her blouse and tossed it on a chair.

"I was wondering where you went."

Is she up to something?

"I came back to change my shirt after I did a bit of window shopping. There's a stain on it." She showed him the spot.

"Better change your jeans, too." He pointed. "There's a mark on the seat, near the pocket."

Cindy twisted looking in the mirror to see the soiled area. "I never noticed."

She promptly unzipped her jeans and stepped out of them. He approached her as she stood in her bra and panties. He put down his drink on the nightstand, then placed his hands on her shoulders.

"What's the hurry?" *She's tense. I can feel it.* "I want you."

He forcibly pulled at the hooks on her bra, releasing the garment. Cindy tried to pull back. He was too strong for her to fight off. He firmly grabbed her breast and gave a lustful squeeze.

"Not now, JC. I don't like this." Slight fear showed on her face. "You tore the hooks off my bra!"

"I'll give you money to buy a new one." *She's not the same.* "What's different? No mask? No restraints?" He pushed her back against the bed. She drew her legs together while he unzipped his pants.

"So you want to play the virgin? As if this is your first time?" *She's such a tease.* "I can play rough. Rough is fun."

She tried to roll off the bed. His hand stopped her. "Not so fast. You need to perfect some skills first." He grabbed the back of her head and pushed his manhood at her lips. "Taste all of me. Suck me hard."

Cindy turned her head away with a disgusted look. "Not like this, JC. Please, not like this. You make me feel cheap and dirty."

His hand slipped into her panties fingering her velvet folds. His words came in deep and lustful pants. "I can make you want me. Make you want me now."

She bolted up, pushed him away with both hands, snatched her clothes and stormed to the bathroom, slamming the door. Jean-Claude turned the knob. It was locked.

"Ma chérie, I was only playing." *What in hell is wrong with her? She used to love sex.* "Open the door."

Her voice trembled, "No. I won't come out until you promise not to touch me—not like you just did."

"I never meant to frighten you." *I hate the idea of using hardcore drugs on her. That might be necessary.* "I wanted to explore new things with you. Sex can become very predictable, and then boring."

The door opened a crack. Jean-Claude could see a sliver of Cindy's face. He pushed it completely open. Tears flowed down her cheeks. Her bottom lip quivered.

"Jean-Claude, I need to get away from you." She wiped her face with a towel leaving a streak of makeup behind. "I can't even look at you. I need to calm down."

She pushed past him, seized her pocketbook and jacket from the entry table and left.

His jaw slacked.

What in hell just happened? She runs from me just because of a little request for oral sex? It's not like she hasn't given me head before. I only wanted to sharpen her skills for the movie.

~~***~~

Cindy sat on a bench in Jardin des Tuileries. Nothing, not even the cute sparrows and pigeons pecking food crumbs, could lift her spirits. The lustfulness that had transpired had created doubt and fear.

If he cares about me, how could he treat me as if I was nothing more than a whore. He talked to me so cheaply. All the times we made love, he was tender and caring. Now he's like a Jekyll and Hyde. Is JC on something?

Crunching sounds of gravel took her attention. She looked to her side and watched a mother pushing a stroller with her toddler nodding off. The mom also held a leash attached to a small poodle, who walked obediently, frequently looking up at the woman. After they passed, Cindy stared out into space. She didn't care to enjoy the beauty of the various flowers planted in precise and effective patterns.

Maybe this is me and not him? Am I subconsciously reeling from Vic's rejection? Am I a prude? I never thought I was close-minded. The sleep mask routine didn't freak me out. What has changed? Sex is great with JC. Why didn't I want sex with him now? Surely, he must love me. If he didn't, why would he want to sleep with me—not when he can have any woman who breathes? Was Fred right? What he said about JC being dangerous?

Cindy drew the front of her light jacket closer together to hide the stain on her blouse and the fact that her bra was no longer fastened.

This stewing is getting me nowhere. A splurge at Galleries Lafayette will do the trick. I won't stop at Stu's—I can't bring my problems to him—especially when it's all in my head.

Crowds of local shoppers and tourists crammed the aisles of the famous department store, each seeking a highly desired sale item. This reminded Cindy of holiday sales in Gérard's when she would visit her mother.

Mannequins displayed the most expensive, and exquisitely styled trending fashion. Passing a perfume counter, she inhaled deeply and recognized her mom's fragrance.

I wish Mom was here. We would have a nice time.

The escalator took her to the women's lingerie floor. She went to the area of expensive bras and panties. A printed conversion chart stood alongside which compared American and UK to European sizing. Cindy read the information and memorized the sizes to look for.

A saleswoman came up to her. She spoke in perfect English and was clearly accustomed to dealing with foreign clients. "May I help you in selecting an item?"

"No thank you." She brushed the hair away from her face. "I'll let you know if I can't find something."

The woman stepped away.

I hope she doesn't hang behind me watching my every move. I'm not about to steal anything.

Cindy examined the various bras and panties. Her attention was drawn to a new ensemble; a black lace demi-bra with sequins and beads of the same color, and skimpy panties to match. Her fingers touched the fabric.

This feels nice—like wearing nothing. How can something so flimsy give any lift, even with underwire support?

Careful not to disturb the arrangement of various sizes, she found what would be equivalent a to 34D bra and size small panties.

Hmm, what Stu would say or better yet do, if he saw me in only these?

She dropped the items on the table.

Why did I think of Stu and not JC? Stu is just a friend, though he'd like to be more.

The same saleswoman came up to her. "Has mademoiselle made a selection?"

"What?" Cindy still felt shaken by her recent thought of Stuart. "Oh, yes, yes." She handed the two items to the woman and absently followed her to the cashier counter.

"Is there anything else? A scarf?" Clearly she noticed the stain on Cindy's shirt. "Perhaps a new blouse?"

She looked down, and then quickly closed her jacket. "Yes. A blouse would be nice. A black blouse." Her chuckle indicated embarrassment. "I was clumsy with my coffee."

"Bien sûr, mademoiselle." The woman grabbed her phone. "The blouse section is on this floor, opposite side. I'll call that department and they will bring some black blouses over for your choice. Do you like it slip over your head or button in the front?"

"Button in the front is best."

She's certainly helpful. Cindy thought a moment while the salesperson made the request in French. *I never checked the price. Silly. How expensive could a bra and panties be?*

Moments later, another female store associate appeared with a selection of three garments. Two were made of satin, and the third was crepe. She checked the price tags discreetly.

Blouses ain't cheap. These are even more expensive. Three hundred euros for one blouse? Ouch! It's a good thing I'll be working at the bookstore. What on earth are the prices of the bra and panties? I hope I have enough left of what JC has given me. I hate to use my emergency fund.

She chose the less expensive crepe shirt.

When the saleswoman handed her the slip, Cindy swallowed hard and tried to act nonchalant.

The employee must have seen her reaction. "Is there a problem, mademoiselle? Would you rather choose from our sale items?"

"No, no." Cindy felt color come to her face. "This is fine."

She handed the six hundred forty-seven euros to the woman.

I'm nearly totally wiped out. All I have is three hundred fifty-three euros left and that's not going to take me very far. If I have to use Mom's money until Stu can pay me, well … I guess I will. I don't want to take anything more from JC.

She bit her lip while the woman packed up her purchases.

Why does JC have to be so darn handsome? That body and those eyes! He's one hard man to resist. Was it like that for Mom when she met Larry?

The saleswoman handed the bag to her. Cindy made her way through the throngs of shoppers and took the down escalator to the ground floor. She decided to exit on a side street, *rue Charras*, separating Galleries and Magasin du Printemps, another famous department store.

Outside, a warm breeze kicked up and blew her hair into her face. She swiped it away. Pedestrians bumped into her as they walked by, seemingly with some form of urgency as she stood there trying to decide which route would be the most pleasant for her walk to the bookstore and then home.

A man in a black leather jacket, black hair and cold eyes charged toward her.

My God! He's going to rob me! No one is noticing.

Fear gripped her. She was trapped.

She couldn't move backward without stepping on another person.

"Tell Jean-Claude to pay up or else!" he said in a low menacing voice in clear English. His breath smelled of stale tobacco.

Something hard and sharp touched her arm.

The assailant vanished as quickly as he had appeared.

Cindy's arm burned fiery hot. She looked down at it and gasped in horror. Blood seeped through her jacket sleeve. She felt warm liquid trickle down to her fingertips, leaving red drops on the sidewalk.

Oh God! What hell have I gotten into? Fred was right. JC must have dangerous friends!

Intense sharp pain took over her senses. No one seemed to notice how she was shaking nearly uncontrollably as she took a wad of tissues from her pocketbook and pressed it tightly to the wound.

An old lady stopped and spoke to her in French. She shook her head and denied what she figured must be the woman's offer to help.

I've got to get to Stu. He'll know what to do. What does JC have to pay up? Gambling? Is he just another Vic in a handsome body?

Forty - Four

CINDY STOOD QUIETLY as Stuart dressed the wound using the first-aid supplies he had in his store. They were in the back lounge. His gentle and loving touch comforted her. The antiseptic stung as he dabbed the cut with a cotton swab.

"Did you get a good look at his face?" He continued to clean the bloody area and glanced up at her several times while cleaning the wound.

"Yes, I think so." She still couldn't control her shaking, and was glad to be leaning against the wall. She didn't think her legs would hold her. "He-he had black hair and these intense fearsome eyes." Cindy looked at her gaping flesh. "Ouch!" She started to pull back as he applied more antiseptic.

"Don't move." Stuart smoothed on antibiotic ointment with a clean swab. "This was just a warning. The cut is too shallow for a large knife—maybe a razor. I still think you should go to the police and the hospital—at least an emergency center. You might need stitches if the bleeding doesn't stop. I'll pay."

She hardly heard Stuart's words. "He saw my face and obviously knew me. If not, why would he give me a message for JC?" She stared at the wall. "If I report this to the cops, then whoever he is could come back to finish the job—kill me!"

"'A message for JC'?" Stuart's eyes popped as he held the wound edges together with one hand and applied steri-strips with the other so the cut would heal together. "How does Jean-Claude figure into this? What did he say?"

"His exact words were 'Tell Jean-Claude to pay up or else!'" She paused with a realization. "He spoke in English. Oh God! He must've been following me. How else would he know to say something to me in English?" She took a deep breath. "He might kill me next time. This is bad! Very bad. And I'm in the center of it."

"You can't go back to him." Stuart applied a gauze dressing and secured it with white silk tape. "It's not safe for you."

"I don't want to return home to the US." Her eyes watered. "Bel-Air is taking a step backwards for me."

"You can stay with me." His expression told her he wanted to say more. "The sofa bed is quite comfortable." He took her hand in his. "Cindy, I make no demands on you. I won't hide my feelings—that I wish we were more—much more than friends."

"I don't want to impose. You always seem to be there for me and I make no promises that we will ever be lovers." Her lips trembled. "I'm not even over what just happened. I never expected this in Paris."

Stuart kissed her temple. *Mom always kisses me there.* "Cindy, there are bad people everywhere, even in Paris. It's no different from anywhere else in the world."

"I'm still going to confront JC." She clenched her fists with determination as she eased onto a stool. "I must. He has to know what his so-called friends have done to me and the danger he placed me in."

"Let me go with you. I don't want you to face him alone." He leaned down and hugged her tightly. "If he has dangerous friends, he could have a dark side you haven't seen yet."

"I don't want JC to think I'm your mouthpiece—just saying what you instructed." Cindy snuggled into his chest.

All her fear came to the surface. Tears ran down her cheeks. She sobbed on his shirt. Sobs not only for her shattered dreams with Jean-Claude, but shattered dreams of her ruined marriage and dead baby. Everything seemed to well up in her all at once.

I thought I was so smart and I had all the answers. I'm such a fool. I wish Mom was here.

Stuart kissed the top of her head and stroked her hair.

I think Stu loves me. Is there enough of me left to love anyone?

Hugo jumped onto her lap and snuggled to her waist. She found his purrs comforting.

"I insist, Cindy." He lifted her chin so she'd look at him. "I *will* go with you. You will not face Jean-Claude alone. You mean too much to me."

"I know, Stu. I know." Her tears wet his shirt. "This time, I'll listen to you." She noticed the freshly opened cuts on his knuckles. Her fingers gently touched his wounds. "What happened? Did JC have something to do with this?"

Stuart swallowed hard. "I had to control an unruly customer."

~~***~~

Cindy's fingers fumbled as she tried to insert the key into the lock of Jean-Claude's apartment. Her hands shook so hard she couldn't do it. Stuart took the key from her and opened the door. Her heart pounded knowing the drama that would unfold. She feared for herself and for her friend. Mixed with that fear, was a slow-burning anger at her lover for not valuing her, nor their relationship.

Stuart started to enter first. She pushed in front of him. "No. This is my problem. I need to deal with JC."

Still in her blood-stained jacket and shirt, she stomped into the living room. Jean-Claude sat at the piano playing a song. He wiped his red nose with a tissue.

He never stood up when I entered. I left in a huff after our argument and he never cared.

"You don't even look up?" She walked to the piano and Stuart followed. "You never gave a second thought to where I was or what I was doing after I stormed out?"

Jean-Claude stopped playing. His eyes remained on the keyboard. "You went shopping, I presume. Isn't that what all women do to solve their problems—an expensive purchase puts everything right again?"

He's a condescending asshole!

Coming from behind, Stuart stood next to her. "Look at her! Cindy's been stabbed!" She saw the bulging vein in his forehead.

Jean-Claude studied the evidence of her wound. His mouth opened as if to speak.

She prevented his words. "I was stabbed by a thug because of you. I've been followed because of you. And for all I know, my life could be in danger because of you!"

An innocent expression veiled his face. "How is this about me? I know no such persons. My associations are with people who perform and are in music."

"Your so-called 'associations' run more deadly than music." She took a step closer. "The thug said to me, 'Tell Jean-Claude to pay up or else!' If he didn't *know you*, there is no reason for him to speak your name, nor say that statement in English to me." She was in his face now, Stuart right behind her.

"He *followed me!* He knew exactly where I was on that sidewalk outside of Galleries Lafayette—he probably followed me all through the store. This low-life thug waited for his chance to accost me in a crowd where he could make an easy escape. I saw him clearly and I can describe him to the police if I need to. He had black hair and a tattoo on his neck—some sort of spider thing. He wore a black leather jacket and reeked of stale cigarette smoke." She took a deep breath. "Where did you get that swollen nose and black eye—from a jealous husband or boyfriend when you were cheating on me?"

"This isn't possible. There has to be a mistake." Jean-Claude went to the bar for a drink. The way the bottle rattled on the edge of the glass told Cindy his hand was shaking as he poured the vodka into it. "Maybe you looked like someone else."

She laughed. "Yeah, right. And that 'someone else' just happens to have a friend with the same name as yours? Get real, JC! There's no mistake here." She backed up a few steps. "We're over! I'm getting my things and moving out! Let that blond warm your bed tonight!"

"No. Wait." Jean-Claude started to follow her. "This can all be explained."

"You can't explain any of this …. I noticed you didn't once ask about my injury." Cindy clenched her teeth.

He pleaded with an upturned palm. "You didn't give me a chance."

"That should've been your first concern—not trying to find a way to cover your ass." She pointed her finger with fury and hatred flaring from her eyes. "It's been all about you and your French Don Juan ego. I was something new and different. You never cared about me."

He took a swallow of his drink. "But, but—"

"No more! I don't want to hear your excuses." She turned on her heels and saw Stuart wanting to speak. "Stu, don't say anything. Just keep out of this."

Cindy rushed to the bedroom, leaving the door open. Stuart stood in the hallway, seemingly as a buffer between her and Jean-Claude. She opened the closet to retrieve her carry-on bag and stopped dead in her tracks. She stood there staring.

Am I really seeing this? I'm not believing my eyes! What a bastard!

"Stu! Come in here!" Her voice held a new fear.

He quickly entered. "What is it? What's wrong?"

She pointed at the closet. "Look! Look at what the bastard was planning—maybe already used!" Her eyes lit with fire and outrage. "Music isn't his only business!"

Jean-Claude entered and looked at the compromising evidence. "You're making assumptions."

"No I'm not!" She panted angry breaths. "That is a movie camera on a tripod all set up and ready to go!"

A dumbfounded look came to Jean-Claude's face. Stuart glared at the singer. Cindy threw her clothes into the suitcase and went to the bathroom for the rest of her belongings.

Jean-Claude followed her. "Why are you doing this? You just assume I was taking pictures of you? You're wrong. Photography is a hobby of mine. I never took photos of us as you are accusing."

She sneered with deep breaths. "Women and sex is your hobby."

With her toiletries in her arms, she pushed past and nearly shoved him against the door jam with her right shoulder. Cindy tossed the items in her case, and closed the latches.

Stuart stood with thinned lips and twitching jaw, clearly wanting to speak his say.

Jean-Claude pleaded his case. "You're not being fair. Hear me out."

"No words. No excuses." She jerked the carry-on off the foot of the bed. "Stu, we're leaving."

Cindy scurried down the hall with Stuart close behind her.

Jean-Claude stood, as if frozen at the bedroom doorway. She opened the door, then turned and looked at her now former lover. After a short silence, her grip tightened on the handle of the carry-on while she took a labored breath. Cindy yanked her purse from the entry side table, fished out the apartment keys, and threw them at Jean-Claude.

"What we had could have been beautiful. It could have been something to last a lifetime." A tear rolled down her cheek. Her bottom lip quivered. "You threw it all away. I was a fool to be taken in by your looks and your charm, and your insincere words."

Cindy gave the door a resounding slam.

Stuart pulled her into him and held her tightly. They stood there like that for a few moments.

The truth is so hurtful. JC never cared for me—not the same as I cared for him.

She pulled away from him and he wiped her tears with his fingertips. He smiled at her with kindness and love, and kissed her gently on her mouth.

"Let's get the hell out of here." Cindy pecked his cheek and strode purposefully toward the elevator.

In the courtyard, she took one last look at the cheerful surroundings that she used to call home.

"Stu, this is another closed chapter in my life." She walked to the main entry and pushed the door open. "I hope one day there will be a new happy chapter with no ending. I've had a gutful of pain."

She stepped onto the sidewalk. He put his arm around her shoulder and gave a squeeze.

"Cindy, you will have a happy chapter. You need to give life time." He took her hand. His clasp felt good to her.

She glanced over at him as they walked.

Stu is so kind and giving. Why was I so blind to his qualities?

They came to the corner, turned right onto *rue de Rivoli* and headed to his home.

"Looks mean nothing," she said as they strolled.

He looked straight ahead. "Never have with me."

She watched his slow smile emerge.

I feel safe with Stu. "I guess Don Draper only exists on the screen. I saw someone who wasn't there—a handsome and dashing illusion."

He chuckled. "Ah yes, Mad Men. I watch American television shows, too."

"Funny," she smiled weakly, "even though you have an English accent, you seem so American to me."

They turned the corner to his apartment entrance. "Don't do what you did with Jean-Claude. See me with clear and truthful eyes. I offer no pretense." He unlocked the main entry door. "I'm not handsome or wealthy. My face is plain. My life is very dull and ordinary."

"You're not to me. Your truth and honesty make you handsome ... to me." She kissed his lips with genuine emotion and no trace of passion.

If Stu is my ticket to happiness, I'm ready to take that ride with him.

Forty - Five

JEAN-CLAUDE SAT on the sofa with a glass of vodka in one hand and an e-cigarette in the other. He still shook. With the realization that his former lover's death in the Seine was not an accident and now with the attack on Cindy, his fear ran icy cold and dark.

Am I next? Will the newspapers post photos of my dead wet body being dragged from the river? He took a swallow of his drink. *Why didn't they kill me after my girlfriend? I must've made a payment shortly after her death—that's what saved me. I need to pay my debt. How? The blackmail scheme is dead, and I don't want to end up the same way.*

He took his phone and dialed. It rang several times before he heard an answer.

"We have to meet. Now! No arguments. *Place de la Concorde,* where it's public. I need a crowd for protection." He puffed rapidly on his e-cigarette.

"What's with you? You can't make payment to me in a crowd." Maurice sounded confused.

"Not the payment!" He stood up and walked over to the window. "Cindy was stabbed as a warning for me to pay the tac-tac debt."

I better stay clear of a window. A sniper could be gunning for me.

He moved from the window and walked to the hallway.

"I told you they play for keeps. My guess is your father is next." Maurice puffed on a cigarette.

"Look. I don't want to stay here now. I'll meet you at Tuileries in fifteen minutes—the fountain closest to the Louvre." He hung up.

Perspiration beaded on his forehead. He took his jacket and left the apartment. He didn't care if his fans recognized him or not.

It might be a good thing if devotees spot me. No hit man will take a chance with adoring fans in the mix.

Jean-Claude hurried across the street and entered the garden. It was only an hour before closing time. He checked his watch frequently.

Come on, Maurice. Where in hell are you?

He walked purposefully on the gravel paths.

It's harder to hit a moving target. I have to keep moving.

His vision sharpened as he studied every face he passed, on the alert for anyone or anything suspicious. At the entry gate near Tuileries Métro stop, he spotted Maurice. He nearly ran to him, kicking up dust. His friend clearly saw him, as a smile emerged.

"Calm down, mon ami. All is not lost." Maurice gave a warm hug. He started walking to a couple of green metal chairs under an oak tree.

"Shouldn't we keep walking? What if I'm a target?" Fear dwelled in Jean-Claude's eyes.

"You're safe with me. No one will take that chance while I'm around." Maurice settled on the seat. "So, tell me about this stabbing of your American lover."

He sat in the chair beside his friend, took a deep breath, and stared down at his shaking hands. "She was on the sidewalk outside of Galleries. He probably followed her through the store. In the middle of the crowd a man came up to her, told her in English 'Tell Jean-Claude to pay up or else!' Then he stabbed her left arm—only a flesh wound, but deep enough to cut through her jacket and blouse."

"Could she describe him—what he looked like, what he wore?" Maurice placed his hands on Jean-Claude's. "Stop shaking. It will be okay …. Do you need a hit? Is that why you're shaking?"

"I don't need a hit. I have plenty to last for a while if I don't share." His jaw twitched. "She said the man had black hair, scary eyes, smelled of old cigarette smoke … and he had a tattoo on his neck."

Having enough tac-tac is the least of my worries now.

"A tattoo?" Maurice's eyes narrowed.

Jean-Claude looked at his friend. *Does he know this man?*

"Yes. She said it was a spider design of some sort …. Isn't that a common description of most mob types?"

"Yes." Maurice rubbed his hands together. "It might be Guy."

"Guy? Guy who? What's his last name?" He inched to the edge of his seat. "Who does he work for?"

Maurice leaned closer to speak in his ear in a low voice. "Guy Cloutier, *The Nail*. He's an enforcer and major hit man for the organization."

"What organization? I know of no such group." His eyes moved back and forth taking in Maurice's reaction to his questions.

"You don't need to know." Maurice looked around, clearly to

see if anyone could overhear him. "Maçon calls all the shots. When he says you're done—you don't see another sunrise."

"That's what I'm afraid of."

How can he be so damn casual about this? My life is on the line!

He looked down at the dirt under his feet. "This was a warning. She only had a flesh wound. You still have time to get the one hundred thousand." He let out a chuckle. "Maybe he'll take installments." Maurice cocked an eyebrow. "It's worth a try, though no one has been successful with a payment schedule."

"Would you please ask Maçon for me?" A mask of horror lined his face.

"I'm in no position to talk directly to the man." He shrugged. "My contacts can pass the message."

"You're my only hope." Jean-Claude grabbed his friend's wrist in desperation. "You must do this for me."

"Your best hope is to pay up, and soon." A park official headed to the gate with keys in his hands. "We better leave." Maurice tilted his chin in the direction of the man standing by the entry. "They're getting ready to close up."

The two men made their way to the exit.

"Maurice, should I return to my apartment? Am I safe there?" He stared into Maurice's eyes. "Tell me the truth."

His friend scuffed the dirt and studied his feet. "Yeah, sure. You're safe there." He looked at his friend's eyes. "I'll start passing the word tonight. How much can you get for a down payment?"

"Not more than five thousand, maybe ten if my father helps."

I don't own enough to sell anything.

"Twenty-five would be better." He patted his back. "Would show more good faith on your part."

"Whatever you do, don't commit me to any set amount yet. I know I can get five."

I'm going to be murdered. I know it as much as I know my own face.

"Mon ami, you don't give me much to work with, but I'll do my best."

Jean-Claude glanced nervously from side-to-side, wary of suspicious faces. He wished the street he lived on had more streetlamps. He watched his drug buddy head down the street in the opposite direction.

Everything would have worked out perfectly if Cindy had cooperated. I could have the money to pay off this Maçon ghoul. I never wanted Cindy hurt. That was never part of the plan. There's no way I can make it up to her.

What was the name of that American movie? Dead Man Walking? That's me. I'm a dead man, tonight, tomorrow, sometime in the near future.

Forty - Six

CINDY ENJOYED A tour of Stuart's tiny apartment.

"This is the living room, as you already know." He chuckled. "The view of the Tuileries and the Eiffel Tower from the bedroom window makes up for its compact size." He continued to lead her as he talked. "This is the kitchen—very efficient despite its step-save dimensions." Stuart led her down a short, skinny hall, then opened a door. "Here's the bath, loo as the Brits say. I hope you don't mind a small stall shower. There was no room for a tub."

"I find your apartment cozy." Cindy eyed the hand-held shower appliance.

How does he ever fit in that stall? His shoulders are so broad. I bet turning around is a real squeeze.

"You're being polite." Stuart looked at her. "It's okay. I know it's small. But, the location is fantastic. I love the view."

He guided her to the last room. "Voilà. The bedroom. Besides the view of the Eiffel Tower, I have a built-in closet. That's a special treat." He opened the door and smiled with pride. "You can even walk into it."

"Very nice." She chuckled. "The closet is bigger than the bathroom. I'm glad I don't travel with a lot of clothes."

Stuart's hands rested on his hips. "I'll clear out a couple of drawers for you. My everyday clothes will fit in the living room chest. That way, you can make the boudoir yours."

"Stu, I don't intend to move you out of your own bedroom." She walked up to him and placed her hand on his chest. "I don't want to impose. I can live perfectly fine out of my carry-on." She brushed her bangs away. "I'm certain the sofa bed will be perfectly fine."

"I won't hear of it." He shook his head. His hands at the small of her waist drew her closer. "I want you to take the bed—my bed." He inclined his head boyishly. "Besides, you're recovering from a stabbing and deserve all the comfort I can provide."

Cindy bit her lip, glanced at the double bed, and looked back at his endearing blue eyes. "If you insist ..."

"I do insist." He kissed the tip of her nose. "Now, how about you get settled in while I brew us a delicious pot of French Press coffee?"

He briskly opened the dresser drawers, gathered his clothes and left the room. Cindy went to her suitcase and proceeded to unpack, guarding the use of her left arm. It still hurt and abrupt movements caused her to wince.

Stu is so generous and kind. I wish I wasn't blinded to his qualities before. I was such a fool. All of JC's falseness! Boy! Was I ever gullible. No more. I guess Mom was right when she said I was vulnerable.

She placed her bras and panties together in the corner of the drawer. She held up the expensive black ensemble.

This was meant for JC to see me wear. I'm glad I didn't give him the chance—even happier that I used his money to buy them.

She placed the costly lingerie in a special area, in the center of the drawer. Her hands balled up.

Stop it! Don't think of him. JC isn't worthy of your time. Don't give him control of your thoughts.

As she unpacked the last item of clothing, Stuart called out to her. "Coffee is ready in the living room."

He's so thoughtful. I made the right decision.

Cindy walked down the hall. She stopped short in the entry. Her eyes widened.

He went to a lot of trouble. Cookies, coffee, flowers, even potato chips.

"Please sit wherever you're comfortable." He placed a few paper napkins on the corner of the coffee table. "It's your time to be pampered."

She sat on the loveseat. "If you continue to spoil me like this, I won't want to ever leave."

His exuberant smile showed his white teeth. "That's the idea. You never have to leave."

He slid onto the seat beside her and poured coffee into the cups. They both reached for the cream at the same time. His fingers lingered on her hand.

Stuart apologetically smiled. "Sorry. You go first."

Cindy poured the cream into her cup. Hugo jumped in her lap. She stroked his back. He rewarded her with loud purring.

"He's missed you." He took a sip of coffee.

Cindy wrinkled her brow as she reached for a cookie from the plate.

"Hugo. He missed you. He and I have two more things in common." Stuart reached over to the cat and scratched him behind the ears.

"What's that?"

He's so charming … such a flirt.

"We missed you and are very happy you have returned to us."
He put his arm around her shoulder.

"I am, too." She kissed his cheek. "This is home for awhile."

"I'll do everything in my power to make this a home you'll
never want to leave."

He kissed her lovingly on the forehead. The feel of that kiss
warmed her.

*Stu gives me a comfort I haven't felt in a very long time. His embrace feels
good to me—something strong and right. Will he be sleeping in my bed
tonight? Or, I in his? I know he won't force me to do anything I don't want
to do.*

Forty - Seven

JEAN-CLAUDE DREW the bedroom drapes, even though it was the middle of the day. His fear hadn't subsided since speaking with Maurice in the park. He couldn't sit still as he went from the bedroom to the living room and back again. He firmly believed his every movement was watched. His paranoia magnified every sound he heard and every passing shadow in his periphery. Sitting on the edge of the bed, he dialed his father's number and waited while tapping his fingers rapidly on his knee.

Damn it, Papa! Answer the fucking phone!

Finally he heard his father's voice.

"What took you so long to answer?" Jean-Claude's voice screamed urgency.

"I was away from the phone." Charles coughed. "What is so important?"

"I need some money—a lot of money." He made a tight fist, drawing his knuckles white with bulging veins. "I'm in big trouble. You're the only one who can help me."

"How much?" Charles spoke with detached sternness.

Jean-Claude took a deep breath and spoke nearly inaudibly, "One hundred thousand."

"Did I hear you correctly?" A moment of silence showed his disbelief. "One hundred ...*thousand?* What fancy abortionist charges that amount of money?" He paused. "Or are you being blackmailed for cheating with a married woman? I told you to stick to the single ladies."

"Papa, it's not women. It's worse."

Please come through for me.

"What could be worse than a blackmail threat?"

"I owe the money to a very bad man ... a dangerous man."

Will he believe me?

"What type of man?" Another pause annoyed Jean-Claude. "Son, what have you gotten yourself involved in?"

He nearly whispered, "I use."

"You 'use'? Use what, exactly?" His father's voice grew cold. "Alcohol? Marijuana?"

He took two deep breaths. Perspiration ran down his back. "Cocaine, Papa." He sobbed. "I use cocaine and the man who sells it wants to be paid."

"If that is true, you need rehab." Icy control pierced his words. "Money won't help you now."

Jean-Claude's hand shook as he held the phone to his ear. Tears rimmed his eyes. "Papa. If I don't pay, I will be dead! Do you want to be without a son?"

"I don't believe you." He heard his father's sigh. "Too many times you have tried with your lies and schemes to get money from me for your foolishness. I remember that you begged me for money for your dying girlfriend. That turned out to pay for that racehorse you bought. Another stupid idea that went absolutely nowhere. You ended up with a horse only good enough to use for riding lessons and I ended up fifty thousand poorer."

"I'm serious, Papa." He trembled. "This is no plan to get money from you for a plaything. I'm scared. I've never been this scared in my life." His anger surfaced. "You owe me. It's part of my inheritance."

"Hold on, dear son. You're not entitled to *anything* I own until I'm dead." His voice rose an octave. "I worked for everything. No one handed one penny to me for free. That's a lesson you have yet to learn."

"If I don't pay this man, then you might be dead before me." The vein in his neck throbbed. "Your death would be their way of sending me a warning."

"You are desperate, Jean-Claude." He paused. "You are bluffing to get money from me. No more. Not one single euro. First you say your life is in danger, now you change and say it's me." He let out a sarcastic laugh. "Get your story straight before you try to con me."

"Fous le camp, Papa! You're sending me to my death!" He took a long drag from his e-cigarette.

"Don't tell me to fuck off! Who in hell do you think you're talking to? I'm not part of your 'yes men' entourage." Charles hung up.

Jean-Claude swallowed hard as the phone went dead.

~~***~~

Cindy came from the bedroom dressed in her comfy nightshirt. She stretched and gave an expansive yawn, then headed to the kitchen. Stuart, dressed in pajamas, a terrycloth robe, and worn leather slippers, stood at the tiled counter. He scooped French roast ground coffee into the press and poured boiling water before placing the plunger on the top. He looked up and walked over to her, ready to give a good morning kiss.

"No kisses yet." She turned her head. "I haven't brushed my teeth." She yawned again, placing her hand over her mouth. "What time is it?"

"Eight o'clock. Why?" He took the sugar from the counter and then the cream from the refrigerator. "You have plans?"

"No plans." She took the cups and placed them on the tray he had laid out. "You? Have places to be?"

"None." He poured the cream into a creamer. "It's Sunday, the store is closed. No obligations."

"While you finish up, I'll wash my face and such." She left for the bath.

When cleaning her teeth and brushing her hair, Cindy's mind wandered.

Stu is certainly making an effort to please me. Is this all for show, or is this how he truly is—caring and unselfish? I want to believe he is. I thought so last night. What has changed? Is it me? Am I so hurt and damaged that I can't recognize a genuine feeling in a man anymore? Damn JC for affecting me like this! Stop it, Cindy. Don't let JC control you.

When she returned to the dining area of the small living room, Stuart had the morning meal set, complete with napkins. Cindy smiled.

JC never set out breakfast for me. He gave me money to go to a café for coffee and a croissant. It's always easier to hand out some cash instead of putting in the effort to do something nice.

She sat at the small table while Stuart placed glasses of orange juice, bowls, a box of cornflakes, milk, the steaming coffee carafe, sugar, and cream in the center. He looked proud of his offerings.

"I went to Monoprix when you agreed to stay here, and picked up what I thought you would like." He sat down. "The local markets don't have American style food." He chuckled. "So sorry if it's not to your taste."

"It's exactly what I like." Cindy poured the cereal into her bowl. "I haven't had cornflakes in ages. This is a treat—makes me feel like I'm home."

He filled her cup with coffee. "That's the idea. I'm hoping you'll feel you are home."

"You're too good to me." She added milk to the bowl.

"To the contrary." Stuart took a sip of juice. "You deserve so much more."

Cindy took a mouthful of flakes and spoke between chews. "You didn't come to bed with me last night. Why is that?"

"First, I felt you were still in too much pain from your wound." He chewed his cereal. "Second and more importantly, I felt you need time for your emotions to heal. I don't want to rush you and I only want to share your bed at your invitation." He gazed intently into her eyes. "If that invitation never comes, I will understand. I won't like it, mind you—but, I'll accept it."

"How did I ever deserve you?" Cindy prepared her coffee. "I wish I had met you from the very beginning—before Vic."

"But, if you had, you wouldn't be as you are now." He wiped his mouth with a napkin. "Those experiences—good or bad— have molded you into the person you are now."

"Still, I wouldn't have minded skipping the bad stuff." She took a swallow of coffee. "Whatever good that came of it, I could've done without."

"Cindy," he reached for her hand across the table, "without the pain, the good doesn't taste as sweet nor can it be truly appreciated."

Taking the cup to her mouth, she looked over the rim. "You have such wisdom for someone so young."

"Twenty-eight is not young." He chuckled. "By some people's standards that makes me an old man."

Surprise colored her words. "I didn't know you were older than me."

"That can be a blessing and a curse for me." He took a spoonful of cereal and chewed. "Some don't treat me with the respect due an adult. I get that a lot from customers thinking I'm one of the hired employees. Maybe that's why my writing isn't taken seriously."

"How is that? Age discrimination in Europe?"

He rubbed his thighs. "When submitting my stories to publishers, many will ask for a photo." He laughed. "I thought of sending a false photo, but that didn't feel right—not honest. Besides, if they want to meet me, I would look nothing like the one I submitted. That would end my writing career immediately. Writing and publishing is made up of a close group." He poured more coffee into her cup. "There's always someone who knows somebody from somewhere."

"Have you started your book yet?" She took the last spoonful of cereal. "Is there anything I can read?"

"I only have a loose outline." He refreshed her coffee. "It wouldn't make any real sense, mostly phrases and bullet point ideas."

"What about a plot?" She prepared her coffee with cream and sugar. "I remember you said that you wanted your characters to be set in either English or French history."

"I'm so glad you're interested." His smile broadened. "Yes. I still have much research to do. I think French history—a setting around the time of Louis Seizième during the Reign of Terror."

She tried to repeat the French word correctly. "Say-zee-em? What's that?"

"So sorry. My French sneaks into my English sometimes." He started to gather the used bowls. "That's sixteenth. Louis the sixteenth was very clueless, as Americans say. He had no idea that the populace was starving—literally starving. I read somewhere that the poor would mix dirt with flour to make bread in an effort to get more loaves baked from what they had. People would eat grass, rats, cats, dogs—anything they could get their hands on."

"I can't imagine such horrible circumstances." She pushed her empty bowl and spoon to the side. "Are you going to have your main character be one of the peasants, or one of the royals?"

"I'm not certain." He rubbed his chin. "If I choose a peasant, then I'm just rehashing 'A Tale of Two Cities' or 'Les Misérables'. So that won't work. I'm considering the viewpoint of a middle-class person. Someone who's not a peasant, maybe a professional of some sort. Many in that class were persecuted and singled out by the revolutionaries, and found guilty by association with a royal."

"Where's the sense of that?" *Stu is fascinating. He knows so much.* "Just because a doctor knows an evil royal person doesn't make him evil."

"Ahh," his eyes lit up with enthusiasm, "that's where the mob mentality comes in. All reason is lost. Common sense is lost."

Cindy looked at the worn clock on the wall. "I'd love to read some of your stories."

He made a face. "I have to translate them into English first. I don't know if they would interest you. They're about the human situation and man's search for a better life—the utopian quest."

"That will have to be a subject we discuss later." She stood up. "I need to shower and get dressed …. I'll do the dishes."

He cocked his head as if confused. "What?"

"I'll wash the dishes … It's the least I can do."

I forget he doesn't understand American colloquialisms.

"Next time. Go take your shower." He collected the dirty dishes and placed them on the tray as she started to leave.

"There are clean towels in the cabinet over the toilet."

"Thanks." Cindy went to the bedroom to gather fresh clothes.

Stu is making headway with me by leaps and bounds. He's so wise, as if he's already lived a lifetime. I like him—a lot. Do I love him? I'm not sure. So much has happened in such a short time.

Will I sleep with him?

Forty - Eight

STUART PULLED UP Frédéric's number on his phone. He hoped he would be free to talk while Cindy was in the shower. It rang a half dozen times before there was an answer.

"Fréd, can you talk?" He spoke in a soft and pressured tone. "I need to fill you in on what's happened to Cindy. She doesn't know I'm calling you."

"Is she sick?" He sounded concerned.

"Not sick. But injured." He walked to the kitchen and turned on the faucet to cloud his voice from Cindy overhearing the conversation. "She's physically okay."

"What happened? Should I call her mother?" Faint children's voices came from the background.

"I don't think her parents need to be involved." He poured milk into a small dish. "Cindy was stabbed on the sidewalk outside Galleries by a thug as a warning for Jean-Claude to pay his debt— most likely for drugs."

"Mon Dieu! Is she still with him?" Stuart could hear him puff on a cigarette.

Hugo rubbed himself against his legs. "No, she's living with me. Hopefully, for good."

"Where was she stabbed?" Urgency sounded from the phone.

Stuart placed the dish of milk on the floor and smiled at Hugo, lapping it up. "It was a flesh wound on her left upper arm. I cleaned it and dressed her cut at the store. She refused to go to the police and refused to go to urgent care."

"She's not seeing Jean-Claude anymore, right?" Frédéric's voice sounded clouded as if distracted.

"No. She broke it off with him." Hugo purred loudly. "You sound far away at times. Am I keeping you from something or someone?"

"No. Since it's Sunday, I'm in the park. I was returning a child's ball that landed near my feet." Cheerful children's voices continued in the background. "Then all is well with Cindy?"

"So far." He looked out the window at the side street. "But now, Cindy has been identified as someone important to Jean-Claude. She might be a walking target until he pays his bill."

"Want my PI friend to snoop around and see what he can uncover?" He coughed.

"That will help." He took a deep breath. "Though until that bill is paid, Cindy could still be in danger. I didn't tell her that, though."

"That's best. Don't worry her unnecessarily." He paused. "The safest place for her is back home in Bel-Air."

"Cindy told me she won't return there." Hugo wrapped his tail around his ankle. He heard the noise of the shower stop. "Look. I have to go. She's out of the shower."

~~***~~

A turned up jacket collar, oversized dark sunglasses and a wide brimmed hat served as Jean-Claude's disguise from being recognized by pedestrians and more importantly, anyone who wanted to follow him. His fear mounted with every step as he trudged the steep streets that led to Monique's apartment. The narrow, convoluted streets offered hiding places to those who could follow others, and persons wishing to escape someone watching from the shadows. He held his head downward to avoid eye contact. His heart pounded. Perspiration caused his shirt to cling to his back. Jean-Claude wiped his clammy palms on his pants and beads of sweat trickled down his temples and at the back of his neck. He came to Musée de Montmartre on *rue Cortot* and farther to *rue Paul Féval* where he turned right, and then climbed the steps leading to her apartment. Fear lent an urgency to his steps and inhibited fatigue. He knew the security code and pushed the buttons. When it buzzed, he shoved the door open, and ran to her apartment where he rang the bell repeatedly.

His harsh voice echoed from the close stone wall behind him. "Monique! Come to the door, damn you!"

There was no answer. Jean-Claude pounded with his fist. He turned his gaze from side to side to ensure no strange and suspicious eyes were on him.

"Damn it, Monique! This is serious!"

What am I going to do? Where can I go? She's my only hope!

A faint voice came from the other side. "I'm coming. Wait a minute."

"It's Jean-Claude. Open the fucking door!" His voice shattered the quiet of others.

The door opened. Monique, still dressed in a nightgown, greeted him with a weak smile. He rushed past her while she closed the door.

"Quel problème? All of Paris on fire or something?" Her bedroom slippers made a scuffing sound as she headed to the kitchen, kicking used food wrappers aside as she went.

"Don't you ever clean around here?" Jean-Claude removed the old scattered newspapers from the sofa, clearing a space for him to sit down.

"My maid has been sick." She called back from the kitchen. "I've been partying with friends."

"Men?" He noticed the remnants of tac-tac in lines on a mirror, with a razor blade nearby. "A maid? Since when did you get a maid?"

Monique came from the kitchen with two empty wine glasses and a less-than-full bottle of wine. She shoved a food-stained fashion magazine to one side on the coffee table, placed the wine in the small vacant area, and flopped down next to him on the sofa. She was careful not to disturb the few lines of cocaine on the mirrored tile.

"I was joking about the maid." She smoothed a strand of hair away from her face. "Me partying with men? Would you really care all that much?"

He leaned forward with his arms on his knees. Muscles in his jaw twitched as he stared straight ahead.

"Yes, I would care." He rubbed his hands together. "I have to stay with you. I'm being followed. My place isn't safe anymore."

She placed her hand on his. "What's wrong?"

"Very bad people are after me." His eyes held fearful tears. "I haven't paid for my tac-tac. They're out to get me."

She poured the wine, and handed him his glass. "You've been using too much. You're paranoid. Lay off for a few days."

Jean-Claude turned and looked directly in her eyes. "Listen to me." He started to speak slowly in an effort to control his fear. "Someone is out to kill me unless I can come up with one hundred thousand."

"Euros?" Her jaw dropped.

"I'm not talking about old French eighteenth century sous .... Yes! Euros!" Beads of sweat dotted his brow and hairline. "I've been threatened. Cindy was stabbed. Just before the attack the thug said, 'Tell Jean-Claude to pay up.!'"

Her eyes popped with almost as much fear to equal his. "Is she all right? Is she in the hospital?"

"Cindy's okay. It was a flesh wound." His fingers wiped the

moisture from his upper lip. "She moved out. We've broken up. I don't know where she went. She'll be okay—she's a survivor."

He lifted the glass to his lips with shaking hands and took a large swallow. "My supplier told me I'm next."

"I wish I had the money to give you, but I'm broke until my next modeling gig." She rubbed his back affectionately. "Don't you have any money?" She raised an eyebrow.

He shook his head. "I could ask the same of you. Where did all your money go, besides up your nose?"

She laughed. "I guess we're two of a kind—mixed up, but all in all, not bad."

"So ... can I stay here?" *She must say yes. Monique's my only hope.*

"Bien sûr. What about your father?" She took a swallow of wine.

"He refused. I pleaded, but it was to no use." Jean-Claude looked around at the unkempt room. "Got any liquor? I need a real drink."

"All gone since last night." She bit her lip. "I'll get dressed and go out and buy some vodka—that's your favorite. I'll get clean bed sheets, too." She paused. "You need tac-tac?"

"Brought my stash with me—in my jacket lining." He scratched his forehead with his thumb. "Why get bed linen? Don't you have more than one set?"

What type of binge has she been on?

"I haven't done the laundry yet." She started toward the bedroom.

"Running a comb through your hair couldn't hurt."

Is she hooked on cocaine worse than me? She might need me more than I do her. Will I really be safe here? Could I be putting Monique in danger? Impossible! They think Cindy is my woman—they'll be hunting her.

~~***~~

Early afternoon in Jardin du Luxembourg, in the sixth arrondissement, provided a nice respite from the city noise, congestion in the street and sidewalks as well as relief from automotive fumes. Colorful flower plantings made a beautiful backdrop while children sailed their toy boats in the large fountain amid the lazily swimming ducks. Squeals of tots on the carousel or swings denoted their joy. Green benches provided a welcome rest for tired parents, or a cozy meeting place for lovers.

Frédéric waited on a bench by the Fontaine de Médicis. He glanced up at the sound of gravel from every approaching footstep.

His senses grew keener with each passing minute. He checked his watch, and then checked his phone for any missed calls or new text messages. There were none.

Claude sat down beside him. He held a newspaper, opened it up and appeared to be reading.

"What's with the cloak and dagger routine? I didn't hear your footsteps." Frédéric looked around. "Is someone following you?"

"Habit." He talked into his paper. "I'm never certain who's lurking somewhere. Pick up your phone and act like you're texting someone. Don't speak directly to me."

He did as Claude requested. "What did you find out?"

"The girl in the Seine was Jean-Claude's lover. Her death was a warning for him to pay his debt." He angled his back slightly to Frédéric. "Cindy's in danger and should go back home where's it's safe."

"I already figured that out. She was stabbed as a warning to that bastard." He continued to play with his phone. "She broke up with him, is living with Dumont."

"How bad was the cut?" He turned a page.

"Just a flesh wound." Frédéric looked around to check for an eavesdropper. "She refuses to leave."

"Not good for her." He checked his watch. "They play rough. Life means nothing."

"What about Charles? Wouldn't his father be in danger, too?"

How am I going to get Cindy to understand the danger?

"Maçon knows he and his father don't get along." He paused. "If he whacks his father, the message wouldn't be as strong— whack someone he loves—well, that's different."

"He's no longer seeing Cindy, that makes no sense to harm her." He thought a moment. "Unless they don't know they've broken up."

"Exactement, mon ami. Exactly." He folded his paper as if getting ready to leave. "Reasoning and what makes sense to you and I, are not the same for them."

Claude stood up and walked away leaving Frédéric with more worry.

What on earth am I going to do? Cindy is just as headstrong as her mother. I must impress upon her that her situation is worse than dangerous—it's now deadly.

Forty - Nine

JOE RESTED IN a chaise lounge by the Davis' pool in Bel-Air. His eyes squinted from the bright morning light dancing from the water's surface. Worry about Cindy lined his forehead while he petted Gigi and Jacques in his lap. His cell phone rang. He eyed the caller ID.

"Sal, what's the news?" He uncrossed his legs and leaned forward, causing Gigi and Jacques to jump down.

"Not good, ol' friend." He took a deep breath. "Cindy's been stabbed."

Joe jerked forward in his chair. His eyes grew wide and his mouth opened. "Stabbed? How? Who did this? Did they find him?"

"Calm down." His voice was low and reassuring. "She's okay. Didn't have to go to no hospital."

"Was this random?" The muscles in his jaw tensed. "Does this have somethin' to do with LeGrand?"

"Seems this Jean-Claude guy has unpaid cocaine debt." He heard his friend puff from a cigarette. "The hit man gave a message to her before the stabbin'. Somethin' 'bout Jean-Claude payin' what he owes to Maçon."

"Will he carry through on his threat?"
She's too far away for me to help her.

"He's known to be a man of his word on occasion." Sal took a deep breath. "Look, if LeGrand pays the man, everythin' will be okay. Then again, one of LeGrand's old lovers paid the price of endin' up in the Seine—dead and bruised. Was written off as an accident by the French cops."

"That's a damn big 'if' to be goin' on." Joe rubbed his chin. "I don't know how I'm gonna tell Lar 'bout this. It could kill Taylor. She's got a bad heart."

"Can't help you there." Background honking horns came over the phone. "You know what's best. If it was a kid of mine, I'd get her home—like yesterday."

"She wouldn't come home on my sayin' so." The poodles reached up to be petted, and he mindlessly patted their curly heads. "Cindy's stubborn and independent like Tay."

"Ah, like mother, like daughter." He chuckled. "Why don't y' text her? Or better yet, call her?"

"Stupid me. I don't have her number. Tay and Lar have that

info." He took a deep breath. "I can't ask for that stuff without raisin' questions from both of 'em."

"Looks like you're in a real pickle." A sipping noise came over the phone.

"Cindy's in the pickle—the whole damn vat! Wish I knew how to get to her." Joe rubbed his chin. Worry lined his eyes.

"Gotta go and make a delivery for my boss." Sal chuckled. "I'm still a runner."

Joe hung up his phone.

I don't see any way around this but to tell Lar. Tay can't be told at all costs. She's too fragile. I can't risk makin' Lar a widower.

~~***~~

Maurice waited for Guy in his favorite hangout bar in Pigalle, not far from Montmartre in the eighteenth arrondissement. He sat on a stool nursing his drink. He checked his watch. It was a quarter to two. He fidgeted and wondered if Maçon's man would show.

If he doesn't come, all will be lost for Jean-Claude.

The clock over the whiskey bottles ticked the torturous minutes as they passed one by one.

Two o'clock. Still, Guy Cloutier had not crossed the entry. Maurice's eyes darted repeatedly from the clock to the front door.

At two-ten, the door opened. Guy stood there for a moment before making eye contact with Maurice. He remained silent, and angled his head in the direction of the alleyway through the back access, indicating that Maurice should follow him.

Once outside, Maurice followed Guy down a narrow and dirty path littered with dumpsters that flavored the air with the stench of rotten food and spilled alcohol. Guy didn't appear distracted by the street prostitute orally servicing her customer. He stopped and faced Maurice, then took a long drag on his cigarette, clearly waiting for his pseudo friend to speak first.

"LeGrand wants to work things out." Maurice shoved his hands in his pockets.

"How?" He shrugged. "Only one way. Pay up."

"He can't get all the money at once." He kicked at some dirt. "How about time payments?"

"My boss ain't a damn bank." His eyes narrowed. "How much down payment?"

"He can get five thousand right now." Maurice fingered his trusty jackknife in his pants pocket.

Guy laughed and then sneered. "That's only a token. Not even good faith." He cocked his head. "Guess his lady will have to receive a stronger message next time."

"C'mon, man." Fear clutched him. "He's been a good customer for years. That should count for something. Buy him some time. Look at all the new business he's brought in."

Guy raised his hand. Maurice flinched and gripped his knife tighter in his pocket.

Is he going to hit me?

"Calm down." He chuckled. "I have no problem with you. You're safe."

"You raised your hand." Maurice still gripped his knife.

"Only to pat you on the back." He glanced at another prostitute and then motioned to her. "I know the man won't accept less than what's owed him." The prostitute came to his side. "I've explained all LeGrand's begging efforts, and it's a no-go."

"I'll tell him and see what he says." *Cindy's dead—no other way around it.* "When will the hit be?"

"You take me for an asshole?" He scoffed. "I tell you that so you can get rid of her? I'm not dumb. Besides, the man tells me when. I merely carry out orders."

"Got it." He shook his head. "Too bad. She was a nice girl."

Maurice backed away from Guy and stopped in the bar's back door, watching the street-walker unzip Guy's pants, kneel down, and service his needs. He shook his head.

I bet with his power he doesn't even pay her. He gets off whenever he wants.

Maurice passed through the bar and out the front entrance. He strode along *Boulevard de Clichy* dreading the call he must make to Jean-Claude.

There's no way I can save him now. If Cindy takes the hit and he doesn't pay up, he could be next. Maçon might want to make him an example to others.

He came to a neighborhood café and sat down at an outside table. A waiter appeared and took his order for a beer. Taking his phone from his pocket and with a heavy sigh, he dialed.

"Jean-Claude, it's a no-go." The server brought his beer.

"What about the five thousand?" His voice sounded urgent.

"Won't hear of it." He sipped the tepid brew. "Looks like your girlfriend is going to get a stronger warning."

"I never wanted that for her." He sighed deeply. "My hands are tied. What about my father? Any mention of him?"

"None." He took a large swallow. "The target is your woman."

"I'm so sorry for Cindy." He paused. "She was a nice girl. I can't get the hundred thousand to save her."

The phone went dead.

Fifty

LA DÉFENSE'S STARK modern and enormous buildings reaching to the Paris sky created a noticeable contrast to the traditional and romantic aspects of the city. Cindy craned her neck as she looked at the looming, yet spacious Grande Arche. This was a cityscape she embraced and demonstrated that fact by taking numerous photos of the architecture. Stuart posed at her request by a sculpture near the modern colorful fountain. In a few photos he sported a funny face or position. She continued taking pictures of the vista from the arch to the Arc de Triomphe, and farther on to the famous Oblisque of *place de la Concorde*.

"Haven't you taken enough photos?" Stuart sat on the steps leading under the arch to the platform. "Aren't you fearful about that thug spotting you out in the open—sending Jean-Claude the same message as when you were outside Galleries?"

"I won't live in fear. Someone in his circle must already know we've broken up. JC is probably with a new woman. Besides, I'm with you and I know you'll protect me. Especially after you decked that drunk at Le Garage and that obnoxious customer in your store." Cindy turned slowly as she took video on her phone. "I love the mix of extreme modernity and the old world buildings. What's the name of the street that connects this arch with the smaller one?"

Stuart stood up and peered in the direction she described. He shielded his eyes from the sunlight.

"Oh. You must mean the arch built by Napoléon—Arc de Triomphe. That street is a boulevard. It's the *Champs Élysée*—the most famous street in all of Paris."

She put her phone away. "So this place is all business buildings? Anything to check out besides the outside sculptures and that cool fountain?"

"There's a lot to see." Stuart discreetly gestured to the points of interest as he spoke. "The carousel over there, the underground is a vast labyrinth of shops, the Métro, RER, eateries of all descriptions. I buy most of my clothes here—far cheaper than any place else in the center of Paris."

Across the vast open area, she noticed the Air France offices.

If I ever need to go home, at least I know where to get a ticket. Stop guessing! Paris is now my home and Stuart's in it.

"Well then, let's go explore." She took his hand. "Lead on."

They rode the down escalator to the underground mall. Cindy discovered that this subterranean shopping experience was several levels deep. Looking through the various shop windows reminded her of a past.

Mom and I would have shopping days. That was nice. Talking fashion and having lunch together.

Impulsively, she stopped into an art supply store, bought a sketch pad and some drawing pencils.

Dad always encouraged my art. It's time I return to that passion.

Cindy and Stuart took a break at a fast-food eatery. Discovering that this McDonald's had the same menu offerings as the States delighted her. She noticed the only difference was that wine was listed. They placed their orders. Cindy insisted on paying for lunch.

After locating a table, they settled down to enjoy the American fare. She ate with relish, savoring the first bite with closed eyes.

"It seems like ages since I had crispy fries and a good burger without a fancy sauce." *JC didn't give me a McDonald's treat.* "I'm so glad I know where this place is."

Stuart chuckled. "You don't have to come all this way for this indulgence. There's a McDonald's near us. At the corner of *rue de l'Échelle* and *rue de Rivoli*. Only about seven blocks from us, toward the Louvre."

"Good to know. Every now and then I need a shot of American in my stomach." She dunked a French-fry into a pile of ketchup on the hamburger wrapper. "I've been thinking about Mom quite a lot."

"Is that a good thing for you?" He dipped his potato piece into mayonnaise. "I recall you said you and she had a difficult past."

"Yes. That's true." She sipped her cola. "But I-I think it's time I do the old forgive and forget routine—though forgetting isn't an option."

"Your forgiveness is more of a gift to you. It's the first step to slay those demons." He touched the top of her hand with a soothing movement. "Do you want to tell me what happened between you and your mum?"

"No. It wouldn't be fair to her. Those are things I have no right to share with anyone." *I wish Mom was here.* "I love her very much."

"You need to say those words to her as much as she needs to hear them." He lifted her chin with his fingers. "Those unfalling tears are for your mum. Call her."

"I might text her." Her chest heaved as she wiped her eyes with the paper napkin. "Texting is an easier first step."

I'll reach out to her when I'm stronger and can truly accept all her wrongs.

"Make certain that you do." He inclined his head. "I'll be your strength to take that first step. There are times I wish I knew my birth mother. I don't even know if she's alive. It would be nice to meet her—if only once."

"Maybe someday you'll find her."

I'm lucky. I have Mom. Stu has an adoptive mother—still, that's not quite the same.

~~***~~

Larry sat at the electronic keyboard playing a chord sequence. He looked up as Joe entered the home studio and shut the door quietly.

"Lar, got some bad news."

Joe's solemn expression yanked at Larry. "You look as if someone died."

"Not yet." Joe looked at the floor. "It's about Cindy and Jean-Claude. Not good."

"Out with it." Larry stopped playing the melody. "Is she hurt?"

"No. Seems Jean-Claude is usin' cocaine and ran up a big debt." Joe's eyes watered.

"How does that affect Cindy?" His eyes showed alarm. "Has he gotten her hooked? My God is she snorting that crap, too!"

"No, boss. She's clean, but, but …" he hesitated.

"But what?" Larry stood up and grabbed his brother's shoulders with both hands. "Tell me, Joe. What is so bad that you're having trouble telling me?"

Joe took a deep breath. "She was stabbed—just a flesh wound. She's okay."

"Stabbed!" Larry flopped back down on the piano bench. "How? When? Where?"

"On a public sidewalk, I guess." Joe patted his shoulder. "It wasn't random."

"You mean she was a target?" He grabbed his brother's arm. "Why would anyone want to hurt her?"

Joe sat down in the chair next to him. He interlaced his fingers while leaning his arms on his thighs. "You know I got this friend in New York?"

Larry nodded.

"Well, I called Sal and had him do some long-range snoopin' to Paris. He's got contacts all over."

"Go on, Joe. Get to the point. How bad is this?"

"Bottom line is, Cindy's stabbin' was a warnin' for Jean-Claude to pay up." He shook his head. "I'm damn frightened for her. These guys play dirty and send ugly messages when someone owes money."

"Joe, Cindy needs to come home. I need to go and get her."

Poor Tay. This will devastate her.

"Chief, she didn't want to return home when she was attacked." He laughed lightly. "I doubt she'll want to return now. Might think nothin' more will happen to her."

"How ugly are these 'messages' that the drug cartel sends to Jean-Claude?" He saw Joe bite his lip. "Tell me. I need to know!"

"Pretty ugly." Joe's eyes reddened. "His last girlfriend was found dead in the Seine. The French cops ruled it an accident because of an overdose. Guess she had a lot of coke in her system. My source said it was because Jean-Claude hadn't paid his drug bill."

"Oh my God! Joe, I have to do something, and quick." Larry stood and started pacing in the small room.

"How you gonna do that without tellin' Taylor?" He upturned his palms. "She's got a bad heart. This could kill her."

He looked straight into Joe's eyes. "The death of her daughter could kill her, too."

"Short of flyin' over there and forcibly takin' her, what's the answer." Joe grabbed Larry's upper arm. "You can't fly there without Taylor hammerin' you with questions. You got no answers except the truth—and that's not an option."

"Can't your contact buddy keep her safe?" Larry felt helpless. "Maybe follow her in some way so no harm will come to her?"

Joe watched Larry's continued pacing. "My guy doesn't have that kind of power. He called in a lot of big favors to get this much info."

"I'll pay whatever it costs to protect her." Larry's fists tightened and released repeatedly.

"This time, your money won't help, not without jeopardizin' Taylor." He paused. "Are you willin' to take that chance?"

Larry took his phone from the top of the electronic keyboard. He dialed Cindy's number. Voicemail answered.

He left a message, "Cindy, call me. It's important. You need to return home. All will be forgiven. We love you. Please come home."

Next, he sent her a text with the same message.

His worry plagued him.

I don't expect her to reply. She's too stubborn and self-confident. Too damn independent and certain she'll always be safe.

Fifty - One

GUY'S STEALTHY STEPS took him along the path. He kept his head down and only snatched sideways peeks through his sunglasses at anyone who might observe him. He was in luck. The courtyard and surroundings were vacant of a soul, save for a yellow tabby cat curled up at another door. He came to the entry, put on latex gloves from his back pocket, then covered his black boots with surgical coverings. He knocked on the door.

A female voice came from the other side, "Un moment."

While waiting, he pulled up his collar around his neck even higher than before. He tugged his leather jacket sleeves downward to obliterate any trace of skin.

She opened the door and smiled. "Bonjour, Guy. Come right in. I have the money if you have the tac-tac."

He said nothing and watched the young woman grab her purse from the cluttered coffee table. She took out a wad of euros. Guy stuffed the money into his pants' pocket. She held her hand, palm up, in anticipation. He stepped forward to her, forcing her to move backwards until the back of her legs rubbed the edge of the sofa.

Her voice quivered. "What's wrong? Why are you like this? Where's my tac-tac? You want to play first? I can play as long as you give me my stuff. Afternoon sex is always fun."

His hand grabbed the back of her neck.

The young woman froze. Her eyes opened in pure panic when he drew the .38 with silencer attached. She seemed to be rigid with terror. Guy easily held her with one hand, which made his job easier. It was more fun for him when they struggled. With cold precision, he placed the gun at her forehead. His mouth widened in a sardonic smile of pleasure. He enjoyed the thrill and power as his index finger caressed and then slowly squeezed the trigger.

A muffled explosion pierced the air. Bits of brain tissue, bone fragments, and blood splattered the walls.

Guy dropped the girl's body, her eyes wide open in a dead stare, and let it fall backwards onto the sofa. Her limbs flopped grotesquely like a discarded puppet.

~~***~~

Jean-Claude's stomach clenched as he climbed the few steps to Monique's apartment. Yellow and black crime scene tape quartered off access to her door. Police milled about taking notes on pads, some gathering evidence, taking photos, and others questioning bystanders.

Was there a burglary? That would be typical for this neighborhood.

A uniformed flic stood in the open doorway as he approached and turned to him. "No one is allowed to enter."

What the hell is going on? Did Monique get busted for possession? Never! She's too smart for that.

He looked over the policeman's shoulder and almost threw up. Monique lay half on the sofa with her arms and legs sprawled outward. Her dead waxy color sent shivers through him.

No. She can't be ...

"Oh my God! Monique!" His eyes opened wide. *I loved her. I now know that I loved her. I wish I had told her.* He cried out, "Monique, I love you. I always have."

He lunged toward her body, but the detective grabbed his arm and pulled him back. "You can't go to her. We're still processing the crime scene."

Jean-Claude could see no sign of a struggle. Crime investigators took pictures of Monique's body and in particular, the paper note protruding from her open mouth. She had been shot. He could see a bloody bullet wound between her lifeless eyes.

A plainclothes detective put on rubber gloves, removed the note from her lips and proceeded to read the scribbled message, then placed it in a clear plastic evidence bag.

Jean-Claude jerked his arm free and pushed through the doorway, ignoring protests from the police. His heart was beating way too fast and he could taste bile in his mouth.

The detective studied his face. "You're Jean-Claude LeGrand?"

He nodded. He couldn't speak. Had the flic recognized him, or had they already researched her friends? Looked at her phone contacts? He had been photographed with her on more than one occasion.

"When was the last time you saw the victim?" He held a small notebook and pen in his hand.

Jean-Claude swallowed hard. "A couple of hours ago." Sweat formed on his forehead. He felt weak. *This is a dream ... a horrible, horrible dream. She can't be gone from my life.* The weight of tears filled his eyes.

"You don't look too well." The detective guided him to a chair near the door and pushed him down. "What was your relationship to Mademoiselle Favreau?"

"We were friends. We'd share a bottle of wine every now and then."

How and why did this happen? Just for a few euros?

"Only wine?" The man cleared his throat. "There was quite a bit of cocaine on the premises." He pointed to the lines of tac-tac on the mirrored tile at the corner of the coffee table.

"She used on occasion to relax—not a real habit." Jean-Claude didn't miss the way the detective rolled his eyes.

"What about this message we found in her mouth?" The man held the plastic bag so he could read the words. "The exact words are, 'Pay up Jean-Claude or you are next.' Know anything about that? Who is threatening you?"

"No one." Sobs flowed as he broke down. "I have no enemies. Monique had no enemies. I don't understand any of this."

My God! They knew Monique was more important to me than Cindy. How? I thought I was careful. I thought I took proper care.

"Do you know of her friends and associates?" He continued to take notes.

He wiped his eyes on his shirt sleeves. "I don't know names. The same faces that she has been photographed with. Everyone loved Monique."

"Apparently, not everyone." He turned toward the body as if emphasizing his comment. "Tell me more about that note, Monsieur LeGrand."

"I have nothing else to say. It's a mystery to me."

He must believe me. Where can I go? My apartment is being watched. I'm certain of it.

"You mean to tell me," his chuckle seemed sarcastic, "you have never used a bit of tac-tac? With all your party connections at the exclusive clubs you frequent?"

"Because I go to a club now and then doesn't mean I use drugs." *He's not believing me.*

"Oh really? And a cat doesn't like cream." The flic bent down close to his face. "Confess, Jean-Claude. This note and Monique's murder was a message to you—a warning for you to pay for your drugs."

"No. I have nothing to do with this." His chest heaved with deep, rasping breaths. "I'm not the only Jean-Claude in Paris."

He won't give up on this.

"Where do you live?" The detective kept his focus on him.

"*Rue Saint Roch*, first arrondissement, off from *rue de Rivoli*." He narrowed his eyes. "But you already know that."

The flics will follow me all over the city. My life won't be my own.

"Do you have any friends or associates who disliked your relationship with the victim?" He analyzed Jean-Claude's reaction.

"No. I don't know how many more times you want me to give you the same answers to your suggestive questions." *Does he think I had something to do with the murder?* "Am I free to go? I would like to grieve my friend's death in privacy."

"Yes. You can go. Don't leave the city without notifying me." He reached into his inside jacket pocket, pulled out a business card, and handed it to him. "There might be more questions for you to answer."

Jean-Claude took the card and shoved it into his pocket. He stood up and left, making his way through the security crime scene tape on rubbery legs.

Thank God there were no drug-sniffing dogs there or else the flics would've found cocaine in my jacket lining. I'm being followed. They followed me to Monique—how else would they know where to find her? Or, did they know Cindy left me, and Monique was the most logical one I would return to as a lover? I'll go to Papa. He's my last hope. I must make him understand.

Jean-Claude went to the closest taxi stand. He was in luck. An available driver pulled up. He quickly got in the back seat and gave Charles' address.

I feel safe here. I can't live my life from the inside of a taxi. Soon, this will all be a dream. I'll wake up and find Monique smiling down at me. Monique, Monique, Monique! I love you so much and never told you. Life is too damn short.

The taxi pulled up to a stop on *rue des Deux Ponts* in front of Charles LeGrand's apartment. Jean-Claude shoved several euros into the driver's hand and walked away ignoring the change due him. He pressed the security buttons on the entrance pad. When the buzzer sounded, he pushed the door open and entered the small, yet stylish courtyard. He took the steps two at a time.

Tears streamed down his eyes. The loss of Monique weighed heavier with every step and every fond memory that he recalled.

I'll never have her back. Forever she's gone. Why was I so selfish? She often said she loved me. Why didn't I tell Monique I loved her. I'll never be able to say those words to her.

He pounded on Charles' door. "Papa, it's Jean-Claude. Let me in."

A voice came from within, "I'm coming. Wait a minute."

A moment passed. Jean-Claude shifted his weight.

Charles greeted with a smile, "This is a special surprise. Come in my son." He opened the door fully.

"Papa, a terrible thing has happened." He rushed to the sofa. His whole body shook.

"What is it?" Charles sat next to him. "It can't be all that serious."

"It is, Papa." He lifted his head and showed his father red and wet eyes. "Monique is dead. She was murdered, all because of me."

"How can that be? Did you shoot her in an argument."

"No. I didn't shoot her. Others did who don't like me." Tears streamed down his cheeks.

Charles went to the bar and poured whisky into two crystal glasses, and handed one to his son. "I don't understand. The only people you know are in the music business. Booze and sex doesn't warrant a murder."

Jean-Claude took a large swallow of his drink. "You may think you know me, but there's a lot you don't know."

Charles sat down beside him. "Why not tell me what I need to know, and then maybe I can help you. Is this something to do with the money you wanted?"

Jean-Claude began slowly, speaking words difficult to utter. "I have been involved with drugs. It started very innocent at first. Only now and then, during parties, or when I needed to relax. Then more frequently. I still believe it has no control over me."

Charles' mouth clamped shut as he looked straight ahead. "If you believe that, then you are a fool like every other user in the world."

"Let me go on." Jean-Claude wiped his eyes and nose with a handkerchief he pulled from his pocket. "I ran up drug bills." He took two deep breaths. "That girl they pulled out of the Seine a while back was my lover. Her death was a warning for me to pay my bill for tac-tac."

"Why didn't you come to me before this, before that girl in the Seine paid the price?" Shock played in his eyes. "And if you had told me this when you asked for the money..."

"I didn't know about it until now—not until Monique's murder." Jean-Claude buried his face in his hands and sobbed between words. "The flics found a note in her mouth …. It said 'Jean-Claude pay up.' … They shot her between, between the eyes. It was horrible for both of us." He looked up at his father. "I loved her, Papa. I never knew I did care, nor how much till this very day. She's been taken from me and for what? A year's worth of snorting? How little her life is valued. I'll never be free of this enormous guilt. Never!"

Charles patted Jean-Claude's arm and spoke softly. "How much do you owe to this filth who supplies you with this vile cocaine?"

His voice lowered as he looked at Charles. "I told you before on the phone. One hundred thousand."

"One hundred thousand?" Charles put his hand to his forehead as if in disbelief. "You weren't lying to me when you called."

Jean-Claude knew his father must be putting two and two together.

"Papa, I'll pay you back, every cent." He swallowed hard. "I'll be going on a European tour in a few months and if I stay here until then, they won't be able to get to me. If you pay them, then I'll be safe for good."

"Jean-Claude, you're not speaking sense. Paying your drug debt is only a small part of what needs to be done." He held his son's hands lovingly. "I will pay your bill—all one hundred thousand. But, there will be no European tour."

"That can't be canceled. Everything is set." He felt new tears well up and blur his vision. His lips quivered. "Papa, you've saved my life."

"You've saved your own life by coming to me and owning up to your wrongs." He sighed. "If needed, I can take over your tour. Maybe it's time for the European youth to hear classic ballads with lyrics that can be understood."

"Don't make light of this … If you pay my bill, then why can't I do the tour?"

I don't understand what Papa's getting at.

"Jean-Claude," he looked kindly at him, "you must get help for this addiction."

"But, I'm *not* addicted!" *This can't be real!* "I told you. It was to relax. That's why I use."

Charles grabbed Jean-Claude's shoulders and shook them. "Son, listen to me. You *are* addicted. Write down the name and number of your supplier. I need it to pay your debt."

Charles handed him a piece of paper and a pen. Jean-Claude scribbled the information.

I can't believe this! I won't believe this!

"What are you going to do? Lock me up in this antique mausoleum?"

"Jean-Claude, you are going into rehab. That's final! It's the price you will pay to me for paying your debt." Charles went to the door and locked it. He placed the key in his pocket, then went back to his son. "Empty your pockets. All of them. Give me your jacket."

He's treating me like a disobedient child! I'm thirty-two, a grown man … and he's treating me like this!

Jean-Claude handed over his jacket and pocket contents. Charles fingered the jacket and discovered the hidden opening in the center seam of the lining. He reached in and pulled packet after packet of white powder. Fourteen of such packets piled up on the coffee table.

He looked at Jean-Claude and pointed to the evidence. "This is addiction—plain and simple. No one carries around this much cocaine unless he is pushing. Are you pushing? Is that the real story here?"

"No, Papa! I swear." New tears filled his eyes. "It's for me. I never sell."

Charles went to his phone on the desk and dialed while looking at his son. "Doctor Marchand. Oui. Cas d'urgence! Emergency!"

Jean-Claude's lips trembled. "Papa, Cindy was stabbed as a warning before Monique was murdered. She's okay, only a little cut. She moved out. I don't know where she is."

Charles placed his hand over the phone's mouthpiece. "Mon Dieu! What have you done! I don't know if I should call Davis."

"I'm certain she's already been in touch with her parents."

Now my hell begins. I've lost the only woman I ever loved, and I might die from the effects of withdrawal. I've heard about that. Some don't survive when trying to get clean. I hope Papa pays Maurice before Cindy is hurt.

~~***~~

Cindy ambled down the sidewalk toward Palais Royal. She noticed a commotion of people clustering around a newspaper vendor. *What's going on? A big news item?* She squeezed closer toward the front. Her eyes scanned the publications on display. A stack of papers stood next to the man quickly taking money for each copy. Sale after sale rapidly dwindled the stack. She saw a large full page photo with a French headline she didn't understand. Cindy looked at the photograph. Her mouth fell open.

My God! That's the same woman I saw JC with! That's Monique! She's been murdered! A bullet in her forehead.

That could've been me.

Cindy briskly turned around and ran down the sidewalk toward Stuart's apartment, bumping into others. She could barely stop shaking and felt her heart pounding out of her chest.

I won't tell Stu. He probably already knows. I bet he never brought it up because he feared I'd be upset. Should I leave Paris? If I stay, will I put Stu in danger?

Fifty - Two

FRÉDÉRIC STOOD AT the back counter waiting for Stuart to finish up with a customer's request of a book selection. They shook hands.

"I hope this visit brings good news on what you've discovered." Stuart rang up the final sale from a lady in line. "I can't really judge from your expression."

Frédéic shrugged. "Some good, some ambiguous. Are you free for a coffee or a bite?"

Stuart checked the clock on the wall. "Hélène, take over the desk, please. You and the new girl can switch out for lunch. I have to leave."

Hélène agreed with a nod.

They left the store and headed around the corner to their previous hangout, Café Carrousel. Frédéric purposely didn't discuss what was on his mind during their walk. They found their favorite outside table facing the Louvre.

Stuart squirmed in his seat. "So, what is so important? Have you gotten any news about my birth mother? Or, is this about Cindy?"

"Cindy seems to be safe. For whatever reason, the focus is no longer on Jean-Claude. All my PI friend would say is, that she's out of danger." He lit a cigarette. "It's about your mother."

"Go on." Stuart looked eager as he edged forward in his seat.

"Like I said, my PI friend had DNA testing done on the sample you provided and the results aren't conclusive yet." A waiter dropped off menus, glasses, and a carafe of water. Frédéric handed one to his friend.

"So, is my mother alive?" He pushed the menu aside.

"If she's who I think she is, then yes. She's alive." Frédéric opened the menu, looked at it briefly, then put it down.

"Is she near? Can I meet her?" His exuberance burst from his eyes. "God, I've got so many questions to ask her."

"Hold on, dear friend." He gave his order to the waiter. Stuart did the same. "To be certain, there needs to be a DNA sample taken from this suspected woman. That involves following procedures."

He wrinkled his brow. "Do you need more money?"

"At this point, it's not a question of money." He took a drag from his cigarette. "It's a matter of time."

Stuart poured water into his glass from the carafe. "How much time? A week? A month?"

"I don't want to get your hopes up, but my instincts tell me that a woman I know of, who is very sick and in a Geneva hospital, *might* be a candidate."

"Geneva?" His eyes grew large. "I was born in a Geneva hospital! Mon Dieu! She has to be my mother. I feel it as certain as I'm here with you."

The waiter brought their meals. He placed a bottle of wine and glasses on the table. "Don't get ahead of yourself. This could all be a coincidence and nothing more."

"Still, it's something to go on." Stuart's words clearly revealed his hopes. "*If* she does turn out to be my mother, then there is a chance I could find my father."

"Précisément! Precisely! *If* is the operative word in this situation." He took a forkful of his cheese omelet. "We could, and will most likely, come to a dead end. This is all based on a hunch of mine." He tapped his finger on the table to emphasize his words.

"It sounds like a good hunch to me." Stuart cut into his ham crêpe. "It's far better than what I had before, which was nothing." He took a sip of wine. "So where do we go from here?"

"Like I said, I and my PI friend would need to go to this hospital and try to get permission for a DNA sample to be obtained."

I hope I'm not revealing information that would cause Claude difficulties in doing his job.

"Can't I go with you both?" He swallowed his food quickly. "I could plead my case to the hospital officials. Surely they wouldn't want to keep a mother and possible son apart any longer than necessary."

"That is true. We might be able to make a case for that. I'll check with my PI friend to see if he thinks you would be a help or a hindrance." He gestured to the waiter for the check. "Don't make more of this than what we know."

"No. I won't. But it will be difficult not thinking of her." He sighed. "Every child should know their mother."

~~***~~

"How's my lovely American saleslady doing? Finding everything you need?" Stuart came up behind Cindy as she opened a box of tourist guide books in the stockroom.

He kissed the back of her neck. She turned and placed her arms on his shoulders. Her eyes returned his intense gaze.

"I'm fine. Learning as I go." Her smile caused him to do the same.

"Learning about the store, Paris, or something else?" His teasing expression amused her.

"Mostly about my feelings and what's important to me." Her tongue ran across her bottom lip.

"Stop teasing me." His arms embraced her waist and drew her closer. "Share."

"Well, … I've learned a lot about the real me inside. The me who has never given a thought about what is important. I'm not talking about others' expectations of how I should live my life or who I should see, like, or love." She bit her lip in thought. "I've given up the old life of social and family beliefs. I want my life to be here—here in Paris."

"That's a big step forward." He kissed her forehead. "Anything else you care to share?"

"Yes …. I-I've given this a lot of thought and I think I want to share that life with you." Her bottom lip trembled. "I was blinded by the glitz and glamour Jean-Claude represented. I can't believe I've been so stupid. And, and I hope you feel the same."

Did I come off as too forward? Will he reject me. Frenchmen don't like pushy Americans.

His expansive smile put her insecurities to rest. "Feel the same?" He hesitated. "I'll have to give that some thought."

A nervous laugh escaped. "Will you have me or not?" She playfully pounded her fists on his chest. "Don't be as stuffy as all those French monuments!"

He let out a loud laugh throwing his head back. "Stuffy? Not very likely." His hands embraced her cheeks. "Yes. I'll have you in all ways possible. The best part of this is, you're in my life. I no longer have to choose my words carefully to hide my feelings."

He kissed her softly. Cindy draped her arms around his shoulders and returned his love. She broke off their kiss.

"There's just one thing that I hope you will agree to."

"Out with it." He kissed her cheek as if to encourage her.

She looked down at his chest. "I don't want us to sleep together yet." She glanced up and saw confusion on his face. "It's not because I don't love you, and not because I'm uncertain of having a future with you. I've been through so much recently at breakneck speed. I need time to do this right—take it slow so we can get to know each other more fully." She twisted her hands together, desperately trying to find the correct words. *I don't want to hurt him.* "I jumped into bed with JC on the first impulse. I don't want to do that again."

"Is that all?" He chuckled. "I thought you might want a place of your own, or take a break from seeing me, in spite of the feelings we have for each other." He looked at her tenderly. "Of course we can hold off on making love—though, it won't be easy."

"The way I feel now," her finger traced along his lips, "it will be near impossible for me."

Stu is so loving. How I wish I'd met him before Vic.

He kissed her softly. "I can see the sofa bed and I will be good friends in the immediate future."

"That played on my mind, too." She raised her eyebrows. "We could take turns sleeping in the bed—every other night or so?"

"It's enough that you said you love me." He kissed her briefly. "I've loved you from the start. I will not have my loved one sleep on a sofa bed." He grinned. "The best of everything is what I want for you—including your comfort. Besides, I haven't suffered from a backache."

"You'll let me know when you do?" Her fingers toyed with the buttons on his shirt.

"Deal. If and when I can no longer tolerate the comfort of that blasted sofa bed, you will be the first to know."

She hugged him and snuggled into his chest.

It feels so right in his arms. He's a good man. I love him. I think he truly loves me. I should share this fantastic news with Mom. Breaking that ice barrier won't be easy. How will I find the words?

~~***~~

"When can we go to Geneva?" Stuart poured dry cereal into the bowl. He held the phone to his ear while seated at the dining table.

"I have to get the tickets first for the TGV. I'd like to check to see if my PI friend wants to join us." Background voices from Frédéric's shop came over the phone.

"I'll buy the tickets." He poured milk into the bowl, then took a spoonful to his mouth. "Just give me a date that's good for you."

"This coming Monday is fine for me." A computer noise sounded as if ringing up a sale. "The earlier the better."

"Okay. As soon as I open the store and the others come in, I'll get our tickets. I'll only buy two since you're not certain about your friend."

I know in my heart that this woman is my mother.

"Good. Talk to you later."

~~***~~

Cindy sat at the small dining table in Stuart's apartment. He wouldn't return for at least two hours. She knew it would be morning, around nine o'clock in Bel-Air. Her fingers held her cell phone tightly as she looked out the window to the street below. Pedestrians walked with umbrellas or hoods over their heads to shield themselves from the light rain. She focused on a raindrop trailing downward on the pane.

Once I felt like that drop. Falling down, inch by inch with no real sense of my own direction, being pushed and pulled by others' will. JC was like that. He tried to mold me into his ideal—what was to his benefit and not mine. He never really cared. I was a diversion. With Vic, I was only worth the sum of my paycheck for his gambling. Stu is different. He sees me as I am and is happy with that. He offers no pretense. There's no illusion with him.

Cindy scrolled through her contacts and punched in the number. There was a pause before she heard the ringing on the end.

How will I find the words?

"Mom, how are you? I hope I didn't wake you."

"Cindy, it's so good to hear your voice. I've been frantic with worry." She heard Taylor cough.

"I didn't want to run up the phone bill with calls and text messages." *I hope her cough isn't because she's back smoking.*

"Don't worry about such things." Piano music came over the phone from the background.

"Mom, I-I need to tell you something." She breathed deeply. "JC and I broke up. He isn't as nice as he looks. I'm living with Stuart Dumont—he owns his own bookstore and has a very nice apartment over the store. It's on *rue de Rivoli* not far from *place Vendôme*. I think I love him—no. I *know* I love him. He makes a comfortable living like Dad did."

"Well, I recall you mentioned him as a friend." Taylor sighed. "You certainly have been going through a lot of changes. Are you safe? Do you need anything? What about money? You can't be living off this Stuart person."

"It's okay." Cindy got up and went to the kitchen for a bottle of water. "I'm working at his store, earning some money."

"But, you don't speak French. How can you possibly talk to the customers? You don't have a work visa."

Mom is full of questions, as usual.

"He runs an English bookstore. Nearly all his customers speak English. And for the ones who don't, Hélène takes care of them. He's paying me cash so it won't be reported to anyone." She opened the bottle of water. "Mom, I haven't gone to bed with him—not yet. I want to wait until I feel I'm ready. Unfortunately, he's going on a business trip of some sort for a day or so and he didn't want me to tag along. I didn't insist on going—not so soon in our relationship."

She heard Taylor's relieved sigh. "I'm so very, very glad to hear you're happy. I always worry about your heart being broken. I only want joy for you. You were right in not pushing him—to join him on his trip."

"I have something else to say that you'll be glad to hear."

God give me the courage.

"Yes, go on." Taylor sounded soft and tentative.

"Mom, I for … forgive you for all that happened with Dad. I have been a selfish and an awful daughter to you. I never looked beyond my own hurt and pain. I don't blame you for what happened. I realize that we don't always have control of our feelings, and sometimes those feelings can force us to make bad choices."

There was a moment's silence.

"Cindy, I know those words were difficult for you to speak. You can't imagine how long I've dreamed of you saying you forgive me." Her voice cracked with emotion. "I love you so very much and always will. I regret my poor decisions involving Paul. I miss him. But, that's a closed chapter in my life, and in yours."

"Mom, don't beat yourself up on what is past." Tears fell on her cheeks. "I want us to be more than mother and daughter. I want us to be friends—friends for life. I miss you, Mom. I want to bury all those bad feelings. Can you forgive me for all my harsh and hurtful words?"

"Forgive you?" She sniffed through the phone as if crying. "I forgave you as soon as you spoke them. Forget the past. How we treat each other from this point forward is what counts."

"Thank you, Mom." *I'll forever have her love.* "You've always been my best friend."

"And, I always will be." Taylor sniffed again.

I made Mom cry.

Taylor cleared her throat. "So when do you want me to come for a visit? I can show you the sites, though you've probably already seen them."

"Not yet, Mom." *I hope I'm not hurting her feelings.* "I want more private time with Stu. He and I are still getting to know each other."

There was a long pause from Taylor. "I see. I understand. But, please don't forget to call or at least text me. We could even do Skype."

"Yes. That would be nice." Cindy wiped more tears away. "I'll set up my Skype with your email .... Mom, I need to go now. I've run up the phone bill enough. I'll call you again, soon."

"Bye, my darling daughter. I love you so much."

That didn't go as bad as I thought. I feel such relief. It's as if I'm at peace somehow. All that built-up anger has vanished.

Then there's the issue of Stu. How am I going to keep him from my bed? I want him so badly. I can't rush into sex. I can't take the chance of ruining something that could be so beautiful and lasting. What should I do? He's going to try to seduce me tonight—I'm certain of it.

Fifty - Three

STUART STOOD WITH Frédéric in the l'Hôpitaux de Suisse's hallway peering through a small square window at the most pitiful woman anyone could have ever seen. Her blond hair mixed with gray was fastened in a bun. Sharp angular arms and legs pulled up to a fetal position hugged a boney frame as she rocked back and forth with vacant and dead eyes.

"Who is this woman?" Stuart shifted his weight from one foot to the other.

Surely this is not the woman I came here to see.

"She is a poor creature who was discarded for whatever the reason." Frédéric touched Stuart's shoulder. "She might be your mother."

"My mother?" His jaw dropped. "She appears half-dead. She looks like she's been wasting away by inches for years."

"She's catatonic." Frédéric shook his head. "I can't tell you further until we know more about her."

"If there's a chance, I need to speak with her." He watched the patient as he spoke. "Even if we're not related. I want to speak with her."

"She won't even know you're there." Frédéric squinted down the hall and spotted a nurse. "As I said, she's *catatonic.* I'll ask the nurse."

He walked a few steps, then spoke with her in French.

The nurse approached with Frédéric. Her tone held a gentleness. "Monsieur said you think you know this woman and want to speak with her?"

"Oui. I was adopted. My parents said my mother was too ill to care for me." He looked at the patient again. "I'm trying to find her."

"She won't respond to you." The nurse took keys from her pocket. "She hasn't said a word since she was admitted many years ago. As you see her now is the way she's always been since her first day here. We did find out that when she did speak, it was English."

The nurse unlocked the door. She entered first. Stuart knelt down in front of the woman, his heart beating way too fast. He stared into her lifeless blue eyes and gently touched her shoulder, feeling the boney prominence.

If she is my mother, I now know why she could never keep me. What type of hell did she endure to become like this?

His words were soft and kind. "Hello. I'm Stuart ... Stuart Dumont. It's nice to meet you."

How I wish you could talk.

The woman looked straight ahead with no movement except for the continual rocking. Stuart looked in her eyes a few moments longer, then stood up.

"I feel so sorry for her. Such a sad and devastating existence." He left a gentle kiss on the top of her head.

"We need to speak to someone who is in charge of this department," Frédéric said to the nurse.

"Certainement, monsieur." The men followed her out of the room.

After locking the door, she spoke with them in the hallway. "What is it that you want to know?"

Frédéric took the lead. "We need to speak to a person about obtaining a DNA sample from this poor woman."

"I see." She checked her watch. "Doctor Fauchon should still be here. I'll take you to his office."

The nurse led them down a long corridor, passing the brightly lit nurses' station, and turned left onto a carpeted hall with closed office doors on the left and expansive windows with bars on the outside to their right. She knocked on the first door.

A low voice responded, "Enter."

Stuart and Frdéric followed her into the room.

"Doctor Fauchon, these men would like to speak with you about a patient—the woman in room 312." She turned and left, closing the door.

"Doctor Fauchon, I'm Frédéric Millet. My friend here, Stuart Dumont, is looking for his mother. He was put up for adoption at birth. He was told that she was too ill to care for him."

"What does this have to do with the patient in room 312?" The doctor leaned forward on his desk and folded his hands on the blotter.

"I have it on good authority that, that same woman was admitted pregnant and gave birth six months later." Beads of sweat collected on Frédéric's brow.

"What can I do?" He looked at Frédéric and then Stuart. "Just because she gave birth does not mean she is the mother of your friend."

Stuart took a step forward. "If I may, Doctor Fauchon, this is extremely important to me. I'm trying to find out about my past and the health history of my parents. A DNA sample of this patient would be very helpful."

"Since she has no person of authority to grant that permission, the decision rests with me. Sit, please." The doctor motioned to two visitor chairs, then opened the desk drawer and pulled out the necessary paperwork. He looked up at Stuart. "Please pass me your identification."

Stuart perched on the edge of the chair, pulled out his wallet and handed over his license and health card.

Doctor Fauchon proceeded to fill out the required information. "All you need is a mouth swab?" The doctor looked up at Frédéric.

"Yes. I have a friend at a Paris lab who can complete the testing." He then turned to Stuart and gave a thumbs up sign.

"Fine." Doctor Fauchon rose from the desk and walked to the door. "Follow me."

Stuart and Frédéric walked behind the doctor to the nurses' station. Fauchon spoke quietly with one of the nurses. She took three sealed cotton swabs, two plastic zipped bags, surgical gloves, and a pair of sterile scissors in paper wrapping from a cabinet. The doctor and nurse walked to room 312, while the two men stood outside and watched the samples being collected.

Moments later Doctor Fauchon talked to them outside the patient's room. "It wasn't an easy process." He sighed. "She didn't open her mouth very wide. I obtained a cutting of her hair in case the oral swabs would be insufficient for the testing." He handed the plastic bags to Frédéric, then looked at Stuart with kind eyes. "I hope you find answers to all your questions."

"Can you tell me her name?" Stuart gazed at her while he spoke.

"If she turns out to be your mother, then and only then, will I tell you her name." He shook Stuart's hand. "This woman is still entitled to patient confidentiality."

"Merci, Doctor Fauchon," Stuart said as the doctor walked away.

Frédéric and Stuart left the hospital. Being so close to having an answer pounded his brain.

If she turns out to be my mother, then who is paying the hospital bills? This is obviously a nice facility and nothing like a free clinic or a community hospital. There must be someone who cares about her—but who?

~~***~~

Although Stuart had waited all his life for the answers, he found himself to be edgy and anxious the entire two weeks before Frédéric called and arranged to meet him at café Les Deux Margots, located on *place Saint-Germain-des-Prés* in the sixth arrondissement of Paris' left bank. They sat at a table in a quiet corner while the waiters, dressed in black with long white waist to floor aprons and black bowties on white shirts seamlessly went about their tasks like well-oiled machines. Stuart had been here before and had believed he felt the old spirits of literary luminaries such as Hemingway and Stein. Today he had more on his mind than ghosts of famous authors.

He had to force himself to take long, slow breaths but he couldn't stop his hands from trembling.

Frédéric made small talk until the food had been served.

Stuart couldn't take it any longer. "Fréd, what news do you have for me? I'm nearly bursting at the seams." The roast beef in front of him looked good, but he had no appetite for it.

"The news is good and bad in a sense." Frédéric motioned to the waiter and ordered two whiskeys.

Stuart put his fork down. "It must be serious if you feel we need drinks. One for your courage to say whatever it is, and one for me, to be able to hear what you have to say."

"I didn't only have your DNA and that poor woman's DNA tested. I also had another man's DNA tested. I have the results." The waiter brought the drinks. Frédéric took a large sip.

"Go on." *I wish he'd hurry up and just tell me.*

"First, that poor creature is your mother." His brow formed deep furrows as his brows knitted together. "There's no doubting that. You have a mama with a serious condition that looks like she will never recover or improve."

"I'm so relieved you've found her." *I felt from the start she was my mum, especially when I kissed her head.* "And that man you mentioned? Is he my father?"

"Yes." He leaned closer to Stuart and lowered his voice. "His name is Clive Bradford, the Earl of Lantham, and Duke of Bryningmead."

"How is that bad news?" He raised his brows and tilted his head. "I'm related to English aristocracy."

Frédéric pointed to the glass. "You better have a swallow of that drink first."

"You're not sounding very promising." Stuart's brows drew together. "Is my father a lunatic of some sort, and that disease is in me?"

Frédéric spoke slowly with a deliberate tone. "Clive is a famous neurosurgeon in London with royal bloodlines going back centuries. He has been conducting neurological research for years. It has been suspected that his wife, Penelope, the woman we saw, was the victim of his experiment gone wrong—though that has never been proven."

"My mum is Penelope. And my papa is a madman?" *This is crazy.*

He nodded and looked at his friend with sympathetic eyes. "I'm so very sorry I couldn't deliver happier news."

"I need to meet my father." Stuart took another swallow of whiskey. "I want to know why he didn't want me and had me adopted by strangers. What type of bastard is he?"

"Don't fly off the handle." Frédéric patted his shoulder. "Take things slowly. You don't know the circumstances."

Stuart's eyes opened wide as his jaw twitched. "Circumstances!" He lowered his voice as to not cause a disturbance. "What on earth is more important than your own child? His busy schedule doing research? And using my mother as his own personal guinea pig?"

"Calm down." Frédéric spoke with conviction. "This man is dangerous. His cousin Amelia was witness to his outrage. Stuart, he won't have any fatherly feelings toward you."

"Then we're even." He huffed. "I damn well have no loving feelings for him either!"

"Promise me you won't show up on his doorstep in the future." Frédéric tapped his finger on the table for emphasis.

"I promise for the immediate future, but not forever." He finished his drink in one gulp.

"I'll keep a copy of the results for safekeeping." Frédéric gestured for the check, then turned over the original test document from his jacket pocket to Stuart. "That's enough for now."

Stuart mumbled between clenched teeth. "Not nearly enough for me."

I must get as much information as possible before I make my move. Right might be on my side, but the facts will be my shield and sword.

Fifty - Four

CINDY LAY ON her side in bed, awake. Stuart climbed in with her, and snuggled up to her back. He ran his fingers up and down her arm, causing her to purr like a cat. She rolled onto her back and fingered his hair. Morning light filtered though the curtains.

"I thought you were going to wait until I felt ready to make love?" Her finger traced the line of his jaw. "You can't do that?" *I want him now, but the time isn't right for me.* "I halfway expected you the other night."

"I have to admit it's been tough. You are so irresistible." His fingers interlaced with hers. "I got some upsetting news from Fréd."

She plumped up her pillow and sat up. "Is it serious?"

"More so for the one who has ruined a person's life …" Stuart rested on an elbow as he revealed his thoughts. "… and deprived another of a true identity."

"Now, you've really piqued my curiosity." She sat up straighter.

His smug smile caused Cindy to playfully slap his arm.

"Don't bruise an up and coming author." His eyes bored into hers. "Leave that task to the critics—they're quite adept at it."

"You're avoiding telling me your news." She faked a pout. "That's not fair. Teasing me and holding back."

"No different than what you did to me in Annecy." He laughed. "You don't like the tables turned?"

"What I think is, you're using this word game to hide something that is troubling you." She drew her brows together. "You've been so distracted these past couple of weeks, I knew something was on your mind. Tell me what's troubling you."

Stuart took a deep breath. "Okay. Here goes." Another deep breath followed. "Fréd and I went to a hospital in Geneva. There was a woman there in the most deplorable situation."

"Wasn't she cared for and fed?"

Was this person his mom?

"No, no. It wasn't that." He rubbed his forehead as if to find the courage to say the words. "She was, is, in a catatonic state. All curled up, arms hugging her knees to her chest, rocking back and forth as if rocking an infant. She is boney, though they feed her on a regular basis …. Fréd said the nurses use a stomach tube for her nourishment. Her blond hair has streaks of gray. This poor woman looks older, way beyond her years. Her eyes are so dead and cold. No expression whatsoever. Just looks straight ahead—trapped in her own hell."

Cindy gripped his arm. She could hear tears in his voice. "You don't have to go on if it's too painful for you."

"I'm all right." He breathed deeply. "The doctor at the hospital obtained a swab sample and a piece of her hair for DNA testing. Today, Fréd gave me the test results."

"Is she your mother?"

This is so difficult for him. I wish I could make everything better.

"Yes. Her name is Penelope—Penelope Bradford. Her husband is Clive Bradford, a famous neurosurgeon in London, with a royal bloodline." He wiped his left eye with the back of his hand.

"That doesn't sound so bad." *Oh my God! Clive! It can't be. Not Clive again.* "At least you know the identity of your parents." She struggled to keep her voice normal.

"I haven't told you the worst part." His voice cracked. "My father knew of my birth and rejected me—left orders for me to be put up for adoption. For me, that was a blessing." His tears began to fall. "It's believed that Clive put my mother in her current condition—a result of his experiment. Fréd did say it hadn't been proven. I think it's a strong assumption."

Should I tell him of my mother and Clive? Better not—that's her secret.

"Oh, Stu. I'm so sorry. So what are you going to do now?"

"I thought a bit of online research would be in order." He wiped his eyes. "I can't confront him without knowing the facts."

"Don't. Let him have his life, and we have ours." *Clive is too big a match for him.* She hugged him tightly. "Stay away from Clive."

Stuart got off the bed and headed to the door.

"Where are you going?" Cindy flung her legs over the side of the bed and slid into her slippers. "It's Sunday. Everything is closed."

"I'm not leaving." He turned back to her. "While you shower I'll do some research online." He smiled. "All good authors do their research."

"As long as that research doesn't include Clive Bradford."

He's not gonna give up on this.

After her shower, Cindy ambled into the living room. Stuart sat hunched over his laptop. His eyes moved side to side as he read the displayed information. The intermittent clicking sound of keys told her he was in deep concentration on a quest. The reflected light from the screen intensified the worry lines in his forehead. She went to the kitchen for morning coffee.

Cindy returned to the dining table, and took a pain au chocolat from the white paper bag sitting in the center. With coffee in one hand and the French pastry in the other, she went to the loveseat and sat next to him.

"What have you discovered?" She took a bite of the French treat.

Stuart didn't look up. "Quite a bit. I think I'm just scratching the surface, though." He glanced at her, then returned his focus back to the computer. "My father has received multiple awards for his research, and humanitarian contributions. He inherited the title of Earl of Lanthan by royal bloodline, and was elevated to Duke of Bryningmead by royal acclaim for his achievements and for doing such good for the poor." He scrolled down the screen. "Seems he divorced my mother on basis of abandonment." He looked at her. "That must've been one of his lies to cover up what he did to her."

"Appears you've learned all about him." *I hope he doesn't find out anything about Mom. Those details should come from her and not a Google search.* "Why don't you investigate about your citizenship in England?"

"I already did." His spirits seemed brighter. "On the British website, it seems that I am entitled to dual citizenship—England and France." He kissed her cheek. "And, my lovely, I'm also entitled to the English title as Viscount of Lantham *and* Marquess of Bryningmead! That's a sweet bit of news." He kissed the tip of her nose. "If we should marry, you would be Viscountess of Lantham and Marchioness of Bryningmead."

"You haven't asked me yet."

What will I say if he does?

"Would you say yes?" His eyes held a hopeful glint.

He's testing the waters.

"Not today." She stood up and closed his laptop. "Let's get dressed and go to the park. The weather is nice, flowers are in bloom, and I want you all to myself. Google has occupied enough of your time. Besides, I want to do a little sketching. I feel close to Dad when I draw—as if he's with me guiding my hand. That's comforting to me. It makes me feel like he's never really gone."

"I'm glad you have found peace." Wistfulness washed over his face. "I hope one day, peace will come to me."

I'm so afraid for Stu. The thought of him meeting Clive—makes me shudder.

~~***~~

Cindy waited for Stuart to leave the apartment before placing the call. She knew he wouldn't be taking a break from work until closing. She looked at the time on her phone.

It's five pm here. In Bel-Air, it's eight am. He must be up by now.

After dialing, she waited for him to answer.

"Larry?" She cleared her throat. "This is Cindy."

"How are things? Everything okay?" He took a sip of something.

"I'm fine."

I hope he can help.

"You want to talk with your Mom? I can wake her." Barking came over the phone. Distantly, she heard, "Gigi and Jacques, quiet. I'm on the phone ...Sorry about that. The poodles are frisky this morning." He coughed. "So, do you just want to chat? Feeling homesick, or something else?"

"I'm afraid to say 'something else'." Her chest heaved. "I'm in love with Stu Dumont."

"Yes. Tay said something about that." His voice faded. "Is that the reason you're calling? Are things going okay with him?"

"Stu and I are very much in love .... Your voice fades at times. Am I keeping you from something?"

Maybe I'm taking him from his work in the studio.

"I'm filling up the coffee maker. Go on. You and Stu are in love, and?"

"Stu found out his father is Clive—Clive Bradford." She took a deep breath.

"Clive Bradford!" There was no sound from Larry for a moment. "That's... Tell Stu to keep the hell away from him."

"That's the thing." Her fingers twirled a strand of hair. "He's been on the Net searching everything he can find, taking notes. He wants to confront his father."

"What the hell for?" She envisioned Larry's bulging eyes. "That won't prove anything and only bring a shit load of trouble to him."

"I tried to tell him that."

Maybe I shouldn't have called Larry.

"Well, tell him again." She heard his sigh. "Keep stressing that Clive is dangerous."

"The other problem is, he saw his mother, Penelope in the hospital. He has good reason to believe that Clive put her in her present condition."

He might as well know all of it.

"Stuart knows all these facts, and he still wants to confront Clive?" His voice rose. "That's totally unbelievable! Where is his common sense?"

"I guess he has none, where Clive is concerned." She started pacing. "I didn't know who else to call and I didn't want to bother Mom with this."

"You did right in calling me." He took a breath. "Tay shouldn't learn about any of these details, if it can be helped. I hate to think what the talk of Clive would do to her heart. It took her six months before the nightmares stopped."

"Do you have any suggestions?"

Larry, please come up with a plan.

"I have one you won't like." He took a deep breath.

Here it comes—the lecture.

"Come back to Bel-Air, and you can bring Stu with you. I can have the jet ready within seventy-two hours. Don't get mixed up with Clive. Clive doesn't need Stuart to ruin his life, he's doing that quite well on his own." Fear colored his words.

"That won't work." She walked to the kitchen for a bottle of water.

"Why not?" Larry chuckled. "He has something against American chow? Tim, our houseman, cooks French food, too."

"Larry, Stu is in no position to start a new life. He has a business and has set down roots." She opened the bottle.

He let out a large sigh. "He's too young to be so settled."

"True. But, I know he won't go for any of it." Cindy took a swallow of water.

"Do you want me to come over there?" He sounded tense. "It wouldn't be a problem."

"And how would you manage that without telling Mom all of it?" *He's not thinking this through.* "You know Mom is like a dog on a bone. She keeps picking away at something until she knows all."

Larry sighed. "Yes. That's true. I wish I could be of more help. How about Joe going over there?"

"Joe wouldn't be able to do any more than you." She sat on the loveseat. "Calling you was a shot in the dark—hoping you would think of something I hadn't already thought of."

"I'm sorry, Cindy." He spoke softly, "Promise to call more often …. We love you."

"I love you all, too. Please don't tell Mom I called—she'll only worry."

I should have never called. Now, he'll worry. Damn! Why can't I just keep things to myself!

"I won't tell her." He laughed. "I don't need to be hammered with questions I shouldn't answer."

"Bye, Larry."

The phone went dead.

When will Stu propose? He hinted at it. I hope it's not before I'm certain of my feelings. I'd hate to break his heart, especially with all this Clive business clouding his life.

Fifty - Five

AMELIA RAN HER fingers up and down a young man's firm and muscular chest. Her hand came to rest on his chin as she enjoyed the feel of his afternoon growth of stubble. She relished these diversions. Knowing she could please a man not only with her body, but also with her money, imparted a sense of power, if even only transient in nature. He leaned closer to her when the phone rang. She took it from the bedside table. Her lover made a face and rolled to his side with his back to her.

The male voice held a tone of urgency. "It's Fréd. Are you free?"

"Yes." She glanced at her lover's back. "I'm not in the middle of something that can't wait for the moment. And by the way, I'm *never* free."

He laughed. "You are a coquette. I'm calling with serious information."

"Truly?" She swung her legs over the side of the bed and sat up. "Deadly information? Or something less dramatic?"

"With your help, I'm hoping for the latter." She heard street noise in the background.

"Tell me, how can I help?" Her lover turned over and ran his fingertips down her back. She ignored his caresses.

"As you English say, the cat is out of the bag." He sighed. "Stuart Dumont is Clive's son, born by Penelope."

"My, my, old Clive has a living blood heir." She chuckled. "So what is the trouble with that? Jolly good for Stuart."

"It won't be good if Stuart goes through with his plan that he's formulating." She heard Frédéric puff on his cigarette.

"Formulating a plan?" She leaned forward. *This is getting interesting.* "Sounds deliciously intriguing."

"He wants to travel to London and confront Clive." Frédéric coughed.

"You need to stop smoking." She sighed with boredom. "The most that will come of it is, Clive will make up some plausible excuse, give him a few thousand pounds, and send him on his way. Where does the seriousness of this grand meeting come to light?"

"I'm not making myself clear." He sipped a drink. "Stuart *knows* the circumstance of his birth. He *saw* Penelope with his own eyes—in the Geneva hospital. Now he's riled up to get as much information as he can before meeting with Clive."

She bit her bottom lip in concern. "Does he know how Penelope came to be admitted to hospital?"

"He only knows that it is suspected Clive experimented on her with some formula he was working on." A honking horn disrupted her hearing. "I didn't tell him anything definite."

"Did you tell him not to see Clive?"

Would Clive murder his own son?

"What do you think?" He chuckled with disdain. "Of course, I did. He wouldn't listen to reason."

"Is it just his anger about his birth circumstance, or does he seek something more?"

Stuart does have a birthright, but will Clive allow him to live long enough to enjoy it?

"Cindy dropped by the shop and filled me in." He puffed his cigarette. "He's been on the Internet and discovered he's permitted to be called Marquess of Bryningmead, and Viscount of Lantham."

"My, my, he has been an industrious little chap." Her lover rolled back over to his other side and cupped her breast. She moved his hand away and shook her head slightly. "Those titles are rightly his after proof of the parentage is presented to the court. My solicitor could handle that …. How old is Stuart?"

"I'd say thirty or so, why?" Frédéric sipped again.

"Well, I'm trying to get the dates straight in my head …" She thought aloud over the phone, "I married Alistair when I was seventeen and Penelope was already missing. I was eight or ten when she left." She counted on her fingers. "Yes, that would make him in his late twenties or early thirties. The gossip was so vivid that I can see the occurrence so clearly in my mind as if I witnessed it."

"Whatever his age, DNA doesn't lie."

"Quite right." She turned back to her lover and ran her hand on his abdomen in slow teasing strokes. "Tell Stuart that when he's ready to come and meet dear ol' daddy, to let me know and I will make all the arrangements. He—or they are to stay with me. Give him my number. He can ring me anytime."

Frédéric sounded amazed, "Are you certain?"

"Quite certain." She chuckled. "It will be fun to see Clive get his comeuppance. Speaking of fun, there's a bit of fun I need to continue. Bye, Fréd."

Amelia's lover placed her hand on his penis. She licked her lips. "Hmm, I fancy a lolly in the afternoon. Always tastes sweeter when one has to wait for the treat."

~~***~~

Cindy and Stuart sat on the Paris RER train, their small carry-ons between their knees, headed to Charles de Gaulle airport. She had no idea what Stuart had planned for this excursion and he sat smugly next to her watching the various passengers. Pungent exhaust fumes assaulted her nose at every stop when the train doors would open for passengers to enter or exit. She obeyed Stuart's request not to ask him for the umpteenth time what would be their destination. Curiosity about his secret excited her and at the same time gave her concern.

What is he up to? Why all this mystery? What if he proposes? Does he have a dark side? I thought JC was wonderful and look what happened. Ridiculous! Stu is way too loving to be unkind.

The train came to the terminus at the airport. They took firm hold of their luggage. Stuart grabbed Cindy's hand as they wedged through the throngs of passengers. On the platform, he looked at the overhead signs indicating the various exits. In the hurry, she didn't pay attention to what the signs designated.

"Stu, are we going on a plane?"

He's so quiet.

"You'll find out the first part soon enough." He picked up the pace. "All things in good time."

"First part?" *I hope whatever he planned didn't cost him too much.* "How many parts are there?"

"You'll find out later." He approached the car rental counter.

"Where are we going that you need to drive?"

His finger playfully touched the tip of her nose. "No more questions. Sit back and enjoy the adventure."

Cindy faked a pout. After signing the rental paperwork and obtaining the keys, he spoke with the representative in French, then located the car. When Cindy saw the sporty red two-seater convertible, her jaw went slack.

This car looks expensive. Does Stu make that much from the bookstore? I don't want him spending money on me that he doesn't have.

Stuart maneuvered the various airport exit and entry ramps until they were southbound on A10 and then westward. Cindy lost track of how many other roads they had turned onto and enjoyed the lush countryside of soft rolling hills and colorful wildflowers. Traveling the D33 route, they seemed to be approaching their destination. For Cindy, the ninety minute car ride felt to be much less.

The open convertible slowly made its way down the narrow road flanked by dense forest. Stuart parked the car in the lot of a charming and rustic lodge. She looked at the sign near the entry, Hôtel St. Michel. Cindy stopped for a moment after turning her eyes to the most beautiful architecture she had ever seen.

"Stu, that castle is magnificent!" He pulled the carry-ons from the small trunk. "It's so intricate."

"That's Château de Chambord." His eyes glazed and for a moment he seemed to have been transported to another era. "The most beautiful château in this area if not in all of France— not including Versailles, of course." He handed her, her luggage, then reached for her hand. "Let's check in and find out where our room is located."

Cindy followed him with rapt attention to the beautiful and lush surroundings.

Stu is certainly full of surprises. I've never been one for the country scene— with him, all things are different.

In the black and white tiled floor reception area, while Stuart stood at the massive mahogany counter and signed the registry, she looked up and spied deer trophies on the walls in the lounge and dining areas. She grimaced and tugged on his shirt sleeve.

She moved close to his ear and spoke in a low tone, "I don't like that. They kill animals here."

He took the room key, then looked at what she had mentioned. He chuckled. "You're out in the country. The French only hunt for the good of the herd, and they *eat* what they kill. Shooting isn't as much of a sport in France as it is a necessity. I promise we won't go on any hunting expeditions. The only hunting I want to do is of the amorous variety."

"Hmm, that might be arranged." She flashed him a suggestive glance. "Maybe the country will bring out my wild side."

"I didn't know Mademoiselle Cindy had such an adventurous nature." He took her hand. "Let's find our room. It's number five. The concierge said it was upstairs."

"Isn't anyone going to show us to our room?"

This is rustic. I hope the bathroom isn't down the hall where everyone shares.

"This place is a lodge—not a city hotel." He led the way up the stairs. "It is very old and quaint. This lodge was a stable back in the day when royals lived in the château—centuries ago."

They reached the dimly lit carpeted hallway. He found their room on the right. Opening the door, Cindy nearly stopped short at the view from the bedroom windows.

"Stu! This is absolutely beautiful." She walked to the window and peered out. "We must have the best view of the château in the entire hotel. How did you manage this?"

"All I said was that I wanted a special room for a special lady to celebrate a special weekend." He looked smug and boyishly charming.

"You did, did you?" She walked to him, rose on tiptoe and draped her arms around his neck.

He embraced her waist and drew her closer. "This is just the beginning of what I hope will be a wonderful and memorable future."

"What future is that?" Her finger traced the outline of his ear.

"That answer rests with you." His eyes held onto hers.

Stuart kissed her gently. Cindy melted in his arms. She enjoyed the feel of her breasts on his chest. Her lips parted as an invitation to give her more. His tongue searched her recesses. Her heart beat faster. She pulled from their kiss with a heavy pant.

"Wow! Stu, you make my head spin, besides having a wondrous effect on me." Cindy stroked his cheek. "I think we better unpack. Let me catch my breath." She looked up at him. "We don't need any extra pillows between us tonight. Things have changed for us since Annecy."

"For the record," he smiled, "I didn't request anything from you."

Is he trying to be coy—acting as if he doesn't care if I refuse him?

"So tell me a little about this place." Cindy placed her suitcase onto a chair.

"The château was set in the middle of a royal game forest, built in the sixteenth century. It has four hundred forty rooms and three hundred sixty-five chimneys." He began to unpack. "Under François I, building started in 1519 and took twelve years to complete."

"You sound like a walking travel brochure." She stopped with a shirt in her hands and looked at him. "You devil." She playfully slapped his arm. "You *are* reading from a brochure. Here I thought you were speaking from what you knew."

"I found the flyer sitting here on the dresser." He continued to read aloud. "There's an enormous double helix staircase inspired by Leonardo da Vinci. Louis XIV had Molière perform here .... Most of the other information is a bit staid—full of dates and who slept where."

"Mom is related to Louis XIV." She hung up her last garment in the closet.

"Surely, you're joking." He placed his hands on hips. "Really?"

"Yup. She is." She walked to him and embraced his broad shoulders. "Some frou-frou courtesan took the king's eye, and poof, the unofficial bloodline was born. I think her name was Madame Montespan—his longtime mistress. Mom's one hundred percent French."

"That makes you half French. What's your other half?" He looked intrigued.

"My other half is English and hungry." *I don't want to talk about Dad.* "Where do we eat?"

"Here. I booked us for breakfast and dinner each day." He shrugged. "We're a bit of a drive from anywhere to find a restaurant."

Cindy checked her watch. "It's too early for dinner. What shall we do?"

He glanced at the bed. "Well, we could ..."

"Not just yet." She ran her tongue along the top edge of her teeth. "I think a drink on the terrace would be nice. You can tell me about that novel you're ruminating on as we enjoy the view of the château. It would be a nice beginning to our mini vacation."

The low sun cast dramatic shadows and played with the intricacies of the château's sculpted spires as they sat on the terrace sipping Kir Royales.

"Stu, you couldn't have chosen a more perfect place." Cindy reached for his hand across the table. "I'm such a city girl at heart. I'm surprised that I'm actually enjoying the view. It's overwhelming that such a masterpiece was constructed all by hand without modern machinery."

"I'm glad I could please you." He sipped the drink. "I hope there will be other opportunities ... to please you."

"Maybe." *Is it just sex for him? Or is it more?* "The evening is young. We could take a walk around the château after dinner."

"Or we could do something else." His thumb stroked the ridge of her middle finger. "You're the one to decide."

Cindy smiled seductively as she sipped her drink.

Should I give in? I want to so badly. My impulses haven't always been good for me ....

After enjoying a delicious meal of poussin, steamed fresh haricots verts, and a dessert of cheese and fruit taken on the terrace, Cindy wiped her lips with a napkin.

"That dinner will live in my memory. Who could want for more? You, a fabulous view, and a country gourmet feast." She sipped her coffee. "This culture is so rich. I understand what Mom has been saying all my life."

"I'm glad I could create a beautiful experience for you." He rubbed her hand and gave it a squeeze. "I hope there will be many more memorable experiences I can give you."

He leaned closer and kissed her lips gently.

"Stu, I think we might better go to our room."

He raised his brows. "No walk around the château?"

"I feel the energy needed for walking is better spent elsewhere."

I can't seem to resist him.

Stuart helped Cindy from her seat before they walked back to their room.

~~***~~

Cindy came from the bathroom dressed in her nightshirt. Stuart, in undershorts, stood at the window with his back to her. One lamp provided a soft glow to the room. She pensively looked at his form.

Is he really as gentle, kind, and honest as he appears to be? Will he break my heart? Am I seeing what I wish, or what is?

She saw the condom on the nightstand.

He seems extremely hopeful.

"I'm squeezing in one more view before the sun sets." He turned from the window as she approached. His smile warmed her. "This view is far more appealing than any château."

"Are you referring to that old painting on the wall behind me?" She knew he enjoyed her teasing.

"Not a chance." His hands on her waist sent warm waves through her. "The beautiful view that I'm about to kiss with all the love in my being."

Stuart leaned down and kissed her fully on the mouth. Cindy gave in to her need to be loved and held. His hand caressed her breast over the fabric's silkiness. She ended their kiss, then led him to the turned-down bed. She lay on the cool sheets and reached her arms out to him. He rested on his side. His kisses flowed from her earlobe to her neck, and then her throat.

He fumbled with the buttons on her shirt, while she tugged at his shorts. He kicked them off at the ankles. Her hands stroked his back. Stuart lifted himself on top of her. He kissed her breasts, and teased her nipples as his tongue made circular movements. She felt his firm manliness against her thigh. His kisses traveled downward to her abdomen, mouthing her soft flesh, then farther, and farther to her seat of utmost enjoyment. Her pants came in waves as her desire rose higher than she ever thought possible. Cindy parted her legs farther, begging him to be one with her. His kisses continued to tease her as he lingered to give her the greatest sensation. She let out a loud ah in response to his teasing.

She felt his firmness grow at her swollen folds and then eased inside to fill her inner being, stretching her and bringing her desire higher. Every movement made her want more. His thrusts grew firmer and quicker. She moved in rhythm to his urgency. Her fingers dug into his buttocks and drove him faster. Her fire-hot nerves teetered on the brink—ultimate pleasure was within her grasp. His rapid breaths echoed in her ears and were in tandem with her own. Her gasp caught in her throat as the pinnacle of ecstasy consumed her entire body. She shared spasms with him in the heated bliss of passion and love. He lifted his head and looked down at her face. He kissed her eyelids tenderly, lovingly, as if she held his heart in her hands.

"You certainly know how to please a mademoiselle." She fingered the damp hair at his temple.

"And you, you know how to please me very well ... very well, indeed." He kissed her fingertips.

"I wanted to give you kisses on your ... your," she giggled, "your love wand."

Why did I say "love wand"—I'm a real dork!

He laughed. "You are such a delight .... I wanted you too badly to give you the chance. But mostly, I wanted our first time to be about you and your pleasure. It's important to me that I make you happy in all ways." He interlaced his fingers with hers. "Cindy," he looked in her eyes, "I love you. I have loved you from the first time I saw you in my store."

"I love you, too." Tears filled her eyes. "Saying those words feels very right for me. I don't say them lightly. I'm committed to you for as long as you want me."

This was more than sex for me. My heart is bonded to Stu. I've never felt so close to another man.

"I want you forever." He wiped a tear from the corner of her eye. "I won't be the one to walk away."

"Neither will I."

Stu, please don't break my heart—I wouldn't be able to survive that.

Fifty - Six

"STU, WHY DID we have to leave so early?" Cindy gazed out the window as Stuart drove with the top down. She enjoyed feeling the rushing wind on her face. "You barely gave me time to make up my face and wolf down breakfast. I wanted to enjoy the view of the château."

"It's not like we're leaving tomorrow. We'll have plenty of time to enjoy Chambord's view." He turned off the main highway and onto a country road. "This area is rich with history and beauty. I want you to see the French country that I have come to love."

She noticed a road sign. "There's the exit for Tours."

He sported a smug smile. "We're not going to Tours."

She brushed a strand of hair that had blown across her face as they passed the exit. "Obviously. Where are we heading? Or is it another mystery?"

"It's Château d'Azay-le-Rideau. Not as magnificent or as large as Chambord, but is still worth a visit." He glanced at her and then back to the road.

Cindy enjoyed the vast bright yellow roadside fields. "That must be a sunflower farm of some sort."

"Sunflowers are a big crop in France for seeds and oil." He gave her a sideways glance and smiled.

Stuart turned onto a minor country gravel road. Signs of their destination appeared in the distance.

He parked in the lot, got out and hurried around the car to assist Cindy, opening the door for her.

"We're lucky," he said. "Because we started out early, the crowds haven't formed yet. We won't have far to walk."

He took her hand as they walked the well-traveled path over a small bridge. Cindy paused to look at the graceful swans in what she assumed was a lake.

They made their way to the entrance. Stuart paid the admission fee. Armed with informational flyers written in French, he translated for her.

"This was originally a medieval fortress. Passed through many French landholders and some royalty. It is actually built on a small island. The Indre river creates a natural moat. Louis III spent a night here." He stopped and looked at the large rooms with sparse furnishings. "This is an example of French renaissance under the reign of Francis I."

Cindy pointed to a sculpture on a pediment. "What's the meaning of the lizard?"

"That's the salamander relief of Francis I. You'll see the same icon in the château at Blois. The same salamander is on one of the fireplace chimney breasts here, too." Stuart read from the flyer. "In 1905 the château was purchased by the state and became a listed historical monument." He inclined his head while looking at her with love. "Are you enjoying yourself? I'm not boring you?"

"You could never bore me." She reached up and kissed him softly. "You have opened my eyes to appreciate all things in culture that I resisted before—before loving you."

"You're prejudiced." He smiled with warmth. "Our relationship took a deeper meaning and made a lasting commitment." He chuckled. "In time you might tire of my historical ramblings."

"I doubt that. What's next? We seem to have covered most of this castle."

"I have one more place in mind." He looked at his watch. "Not far from here. We can have lunch there before returning to Chambord for dinner."

"Sounds fine by me." Cindy placed her hand in his. "Bring on more history! I'm ready for another lesson ..." She smiled flirtatiously. "... among other things."

He laughed. "You are such a devil—and I love it!"

~~***~~

Cindy stood in the central entry and took in the majesty of Château de Cheverny. The stone carvings made an impressive and wondrous site. Stuart and she strolled from room to room as hushed tourist voices waved over them. Tapestries of intricate detail covered some of the walls while others supported fine portraiture of French notables in history.

Cindy nudged his arm. "Where do we eat ... and when?"

In keeping with the museum environment, he spoke in low tones. "There's a nice snack shop behind the château, along with a gift area. It used to be an orangerie."

Stuart took her hand as they walked out the entrance and then around to the back.

Inside, Cindy looked at the selection of offerings. She opted for the same as Stu. Seated at a small table, he sported a playful glint in his eye.

She chewed then swallowed the bite of her ham sandwich. "You have something up your sleeve. I can tell by your devilish expression."

He mockingly looked under his shirt cuff. "No. I don't see anything hiding there. Nothing up my sleeve." He chuckled. "There is a tidbit about Cheverny that I think you might find interesting."

"I'm all ears." Cindy sipped her cola.

"The French Crown got the château due to fraud. Henri II gave it to his mistress, Diane de Poitiers. She didn't care for it and sold it to the former owner's son." He took a swallow of water from his bottle. "It was one of the first chateaus to open to the public as an attraction with the family still living in it." He chuckled. "Need to pay for the electric by one way or another."

"I don't need to read any books about French history." She rubbed his forearm. "I have you as my special professor."

"There's one more excursion for us." He kissed her cheek. "Don't ask. It's a secret."

Hand in hand, they walked back to the entrance, down the gravel walkway, crossed the narrow street to a grassy park. He looked up at the clear blue sky and smiled.

Cindy noticed the Golf de Cheverny sign and tapped his arm. "Are we on a golf course? Are we allowed to even be here? What if a golf ball comes flying through the air?"

He laughed. "The golf course is not even near us. We would have to walk quite a distance to see any players."

She purposely didn't say a word during the fifteen minute walk.

I feel so comfortable with Stu, even when we're quiet like this. We don't need words. I've never felt so in sync with a man before—not with such a secure feeling.

She looked up from the gravel path. A hot air balloon in bright colors of red, yellow, and blue, and with a woven wooden base sat on the lawn in front of them. Stuart picked up his pace.

He firmly took her hand. "Let's check it out."

Cindy followed. "What are you thinking? Don't people make reservations for those rides?"

"Yes." He glanced back at her. "It's fun to see them take off."

A group of men finished filling the balloon with hot air from the burner. Stuart took two pieces of paper from his jacket pocket and handed them to another man standing near the passenger gondola. They spoke in French.

What's going on? Stu planned a ride for us?

The man pointed to the toeholds in the balloon basket. "Entrez-vous, mademoiselle."

Cindy gingerly climbed over the side into the gondola. She noticed a cooler on the floor and assumed it must have something to do with putting out a possible fire. Stuart followed her and kissed her cheek.

"You devious little devil." She smiled broadly. "You had this planned all along. I've never been on a hot air balloon ride. This is fantastic!"

"I like to keep you off balance every now and then ... in a good way of course." He wrapped his arm around her waist. "It won't be long now and we'll take off."

"How far up do we go?" She brushed her hair away from her face due to the light breeze.

"I think over the rooftops." He watched the pilot secure and adjust the ropes.

Slowly, the balloon lifted them up into the sky. The rushing of air from the burner was the only sound as they gained altitude, obliterating all noise of the community below. The buildings reduced in size as they traveled higher.

This must've cost Stu a mint. Should I offer him some money? I don't want him to feel he has to pay for everything.

The peaceful ride gave the illusion that with a little stretch, they could pick the leaves off the treetops. Stuart pointed out the famous sites while Cindy took photos and video with her phone.

"Look there." He squeezed her waist. "That's Château Chenonceau—the one I told you about involving Henri and Diane de Poitiers. It's the only château that has running water under it. That's the Cher river. In World War I, Chenonceau was a military hospital. Wait, I could be wrong, maybe it was the Second World War."

"It doesn't matter." *He's wonderful.* "Facts and dates don't matter—it's the man speaking who does."

He kissed her passionately. "I love you so very much."

"I love you, too."

How I wish I had met him years ago.

Château de Chambord came into view.

That place is special for us. That's where we first made love.

She took photos and more videos of their cherished love nest.

Stuart nodded to the pilot and spoke something in French. The man gave a thumbs up sign.

What's going on? What did Stu tell him? We can't land here—not with the car in Cheverny.

The balloon slowly circled the château and hotel. Stuart reached in his pocket and took out a small black velvet box. He took Cindy's hand and looked deeply in her eyes. Her heart beat faster in anticipation.

"Cindy, you have brought a light and love to my life that I never thought I'd be blessed to realize." She started to speak. He took a deep breath. "Please let me finish." He cleared his throat. "With all my heart and being, I can't see my world moving forward without you. You are my raison d'être, I mean, my reason for being. I love you as you are and will never thrust my expectations onto you." He cleared his throat again. His hand trembled. "Cindy, will you share my life as my wife? Will you marry me?"

Cindy couldn't speak for a moment. "Stu, you've taken me by surprise, and how wonderful to do it in a balloon ride, but not your question." Tears blurred her vision. "Yes. I would be very proud to be your wife with all the love in my heart."

His shaking hands opened the box. He lifted out the impressive diamond ring from its hiding place. It sparkled and reflected rainbow colors. Gingerly he placed it on her shaking finger. She snuggled into his chest. Tears streamed down her cheeks and fell onto his shirt.

"Stu, it is beautiful, absolutely beautiful!" Her bottom lip quivered. "I'll never take it off—never!"

He wiped her tears with his handkerchief. "The setting is okay? I was told platinum was the best, and that's what I wanted for you—the best. It's two carats." He looked sheepish. "I found the ring in that mall at La Défense. I'm sorry that I couldn't afford a jeweler in *place Vendôme*. That square shape is called a 'princess' cut. In my mind, that was perfect for you, because you're the princess of my heart."

"Stu, I would love it just as much if you placed a rubber band on my finger." *He's so sensitive.* "It's *you* I'm going to marry, not the ring."

They shared a passionate kiss as the pilot steered back to their starting point. The late afternoon sun cast a soft glow on the

Loire Valley's chateaus below. All the world glowed for her.

I want to call Mom. At the same time, I don't. This is our special and private moment—a moment we will always remember.

The pilot guided the balloon back to the landing target. A crew of men came rushing to them and secured the passenger basket. Cindy and Stuart climbed out over the sides. A balloon employee spoke to Stuart in French, and they followed him to an open pickup truck. Another man brought the cooler out from the gondola.

The pilot trailed a few steps behind before reaching them. "I'm sorry sir, for not serving the champagne when we flew over Chambord. I felt the wind too unsteady to leave the controls to open the bottle."

Cindy answered for Stuart. "That's all right. I'll take a proposal over a glass of champagne any day of the week."

The man expertly opened the bottle and poured the effervescent liquid into slim flutes, then handed them each a glass.

Stuart made a toast. "To the most beautiful, sincere, and wonderful woman in my life …. I wish you could see yourself through my eyes, then you would know how beautiful you are."

Cindy stopped him from taking a sip with her own toast. "To my future husband—a man I've waited all my life to find. I love you with all my heart."

With entwined arms, they each took a sip. Her emotion and tears welled up. A thick lump formed in her throat.

Stuart kissed her tenderly. She felt the love in his kiss and knew her decision was right and would forever change her life.

Fifty - Seven

"I HOPE YOU won't miss me too much." Larry sat at the kitchen counter while Tim brewed coffee.

"Where are you going?" Taylor put the newspaper down beside her orange juice. "Another tour?"

"I have a commitment in London that I can't ignore." He took the arts section from the paper she was reading.

"When's our flight?" She stared directly at his face.

"I thought it would just be me and Joe." He leaned over and kissed her forehead. "London didn't leave you with good memories."

Uh oh. Tay's going to be difficult.

"That's true. But I want to *go*." She pouted as a little girl.

"Not a good time." *I can't tell her the reason.* "I will be back before you'll ever know I'm gone."

"That old chestnut!" Her lips thinned and eyes narrowed. "You're hiding something Larry Davis, and I want to know what it is—*now!*"

"I don't want to upset you." He stroked her hand. "I'm concerned about your health."

"My health won't benefit from worry." Her brows drew together as her pupils dilated. "Tell me!"

I pray I don't regret this.

"This is a long tale that has some good and possible bad in it."

"Tell me the bad first." She leaned closer to him.

"I can't separate the parts." He took an enormous deep breath. "Cindy and Jean-Claude called it quits. She's now deliriously happy and in love with Stuart Dumont—an English bookstore owner."

"So far, so good. Cindy told me that she and Stuart started out as friends." Her face brightened. "She called me about Stuart. Remember? I told you about the call when she and I made up—resolved all that pain—nothing bad about that. I always felt Jean-Claude was bad news."

"I haven't gotten into the meat of the issue yet." He took a sip of coffee and bit his lip. "Jean-Claude was, is a drug user. He had a big drug bill, and Cindy was singled out. Someone attacked her with a knife as a warning to him to pay his debt. Thankfully, it was just a small flesh wound on her arm—didn't need stitches—

she's safe now and off the grid, and no longer a target."

I hope Cindy is no longer in the drug cartel's crosshairs.

Tears formed in her eyes as she gripped his arm. "She needs to come home."

He negatively waved his hand. "Let me finish .... Apparently, Stuart has always been curious about his birth mother because he's adopted. He contacted Fred, and after DNA tests, which I'm guessing Amelia assisted with, it's been proven that Penelope Bradford and Clive Bradford are his parents. Now, he wants to go to London and confront Clive. I'm certain Cindy will go with him." He touched her shoulder to emphasize his words. "I don't want you to have any contact whatsoever with that bastard. He's not worth the consequences to your health."

"I can't believe it. Clive? Am I ever going to get him out of my life?" She gazed into the distance as if deep in thought. "I'll stay in a hotel. Cindy and Stuart can be there with me." Pleading showed in Taylor's eyes.

"I've already talked with Amelia. I plan to stay with her." He took a breath. "If Stuart goes through with his plan, she wants to be with them as a buffer. I feel the same. I don't want Stuart to confront him alone."

"What do you think he wants—Stuart, I mean?" Furrows formed across her brow.

"I imagine acknowledgement of his birthright and an explanation as to why he was put up for adoption, not to mention, the reason his mom is in her current condition."

"Clive will have a bucket load of excuses." Her narrowed eyes showed seething anger. "He deserves every nasty thing Stuart can fling at him."

"Calm down." He took her hands in his. "You're getting upset. That's what you shouldn't do—letting Clive have power over you."

"I'm going with you." Her jaw set. "No ifs, ands, or buts about it. I'll pack Cindy's things with ours. Then she'll have them safe and sound. We must protect her at all costs. When do we leave?"

"I'll have to get in touch with Amelia. She'll know when Stuart plans to make his trip to London."

Can Tay's heart take the stress of meeting Clive again? Will my poor judgment leave me as a widower? I would never forgive myself.

~~***~~

"We're all set." Stuart came up behind Cindy as she placed a new shipment of books for the store on the self.

"Set for what?" Her eyes held a curious gleam. "It wasn't that long since we returned from our jaunt in the countryside."

"Our trip to London—to meet and question my father." *I hope she doesn't try to talk me out of this.* "There are answers I must have. I've waited all my life wondering."

She grabbed his arm. "Just let sleeping dogs lie. We have a good life here and a future to build. Please don't take chances with that."

"Nonsense. My newly found cousin, Amelia, will arrange everything. We take the train to Calais where we get on her yacht and off we go to South Hampton, and from there her driver will take us to London. We'll be staying with her."

"What about Hugo? Hélène will care for him?" Cindy crossed her arms across her chest.

As if he knew what she had said, Hugo came running and rubbed up against her legs.

"No way. He'll come along, too." Stuart reached down and picked up the cat, giving him loving strokes. "Amelia said that she has connections and he won't have to go through a six month quarantine." He straightened some leaning books on the shelf. "She sounds like quite a woman. Thank God she has contacts with the English officials." He sighed. "I imagine she has a great many favors she can tap into."

Cindy's trying to find obstacles—a reason I shouldn't go.

"I still don't feel good about this." Worry settled in her eyes. "Mom and Larry said very bad things about your father."

How much worse could he be?

She stepped closer. "I'll tell you this—he has a violent temper. The rest is for Mom to tell. I won't betray her confidence."

Hugo purred loudly and reached out for Cindy to hold him. She scratched behind his ears.

"I'll deal with that when it happens." He looked at the calendar on his desk. "We leave next Monday at seven in the morning. So you better pack."

"That's only two days away. I don't have much to pack, though." She made a face. "Better get a health certificate for Hugo—just in case."

"Already done. As soon as I knew of the date, I took him to the veterinarian." He kissed Hugo's head. "He's good to go, too."

"Looks like your mind is made up." She kissed his lips. "I pray your decision doesn't hold negative consequences."

"If it does, I'll deal with it them." He drew her close with his free arm while Hugo purred loudly between them.

~~***~~

Cindy had resigned herself that Stuart's stubbornness would not be swayed. She folded her few clothes and placed them neatly in her carry-on. Hugo watched her every movement and then curled up into the luggage, turning belly up, begging to be petted.

"Not now, Hugo." She picked him up and placed him on the floor. "I need to pack before your daddy returns. We're leaving soon."

I pray my worry is for nothing. Though, I can't imagine Stuart's father will give him a warm welcome.

The cat returned back to his comfy position on top of her clothes. Cindy smiled at him and picked him up. "Well, I guess I'll have to finish packing with you in my arms." She kissed the top of his head and walked to the bathroom. Balancing Hugo and her toiletries wasn't easy for her. He purred loudly as she tossed the items onto the clothes in the carry-on.

Cindy reached down for the cat carrier to make certain it was clean. Hugo's eyes grew large and his ears flattened back. He jumped out of her arms and hid under the bed, then meowed loudly, as if frightened.

"Hugo, don't be afraid." She knelt down to peer under the bed. *He won't come out for me.* "We're going to a nice place. You'll enjoy all those tasty kippers in London." *I wouldn't walk across the room for one of those fishy things.* "Have it your way, Hugo." She placed her brush and comb in the case. "Daddy will get you out of there when he comes home."

Cindy picked up her cell phone. She thought a moment, then scrolled through her contacts and hit her mom's number. She waited for the ringing sound on the other end.

"Mom, I wanted you to know that Stu and I will be leaving for London on Monday. I don't want you to worry. We're staying at his new cousin's, Amelia's place."

"Lar filled me in on the details. We'll be there, too. I don't want you to be in a dangerous situation." Cindy heard the tenseness in Taylor's voice.

"Please don't worry. I, we'll be fine." She sighed. "I think too much is being made of this whole situation. You and Larry don't need to come."

"Cindy, this is not up for debate. We will be there at Amelia's when you arrive. You and Stuart should not meet Clive alone." She took a deep breath. "I know what I'm talking about. I won't go into the details, but trust me in this. You and Stuart should just let it be. If you or he feels you must go to London to meet his cousin, Amelia ... well, that's different—but give up the idea of challenging Clive—he's bad news. Stay with Amelia and enjoy the sites. Keep Stuart away from Clive."

"Mom, I already tried to reason with Stu." She sighed. "It's of no use. I won't let him go there alone. I don't want to be a widowed fiancée before I'm married."

"Fiancée?" She gasped. "You're engaged?"

"Yes. I was waiting for the right time to tell you, but I guess you know now. I'm so thrilled. Stu picked the perfect place at the perfect time." *I hope Mom's happy for me.* "We took a balloon ride over Chambord. He proposed over the chateau and placed a princess-cut diamond on my finger—it's beautiful. You'll be able to see it." She wiggled her finger and watched the sparkling reflected light. "We stayed at a small hotel that faced the castle—Hôtel St. Michel. Room number five. That is now my new lucky number. It was *so* romantic."

"That's the same hotel where Lar and I honeymooned and in the same ..." Her voice softened. "He couldn't have chosen a more romantic setting."

"You're happy for me?"

What luck ... Mom and Larry stayed there before us and I bet in the same room by the way she didn't finish her sentence. I wanted Chambord as our special place without sharing a memory.

"Of course. I'm happy for you." She lowered her tone. "If this is what you truly want. It hasn't been that long since your divorce. You seem to be jumping from one man to another. How can you be sure Stuart is someone you want to spend the rest of your life with?"

"Please don't go there, Mom."

After we made up and I said I was sorry, she's going back to her old ways—lecturing.

"I only want you to make choices that are right for you." She breathed deeply. "I love you, and I worry."

"*Don't* worry. Besides, Stuart will be titled twice after the legal papers are in order with the London courts. That will make me a Lady in British society."

I hope she doesn't expect Stu and me to return to the States.

"Are you in love with the man or the titles you'll have after you're married?"

"I love Stuart, the man. I loved him before I ever knew he was the son of royalty."

I wish she would give it a rest.

Taylor's voice cracked. "Whatever happens, you always have a home here—remember that."

"I know, Mom. Look, I've got to finish packing. I'll call you again if anything changes." She started to pace in front of the foot of the bed. "I love you. Don't worry."

She hung up the phone.

Maybe it was a mistake calling her. Now she'll worry herself sick. She has a heart condition. I can't stress her with bad news. I wish Stu would listen to me and not go to London. What hell am I walking into?

Fifty - Eight

"I'M DELIGHTED TO see you both." Amelia greeted Larry and Taylor in her Mayfair townhouse's foyer. "And you, too, Joe. I take it that my driver had no difficulties in finding you at Gatwick?"

Her housemaid, Elizabeth took their jackets and hung them up, while her Cavalier Spaniel, Rodney, followed them into the living room. She had instructed Harold, the multitasking male servant, to take their luggage to their respective rooms.

"No problems at all." Taylor went to the sofa. "Uneventful, but I'm afraid the purpose of this visit won't have such joyful results."

Larry sat next to his wife, while Joe sat on a wingback chair. Rodney curled up at Taylor's feet and raised a paw. She patted his head lovingly and said softly, "I've missed you. You're such a baby."

Amelia seated herself in an overstuffed leather chair by the fireplace. "Yes. You're referring to Cindy, Stuart, and Clive? That could be a problem." *I hope they like what I've planned for Clive.* "However, my brain has been as busy as the boats on the Thames."

She couldn't help notice Larry, Taylor, and Joe exchange glances.

They know me and are worried. She grinned.

"What plans are those?" Larry inched forward.

Elizabeth entered with a silver service of coffee and tea on a tray with cups, saucers, and a plate of shortbread biscuits, and placed them on the tea table. Rodney stood up and wagged his tail, clearly anticipating a treat. The servant quietly exited the room.

"As you Americans say, I've done my homework." Amelia turned the teapot around three times. She held a cup of coffee, then raised an eyebrow at Taylor. "Milk?"

"Yes, please," Taylor said. "Larry also takes milk in his tea."

She stared at Joe.

"Black coffee for me, thanks."

Amelia served the cups to each of them. She stirred a teaspoon of sugar for herself.

"Please help yourselves. The shortbread was baked this morning." Amelia took a biscuit and set it on her saucer. She sat back in her chair and waited until everyone had taken their tea and biscuits. "I've been talking to my solicitor. He assured me that, based on dear Stuart's evidence, he is indeed due the titles of Marquess and Viscount."

Taylor looked at her intently. "Is that all? Just the titles?"

"That's only the froth on the cauldron." She chuckled. "If Clive doesn't back off and give the boy all that is due him, then I'm fully prepared to go to the papers *and* the crown." She looked at Larry's brother. "Joe, you're so quiet. You have any thoughts on the situation?"

He shrugged. "I just go along for the ride. For my two cents, I'd say keep the hell away from Clive. Nothin' good can come from him."

"On the surface that may be ... but I think he owes his son a lot more after neglecting and rejecting him for his entire life." She sipped her tea. "After Stuart and Cindy arrive and are settled in a bit, we all will pay a visit to my dear cousin. My solicitor will be there, too." She smiled smugly. "Strength in numbers, my pets." *I hope they will agree to what I've planned.* "Stuart and Cindy are traveling from Calais via my friend's yacht, dock at South Hampton, and then a drive to here. They should be chiming the doorbell tomorrow."

Taylor knitted her brow. "What do you expect to achieve? Is all this drama worth a couple of titles and a few British pounds?"

Amelia took another biscuit, broke it in half and gave a piece to Rodney. "There's the financial wealth that Clive has been hoarding all these years. Stuart has been denied his birthright of a quality education had he been brought up here—that has to account for something."

"But, remember how violently he reacted before," Larry refilled his cup, "when challenged by something or someone he didn't like?" He shook his head. "I don't want Tay exposed to that."

"Not to worry." Her voice rang with confidence. "We will be a force. Clive wouldn't dare make a scene—not with so many witnesses, plus the security of my solicitor." She laughed. "If there's one thing I know about my wicked cousin, social appearances are everything to him. If the truth ever leaked out, his life would be in shambles—career, standing at his club, and his all-important title of Duke of Bryningmead." She chuckled again. "That is the most precious jewel in his crown."

Larry looked downcast. "I hope you're right. I have my doubts about this." He glanced at Taylor.

Amelia leaned forward in her seat. "Dear friend, put those concerns to rest." She smiled in thought. "This will be fun, and I'm the ringleader."

~~***~~

Stuart and Cindy rode in the backseat of the hired car Amelia had provided. Stuart's heartbeat quickened as the scenery changed from rural to suburban. He held Cindy's hand and glanced at her worried face. Meows from Hugo, still in his carrier on the seat beside them, punctuated their concerns. He put his fingers through the grills and felt the cat rub up against them.

"Do you know what your cousin looks like?" She angled her body to see his face.

"She sent me a selfie on my phone. Seems like a nice person. Thirtyish, red hair." He smiled. "I believe she is someone who I'm glad to be related to."

The passing sights indicated they were in London. Cindy looked out the window. Stuart leaned forward and tried to make mental notes of landmarks he might need to recall in the future. The car came to a traffic jam. The sight of traditional black cabs and English pubs churned his blood.

This is where I come from. London is my roots. I'm no longer a Frenchman who feels adrift.

There wasn't a detail he missed. He took it all in—people, street names, and buildings.

He asked the driver, "Where are we now? What part of the city?"

The driver glanced back through the rearview mirror. "Piccadilly, sir. We're not far from your destination. Just a few blocks more."

Stuart noticed Cindy's furrowed brow. "Cheer up. You're about to meet my cousin." He bit his lip. "I'm so excited. I feel like it's Christmas morning."

Cindy squeezed his hand. "I hope this visit has very positive results for you."

The car pulled up to the curb. The driver swiftly got out and opened their doors.

"This is the location I was given, sir. I'll be just a moment getting your luggage." The man went to the trunk. Stuart carried the cat carrier. Cindy started up the steps. He pressed the doorbell. Barking came from the other side.

A young girl greeted them, a spaniel sitting at her heels and letting out playful whimpers.

"I'm Stuart, Stuart Dumont from Paris." He fidgeted. "I'm here to see my cousin Amelia Hollingsworth. I believe she's expecting me."

I hope this is the correct place.

"Oh, yes, sir." She made a slight curtsey. "Lady Steffenfordshire is awaiting your arrival."

"Lady Steffenfordshire?" He cleared his throat. "Maybe I didn't make myself clear. I'm here to see Amelia Hollingsworth."

"So sorry, sir. Lady Steffenfordshire is her royal name. Her ladyship is Duchess of Steffenfordshire. You may call me Elizabeth." She opened her hand to indicate the dog. "Her grace's dog is named Rodney." The girl motioned for them to enter the foyer.

Cindy's wide-eyed expression indicated she was impressed by the lavish surroundings. A servant who introduced himself as Harold took their luggage to their rooms. Stuart still carried the cat carrier. Rodney sniffed at the grill and wagged his tail as if wanting to play. Hugo let out several meows.

"Please follow me to the library," Elizabeth said. "Everyone will be so happy to see you both."

"Everyone?" Stuart glanced at Cindy and then returned his attention to Elizabeth. "Who is 'everyone'?"

"Taylor, Larry, Joe, and Lady Steffenfordshire." The girl opened the door.

Taylor stood up and embraced her daughter. "It feels so good to hug you. It's been so long—too long." She kissed Cindy's cheek.

Stuart observed their interchange.

"It's good to see you, too, Mom … I love you. I'm so sorry for, for all of it." Her eyes filled.

"Hush." Taylor hugged her again. "None of that. All is good between us."

Cindy wiggled the fingers of her left hand. "Look at what my wonderful husband-to-be graced my finger with."

"It's absolutely beautiful!" She smiled at Stuart. "You have been wonderful to my daughter. Keep up the good work."

He stepped to Taylor. "That's my intention, Mrs. Davis. She

will always have the best of me."

She shook her head. "Please. No 'Mrs. Davis'. You can call me Taylor or Mom, if you're comfortable with that." She gave him a firm hug.

He nodded. Amelia motioned for Elizabeth to leave and then invited her guests to sit down as she continued with the introductions.

Joe smiled broadly. "Glad to know y'. I'm Lar's adopted bro."

Larry gave Stuart a warm handshake. "I'm Larry. Welcome to Cindy's family."

Stuart placed the carrier by his feet. Rodney continued to sniff the container while Hugo voiced his meows.

Amelia stood up. "Give me a hug. I'm your cousin—your blood. I'm here to help you in any way I can."

"It feels a bit odd to me—this instant family—but in a good way. I must apologize for the noise." He pointed his chin at Hugo's carrier. He raised his eyebrows in question. "Is Rodney agreeable with cats? Can I open the crate's door? I have a harness on Hugo and a leash in my pocket. Hugo is a Parisian cat and loves the dogs in the parks. I often take him on walks."

Amelia chuckled. "A cat? I don't see why not. As long as you keep him on leash until he's settled in. Rodney likes to play with the neighborhood cats. He gets along famously with them."

Stuart opened the carrier and attached the thin leash. Hugo crept out cautiously and gently reached out with semi-concealed claws and patted Rodney's nose.

Amelia laughed. "They're getting on already." She looked at Stuart. "They'll be the best of friends in no time."

They all watched the game of soft nose-swatting that Hugo had devised.

It's almost a sign that I'm meant to be here.

"Stuart," Amelia looked directly at him, "what is your occupation in Paris?"

"I own an English bookstore and the apartment above it on *rue de Rivoli*." Elizabeth brought in refreshments of tea, sandwiches, and coffee on a tray. "It does quite well. There are many who treasure the English word in Paris. My real passion is to write a novel."

Taylor spoke to him. "So you speak French, too? Your accent sounds English to me and not French."

Amelia cleared her throat. "Please take a seat, and let's discuss our plans over tea." The duchess poured the tea and handed the plate of sandwiches to Stuart. He took a sandwich and slid onto a loveseat beside Cindy, then handed the plate to her.

"In answer to your question," he said to Taylor, "My adoptive parents are French, but had me schooled by an English nanny out of respect to my poor mother … Penelope. So, I'm fluent in both languages."

Taylor clapped her hands together. "Fantastique! I have a future son-in-law who I can speak French with." She beamed. "Though I think that might bore Cindy."

"Mom, you'll force me to learn French so I'll know what you two are discussing." She snuggled closer to him. He smiled to himself at her eye-roll.

Amelia shifted uneasily in her seat. "Not to put a damper on this jovial meeting, Stuart, but you need to know what is planned. First, please don't interrupt me and second, if you don't agree with me, by all means, please say so."

Stuart leaned forward with his arms on his knees. "Please go on, cousin Amelia."

"Tomorrow afternoon, we will all arrive at Clive's townhouse, a quick walk—only a few blocks from here—at one o'clock. My husband, Alistair who works with Clive, said he would be home at that time as it is his day off and Clive mentioned to him that he planned to stay at home to catch up on medical journals." She took a breath. "My solicitor will meet us outside his door on the sidewalk. We will confront him en force. I have the proof I need. Did you bring the DNA documents with you?" Stuart nodded and patted his shirt pocket. "Good. You will need those. I will do the talking. Stuart, you can have your say at the end. If you start the discussion, Clive will fling millions of excuses at you. He will do no such thing with me. Hear me clearly on this. Your birth father has robbed you of your birthright, wealth, an Oxford education, and a social standing. The only good thing that came from his hellish nature was that you had the good fortune to be brought up by wonderful people who loved and cared for you. With the proof I have, Clive will be forced to move out and live wherever he wants, while you and Cindy will have the right to move into his home—the family home."

Stuart's jaw dropped. "I see you've given this a great deal of thought. This is a lot to take in." He eyed his love briefly. "Cindy warned me he could be dangerous with a violent temper."

"Leave that to me. He's not about to show his colors with so many witnesses about." She sipped her tea. "I most decidedly know how to take the wind out of his sails, right enough." She looked at Taylor and said, "If you don't want to go, I completely understand." Then to Joe, "The same for you, Joe."

Joe answered first, "That bastard doesn't scare me. I'll be there for support."

Taylor looked at Larry. "I'll be there. I wouldn't miss his downfall for all the gold in Fort Knox."

"Brilliant! We're all agreed?" Amelia stared at Stuart.

"Definitely." He took a bite of his cucumber sandwich.

Amelia smiled. "When you're quite ready, I know a great many influential publishers in London, some on Fleet Street, who can help you get your novel published, and provide the editing support. One must keep the fame and fortune in the family."

"Thank you so much." His gaze went from Cindy and back to his cousin. "I appreciate all the help you can offer."

"What name will you go by?" Amelia swallowed her coffee. "You can't very well not use the Bradford name."

"I had been thinking about that." He bit his lip. "I've been Dumont all my life and out of respect to my parents, I want to keep that name. I thought that a combination would work for me—Dumont-Bradford or Bradford-Dumont?" He inclined his head as in a question. "I don't know if that's possible."

Amelia wiped her lips with a napkin. "Of course it's possible. Hyphenated names abound in the British realm. The latter sounds better to the ear, but Dumont-Bradford will be more recognizable and influential in British society. My solicitor will take care of the details."

He glanced down at Rodney. Hugo slept with his head on the pup's nose.

I can tell they're friends. There won't be many friendly feelings in the Clive household come one o'clock tomorrow. His stomach knotted. *I pray he's not as dangerous as I've heard. Just how far would he go to protect what is his?*

Fifty - Nine

STUART STOOD ON the front door portal behind Amelia. Cindy leaned on his arm. He felt her trembling as beads of sweat glistened on his brow. He took several deep breaths. Mr. Hargrove, his cousin's solicitor, waited next to Amelia. Stuart was comforted by the knowledge that Larry, Taylor, and Joe stood behind him on the steps.

Amelia turned to him. "Are you ready?"

He nodded.

"Right then." Her finger pressed the doorbell button.

A Winsor knot formed in his throat as his heart pounded.

God, please let this turn out to be easy. I don't want shouting and angry voices from a father who's a stranger to me.

A tall young man, dressed in a uniform, opened the door. Amelia pushed her way through and said in passing, "No need for introductions. I know my way."

She went directly to the library on the right. The entourage obediently followed. They stopped near the room's entry, glaring at the man sitting behind a desk, who had to be Clive.

Amelia's solicitor stood on her left, and Stuart took his place at her right with Cindy at his side.

Clive jolted up from his seat and stepped around the desk. "What is the meaning of this outrage? Amelia, what have you been up to now? A new clever way to ruin my life?"

"That's rich coming from you, dear cousin. 'Ruin' one's life?" She broke from the rest and moved closer.

"What are all these uninvited people doing here, in my home?" His eyes widened with fury. "Taylor, you have no business here. Larry, I owe you in spades for that bloody nose you landed on me for no reason. I see you still have your lapdog, Joe." He scanned the unfamiliar faces. "Who are the other three?"

Amelia smirked. "This is Mr. Hargrove, my solicitor. Then Cindy, Taylor's daughter, and Stuart Dumont, your son and heir. We're here to see he gets his rightful inheritance."

"Bloody ridiculous!" He stood pencil straight and jutted his chin forward. "I have no children, least of all a son who couldn't dress better than a street peddler."

Stuart stifled his words. *That pompous bastard.*

Amelia stepped forward and met Clive head-on with barely

twelve inches separating them. "There is documentation—DNA tests that you *are* Stuart's father and poor pitiful Penelope is his mother. DNA doesn't lie, dear cousin."

"If Penelope was pregnant, then this man is a bastard by her lover. She left me for a gigolo." He went back behind his desk. "Besides, Amelia, you haven't been near me when you could get a sample of my DNA. This is all an elaborate farce for whatever sick purpose that has come into your simple-minded heads."

Amelia leaned on the desk with her knuckles balled into fists. She grinned as if she enjoyed this confrontation. "Remember when I stopped at your lab? You were drinking water from a bottle. I took it for DNA comparison."

Clive reached for the top drawer of his writing table. Stuart moved closer behind Amelia as she spoke. "Don't think about pulling a revolver, dear cousin. Mr. Hargrove has a pistol of his own and will call the police before you can even pull the trigger."

Clive put his hand back on the desk when the solicitor reached into his pocket. "So what do you want? An acknowledgement of some kind? Have Stuart put in my will?"

Amelia laughed loudly, throwing her head backwards. "Do you really think you'll get off so easily?" She strutted in front of him.

"Did my bastard son put you up to this?" He glowered at Stuart. "He came here to pick the old man clean?"

"You couldn't want for a nicer son than Stuart." She flashed him a snide smile. "No, this was all my doing. Time to pay the piper for everything you've done to Penelope and Taylor."

"There was no proof that I did anything to Penelope." He scoffed. "You have no *proof!*"

"Maybe not for her, but there is proof about your deadly dealings toward Taylor." She took a breath. "Now if you don't want me to go to the crown and reveal what I know, you will leave this house and move to wherever you please. You have three days—so after we leave, you had better get cracking."

His jaw dropped a moment. "You're completely daft, Amelia. I had no association with Taylor. Tiffany left me…. And what will happen if I don't?"

"As I said, I will tell the appropriate royal personages and your title of duke will be stripped. You will be a social outcast, your club will not receive you, and I will, with Mr. Hargrove's assistance here, go to the police and tell them everything I can *prove.* Your medical license will be lost while you contemplate your fate in Her Majesty's custody, confined behind bars until you rot!" Amelia leaned across the desk. "And, you will provide the most lavish wedding London has ever seen for Stuart and Cindy …. Oh, I nearly forgot the most important bit—you *will* give fifty percent of all your holdings to Stuart—including the bank accounts."

Clive flopped down in his chair as disbelief wiped across his face. "I-I …"

"Yes is all you need to say, dear cousin." She turned to Stuart. "You have any words for sweet dad?"

Stuart stepped forward. "In all my life, I have never seen anyone so despicable with so much disregard for human life. You call yourself a doctor? Doctors heal, not destroy. I am ashamed to be your son." His fists clenched as his voice shook with anger. "The only saving grace is that I might be able to bring honor to the Bradford name through good deeds and an honest life. Remember this, humans are here to help each other and are not for the sole purpose to serve you at whim."

Clive spoke through clenched teeth. "I don't believe any of this. My solicitor …" He appeared to be thinking.

My bastard father is sizing up his options. He doesn't want to tell his attorney everything of his dirty dealings.

"When will the papers be filed?" Clive almost appeared to have shrunk.

Amelia's voice rang with triumph. "Mr. Hargrove will file them this afternoon." She turned to Stuart. "Henceforth, Stuart will be officially known as Marquess of Bryningmead and Viscount of Lantham. Chew on that crumpet, Clive!" She gestured for the others to leave and then turned at the library door. "Also, Clive … Stuart had better be receiving invitations from your noble and royal colleagues for the proper introductions. You can always say he's your estranged son from Penelope—not one word maligning her character!"

Stuart made his way with Cindy to the front door. The others had already left. He felt a hand on his shoulder. He turned his head. It was Clive.

Is he going to hit me? Shoot me?

He turned around.

Clive offered his hand. "For what it's worth. You're my son."

That bastard! "Not worth a cent in my estimation."

Sixty

CINDY HEARD THE shower turn off in the adjoining bathroom. Her lips curled into a smile in anticipation of him coming to bed. *This is our first night in our home. It feels so right, even though the wedding is still months away. I love Stu so much.* She and Stuart had moved into Clive's townhouse but she had requested that they stay in a guest room, explaining that she couldn't bear the thought of sleeping in an evil man's bed.

She looked up. He stood in the doorway with only a towel wrapped around his waist. His muscles glistened from the remnants of water. She licked her lips.

"I could look at your body all day and all night." She patted the mattress on his side of the bed.

He approached her. "You wouldn't see much at night."

Her hand felt the firm muscles of his thigh. "No. What I can't see, I can feel." Her fingers caressed him under the towel. "And, what I'm feeling now is very nice." She gently massaged his hardening manhood.

"That's not fair." He leaned over and kissed her. "I don't have anything to massage. You can't have all the fun."

Cindy brought his hand to her bare breast. She relished the feel of his gentle kneading of her flesh. She kicked off the covers. He dropped his towel and then climbed into bed beside her.

He kissed her fully on the mouth. His tongue mingled with hers, sending delightful shivers through her. Then the soft brushing of his lips on her breasts spurred her desire further. Her breath quickened as his mouth traveled downward, lower and lower to ... Yes, that was what made her writhe in joy. He teased her, withholding his moist caresses and then giving her more. His fingers fondled her soft and swollen folds. She moaned as she grabbed the sheets with heightened desire. She needed him, and she needed him now. Stuart lifted himself onto her. She opened her legs wide to receive him. He entered her slowly and then pulled back. She tugged at his hips to bring him to her, deeper. He seemed to purposely slow his movement. This drove her wild with passion. Her hips moved faster to feel all of him, to feel him swell within her. His rhythm increased to her demands. She grabbed his buttocks frantically. The more he gave her the more she craved. The pinnacle was in her reach. Her entire focus was on the pleasure he gave her. His pace increased to meet her desire. She gasped as the wave of spasms swept over them. His panting breaths met hers. Perspiration from his hair fell onto her temple. She wiped away a strand of wet hair from her forehead. He lifted his head and looked in her eyes.

"Cindy, I love you. You are the sole purpose for my existence." He kissed her gently.

"Stu," she caught her breath, "you and I will grow old together. There will be no others."

"In the beginning, I didn't have much to offer you, but my love." He stroked her cheek with his thumb. "Now I can provide for you properly and give you royal titles."

"Your love is all I need." She fingered the hair at his temple. "All the rest is not important."

~ END ~

The story continues in "*Dangerous Reach*", book 4 in the Forbidden Series. Read on for chapter 1. Release date yet to be determined.

"In the pit of darkness ...
lies heaven and hell..."
~ CB Ainsworthe

DANGEROUS REACH

One

"DON'T GO NEAR that hell cat, Trenton," David Carson advised. "Amelia will have you for dinner and will then expect you to thank her for the privilege of being devoured."

I hope she's single. What a knock out!

Trenton Lowe fought the beginnings of his arousal as he scrutinized her flitting around the cocktail area filled with royal and prestigious wedding guests. He stood next to David, his London friend and co-producer outside the ballroom at Claridge's in Mayfair, London, enjoying the champagne and delicacies served on silver trays by white-gloved waiters. He didn't know many of the guests.

He nudged David's elbow. "I have no idea why I'm invited. I have no connection to these people."

His friend spoke softly, careful not to be overheard. "You are here to meet the groom, Amelia's cousin—Stuart Dumont-Bradford, ol' chap. He's written a novel or has nearly completed it and she most likely hopes that you will produce the blasted thing, making it the next blockbuster on the big screen." He chuckled. "The groom is a new marquess and viscount. He's not properly royal."

"How's that?"

British doubletalk drives me crazy.

"He doesn't request to be *addressed* as a royal." He took a hefty swallow of champagne. "Prefers to be addressed as 'mister' of all things—ruddy damn improper if you ask me—damn improper."

"Who put me on the guest list?" Trenton took a sip from the slender flute.

"That vivacious redheaded lovely over there—the one in the bright green dress." David lifted his glass slightly in her direction. "That spitfire and devil-may-care vixen—Amelia Hollingsworth, the Duchess of Steffenfordshire." He chuckled. "You're in bloody good company. Mostly nobles and royals here, save for the bride and her relatives. Though, the bride's father is the renowned Larry Davis—Yank singer and composer extraordinaire. When you meet her, address her as 'Your Grace'. If you yourself were royal, then you would call her 'duchess'."

"I had no idea." He chewed on a shrimp canapé from the rounding waiter. "Tell me more about the duchess. She free?"

"Only if you're young." He eyed his friend's face. "You don't fit into that category."

Trenton studied her from across the room. "She married?"

"Oh yes, to the duke." David seemed to delight in relating the gossip. "Alistair doesn't care for her. He has … other interests."

He licked his lips. "If I had a wife like Amelia, I wouldn't leave her alone. I'd have her in the bed, on the sofa, wherever I could find privacy."

David stared at his friend. "Feeling a bit randy? She's more than a handful—too much for me."

"Sounds like my kind of woman." Trenton gazed at her, contemplating his new quest.

"You haven't been divorced that long. You're ready to jump back into those same old brambles?" David laughed. "What are you, masochistic?"

"There's a mystique about her." He wet his lips and ran his finger between his neck and shirt collar.

"Yes. She does have that—in spades." David finished his drink in one swallow. "It's well-known she pays for her young lovers."

Amelia smiled beguilingly at one of the young waiters. Trenton watched her slip a card from her purse onto the tray. The youthful man smiled and tucked the card into his uniform jacket pocket.

She's smooth. Doesn't she realize that most in this room know what she's up to? Does she care about negative gossip?

"How about an introduction?" His eyes remained fixed on her.

"That's easy." David placed his empty glass on the waiter's passing tray. "Follow me."

The two men squeezed through the milling guests, making apologies as they approached her. David lightly tapped Amelia's shoulder. She turned to him and flashed an electrifying smile at Trenton. Her eyes gave him a brief once-over.

"Your Grace, may I introduce you to a dear American friend of mine?"

She smiled with an arched eyebrow. "By all means."

He continued, "I'm pleased to introduce Mr. Trenton Lowe, Hollywood producer and a fine connoisseur of all things beautiful and creative."

She spoke before David could complete the introduction. "Very pleased to meet you, Mr. Lowe. I'm Amelia Hollingsworth, the Duchess of Steffenfordshire, and a connoisseur of all things pleasurable and tasty. Please call me Amelia. I find titles such a bore, as well as those who have them, equally so. Of course there are exceptions—my cousin Stuart Dumont-Bradford, for one. He's an extremely talented author."

She's certainly direct.

"I'm very happy to meet you."

She extended her hand. Trenton took it gently in his, not certain if he should leave a kiss on her glove. Her middle finger gently stroked his palm.

"So you make movies?" She stepped past the two men and gestured for them to follow her to the edge of the room. "I find that utterly fascinating."

"Your Grace, a few movies have my name attached to them."

Any minute she'll serve me the pitch on a silver platter.

He took a glass of champagne from the waiter's tray.

David left, apparently to socialize with the other wedding guests.

"Please, call me Amelia. I already told you that. Titles and royal protocol are tiring and meant for stuffy snobs." She edged closer. "I've never had a Hollywood producer before." She sipped her drink and looked up at him beneath her long false eyelashes. "Are you tasty?"

Trenton coughed loudly and nearly choked on his swallow of

the effervescent liquid. He took a napkin to his mouth. "No one has evaluated me in those terms. You are very frank in a refreshing sort of way." He glanced at her cleavage. *She does have nice tits.* "Back to your question. I haven't had any complaints."

Amelia inclined her head and raised an eyebrow. "You haven't been evaluated by me. I have very high standards."

Trenton stepped back to the point where he felt the seat of a chair against his legs. "You are assuming that I would want your critique."

Amelia smiled and ran her tongue along the upper edge of her teeth. "You like the chase? A bit of a challenge induces or strengthens a rising?"

He brows arched. "'A rising'? I don't understand."

She chuckled and fingered his jacket lapel. "That's British talk for an erection ... I assume you still have them?"

Trenton felt himself blush. "Yes. But, that isn't something I normally discuss, especially at a wedding reception."

What will she do? Pitch Stuart's novel through the back door? Trying to keep me off balance?

"I never go for soporific party talk." She winked. "Too much time can be wasted with the superficiality of niceties, only to be left wanting when the meat is separated from the bone." She touched her décolletage suggestively. "The bone is what counts. Don't you agree, Trent?"

He cleared his throat. "It depends on which perspective. By the way... my name is Trenton."

"To me," her tongue slowly ran across her lips, "you are Trent. That is the name I've chosen."

"You have, have you?" He glanced briefly around the room. "What if I don't like to be called Trent?"

"After one night with me, you would like any name I call you." She sipped her champagne. "Yet, it doesn't have to be at night. Mornings and afternoons are good, too."

"Amelia, how can you be so blatant?" *Is her husband near?* "Aren't you worried about gossip."

"I swim in gossip—especially if it's about me." She took her calling card from her purse and slipped it into his inside jacket pocket. Her fingers lingered on his chest. He enjoyed the warmth of her touch.

"I was told you're married." He took another swallow. "What

makes you think I'm interested in a married woman?"

"If you weren't, you would have left after the first introductions." She took a step closer. "Alistair has his diversions, too. We have an understanding. He doesn't mind in the least."

A young man came to her and whispered in her ear. She flicked him off as if he was an annoying mosquito.

"Am I keeping you from something, or someone?"

I bet he's one of her diversions.

"Oh, him?" She turned and looked at the man walk away. "They're a penny a dozen. Like Alistair, he understands. He'll be replaced when I tire of him." She turned back to Trenton, inclining her head in a beguiling fashion. "I might have found his replacement already."

"I'm pushing forty and don't intend on being a plaything for a bored woman who has nothing better to do than to pay young men to entertain her."

She is totally off the wall and extremely spoiled.

"I never said I paid anyone!" The seductiveness in her face faded as her eyes pierced his, and she spoke with steely softness. "Before you listen to gossip, Mr. Lowe, you had better verify your sources. I don't have to pay anyone. Men clamor for my attention."

I hit a hot button there. "I apologize. I was way out of line."

"Quite right." She pouted as her fingertip drifted to her cleavage.

"Maybe we could meet for a, a cup of tea?"

I can't believe I'm asking her out. She's a married woman, and a royal at that, not to mention a spoiled brat.

"After insulting me, you plan to make up for that verbal assault with tea?" A small smile curled the corners of her mouth.

"I'm in London for a while, working on a movie deal." He rubbed his forehead. "Lunch? Maybe dinner would be better for you?"

"Your proposal is sounding better by leaps and bounds … almost as good as what it takes to rumple the sheets." As she talked, he watched her breasts rise and fall with each deep breath. "I prefer dinner. My afternoons have been rather booked with one charity or another, not to mention the boys."

Trenton pulled out his phone and checked his schedule. "Next Thursday is open. Where should I pick you up—at your place?"

"Where are you staying?" Amelia took a swallow of champagne.

"The Corinthia. You know where it is?"

That was dumb. Of course she knows where it is. She lives in London."

Her smile held a trace of a smirk. "I think I can find it." Her fingers slowly stroked the stem of the flute. "Shall we say seven for next Thursday?"

"Seven it is. Unless you want to come sooner." He inclined his head with inner confidence.

"'Come sooner'?" She chuckled. "I like your choice of words. I had better come first, if you get my drift." The tip of her tongue slipped between her lips.

"You may be disappointed." He moved closer. "I have no intention of bedding you."

"That's your lack of intention—not mine." Her fingers traced his jaw slowly. "The duchess always gets her target ... and the target is grateful for it."

"I'm only taking you out to dinner as an apology—nothing more."

Why am I so attracted to her?

Amelia patted his chest. "Yes. That's the premise to fit with social convention."

Her lips are like raspberry jam dropped into a bowl of cream. I could watch her mouth move all day, not to mention those tits. Are they real?

"As I mentioned before," *How am I going to make her understand?*, "you are married. I'm not comfortable getting involved when a husband is in the picture."

"You'll have to do better than that." Her free hand brushed against his thigh, and then gave a seductive squeeze.

Is she gonna grab my dick next? No one seems to notice her, or if they do, they don't care.

"Seriously, maybe dinner was a bad idea."

I want her. Why? She's forward and obvious.

"Ridiculous! We can have a nice friendly dinner." Her enticing smile intrigued him. "Besides, I might have been only playing with you. I love games of all sorts. Just because I suggest something doesn't mean I'm serious."

"I-I have never met anyone as free-spoken as you."

Her body is driving me insane. I want her!

"Yes. I'm a rare breed." She looked about the room. "I must go and mingle. Time to check up on the bride and groom." As she started to leave she called back to him. "Thursday at seven. Don't keep me waiting."

Trenton nodded.

Is she just one big tease wrapped in one gorgeous British package? Will I give in to her? I want to. No woman has ever gotten the better of me, except for my bitch of an ex.

~ END ~

~ Release of *Dangerous Reach* yet to be determined. ~

MEET CYNTHIA

Cynthia B. Ainsworthe and Barry Manilow

Cynthia has longed to become a writer. Life's circumstances put her dream on hold for most of her life. In 2006, she ventured to write her first novel, **Front Row Center**, which won the prestigious **IPPY Award** (Independent Publisher), as well as garnered numerous 5-star reviews, one from the well-known **Midwest Book Review**. **Front Row Center** is the first book in the *Forbidden Series; a* script is in development by her and notable Hollywood screenwriter, producer, and director, Scott C. Brown. Cynthia has been a guest on several talk radio shows. As a retired cardiac RN turned author, Cynthia enjoys her retirement in Florida, caring for her husband and their five poodle-children.

The second book in the series, **Remember?**, received many 5-star reviews, in particular from the well-known **Huffington Reviews**. Ms. Ainsworthe has been a guest on several talk radio shows. As a retired cardiac RN turned author, she enjoys her retirement caring for her husband and their five poodle-children. Cynthia is currently writing **Dangerous Reach**, book four in the **Forbidden Series.**

Dear Reader Friend,

Thank you for reading my book. I hope you have enjoyed my story. I had a few laughs and some tears while writing this novel.

Please visit my website and sign the contact form so that we might keep in touch through my newsletter.

If you enjoyed it, won't you please take a moment to leave me a review at your favorite retailer? Don't hesitate to reach out to me on social media. My links follow on the next page.

Thanks!

Cynthia

Author Awards

2008 Prestigious IPPY Award in romance, *Front Row Center*
2013 Reader's Favorite International Award in fiction anthology, *The Speed of Dark* for two contributing sories: When Midnight Comes and Characters.
2013 Excellence in Writing Award, It Matters Radio, short story It Ain't Fittin'

Visit Cynthia at:

Check out my website and sign up for my newsletter:
http://www.cynthiabainsworthe.com/

Please follow my Amazon Author Page:
https://www.amazon.com/Cynthia-B.-Ainsworthe/e/B00KYRE1Q8

View my book trailer/s:
https://www.youtube.com/watch?v=qhK7prWYxhk

Friend me on Facebook at:
https://www.facebook.com/cynthia.b.ainswortheauthor

Please like my Facebook Fan Page:
https://www.facebook.com/pages/Cynthia-B-Ainsworthe/38240446635

Follow my Blogs: http://ainsworthe1.wordpress.com/ And:
http://cynthiaswordsandpassion.blogspot.com/

Follow me on Twitter:
https://twitter.com/CynB_Ainsworthe

Follow me on Google+:
https://plus.google.com/+CynthiaBAinsworthe/posts/p/pub

Be my friend on Goodreads:
https://www.goodreads.com/CynthiaBAinsworthe

Let's connect on LinkedIn:
https://www.linkedin.com/in/cynthiabainsworthe/